BLACK TIDE

SOMEWHERE IN THIS xenos warren, somewhere deep in the gloom, an arch-traitor, the self-styled Primogenitor of Chaos Undivided, former lieutenant of the Emperor's Children, a twisted Apothecary, a murderer and torturer of men, was working his evil.

Rafen glanced down at the oath of moment adhered to the vambrace of his power armour. The strip of sanctified parchment bore a spot of dark colour, a droplet of blood from the veins of Corbulo himself, the Master of the Red Grail and lord of the Chapter's sanguinary priests. The oath-paper was Rafen's vow, committed to words and sanctified in the sight of the God-Emperor of Mankind.

A promise to find and to kill the man known as Fabius Bile.

A WARHAMMER 40,000 NOVEL

BLOOD ANGELS

BLACK TIDE

James Swallow

A BLACK LIBRARY PUBLICATION

First published in Great Britain in 2010 by
BL Publishing,
Games Workshop Ltd.,
Willow Road, Nottingham,
NG7 2WS, UK.

10 9 8 7 6 5 4 3 2 1

Cover illustration by Adrian Smith.

A CIP record for this book is available from the British Library.

ISBN: 978 1 84416 805 7

Distributed in the US by Simon & Schuster
1230 Avenue of the Americas, New York, NY 10020, US.

See the Black Library on the Internet at
www.blacklibrary.com

Find out more about Games Workshop
and the world of Warhammer 40,000 at
www.games-workshop.com

Printed and bound in the US.

IT IS THE 41st millennium. For more than a hundred centuries the Emperor has sat immobile on the Golden Throne of Earth. He is the master of mankind by the will of the gods, and master of a million worlds by the might of his inexhaustible armies. He is a rotting carcass writhing invisibly with power from the Dark Age of Technology. He is the Carrion Lord of the Imperium for whom a thousand souls are sacrificed every day, so that he may never truly die.

YET EVEN IN his deathless state, the Emperor continues his eternal vigilance. Mighty battlefleets cross the daemon-infested miasma of the warp, the only route between distant stars, their way lit by the Astronomican, the psychic manifestation of the Emperor's will. Vast armies give battle in His name on uncounted worlds. Greatest amongst his soldiers are the Adeptus Astartes, the Space Marines, bio-engineered super-warriors. Their comrades in arms are legion: the Imperial Guard and countless planetary defence forces, the ever-vigilant Inquisition and the tech-priests of the Adeptus Mechanicus to name only a few. But for all their multitudes, they are barely enough to hold off the ever-present threat from aliens, heretics, mutants – and worse.

TO BE A man in such times is to be one amongst untold billions. It is to live in the cruellest and most bloody regime imaginable. These are the tales of those times. Forget the power of technology and science, for so much has been forgotten, never to be re-learned. Forget the promise of progress and understanding, for in the grim dark future there is only war. There is no peace amongst the stars, only an eternity of carnage and slaughter, and the laughter of thirsting gods.

ONE

Everything is madness.

That was the clearest explanation, the simplest, most logical answer. There could be no other truth; any alternative was impossible. The undeniable fact was that the universe turned on an axis of insanity, and any being who struggled to deny that fact was utterly doomed.

Understanding of this truth was no reward, however. Moving through the thick, sticky silt that coated the surface of the effluent channel, La'Non paused and looked down at his right hand, the spindly grey fingers caked with filth and dried bloodstains. The other arm – *the alien thing* – hung limply at his side, the grotesque greenish-brown bulk of it forever pulling him off balance, upsetting his gait and motion. It reached up to wipe muck from his forehead, but he slapped it away and used his good, true tau limb to do the job. La'Non didn't like to stop too often. If he kept moving, then the voice in his head stayed away. He imagined it like a phantom, a spectral thing that moved as he moved, in perfect lockstep; but it was slow, and he could outrun it. For a time, at least.

Time enough to understand that the mad universe hated him. Hated him and wanted him to suffer, so much so that it had broken off pieces of itself and sent them here, to this place, where they might torment him to death.

He felt the voice coming, and shouted a curse at it, the snarled words echoing down the channel. With a hard effort, La'Non kicked out the service grille above him and hauled himself up, on to the work gantry. He allowed the alien limb to help; he would not have been able to make it otherwise.

From there, he moved up and up, spiralling through the turned tubes cut through the rock, passing once or twice through voids where great deposits of nickel-iron ore had nestled, back when this place had just been a vast stone adrift in the void.

La'Non stopped once more and started to weep. This he did for a few minutes. He couldn't be certain why these intervals came and went without pattern or regularity. Instead, he sat through them, let them take their course. It had become possible, ever since the day he had awoken with the limb grafted to him, to compartmentalise himself in this way, distancing the functions of his body from his mind. Eventually, as they always did, the racking sobs went away and he moved on, towards the surface. The tracks of tears cut lines down his dirty cheeks, and he noted the pattern as he caught his own reflection in a large piece of glassaic, broken off from a window. He was a sorry sight. The robes he had once worn in his role as a minor earth caste functionary had been replaced by the ripped oversuit he had taken from a dead kroot, and it was only the broken pieces of his necklace, balled up in a pocket, that recalled his rank. His drawn face was pallid, the flesh hanging from his skull like an ill-fitting mask made from parchment. The big arm at his side swung back and forth; it was heavy with muscle, twitchy and hot to the touch. La'Non didn't dwell on it, looking away from the shapes of alien flesh, the places where implanted things beneath the surface hissed and bubbled. He padded, feet bare, through the splinters of the rest of the glass, and felt nothing. He pressed his weight down deliberately, but felt no pain. Blood was there, pooling between his toes, but no sense of it reached him. And so he moved on. Upward. Outward.

The colony was like a kittick fruit from a tree infected by boreworms. Oblate in a rough sense, lumpen across its outer skin, inside the asteroid was all tunnels and voids, eaten through and cross-connecting. Factories and oxy-plants, arboreas and habitat pods, places of exercise and teaching and leisure, the home to a hundred thousand tau… Or at least, it *had* been.

La'Non had come when the colony had been opened, drifting out at the farthest edge of the Tash'-var system. He'd lived a good life here, until the tempest had arrived.

He remembered little of it. He learned the story later, in fragments. A warp storm, sudden and terrible, swallowed up the colony and tore it away, spat it back out like indigestible food into some other part of space. Far from home. Far from T'au.

And there, while they were alone and lost, the strange gue'la had come, the human with his many devices of pain and his army of freaks. The madness came with the invader, the great revelation.

How long ago was that? Days? Years? La'Non had lost his sense of the passage of time, and he recalled old wisdom that said a being should recognise such a thing as the first roadstone on the path to insanity. Perhaps, if and when he reached the outer tiers, perhaps when he saw the dark sky again for the first time in... however long it was, he would know. But so many things had kept him from moving forward. The nest of crazed vespids that blocked his path down in the food stores. The crippled and near-dead kroot he had killed with a broken chair. The thing that had seemed to be a female of the air caste, but was actually a bag of meat and blood. She took the most of his time. Talking to him, being a friend to him. When the alien limb had driven her head into a stone wall and crushed it, La'Non had watched with dispassion, still reaching for an understanding at that point in his journey.

The colony was a place of death and decay now, the survivors of the strange gue'la's horrific experiments discarded to perish, ejected into the bleak corridors to live or die at the hands of those who had escaped his knives, or the other victims. For the longest time, La'Non had lived in fear of being recaptured, submitted once more to the white-hot pain and endless agonies. His hand – his good hand – moved to his throat, as he thought of how he had screamed himself ragged. As he did this, the voice whispered in his ear. It had caught up to him.

It told him the same story again. The voice liked this story, liked it a great deal; that was the only explanation he could think of, for the repetition and the endless recurring talk of the same motifs, the same images. The voice told La'Non of another tau who was also called La'Non, who had a pair-bond and a habitat that was small but comfortable, who was respected for his work ethic even though he was not a being of outstanding nature. A tau who was a fair husband to a quiet wife and a careful father to a lone child who was troublesome as all children are. This other La'Non – which could clearly not be him, because he would have remembered if he had a wife and a son – had lost all that was important when a great storm came and split his home asunder. The voice came to the end of the story and began to tell it again. It never tired of the tale.

La'Non started shouting wordlessly and banging his head against the deck. Presently, the voice went away again. Perhaps it had other people to talk to. Others who liked the story of this different La'Non better. Dizzy, wiping away his blood, he moved on again, grateful for the silence.

He ate something that resembled vegetable matter, a hank of it he found rotting in a shadowed corner of a corridor, then supped spoiled water from an overfilled bathing sphere in a collapsed hab pod. La'Non followed the sign-lanterns up the slow, long ramps, spiralling around and around. The light tug of gravity generators, power still flowing to them from the mighty fusion reactor in the colony's core, enabled him to walk the inner circumference of the corridor-tubes; the technology let the tau use every iota of space within the asteroid for living and working.

No life now, though. Instead the colony was a corpse, and all the things swarming inside it just pests and vermin. La'Non was like that, a maggot inside dead flesh. Not a living thing, not like he used to be. Not like the other La'Non spoken of by the voice in his head.

But he was at peace with that. Understanding had given him contentment, if that was what a being could call it. Before, La'Non had been afraid he had lost his mind, been driven into lunacy by the agony and the limb. He thought better of it now, though.

He had gone *sane*. Yes. Clear to him. It was just that everything else was madness. Once he faced the night beyond, he would be certain of it. The last iota of doubt would be banished. If only he could find silence, find a way to end the pain, then he would be content.

Hours or days or years later, the tau found himself at the shipgates. The alien limb was scratching at the walls as he passed along them, rapping greenish knuckles on oval portals webbed by fracture damage. Presently, La'Non found what he sought. A hatch, an iris of dense metal alloy, each oiled leaf of it tight and closed. He didn't remember the sequence to open it, but his good hand did, and worked the hooded key-pad in the wall.

Through the fractured window, past the frosting of oxygen ice, he could see the black beyond. But not really. He couldn't really, *truly* see it. Not with the naked orbs of his own eyes. To really understand, to look the mad universe in the face and know it, he had to go out there. Or was he really venturing *inside* for the first time? La'Non wondered if the voice knew the answer. He smiled. Soon the pain would be gone and the voice would never trouble him again.

Busy with the sequence, he glimpsed but ignored the motion of a red shadow beyond the portal. It wasn't important; like the other La'Non and the wife and the child, it was a forgettable thing. Only this action, this moment, was significant.

Sound and vibration reached him, and his grey face twisted in confusion. Beyond the iris hatch there were noises, heavy footfalls and grinding impacts. That did not seem correct. On the other side of the iris there should only have been a stark white anteroom, the decompression chamber and the racks of skintight environment suits. The space should have been empty and ready for La'Non. The last barrier between him and the mad universe, waiting out there for him to arrive. For the tau to tell it he understood.

Then the iris keened as its metal blades came open and retracted into the stone walls. La'Non felt the alien limb twitching as he turned from the panel to take the next step.

The open hatchway was blocked by a statue made of crimson. La'Non looked up at it, taking in the form in a glance. It was humanoid, all curved shapes and hard edges. A heavy thing, carved to resemble arms and legs of bloated muscle, a small and fierce head sporting eyes as sharp as gemstones, a breath-grille mouth set in permanent grimace. Across its chest, a symbol; wings made of beaten gold growing from a wet, glistening droplet of ruby. And in one hand, the largest weapon La'Non had ever seen, a great steel block of mechanism bigger than any common pulse carbine. The yawning muzzle presented a black tunnel towards him.

There were others, too, more of the same crammed into the airlock space, stooped. Barely contained by the walls, hard and menacing. They sparked memory of the gue'la who had brought all the pain and understanding to the colony – these things were the same but different. The same mass, the same form. La'Non wondered if they shared the same cruelty as well. He asked the voice in his head if it knew the answer. Had the universe sent these new monsters to follow in the tracks of the pain-bringer? Were they the next act in its insanity, a new anguish for him to endure? And in doing so, learn a new truth?

La'Non offered his good hand in a gesture of greeting, but the alien limb wanted to participate as well, and rose in a fist.

BROTHER AJIR'S BOLTGUN rose, and in that moment Brother-Sergeant Rafen snarled out a command word. 'Hold!'

Ajir gave no sign that he had heard the order, and simply extended the motion of the gun, using the butt of the weapon to strike the alien away instead of killing it outright. The dishevelled tau was projected backward into the corridor of polished rock beyond the airlock antechamber, and it clattered to the deck in a heap of spindly limbs. For a moment the only sound was the scrape of the alien's feet as they skittered over the floor, failing to find purchase. Thin blood from a new cut oozed across the tau's dirt-smeared aspect. A moan escaped its lips.

With careful, spare motions, Ajir flicked his weapon to discard the dash of alien blood that had marked it. Brother-Sergeant Rafen heard him give a quiet sniff of disdain. 'It lives still,' said the other warrior.

Rafen's helmeted head turned and found Brother Ceris. The Codicier gave a nod, sensing his commander's unspoken instructions before he gave voice to them. Ceris pushed forward to the front of the group; of all the Adeptus Astartes in the antechamber, he was the only one not clad head-to-foot in crimson battle armour. Ceris's wargear was indigo, with only his right shoulder pauldron toned blood-red. The warrior removed his helmet and turned a narrow, flinty gaze on the alien. Crystalline devices surrounding the back of his head glowed gently, the contacts and mechanism of the psychic hood built into his power armour working their arcane science. The tau shrank away from him, muttering, and threw a worried glance towards Rafen.

The sergeant followed Ceris's example and detached his own helm, dark shoulder-length hair falling free as he did so. Rafen studied the alien without pity. 'Can you understand my words, xenos?'

The tau didn't respond; after a moment, Ceris spoke. 'It does.' The crystals pulsed slightly, and Rafen sensed a faint tang of ozone in the cool air, the overspill of the Codicier's careful psychic pressure on the alien creature.

'La'Non speaks your tongue, gue'la,' it said, in a papery, weak voice.

'We seek something,' Rafen told it. 'Here, on your colony. You will be compelled to help us find what we are looking for.' He inclined his head towards

Ceris, the inference clear. The psyker leaned in, unblinking, glaring at the trembling tau.

'This place has nothing but agony within it,' rasped the alien. 'Nothing for you. Only the agony and the voices.'

Rafen continued, ignoring the interruption. 'We are looking for another... Another *gue'la*.' He grimaced, the xenos word tasting foul upon his lips. 'Tell us what you know.'

'Pain-bringer!' The name was an abrupt snarl. 'You... You are the same!'

From behind him, Rafen heard a gruff growl of annoyance. 'We are nothing like *him*,' spat Brother Turcio.

'Show it the image,' continued the sergeant. He turned to Brother Kayne, who stood nearby with his rifle at the ready. 'We must be certain.'

Kayne's face was hidden behind his helmet, but his motions betrayed his irritation. Like the others, Kayne shared the ingrained urge to terminate any alien life he encountered, and it came hard to resist it. Rafen understood; he felt the same way, but the mission took precedence, and to prosecute that to its end he would do whatever was needed – such as allow an undeserving xenos a few more moments of life.

The younger Astartes produced a disc-shaped pict-slate from a pocket on his belt and stepped forward, offering it to the alien at arm's length.

The tau blinked blood from its eyes and peered owlishly at the screen; and in the next second what colour there was in its corpse-grey flesh faded. Rafen recognised the expression on the creature's face; horror, it would seem, looked the same no matter what species you belonged to. The alien brought up its hands to cover its eyes, one of them spindly and skeletal, the other thick-set and muscled.

'The creature's arm.' Turcio's voice came over the vox in his ear-bead, on a general channel that only the other Space Marines would hear. 'It's wrong.'

At Turcio's side, steady as a statue, a heavy bolter in his grip, Brother Puluo offered his taciturn opinion. 'Mutation?'

'No,' said Ajir, with a bored tone in his words. 'I've killed enough of them to know one from another. That's something different.' He glanced at his commander. 'Perhaps we ought to slit its throat and return it to the ship, give the sanguinary priests a curio to toy with.'

The tau watched them with a strange mixture of terror and compulsion, likely aware that they were talking about it, even though no sound escaped the sealed helmets and ear-beads of the hooded Space Marines. Gingerly, it got to its feet, blinking. The alien's breathing was shallow, and it was stooped. It extended a trembling finger into the darkness. 'Below, below,' it muttered. 'Pain-bringer. Below.'

'You will show us,' Ceris insisted, his gaze never wavering.

'Gue'la, the word is no. No. No.' The xenos began pulling at itself with the thick, distended limb. 'Cannot go back. Will not.' It pointed past the Astartes, to the outer airlock doors. 'Outside. Yes. To see the universe, face it. Stop the voice. Voice voice voice…'

'The creature is unhinged,' Ajir sniffed. His bolter rose again. 'What do we need with a guide, lord?' He glanced at Rafen.

'It is afraid,' Ceris noted. 'The torments of fear have pushed it over the bounds of sanity. The creature believes that it will be forced to live through more pain if it returns to the inner tiers of the colony.' He grimaced, as if reading the thoughts of the tau sickened him.

The alien waved its hands. 'Yes. Yes. No more pain.'

Rafen gave the tau a hard look. 'La'Non. Do as I say, and I will end your agony. Forever.'

When the tau looked up at him, the beseeching look in its eyes was pathetic. 'You swear this? On your deity?'

Ceris's eyes narrowed, his subtle power pressing down on the creature's weakened will.

Rafen gave a nod. 'Show us,' he demanded. 'Take us to the pain-bringer.'

THE MUTTERING, STUMBLING tau led them on, wandering back and forth down the corridors in a meandering course that at first seemed aimless. Ceris walked behind it, the faint glow of blue about his head and the tightness of his expression signifying the constant telepathic force he was keeping on the alien.

Rafen walked a few steps behind, his boltgun cradled in a barrel-low grip across his sternum. The sergeant was still finding the measure of the Codicier; his recent assignment to Rafen's unit had come on the orders of the Chapter's chief Librarian himself, the psyker-master Mephiston. Ceris, so barrack-room rumour had it, was one of several psychics personally selected by Mephiston to act as his eyes and ears throughout the Chapter; and Rafen could not shake the sense that in some way, everything he said or did within sight of the olive-skinned Codicier was somehow being observed by the man the Blood Angels called the Lord of Death. The ways of the witch-kin were beyond his experience, but Rafen did not find it difficult to imagine that Mephiston's great distance was no obstacle to the preternatural power of the mind.

Ceris cast a brief glance over his shoulder, and then away, as if giving some confirmation to Rafen's thoughts. When he spoke, the Codicier had a soft voice that seemed oddly out of place for a man from the heavy stock of Baal Prime's equatorial tribes; and his flat, hard gaze seemed to take in everything. Emotion, when the psyker cared to show it, was vague and undefined upon him. It was this, more than anything, that sat poorly with the sergeant. Every other man under his command, even the reserved Puluo, wore their spirit and fire openly. Ceris was an enigma, and Brother-Sergeant Rafen was ill at ease with the man.

'Sir.' Brother Puluo's voice issued from Rafen's vox bead. An indicator rune glowing on the inside of his gorget showed that the communication was coming in on a discreet channel from his second-in-command.

The sergeant knew Puluo had a question to voice. 'Speak,' he ordered.

The other warrior marched at his side, the blue helmet that marked him as a heavy-weapons Devastator Space Marine near-black in the shadows. 'Ajir had a point. We can find our way through this maggot-nest without the help of a xenos.'

'It is my prerogative,' Rafen replied, sub-vocalising the words so that they would be picked up by the vox but not heard by anyone else. 'It is a matter of expedience, brother. The alien will serve a purpose.' His face tightened into a frown. 'Too much time has been wasted on unsuccessful pursuits. If we must tolerate this creature to live a while longer in order to complete our assignment, so be it.'

'As you wish,' came the reply, but Rafen could tell Puluo was unsatisfied with the answer.

Truth be told, so was Rafen. But it had been several months now since he and his squad had left the Chapter's home world Baal aboard the warship *Tycho*, and in those days and weeks their victories had been few. Their mission, charged to Rafen from the lips of Chapter Master Dante himself, had proven every bit as difficult as the Blood Angels had expected. Their quarry was, if anything, even more elusive than his reputation suggested. They were chasing a shadow across the deeps of interstellar space, and to date they had constantly been one step behind him.

He threw a look back down the skirmish line of his warriors. Behind Puluo, who walked steadily with his heavy bolter held at arms, Ajir strode boldly down the middle of the corridor, glaring into each branching tunnel or open doorway, looking for an opportunity to engage an enemy. Kayne, the youngest of Rafen's squad, followed on with careful, wary footsteps and Turcio took up the rearguard, silent and watchful. In the gloom, Turcio's extended arm was rock-steady, the dull steel and heavy carbon of his augmetic limb hidden under his armour, a bolter in his iron-fingered grip. Each man, in his own manner, kept his focus on the duty at hand; but Rafen knew them well enough to sense the tension in them all, the tension he mirrored. Something that might have been called *unease* by lesser men, the edges of a disquiet that had been slowly growing as each avenue of their hunt had drawn closed, one after another.

Was *he* here? The question was one Rafen had asked himself a dozen times over the course of the *Tycho's* mission. On the surface of Seyrin Minoris; amid the ruins of a Dark Eldar slaughterdome; in the depths of Nadacar hive city; and through the rolling madness of warp space. A dozen leads, fragmentary sightings and half-truths drawn from a network of spies, scrying viewers and Imperial intelligence reports. Every one of them had proven to be a dead end, a wasted journey. Each time, the question. Each time, the search unfulfilled, the target lost.

Or was it that the subject of the hunt was just as fearsome and as clever as his enemies said he was? At Nadacar, Rafen had been certain he had seen him, glimpsed the hulking figure forcing its way through a mass of penitents. In the makeshift laboratory they had found, adorned with the wet remains of a Hereticus Inquisitor and his retinue. A goblet of wine, still warm to the touch. The smell of him lingering in the room. So close; but not close *enough*.

And with every disappointment, Rafen felt the blade of failure push deeper into his heart. For all the forgiving words of his master, it had been *he* who allowed the quarry to first make his escape from Baal. Even if no one else blamed Rafen for it, he laid the heavy responsibility upon himself. For a moment, a blink of memory clouded his thoughts, the recollection of a thing made of psy-smoke and ectoplasm hanging in the air before him. *A howling skull-shaped gateway*.

Rafen's hand drew tight around the grip of his bolter, and he tried to dispel the thought. It did him no good to torture himself with recriminations. Instead, he used the anger he felt as fuel, to power him on, to sharpen his senses.

They had been reduced to sifting through a detritus of information culled from sources so widespread and unreliable, that their veracity barely rose above the level of tall tales spun by tavern drunkards; and yet, as they had crossed the span of vacuum towards the hull of the drifting tau colony, something in Rafen's spirit had resonated like the strings of an electroharp. The renegade was close. He felt it in his bones.

Somewhere in this xenos warren, somewhere deep in the gloom, an arch-traitor, the self-styled Primogenitor of Chaos Undivided, former lieutenant of the Emperor's Children, a twisted Apothecary, a murderer and torturer of men, was working his evil.

Rafen glanced down at the oath of moment adhered to the vambrace of his power armour. The strip of sanctified parchment bore a spot of dark colour, a droplet of blood from the veins of Corbulo himself, the Master of the Red Grail and lord of the Chapter's sanguinary priests. The oath-paper was Rafen's vow, committed to words and sanctified in the sight of the God-Emperor of Mankind.

A promise to find and to kill the man known as Fabius Bile.

* * *

THE VOICE TOLD La'Non where to take the gue'la. After hours – or was it days? – of loping along the spiralling corridors, the tau brought the armoured humans to one of the largest of the colony asteroid's interior spaces. An elliptical cavern tapering to a point, the bulk of the open void was taken up by a faceted orb built of the same bland polymetal that so much tau construction was made from. Thick rods extending from the floor, the walls and ceiling held the bone-white sphere in place. Fixed focus gravity generators made it possible to walk up and over the surface of the orb, as if standing on the face of a tiny moonlet. Inside it, La'Non knew, there were vertical floors stacked one atop another. It had once been the colony's infirmary, now become a place of horrors.

The gue'la who came after the storm had spat them out, the pain-bringer, he had made his home here. All the politic words and platitudes at first, all the masks he wore and the honest entreaties to help the lost colonists, his lip service about wanting to join them in the service of the Greater Good. All lies.

La'Non heard the voice urging him on and he began to tremble and shiver. He felt the mind-force of the blue-armoured human at his back, making his legs move like stuttering pistons. Between the two opposing pressures, the tau felt as if his skull was about to burst. He whimpered, remembering all the things that had spilled from the infirmary. The pain-bringer and the great metal spider emerging from his back, the devices that cut and sliced and stitched. The monstrous pleasure he took in giving La'Non the limb.

And then all the others. The hybrids he built from bits of diverse species, things that never should have shared flesh, melded together by means that were beyond the understanding of a common earth caste clerk.

Another memory pushed itself forward, presenting itself to him as some horrific gift by the chattering voice. Recalling a moment when La'Non spoke, actually managed to utter a few words to the pain-bringer as the gue'la tethered him to an operating table.

The tau had asked him why. What reason was there to come to this lonely knot of star-lost castaways, to give them false hope and then torment them so? What value could it possibly have to him?

The pain-bringer had not lied then. He told La'Non he did these things not only because he could, but because it amused him.

La'Non remembered nothing but the screaming after that. Stumbling along the curved floor, he heard the sound in his head again, the voice wailing in pain. The limb curled up and punched the tau in the face, staggering him, and the shock lit energy inside him. Without understanding, disconnected from himself, the tau began to echo the inner scream with his voice. He pulled at the skin of his face, but the sound would not cease.

'THE XENOS−!' CERIS snarled out a warning as the tau stumbled away, clattering heedlessly through piles of wreckage and alien debris. The creature was shouting into the air, babbling a tirade in its own sibilant, incoherent language.

Rafen was already bringing his bolter to bear, sighting down the scope atop the weapon's frame. Leading the target, he thumbed the selector to single-shot and began to apply gentle pressure.

But in the next second a bolt of blue-white fire lanced through the sullen air and clipped the alien with a near-hit. The tau described a jerky pirouette and went down in a puff of thin blood. Rafen reacted as a second pulse beam went wide of him and cracked into a toppled heap of storage bins.

'There!' shouted Kayne, the youth's sharp eyes catching sight of the shooter. He pointed, and Ajir released a spray of bolt rounds into the low wall the other Blood Angel had indicated. With a cry, another tau exploded from the cover, brandishing a smoking weapon. The alien was clad in pieces of the sand-coloured armour Rafen recalled from hypnogogic training tapes, but the wargear was smeared with dark fluids and in poor order. Strangest of all, the tau warrior's face was oddly proportioned; spindles and bits of chitin festooned the right side of the alien, and when it screamed, the noise from its mouth was a rattle of bones.

Rafen put the xenos down with a single shot to the chest, and it blew backwards into wet rags. The dying alien had not finished twitching when more lines of blue fire probed out towards the Blood Angels. From heaps of wreckage and the shadowed doors of habitat pods, more of the creatures emerged. They hooted and roared, all of them bellowing a shared pain at the Space Marines. Rafen picked out one word being repeated, over and over. *Gue'la. Gue'la. Gue'la.*

'The alien brought us to an ambush!' Ajir snarled, clear reproach in his voice.

'No,' grunted Ceris. 'I would have known it.'

Rafen didn't venture an answer; he only frowned, and began to fire.

THE RAGGED, SCREAMING tau boiled out of the passageways and the fallen heaps of wreckage formed by broken habitat capsules. Some of them were soldiers – the so-called 'fire warriors' of their kind, the line infantry in their strange rectilinear armour sheaths – but more were civilians, functionaries, non-combatants. Many of them bore weapons, doubtless looted from fallen members of their kind or the armoury of whatever xenos garrison had been stationed in the colony. The strident shrieking of pulse bolts echoed around the vast oval chamber, lines of perfect lightning blazing outward, hugging the ground.

Rafen's Blood Angels splintered, moving through cover, pacing up towards the enemy advance. They fell into battle routine with rote precision, ready and geared to give death to their attackers. The heavy crack of bolters warred with the screaming alien guns, and from the corner of his eye, the sergeant saw Puluo plant his boots, lean into his heavy bolter's weight and unleash it. Flame gushed from the flash-hider of the weapon in cruciform flares, great brass casings launching from the ejection port in a fountain of metal, a punishing wave of rounds lashing out as the Space Marine turned slowly in place, tearing down everything in his arc of fire. Unarmoured tau caught in the midst of his kill zone lost limbs or exploded into flecks of meat, while the soldier-xenos went down, howling if they were not already dead.

Puluo's weapon alone should have been enough to put the fear of the God-Emperor into any enemy; but still the tau came on. Rafen had never fought their kind before, and what he knew of them came only second- and third-hand from other warriors, from his late mentor Koris and the indoctrination schema of his training. All of that had told him the tau were a clever foe, wily and careful in battle. That was not what he saw here.

'Rage…' muttered Ceris, close at Rafen's side. 'Nothing but rage.'

The psyker sensed the mindset of the aliens more clearly than the sergeant ever could, and saw what Rafen did. Fury was something the Blood Angel knew well – far *too* well, he admitted – and it was there before him in the tau. Their tactics were blunt and hard, with only the letting of blood on their minds. This was not the combat of a foe defending a location from an invader. It was anger, pure and simple. These xenos had been wronged, and they wanted someone to pay in kind.

The leading edge of the attack wave was downed, dead or dying, and Puluo found his pause, the heavy bolter's muzzle running cherry-red and shimmering with heat. In the moment, the tau advance surged, pulse rounds converging on the Blood Angels in threads of icy energy.

A figure mounted the curved roof of a collapsed habitat pod and flung itself at the sergeant. Rafen glimpsed dun-coloured armour and a curved helmet, featureless but for a peculiar mono-optic eye. The fire warrior led with a pulse carbine and the Blood Angel rocked off a fallen stone roundel to meet the alien in mid-leap. With one arm, Rafen forced the carbine away, shots screaming from it over his shoulder. In the heartbeat-fast pace, he was aware of a particle stream creasing the upper surface of his pauldron. The tau was smaller, lighter than the Space Marine, but its momentum was toppling Rafen backward.

The world tipping about him, he jammed the muzzle of his bolter into the gap between the plates of the alien's articulated armour and pulled the trigger. At point blank range, the tau was bifurcated, its legs and abdomen spinning away in one direction, the remains of the torso falling free, dragging wet ropes of intestine with it.

Rafen landed hard and rolled, coming up in time to see Ceris deploy his force mace in a glittering arc. The blunt-headed weapon grew spikes made of psionic energy, and the Codicier used it in an upward swing that batted another half-armoured fire warrior into a fallen wall. Wreathed in crackling energy, the tau vomited blood and perished.

Nearby, on a low mound of debris, Kayne and Turcio engaged a group of frenzied xenos at close range. The youth brought forward the crest of his helmet and put down a bulky male with a strike against its skull. Rafen's eyes narrowed as he watched the alien fall; like the one he had seen moments before, this tau's body seemed deformed, strange spines sprouting from its back, one arm folded up in a withered curl of bone and talon.

Turcio made a kill with his boot, grinding an armed creature in torn robes into the rock, dodging as its hands flailed at him. In a fluid motion, the Blood Angel followed through and put two more tau to death as they came at Kayne.

On the vox channel, Rafen heard a concussive grunt of anger and moderated pain, and immediately knew it was Ajir. Swinging about, he found the other Space Marine where he had fallen to one knee, the black streaks of pulse hits marring the crimson perfection of his battle armour. The sergeant thumbed his bolter's fire-select to fully automatic and lent his battle-brother support, blazing back towards the trio of fire warriors moving and shooting as they closed in. One went down, then another, bolts slamming through polymer and into meat and bone.

The last round belonged to Ajir, who made the engagement's final kill from where he crouched, taking off the top of the last fire warrior's skull in a low-deflection shot. The alien staggered closer before gravity finally captured it and dragged the corpse to the bloody ground.

Rafen extended a hand to Ajir, but the other Space Marine did not acknowledge it. Instead, he righted himself without assistance and got to his feet. The Blood Angel removed his helmet and spat into the dust. Rafen saw red in the spittle but did not remark upon it.

'Lord,' called Turcio, who stooped to poke one of the corpses with his gun barrel. 'You should see this, I think.' The penitent brand on his cheek was livid with his exertions.

Rafen left the glowering Ajir to his own devices and crossed to where Turcio's kill lay in a crumpled heap. Another anomaly, he noted. This tau bore odd fleshy wattles that spilled out of places beneath its clothing, as if they had burst through like tumours. In patches, the characteristic grey-toned skin veered towards pink. The dead alien had a piecemeal look to it, as if swatches of flesh had been cut from a human and merged with the tau's own skin. But there were no sutures, no marks where differing organic matter had been conjoined. There were simply spaces of meat where tau ended and human began. The sergeant felt his lip curl in disgust as the scope of the discovery became clear to him.

He nodded to himself. The other fire warrior, the one Kayne had killed... The spines upon it could so easily have been from a kroot organism, or perhaps even a tyranid. Here then was the signature of Fabius Bile, the callous experimentation on these pitiful xenos the detritus he had left behind him.

'This is the renegade's work,' he told his squad. 'These are the spoil.'

'Brother-Sergeant!' Kayne called out across the killing field. 'The xenos... The prisoner? It's gone!'

'Must have slipped away during the engagement.' muttered Turcio.

All eyes turned to Ceris, who accepted the unspoken question with a nod. He hesitated, his hooded gaze turning inward for a moment. The force mace, the tip still shimmering with tics of ethereal energy, rose to point towards the sphere-construct. 'In there.'

THE TAU, THE one that called itself La'Non, was not difficult to find. At first, they followed the regular spatters of thin blood that the xenos had left behind it, as it staggered its way up into the construct; but once inside the building proper, the trail of fluid became lost in the layers of older and darker vitae, dried out in a cracked layer over the floor like a coat of ancient varnish. The xenos blood left splash patterns up against the walls that became more pronounced the deeper the Astartes ventured, high-water marks that showed where some vast reservoir of the fluid had been emptied heedlessly into the corridors and left to find its own level.

There were, of course, bodies. Scattered remains of tau and some of their servitor races – the feral kroot and the insectoid vespid – some of them in states of death that defied explanation, others killed in more commonplace ways by shot or blade, or each other. A cloying stink that recalled rotting flowers permeated everything, and presently Rafen replaced his helmet and let the breathing filters do their work. They forded an inner barrier of tightly knit binder fungus, cutting through with swords and knives, boots sinking into the mushy flooring where accursed symbols had grown out of the damp mould. Ajir murmured a litany of protection beneath his breath, and Ceris echoed him on each word; the other Blood Angels kept their own prayers mute.

Kayne pointed out strange capsules lined up on stands through the next ward they entered, their skirmish line moving with steady care. Rafen examined one and found soft cloth bundled within; it was a natal clinic, he realised, and the pods were support units for tau newborns. All were empty, and he did not dwell on what the layer of white ash that lay at the bottom of the pods might have been.

When La'Non's blood trail ran out, they sought him in another fashion. They followed the sound of his lament.

THE IRIS DOORS were open and sagging, bent outward as if by a powerful pair of hands. The keening of the sorrowful tau echoed out to them, and Kayne led the way in, taking point. The pin-lamp atop his bolter searched the damp, close gloom, picking out stone tables coated in cracked enamel, angled to allow fluids to gather in clogged blood drains beneath. Pieces of corpses dangled from makeshift meat hooks on the ceiling – objects Rafen identified as parts of an ork, a human female, tau and orubon and xexet and other species he could not place. Kayne's torch found the corner of a strange design upon the wall and it was only when the youth recognised the sigil of the Eightfold Path of Chaos that he let out a curse and turned away.

The place had the sense of a work interrupted, and Rafen's heart sank. It was Nadacar Hive all over again. Fabius had been here, in this very room, conjuring his horrors, and then fled them.

This thought foremost in his mind, he found himself at one of the tables. Upon it, the tau called La'Non sat, legs dangling like those of a child in an adult's chair. Its shoulders were stooped and it moaned. He saw it had a heavy blade in one hand, almost a cleaver of the kind a butcher might use to cut a carcass. The tau was sawing back and forth at the place where the strange distorted arm had been connected to its body. Blood emerged in rivers, but the alien was making little headway in severing the alien limb. The blade was too dull, too broad, ill-suited for the task.

The xenos looked up at him, as if noticing the Astartes for the first time. 'The voice, gue'la,' it sobbed. 'I can still hear it. It will not be silent.'

'Where is the pain-bringer?' He met the alien's watery gaze. 'Where is Fabius Bile?'

'All around you!' came the shouted reply. 'His lies, his works, all here. All here!' The tau showed him the distended, muscular arm, and the limb flailed weakly, as if it were trying to escape. 'He lied, made us promises. And look what he did!' The creature's reedy, emotion-choked voice was rising. 'Everything is madness, yes? That is true, but all else is lies! Lies!' It rocked forward and tapped a thin finger on Rafen's chest, blinking away tears. 'You lied just as he lied!'

Rafen shook his head, a grim certainty gathering in his thoughts. 'I did not lie to you, xenos,' he told it. 'I said I would end your agony. I will.'

With a swift motion, the sergeant drew his combat knife and buried it in the alien's chest. The tau heart, as he recalled from his training, was in the centre of their torso, beneath a dense, bony plate in the middle of their ribcage. The fractal-edged blade slid easily through La'Non's flesh and resisted a little as it bit into bone; Rafen applied even pressure and the weapon went in to the hilt, the very tip emerging from the alien's back. The incision was clean and fast, cutting the heart in two. La'Non died silently, and Rafen allowed the body to fall off the edge of the knife.

Turcio watched him clean his weapon. 'I didn't know they could weep,' he noted.

Kayne gestured at the room, and his answer was Rafen's. 'Look around, brother. Any creature would weep to have such horrors forced upon them–'

He never finished his words; Puluo, on guard at the door, gave a sudden shout and dragged his cannon up to firing position. 'Movement!'

Rafen's gun came to his hand as a shape shuffled into the chamber from the far side of the room. In the shadows, it was a hulking humanoid form the equal of a Space Marine in stature and breadth, shoulders broad and heavy, a shorn scalp with a halo of long white hair, and raising hands; hands that were fine and clever and capable of such horrors.

'*Fabius!*' The silhouette was the very profile of the man Rafen had pursued through the lower levels of the Vitalis Citadel on Baal, the renegade and traitor. At once, every Space Marine in the room opened fire, and a flashing storm of bolts ripped into the figure, tearing it apart in a razored hurricane.

Rafen was rushing forward even before the body hit the floor, the burning bite of vengeance surging through his veins.

His moment of thunderous elation died, quickly and silently. Kayne's lamp lit the face of the figure, still discernable despite a bolt wound that had eaten away a fist-sized chunk of skull. The face was grey, pallid, a slit down its midline where a human being would have a nose. Eyes, large and wet, bulged out at him.

It was a tau, after a fashion, but monstrously bloated, bulked up by veins filled with generative compounds and muscle transplants. A xenos, made to mimic the mass of an Adeptus Astartes. Perhaps left here to be found so just such a trick could be played on whomever had come seeking the twisted Primogenitor.

Something fell from the freak's twitching fingers and fluttered to the wet floor. A scrap of paper. Rafen knelt to recover it before the fluids scattered all about soaked into the vellum and rendered it useless.

On the paper there were words in high gothic, rendered in a careful, studied hand. Just words, just ink upon a piece of dry parchment; and yet they raised in Rafen a rage so high his vision hazed crimson.

You have failed.

TWO

With a fluidity and pace that belied the bulk of his armoured form, Rafen strode through the corridors of the warship *Tycho*, the hard glitter of chained anger in his eyes enough to ensure that no Chapter serf, machine-helot or crewman dared block his path and question his passage.

His boots ringing on the iron deck plates, the Blood Angel climbed the shallow ramp leading from the cruiser's main spinal corridor, up towards the highest tier of the ship's hull. He entered a cloister lit by windows of starlight and colour, the glow trailing in shafts through the smoky air of the *Tycho's* chapel. Stained glass arranged in intricate designs showed the faces of warriors who had commanded the vessel in the past or commemorated great battles it had participated in. Over the entrance, a hexagonal mosaic showed a portrait of the man the cruiser drew its name from; Brother-Captain Erasmus Tycho, his face partly concealed by a golden half-mask. Rafen did not pause to meet the impassive gaze of the hero of Armageddon. The smell of incense was heavy here, reaching out from the nave, into the ship proper. Through the open doors ahead of him, the heavy copper gates lined with runes and inlaid obsidian, he glimpsed the altar and the statues beyond it.

'Lord?'

The question stopped him dead, and he turned in place. Behind him, Brother Ceris stood, studying him. Like Rafen, he had not yet removed his wargear, and his armoured bulk filled the doorway.

Ceris approached, and the sergeant mused on the realisation that he had not heard the Codicier following him. Perhaps it was because his anger was so fulsome, his attention elsewhere, that the psyker had managed to come so close without registering on his awareness; or perhaps not. The other Blood Angel walked to a bowl protruding from a wall, and reached in. Water – purified fluid recovered from the ship's reaction mass store, blessed daily by the *Tycho's* resident sanguinary priest – flowed from a nozzle in the shape of a cherub's mouth, and Ceris used it to dampen a cloth he recovered from a brass rack. In turn, he offered it to his commander.

Rafen took it without comment. It was protocol; on their return from the tau colony, the brother-sergeant and his squad had undertaken a brief ritual of purification to ward off the influence of the xenos and the stain of Chaos, but even so, it would have been wrong of Rafen to enter the chapel without taking a moment to pass a measure of the sanctified water over his armoured hands. He frowned inwardly; he should not have needed another man to remind him of that, even if Ceris did it without reproach. Rafen's mind was indeed unsettled, and it stoked his ready anger still more that it was so.

Ceris watched him as he completed the brief sacrament. The white cloth in the warrior's hands turned an ugly reddish-black as gummed oils and alien vitae, still caught in the hinges of his gauntlets, were dissolved.

'I spoke with the shipmaster,' began the psyker. 'He has taken your orders, sir. *Tycho* is turning to bear.'

Rafen nodded once. On the floor, the discs of waxen light cast through the windows were moving slowly across the floor as the starship came about. He looked away. 'Once it is done, tell him to prepare the vessel for the warp.' The sergeant balled the cloth in his hand and threw it at a waiting servitor in an alcove. The machine-slave caught the cloth from the air and carried it towards a fire grate for disposal.

Rafen took two steps before he noticed that Ceris had not taken the implied dismissal in his tone. The psyker studied him, and the sergeant found a churn of resentment turning in his chest. 'You have something else you wish to say to me?' he demanded.

'The blame is not yours.'

The statement was blunt and firm. The sergeant's expression tightened. 'You are dismissed,' he growled, enunciating the words clearly so there would be no further misunderstanding.

Still Ceris made no move to obey the command. 'You cloud your thoughts with recriminations, and it does you ill, sir. It takes your focus.'

'Stay out of my mind.' Rafen's voice was low and menacing.

'I need not exercise my abilities to read you, brother-sergeant. You wear your ire upon your sleeve as clearly as our Chapter sigil.'

Rafen took a step closer to the blue-armoured warrior. 'For one they say is a chosen man of the Lord of Death, you seem to lack the sense to keep your opinions to yourself.'

'My master Mephiston expects honesty and directness from his Librarians,' replied Ceris. 'He told me I was to give the same to you.'

'So you have, then.' Rafen gestured at the ramp leading back from the chapel. 'Go now, and be content you have done your duty.' Bitterness laced his words, hard and unexpected.

'I have not,' Ceris continued, remaining irritatingly unruffled, stock-still and fixed upon the other warrior. 'Mephiston bid me to join your squad to aid you in our mission, and this I have not done.'

'The *mission?*' Rafen spat the reply at him. 'The mission is a failure, Ceris! You saw it with your own eyes! Fabius has slipped out of our net at every turn, confounded us. He mocks us, and we have no choice but to countenance it!' He turned away. 'And you are wrong. The blame *is* mine.'

'Can you be so sure?' Ceris asked. 'The renegade Bile has been at large for over ten thousand years, sir. He travelled the stars in the time of the high traitor Horus and the fires of the Heresy. Thousands have been killed at his hands, across countless worlds. He is a singular foe, a man who slipped even the grasp of Chapter Masters and primarchs alike–'

'And you would have me take succour from that, would you?' The sergeant snorted. 'You were not there on Baal, psyker! You did not have him in your sights. You were not the one who failed to stop him!'

For the first time, Ceris broke eye contact. 'I was not,' he admitted. 'I was many light years distant, at the conflicts on Beta Comea. But consider *my* anger, lord. Imagine *my* fury at learning that our home world had been attacked by the forces of Chaos. I and the battle-brothers with me were too far away to lend our arms to the defence of Baal... We could not even see the face of the enemy, let alone chance to strike at him as you did.'

'You're a fool, then,' Rafen grated. 'You ought to think yourself blessed for being spared the shame.'

The same black skein of thought that had plagued the sergeant every night since the *Tycho's* mission began rose in him.

In the wake of the Chapter's losses following the insurrection on Cybele and the dark schemes of a turncoat inquisitor named Stele, the Blood Angels had called a conclave of all successor Chapters. This historic gathering on Baal had but one aim – to bulwark the Chapter's forces by drawing a tithe of warriors from each force of Blood Angels descendants – but the plans of the Chapter Master Dante had been set awry by the blind ambition of a single, misguided sanguinary priest. One man, convinced he could rebuild the Chapter's losses not through a tithe, but by the use of ancient, forbidden science, had unwittingly allied himself to a biologian of the Adeptus Mechanicus; or so he had believed.

The priest opened a door to Baal, joining forces with a magos who called himself Haran Serpens. To their cost, the Blood Angels learned that this identity was merely one mask, one falsehood among hundreds spun by the arch-traitor and self-styled Primogenitor of Chaos Undivided; Fabius Bile.

In the madness that followed, great horrors were wrought. Mutant creatures that merged Astartes DNA with rapacious animal hungers were created, freakish aberrant Bloodfiends running wild, pillaging and despoiling everything the Blood Angels held sacred. In a final battle beneath the Chapter's great fortress monastery, Rafen and his battle-brothers came together with their kinsmen to fight and vanquish the Chaos-spawned monsters. There, in sight of the tomb of their primarch, the golden Sanguinius, father of their Chapter and Lord of the Blood Angels, the invaders had at last been defeated and sanctity restored.

The future of the Chapter was secured; the Blood Angels would live on. But in the anarchy of the battle, slithering through the mayhem he had set in order to hide his crimes, under cover of lies Fabius Bile had stolen a most precious relic. A crystal vial, and in it, a measure of the purest blood plundered from the holy Red Grail. Drops of the vitae of Sanguinius himself.

Even now, after months had passed, Rafen was still sickened to his very core by the thought of this high transgression against his Chapter. His mind reeled at the horrors that a twisted genius such as Fabius might wreak with so rare and powerful an artefact in his clutches. The enormity of this monstrous theft shook him, the resonance so strong it was as if it had happened only yesterday.

To let this sin go unanswered could not stand. The renegade had committed a grave offence that could only be resolved by his execution, and by the recovery of what he had stolen.

Rafen and his squad had dedicated themselves to fulfilling this need; but all they had to show for it were empty hands, spent bullets and a string of failures. Those, and a single piece of bloodstained paper.

'Have you learned nothing?' The psyker's question shattered Rafen's moment of reverie. 'After all that great Dante said, were you deaf to it?'

The sergeant's anger rushed through him, and with a sudden movement, he grabbed the other Blood Angel and forced Ceris back hard against the wall of the cloister, slamming him into a stone pillar. 'Damn you!' he shouted. 'What do you want from me, brother? Answer!'

For a brief instant, there was something like shock on the psyker's face; but in the next moment it was gone, and his blank, steady aspect returned to its place. 'Are you so arrogant, Brother-Sergeant Rafen, that you think yourself elevated above all the rest of us?' Ceris's voice was rough. 'I know Lord Dante's words and I was not even there to hear them with my own ears! Remember what he said, there in the great sepulchre before the battle with the Blood-fiends. *We are being tested!* Every single one of us, not just you!' The psyker shook himself free of Rafen's grip, and he allowed it. 'You have no right to take this burden upon yourself. It is not yours to hold alone. We are the Sons of Sanguinius, we are Blood Angels, and we face challenge every day of our lives. This one is no different, only the scale of it changes.

We find this enemy and we kill him. All of us. *As one.'*

Rafen turned away, the bitterness rising again in his gorge. 'Find him? How? Tell me, Codicier, can you pluck his whereabouts from the tides of the warp with your witch-sight? Do not think to accuse me of wallowing in despair! I do nothing of the kind!' He pressed a finger against the other man's chest. 'Know this. I would take this ship blindfold into the Eye of Terror. I would cut my own hearts from my flesh. I would sacrifice every one of my kinsmen here aboard, and more, if that is what it would take to find this renegade!'

Ceris nodded. 'And no man in this crew would defy you if you did.'

'But I cannot…' hissed Rafen. 'Look around you, brother. We have nothing. Our last lead, wasted on that tau madhouse. And Fabius knows it. He's out there, laughing at us.'

'The Chapter Master would not have charged you with this hunt if it were a simple matter.'

Rafen made a negative noise and angrily stalked away. 'This is not some great and noble quest we can take a century to prosecute! It is an assassination! Time is ranged against us. Every moment that Chaos bastard holds a single droplet of sacred blood, he works his evil. Every hour advances his corruption. We must end this with swiftness, or we are lost!'

Ceris was silent for a moment. Then he threw a nod towards the copper doors and the chapel beyond. 'Why are you here, sir?'

'What do you mean?'

'The chapel, brother. The rest of the squad returned to the arming chambers to doff their wargear and undergo the rites of cleansing. But you came straight here. You did not even take your orders for the shipmaster to the bridge.'

Rafen frowned. 'I came here… For the peace of it. I find clarity in the quiet.' He allowed himself a sigh. 'Perhaps I hoped to find some insight.'

Ceris looked at the statues at the far end of the chapel, the God-Emperor and his son Sanguinius standing like stone titans, offering only their steady and unswerving aspects. 'Then you already have your answer, sir. You already know where our remedy lies. Have faith in the Emperor, brother-sergeant, and the Emperor will provide.' The psyker began to walk away. 'It would be an even greater crime if Fabius were allowed to take that too from us.'

'Indeed.' Rafen found himself nodding. Through his boots, the Blood Angel sensed a subtle vibration in the *Tycho's* decking, and he moved to one of the stained glass windows in the cloister's alcoves. Through the diamond-hard tiles of colour, he saw a flash of light from a launch tube on the warship's flank. Sleek cylinders of metal, pressed forward on white spears of fire, looped away from the vessel, tracking, swarming together. He followed their course, looking ahead of them, and found the murky shape of the asteroid colony caught by the light of distant stars. Without another word, Rafen turned away and walked into the chapel; his anger, for the moment, held at bay.

Silent, hard flashes of refracted illumination reached out after him as the *Tycho's* weapons did their work, and undid that of the traitor.

* * *

IN COARSE ROBES dyed grey and rust-red, there were rank upon rank of warrior-kin. They stood in lines across the sun-warmed flagstones of the great central courtyard, the air dry upon their upturned faces, the glow of the distant Baalite sun a red disc at their backs. Corbulo stood out from them, his robes cut in much the same fashion as theirs, but dressed with panels of white. The brash detail of his gold honour chains blinked as the sunlight crossed them. He walked the length of the warriors, his steady, clear voice carrying far, echoing off the walls formed by the surrounding buildings of the fortress monastery. His hood was rolled back, so that he could look each one of them in the eye.

'There will come a day,' he told them, 'when you will ask yourself a question. Who am I? You will ask yourself where you came from, you will ponder on this and seek an answer.' Corbulo's craggy face pulled in a slight smile. 'And then you will remember what I am about to tell you, and think no more of it.'

The sanguinary high priest paused in the shadow of the great statue in the middle of the courtyard, the winged shape rising high above him. He spread his hands, taking in all before him with a single gesture. 'Where you were born. The tribes in which you grew to manhood. The worlds you called home. The leaders you once gave fealty to...' He looked into different faces, and saw stiff attention, in some perhaps the odd hint of anticipation and awe. 'These things are what made you who you are. But you stride beyond them now. Each of you has been tested to breaking point and emerged the stronger for it. You have fought through the trials and been judged. A great gift is now yours. You have earned the right to live and to die, not as a mere human being, but as an Adeptus Astartes. A Son of Sanguinius. A Blood Angel.' He nodded to himself. 'That is the only answer you will ever need. And be certain in the belief that there are many who envy you. Many who cherish and honour you. But still more, a myriad more, who hate you for what you have become. And against them, every day you still draw breath is a victory.'

Corbulo reached inside his robes, his fingers closing around a bag made of blood-crimson velvet, sewn with threads of gold and platinum, bedecked with rare gems from a hundred conquered worlds. 'You are a victory made of meat and bone and blood. You are kings of war and the battle-lords of all you survey. You stride the stars in one unity of purpose – to fight in the honour of humankind, for the grace of Holy Terra and in veneration of the God-Emperor of Man and the Primarch Sanguinius.' From the robes he drew forth the relic that was his sole charge, an object cleansed and sanctified and made pure as no other artefact could be.

He turned it in his hands, hearing the collective gasp from the warriors arrayed around him. It was flawless and perfect, without any outward sign of the great affront that had been perpetrated against it only months ago. Corbulo refused to allow himself to dwell on that moment of darkness; he held the Red Grail high, and let the incarnadine sun shower it with colour. The same old, giddying elation, the same undimmed sense of power surged through him and, at the sight of the relic, the robed Astartes went as one to their knees. 'In His name, brothers,' said the priest.

They echoed his words in a roar that raised to the sky.

'IN HIS NAME,' whispered Dante, speaking the litany along with them. His hands rested on the balustrade of the stone balcony, the glassy black basalt there polished by his fingers, by the actions of countless such moments when he had stood here and looked down upon his warriors and his Chapter. His keen, hawkish eyes studied the faces of the warriors far below, each of them fully-fledged battle-brothers now and no longer initiates. He mused on Corbulo's words, wondering after the origins of these new Blood Angels. The majority were the intake from the tithes of Baal's two desert moons, but a fair proportion were assignees from the successor Chapters that had elected to bring the Chapter's numbers up to full strength. How many of them had been recruited by the Angels Encarmine, the Flesh Tearers, the Blood Legion or any of a dozen other brother-Chapters? He pushed the question away. Corbulo had been correct. Who they had been mattered not; who they were *now* was all that mattered. All of them, Sons of Sanguinius.

'New blood,' said a familiar voice, from behind him.

Dante nodded. 'Aye.'

Mephiston, master psyker of the Chapter and Dante's strong right arm, joined him at the balustrade and cast his glacial gaze across the crop of recruits. The chief Librarian of the Blood Angels was clothed in a combat tunic and fighting breeches; he had come from the training halls to the presence of his master without summons, and it was a testament to their decades-long friendship that Dante did nothing more than raise an eyebrow at the other warrior's somewhat casual attire. Few Blood Angels were granted the latitude to enter the Master's chambers without first donning all the requisite robes and decorations of fealty; but there were times when such trappings of ceremony and ritual were important, and times when they were not. This moment was one of the latter.

Dante had not been aware of Mephiston's approach, and to admit that was to say much. In over a millennium of service to the Golden Throne, those who could enter Dante's presence without his knowledge could be counted on the fingers of one hand – and of those, three had been killed by the Chapter Master himself. But far from being concerned by such a thing, Dante was pleased by it. If Mephiston was still a mystery to him, after so long, then to his enemies the Lord of Death would be a ghost, unknowable and lethal.

'I make it a rule never to miss this moment,' Mephiston offered, jutting his sharp chin towards the recruits, as far below Corbulo bid them to rise. 'To see our kindred and the grail together...' He trailed off, his voice soft with reverence.

'You may see the Red Grail whenever you wish, brother,' noted Dante. 'Such is your rank, no sanguinary priest would ever dare to deny you entrance to the great chapel.' He nodded towards the spherical nave atop a distant tower.

'It is so,' said the psyker. 'But this is different. When Corbulo shows them the relic, and their hearts rise in its glow...' Mephiston sighed. 'I feel sorrow for you, my lord, that you cannot perceive the colour and play of their emotions as I can. The sense of our battle-brothers and their auras at this moment is... almost transcendent.'

'I feel a measure of that,' Dante noted. 'Perhaps not as you do with your witch-sight, but still the power of it rings in the air. It reminds me that even after eleven hundred years, I am not so jaded that I cannot still be awed.'

Mephiston nodded. 'Just so. We live in a time of wonders, my Master. It is hard to believe that just a season has elapsed since our Chapter stared into the abyss. We faced the spectre of dissolution, but with the grace of Holy Terra, we have dispelled it.'

Dante folded his arms and drew in a slow breath. Unbidden, his mood began to shift and darken. Mephiston sensed it immediately and glanced at him, measuring him with that ever-unblinking gaze. 'Curious,' said the Chapter Master. 'How strange it is that I can at once have such pride in my heart, but also the shadow of something bleak. Something closer to fury.'

And the source of that fury did not need to be given words; both of them shared the same stony ire, the same slow-burning hate at the violations done to their Chapter and their home world.

'It is often the nature of men to be two things at once, in direct conflict with themselves,' mused the psyker. 'When the God-Emperor, His light unbound, first forged the Adeptus Astartes, He ensured that we would keep that duality. It is just and right we do so.'

'Indeed,' Dante replied. 'Better to remind us not to stride too high above the common people we protect.

What becomes of those of us who eschew their humanity?'

Mephiston's face grew a sneer. 'Perhaps that is a question I will put to Fabius Bile when we capture him.'

Dante's reply was cold iron. 'There will be no capture. Despite what the Ordo Hereticus may wish, there will be no trials and imprisonment, no process and public excoriation. Fabius will die wherever he raises his benighted head.' He turned away from the balcony and walked back into the chamber, irritated at himself for allowing his black mood to come to the fore. The pleasure of seeing in the new tithe faded by the second, and that too built upon his hard, precise anger.

Finally, he stopped in the middle of the room and turned a hooded look on his battle-brother. 'You have seen the most recent communiqué from the *Tycho*.' It was not a question.

The other man nodded. 'I have. It is… disappointing.'

Dante gave a gruff chug of humourless laughter. 'A moderated way of describing the situation, if ever there was one. That xenos colony was a solid lead, but like all the others, it has turned to ashes in our hands.'

'Our agents still seek new indications,' said the psyker. 'Every battle-brother listens out for any fraction of information.'

'And what have we learned, Mephiston? What have we gathered but acres of useless data, nothing but hearsay and the ghosts of rumours?' He gestured to an ornate desk in the corner of the room, where a gas-lens viewer scrolled through pages of data in gothic script. Parchments and pict-slates littered the surface of the console. 'I vet this tide of noise myself and pick nothing from it. It is static, and little else. Worthless.'

'Fabius Bile has been sighted,' noted the psyker. 'Those appearances are being researched by our cogitators and a contingent of my best epistolaries.'

'If we were to believe all that we are told, then it would seem that the accursed renegade is active in dozens of places all across the galaxy, all at the same time.' Dante's voice rose in annoyance. 'During the Festival of Ultimate Piety, observers place him in the Eastern Fringes, the Sabbat Worlds and the Damocles Gulf. Which of them is right? To which place do we send our warriors?'

The fact that Mephiston did not offer to supply an answer to his question made the Chapter Master's point for him.

Dante's lips thinned. 'I could dedicate the whole Chapter to the chase and it would still not be enough, damn him.'

'We knew the traitor would not be easy prey when we embarked upon this course of action,' said the psyker. 'He has eluded the forces of the Imperium for lifetimes. It may take that long to exact our full vengeance upon him.'

Dante gave a terse nod. 'And that may be so, but there is the matter of... of the sacred blood.' The warrior's gut twisted at the thought of it. 'And in that, we cannot tarry.' He walked back towards the other man, and when he spoke again, his voice was low. 'Old friend, what robs me of my peace, what keeps me awake in the dark of night, is the question. The question that torments me.'

'What does Fabius want with the blood of our primarch?' asked Mephiston. 'I dread to know the answer, lord. I truly do.'

'And more than that, I wonder if the atrocity he perpetrated against us was some part of a greater plan. Some scheme in which the Blood Angels are but a single element.'

Mephiston eyed him. 'How so?'

'What do we know of this bastard?' snapped Dante, allowing himself to give full voice to his thoughts. 'This so-called Primogenitor, who cuts and stitches the meat of life into patterns that offend all who lay eyes on them? A traitor among traitors, once a sworn Adeptus Astartes of the Emperor's Children before they took the coin of Horus and turned heretic. A genius Apothecary, twisted by his fealty to the Eightfold Path of Chaos. A being of towering cruelty without interest in power or dominion–'

'Only arcane, forbidden knowledge,' said Mephiston, with a nod. 'I have seen the horrors he has wrought and then released upon the battlefield. His freakish "New Men", things that walk like humans, each the equal of an Astartes.'

'Bile has no loyalty, not even to the daemon prince Fulgrim, Emperor blight him, or the rest of his turncoat kindred.' Dante stalked away, his anger animating him. 'He slips through the shadows, prostituting his skills to any Chaos warlord who will pay for them.' The Chapter Master came to a halt and drew in a deep breath, forcing down his building anger. 'This is the traitor we must find and kill.' He looked away. 'If only we could.'

After a long moment, Mephiston spoke again. 'There is another reason I came to you today, lord,' he began. 'In the throes of my battle-meditation, a vision came to me. An inkling. A sense of import.'

Dante watched his comrade intently. The workings of the psyker-mind were a mystery, even to those who had been steeped in their ways for centuries, and yet the Chapter Master knew Mephiston well enough to recognise the import of what the Lord of Death was about to say. 'You... saw something? In the warp?'

'The skeins of past and future are open to some. In rare moments, I have been blessed to be one of them... Although some might think it more a curse.'

'Tell me what you sensed.'

Mephiston hesitated, and in that instant there came a hard rapping against the chamber door. The Chapter Master gestured to one of his helots, and the servitor stepped forth from its charging alcove to answer the entreaty.

A Blood Angel in full wargear, the golden helmet of an honour guard in the crook of one arm, entered and went down on one knee. 'My lord, forgive the intrusion.'

'What is it, Brother Garyth?' Dante failed to keep an edge of irritation from his voice.

'An urgent machine-call from the dock station in high orbit. They relay a message from Brother-Sergeant Kale.'

Dante nodded; Kale was currently serving aboard the cruiser *Dario*, a warship assigned to the picket force that patrolled the rim of the Baal system. 'Go on.'

'Kale is inbound, sir. He brings with him a courier vessel that exited the warp just beyond the outer defence ring.'

'A messenger,' whispered Mephiston, his gaze turned inward.

'Aye,' said the honour guard. 'The craft bears the pennants of the Flesh Tearers. They claim to have come bearing a message of utmost import, from Chapter Master Seth himself.'

Dante looked to the psyker. 'This is what you saw?'

He got a nod in return. 'A swift galleon moving through endless night. On its sails of black sackcloth, a serrated blade touched with a single drop of blood. In its hold, the sound of a voice, whispering a name. *Gabriel.*'

The Chapter Master walked to the doors leading to the balcony and stood on the threshold, looking up onto the rust-red sky. 'Grant them passage,' he told the honour guard. 'I will hear what my honoured cousin has to say to me.'

THE AQUILA-CLASS SHUTTLE dropped like a falling hawk from the low dust clouds and made a leisurely banking turn over the tallest spires of the fortress-monastery, before angling in for a landing on the southern approach. The shuttle settled with a dull thud of compacting hydraulics, fumes and dust swirling around it before the low winds caught them and dragged the haze away.

Mephiston's eyes narrowed to slits as he peered at the craft, pressing through the commonplace metals and plastics of the hull, reaching for a sense of the passengers inside. He found what he expected;

warriors of character, intent and focused on their missions at hand.

The psyker stood at his Chapter Master's side, the pair of them joined by a trio of honour guards; aside from the mindless machine-slaves that skittered out to connect up the refuelling conduits and stabilising tethers, the landing pad was empty. Mephiston knew that as a matter of course, scouts armed with modified Zaitsev-pattern long-bolters were ranged in the upper towers bracketing the platform, watching for any signs of trouble; it was one of many additional security measures that he himself had initiated in the wake of Fabius's infiltration of Baal.

Presently the drop ramp along the shuttle's ventral hull fell open and a lone Blood Angel wearing a veteran sergeant's laurels exited the ship. The warrior came forward and knelt before Dante, removing his helmet and tucking it to his chest. 'Master, my lord,' he began. 'I bring news.'

'To your feet, Brother-Sergeant Kale,' said Dante. 'Speak plainly.'

Kale stood up, and Mephiston noted how the man was careful not to allow his gaze to cross that of the psyker. The sergeant was an old hand at the business of war, and not one to take to fear easily; yet, his aura glittered with trepidation at being in the chief Librarian's presence. Mephiston saw this and accepted it. His fearsome reputation throughout the Chapter had a life of its own, and the Lord of Death saw no reason to do anything to discourage it.

'The *Dario* intercepted a small warp-capable craft exiting the immaterium beyond the orbit of the twelfth planet,' Kale explained. His voice had the sharp edges of a Secundus clan accent. 'It answered challenge and hove to. Aboard we found a contingent of Astartes from the Flesh Tearers Chapter. They would speak only with you, Master.'

'Their diktats and signets are in order?' said Mephiston.

Kale nodded. 'Aye, sir. The messenger bears the seal of Lord Seth himself.'

Dante made a beckoning gesture. 'Bring him to me.'

As Kale returned to the shuttle, Mephiston leaned close to his commander. 'No falsehood here,' he reported. 'Kale believes what he has been told, and those aboard that ship believe it too.'

'What does Seth want?' Dante wondered. 'We parted on amicable terms after the conclave. Perhaps he wishes to ask a favour of me now we have strengthened the comradeship between our two Chapters.'

The sergeant returned, and with him came three Flesh Tearers. Their armour deep blood-red and trimmed with night-black, they largely abstained from the displays of honour chains and heraldry common to their parent Chapter. One of them, a veteran sergeant like Kale, sported a shield-roundel attached to his shoulder guard – on it, Mephiston spied the lizard-claw symbol that was Seth's personal battle emblem. The gold helmet dangling at the Flesh Tearer's belt confirmed it; this Astartes was one of Seth's personal guard.

Kale and the two other Flesh Tearers stood to attention and the messenger followed the pattern as was expected of him, bowing low and announcing himself. 'I am Brother Mazon,' he said, 'I bring word from your honoured cousin, Seth of the Flesh Tearers.'

Mazon met Mephiston's gaze for a moment – a fractional one – and quickly looked away. It was more than enough for the psyker to gain an insight into him. No subterfuge lay in this man's thoughts. Whatever reason his Master had sent him to Baal for, it was not for ill intent. The psyker thought of the fragmentary vision he had experienced and mused on how it would connect to this unexpected arrival.

The Space Marine drew a plain box made of red-enamelled iron from his belt and offered it to Dante. 'This will open only to you, lord.'

The commander nodded and accepted the device. The instant his bare flesh touched the surface, Mephiston heard the quiet click of a bloodlock. With an oiled whisper of intricate workings, the box unfolded to become an oval plate crested with spines; atop the spines, a rarity glittered.

'A hololith diamond,' noted Dante. 'A rare device. Great Seth has clearly spared no effort in bringing this message to me in secure order.' The Chapter Master stroked the facets of the fist-sized gemstone, and it shone as it caught an errant ray of sunlight.

As if from a prism, the diamond's glow grew, emerging from the stone to become a ghost of shimmering light. The ghost stuttered and flickered, becoming a crude image of Seth, armoured but unkempt, as if he had just stepped from a battle. The Flesh Tearers bowed to the hololith, showing it the same fealty they would have the Master himself. Mephiston watched as the message encoded on the crystalline matrix of the archeotech device began to play out.

Seth began with a cold, humourless grin. '*Cousin, the Emperor's light find you well. You'll forgive me the cheap theatre of this message, but it seemed the most expedient means of reaching you. I have something for the Blood Angels.'*

Dante and Mephiston exchanged wary glances. Of all the things the Lord of Death had expected the Master of the Flesh Tearers to say, it was not this.

'Battle chews up all my time and energy, and if it were not so, if it were not a shirking of my sacred duty to Terra, I would follow this datum myself. But I cannot, so I pass this to you.' Seth's face clouded briefly with annoyance. *'I know what you have been doing, cousin. Don't trouble yourself by wondering how I know, just accept it.'*

'He's talking about the hunt for the traitor,' said the psyker. 'How–?'

Dante silenced him with a shake of the head.

'We have made a discovery. A member of the Adeptus Mechanicus, a tech-priest of some great self-importance by the name of Matthun Zellik, has stepped over the bounds of his oath to Mars and Holy Terra. He has been in contact with a rogue tech-lord of your acquaintance. Haran Serpens.'

'Fabius…' husked Dante.

'Granted, this information is old, but the veracity of the source is assured.' Seth gave a wicked, predatory grin that showed his fangs, his right hand straying to scratch at the old scars on his face. *'The informant was… shall we say, drained dry of all he had to give.'*

The commander of the Blood Angels glared at the hololith image, as if he could see into it and through to Seth himself. 'And now comes the price,' he muttered.

As if in answer, the figure in the message nodded to himself, becoming dour and serious. *'I have said nothing of this to anyone. None of the other successors know of what has been under way, or of what has been stolen. I lay no blame upon you, Dante. I understand the import of this. I would have done the same as you do now, if I stood in your place.'* He frowned. *'But I want in. The Flesh Tearers will be a part of this. My Chapter will share in the glory of bringing the quarry to his ruin.'*

Dante nodded slowly. 'Ah, Seth. You know I cannot refuse you. Not now.'

The hololith continued. *'I have already sent a ship to rendezvous with your lad Rafen and his band. The* Gabriel. *The warriors aboard know enough.'*

Mephiston's chest tightened at the mention of the vessel's name.

'You need only tell Rafen to accept the help he is offered. And together, we will right this.' Seth bowed. *'We both know the risk of standing alone, Dante. Our unity will make us strong.'* With a final flicker of colour, the image became mist and dispersed, the glow from within the diamond fading to nothing.

The Master of the Blood Angels allowed the message box to close and weighed it silently in his hands, considering. Finally, he glanced at Brother Mazon and tossed the device to him. Mazon caught it easily, and said nothing, waiting.

Dante walked away a few steps, and Mephiston followed him. 'The God-Emperor's ways are sometimes opaque to us,' offered the psyker. 'Perhaps we should accept that this turn of events is His hand at work.'

'Perhaps,' echoed Dante. 'I wonder, should I be troubled that my cousin knows so much of our endeavours? This is not the first time the Flesh Tearers have shown such… insight.'

'Our search for Fabius cast a wide net, and quickly with it,' noted Mephiston. 'These things could have become known to Seth.'

Dante's patrician face stiffened. 'A matter to be addressed. But first this.' He turned abruptly and crossed back towards Mazon. 'Brother-sergeant. Consider your message delivered. You may leave.'

'Lord,' said the Flesh Tearer, 'if you will. An answer will be requested.'

The commander shook his head, a grim smile playing on his lips. 'You are mistaken, Mazon. Your Master knew my answer before he sent you to me.'

FROM A DISTANCE, both ships appeared almost identical. They shared the bladed prow, the orchard of crenulated minarets along the dorsal lengths of their fuselage, the hammerhead castle rising from their hull. Cannons in brassy, murderous array gave mute defiance to all enemies, engines flaring like captured suns at their backs; these were rapid strike cruisers of the Adeptus Astartes, ships of singular, swift purpose that could turn cities to slag or land armies if the needs of battle demanded it.

Their colours were all that separated them, that and the bold sigils upon their blade-sails. The *Tycho*, red as fury, chased with brass and gunmetal silver, adorned with a winged droplet of blood shining bright in the void. Alongside, the *Gabriel*, black as rage, lined with sanguine among the ebon, with a razor-toothed wheel kissed by a tear of dark blood catching the distant solar glows.

In silhouette, both the same; in light of sun, their characters revealed. The Astartes aboard them did not differ from the ships in which they travelled.

'COUSIN,' SAID RAFEN, 'well met.'

Brother-Sergeant Noxx gave a terse nod. A thin smile threatened to break out across his lips. 'I'll wager you didn't think we would cross paths so soon again, eh, Blood Angel?'

Rafen allowed the other man a nod. 'Just so, Flesh Tearer. I confess, I was surprised to see your ship out here. Is not your Chapter still engaged in the punishment of Eritaen?'

Noxx shook his head, making a show of looking around the *Tycho's* audience chamber. The veteran and his squad had come aboard, claiming the right granted to any Astartes, to meet and speak in confidence with members of another Chapter. The *Gabriel* had left the *Tycho* little choice but to heave to, the Flesh Tearers' ship venturing so close that its mass shadow would make any attempt to enter warp space a dangerous prospect. 'That conflict is ended. But the rest of my kinsmen have been given a new battle to fight, against an ork horde in the Auro Cluster.'

'Such a fitting foe,' sneered Ajir. 'I wonder which side is the more savage?'

Rafen silenced his man with a look, but Noxx seemed to enjoy the barb. 'I only wish I could be there to find out. But sadly, instead I am here to help you where you have failed.'

'You dare-?' Kayne rocked off his feet, and this time Rafen had to take a step up to block the young Space Marine's path.

'Did you learn nothing from what has gone before?' said Rafen. 'Stand down, boy. Keep your mouth shut.'

'Still has some fire in him,' Noxx nodded approvingly. 'I'm glad to see that's not been lost.'

Rafen's gaze dropped to the data-slate in his hand. The device had been presented to him by the runner from the astropath sanctum mere minutes before the cruiser's scrying monitors had picked up the approaching vessel. 'What do you know of our mission?'

'I know that an arch-traitor defiled Baal with his presence,' said Noxx. 'I know you have not yet been able to find him and take recompense for that transgression.'

'You think you could do better?' Ajir grated.

'We could hardly do worse–'

'*Enough!*' snarled Rafen. 'We are Astartes, Sons of Sanguinius all! We have not forgotten the threat we faced together and destroyed in our unity! I will not have us fall back into old rivalries like bickering children.' He turned and shot a hard glare at his warriors, each in turn, ending with Kayne and Ajir. 'Are we so arrogant that we cannot take an offer of help from our kinsmen? I think not.' He was aware of Ceris watching him. Silently, the Codicier gave him a level nod.

Noxx's expression shifted. 'Every man under my command knows the import of this, Rafen,' he said. 'And together, we will take the target we seek.' He nodded in the direction of the *Tycho's* bridge. 'Even now, the *Gabriel's* navigators commune with yours, passing to them the data we have uncovered.'

'Good,' Rafen replied. 'Once we set a course, we'll convene to devise a plan for a joint sortie.'

'Brother-sergeant!' Ajir stepped forward and came across, shaking his head. 'I cannot stay silent on this, even if you order me so!' He stabbed a finger at Noxx and the other Flesh Tearers. 'This is not a matter for others. This mission is ours alone.'

'You're wrong,' Rafen told him.

'Who decides that?' demanded the Space Marine.

Rafen didn't answer him; instead, he thrust the slate into Ajir's hand and let him read it. There, on the display, was the clear and unmistakable cipher of a message from Baal, appended with the highest priority suffixes. Ajir's eyes widened as he realised that the communication had come directly from the Lord Commander himself.

'What does it say?' asked Puluo, speaking for the rest of the assembled warriors.

'*Fight together*,' said Ajir.

THREE

Turcio stood, and he was not at his ease. The two squads faced each other across the tacticarium chamber, and it might have seemed to a passing observer that they had gathered to do battle with one another. Blood Angels ranged to the starboard, the Flesh Tearers to the port, the armoured warriors sized each other up, as was their manner. Recent events on Baal had in some ways built bonds of comradeship between the diverse Chapters that drew lineage from the Primarch Sanguinius; but still the old contentions between the first founding and its successors could not be washed away in a single night.

And never could there be more polar an opposite to the Blood Angels than the Flesh Tearers. The former proud and noble in bearing, the latter feral and coarse – yet the same blood flowed in all their veins.

Outward character aside, they were all sons of the Great Angel, and beyond that they were Adeptus Astartes. Brothers in arms if not in true kinship.

None of the Astartes spoke. Both squads had been ordered to rein in any comments that did not immediately benefit the discussion at hand. Brother-Sergeant Rafen had been blunt about that, and he imagined Noxx had said the same. Rafen had tired quickly of even the smallest hint of divisive behaviour, ordering Ajir and the others in no uncertain terms to direct their energies towards the mission. *Our enmity*, he had told them, *has only one target today*.

That target turned slowly in front of them, suspended in a vapour, conjured by hidden display beams in the base of an ornate, wrought-iron chart table. Rafen circled the table, glaring at the flickering image. Turcio recognised the face of Fabius Bile. It was an artist's impression of the fiend, dispassionately constructed by some machine-slave fed a diet of security camera footage, faded portraits and research data.

It depicted a man with the dimensions of a Space Marine, three metres high and another across the shoulders. Pallid of face, his flesh was pulled tight on his skull and around the rim of a cranial cognition accelerator implant. Strings of white hair fell down upon shoulder pauldrons of bloodstained bronze, blurred where the display engine's self-censorship subroutines masked the eightfold stars etched there. He wore a long coat over his wargear, a patchwork thing made of human skins with screaming faces sewn into the pattern of it. A brass mechanism of limbs and manipulators – a device of mysterious origin known only as 'the chirurgeon' – was attached to his back; skull-topped valves and reservoirs of black fluids, oil-thick and sluggish, chugged as they worked. The functions of the chirurgeon could only be guessed at. Several learned scienticians of the Imperium had attempted to divine its capabilities, suggesting it might be some sort of life-support mechanism, or perhaps even a semi-sentient servitor device. It reminded Turcio of the servo-harnesses worn by the technical adepts of his Chapter, but in a more bloated, grotesque design.

He was considering this as his gaze found one of Noxx's warriors, standing slightly askance from the rest of the Flesh Tearer squad. The warrior had a single servo-arm folded discreetly at his back, and upon his shoulder pad the cogwheel trim of a Mars-trained Techmarine. An angled face robbed of one human eye, sporting an augmetic replacement with a sapphire lens, met his look and gave him a respectful nod.

The fact that Noxx had been allowed to bring a Techmarine with him spoke volumes; the Flesh Tearers, a small Chapter made up of only a handful of companies, had little resources to squander idly – and that included warriors gifted with some fraction of the knowledge and training of the Adeptus Mechanicus. Techmarines were a rare breed among the Adeptus Astartes, inducted into their Chapters in the same fashion as every other initiate, but then trained on Mars to commune with machines... and so some would have it said, never again to be counted as truly trustworthy on their return.

Turcio had never held to that suspicion. He found it hard to believe that an Astartes would ever find something more divine than the God-Emperor of Mankind inside the cogs and coils of a machine, no matter what spirituality the tech-priests of the Mechanicus claimed.

He saw Rafen turn to Noxx. 'I'm eager to see the gift you've brought us, brother-sergeant.' His commander gestured at the viewing table. 'If you will?'

Noxx glanced at the Techmarine. 'Mohl,' he said, 'show them.'

Brother Mohl stepped forward and his servo-arm unfolded with a fluid, almost elegant motion, in the manner of a courtly noble offering his hand before a dance. The movement seemed strange coming from a machine-limb that could crush a man's skull like an egg. The arm presented a mnemonic cylinder to the table and the viewer accepted it with a whine of small motors.

Lenses clicked and chattered inside the table, and the image of Fabius Bile shifted. Particles of magnetic sand inside the viewer's core moved, clustering around the projector head to give out a new, compelling image. The form of a tech-priest shimmered into being before them. A hooded human – but only by the loosest of definitions – the figure wore the familiar robes of the Adeptus Mechanicus and a skull-and-cog sigil denoting the exalted rank of Magos. Turcio caught a glimpse of the priest's face and realised that his head appeared to be entirely coated in chrome. Perhaps it was some sort of mask.

'This is the Magos Minoris Matthun Zentennigan Eight-Iota Zellik,' said Mohl. The Flesh Tearer's voice was quiet, but it carried across the chamber. 'A ranking tech-lord of the Magos Technicus of Mars, he is listed in the rolls as an adept-without-portfolio, with letters of marque from the Fabricator-General to conduct independent operations beyond the Segmentum Solar.'

'In other words, he's a law unto himself,' muttered Kayne.

'Zellik's rank and position allow him a great deal of liberty,' Mohl agreed. 'We believe that the Ordo Xenos have been watching him for some time for overt signs of contamination, but no evidence has been forthcoming.'

'They believe he's treating with aliens?' said Ceris.

'Possible,' came the reply. 'Not confirmed. Zellik's connections have so far enabled him to remain outside the grip of the ordos. But what has been determined, by agents in our employ, is that Zellik is indeed operating outside the letter of Imperial law and Mechanicus doctrine. He fancies himself as something of a collector, inclined to hoard items he considers precious rather than turn them over to his masters. Apparently, he maintains an extensive private museum… In addition, he has been trading in proscribed and rare technologies.'

'The cog-boys would go wild if they knew that,' said Ajir.

Noxx shook his head. 'Don't be so sure. The Adeptus Mechanicus are quite happy to bend the rules if it lets them gather up another dusty relic from the days before Old Night.' He glanced at Mohl and the Tech-marine's head bobbed in agreement.

'So, Kayne was correct, then,' offered Rafen. 'This Magos Zellik is operating on his own… Perhaps at the behest of Mars, perhaps only to enrich himself.' The Blood Angel folded his arms. 'What does that have to do with our hunt?'

'One of the names connected to his trade will be familiar to you,' Mohl explained. 'A Magos Biologis by the name of Haran Serpens.'

'Bile's alias…' Puluo's craggy face hardened. 'This wastrel cog is in league with Chaos?' He spat on the deck.

'We suspect he is unaware of the lie of the Serpens identity. Knowledge of what took place on Baal has yet to filter out into the greater Imperium–'

'It filtered out to you, didn't it?' interrupted Kayne darkly. Turcio found himself nodding in agreement. As much as he knew he should trust the Flesh Tearers, he still found it hard to.

Mohl ignored the comment and kept talking. 'It is likely Zellik has no idea who he was really dealing with.'

'What was the nature of his trade with Bile?' Turcio spoke for the first time. 'Do we know that?' The metallic fingers of his augmetic arm drummed on his vambrace, an unconscious tic he could not seem to excise.

'Unclear,' replied Mohl.

'It is my Lord Seth's suggestion that we approach this Zellik and ask him to tell us all he knows of the whereabouts of one "Haran Serpens"…' Noxx made the statement sound almost playful.

Turcio considered this. 'The Mechanicus are a rule-bound lot. I don't doubt our errant Magos will have chapter and verse on every trade he's ever made, from bolt-screws to battleships.'

'He won't just give it up for the asking,' said Ajir. 'And if he has indeed been dealing off-book, with xenos or any other enemies of Terra, then he knows his life is forfeit.'

Ceris peered at the image. 'Are we to simply confront him with this? Impose the Emperor's authority and arrest him?'

'He'll flee the moment he sees our ships,' added Kayne.

'Perhaps not,' said Noxx. 'Not if he only sees *my* ship.'

Rafen eyed his opposite number. 'What do you mean, sergeant?'

The Flesh Tearer's thin lips parted, revealing his teeth. 'Brother Mohl must take credit for this idea.' He patted the Techmarine on the shoulder. 'We'll bring the *Gabriel* in to his complex at quarter speed, contact Zellik and tell him we want to make a trade. Weapons or vehicles, or some such.'

'You're Space Marines. What makes you think he'd believe that you are interested in an illicit deal with him?' Turcio frowned at the Flesh Tearer. 'It's a lie a child could see through.'

'If it were you making the approach, Blood Angel, I would concur,' Noxx replied. 'But we are the Flesh Tearers.' He took in his squad with a sweep of his hand and gave a chilly grin. 'And as I am sure you know, people are always willing to think the very worst of us.' Noxx glared at Turcio, daring him to disagree; and in all truth, he could not.

The Space Marines were silent, each of them considering Noxx's words. Finally, Rafen spoke. 'Brother Mohl is to be commended. This has the makings of a good plan. So good, in fact, that I find myself wondering why Lord Seth did not simply send you to prosecute it alone, without the involvement of my Chapter at all.'

'Ah,' said Noxx, 'there's more to it than that.'

'There always is,' Puluo said dryly.

'Zellik's base of operations is a mobile platform… It would be a misnomer to consider it a ship or a space station. The Archeohort is neither one nor the other.'

'Archeohort?' The word was unfamiliar to Turcio.

'Show them,' Noxx told Mohl. The Techmarine touched a luminous keypad and the lens viewer shifted again. The new shape was hard to grasp, and for long moments Turcio stared at it, trying to draw meaning from what appeared to be a collection of gigantic derricks clustered about an egg-shaped core. It reminded him a little of the fat dust spiders that lurked in the sublevels of the fortress-monastery. The scale was hard to reckon from the image, however.

'The construct is essentially a mobile processing facility, dedicated to the recovery of lost scientific relics. It moves from star to star, sifting planets for archeotech. Zellik has a small army of skitarii and savants, and the construct is well armed. A single vessel would not pose a serious threat to it.'

'The question answered,' Noxx said with a nod. 'Our Chapter's starfleet is small. It was difficult enough to detach the *Gabriel* for this duty. But in order to hobble Zellik, two ships are needed. One to close to point-blank range and rake the platform with its guns–'

'And another to sweep in and bracket the Archeo-hort, aye. I see.' Rafen nodded back. 'You have this... construct's location?'

'Beyond the Holda and Precipice systems, out on the lip of the void before the Ghoul Stars.' Mohl's answer was immediate. 'Zellik returns there frequently to sift the corpse worlds along that axis.'

Turcio and the others listened as Noxx went on, outlining his plan to attack the Archeohort. There were a few times where Brother Rafen offered observations, largely points of finesse where the blunt, unchained approach of the Flesh Tearers could benefit from the more aloof viewpoint of Blood Angel thinking; but as the meeting drew to a close, he saw a slow hunter's smile forming on his commander's lips, the mirror of it on the faces of the other Astartes.

It *was* a good plan. It would work. And for the first time in what seemed like forever, the black mood that had gripped the Blood Angels on their return from the tau colony lifted a little. The distant call of battle was coming, and Turcio felt it in his hands as they itched to hold a weapon.

At last, Rafen stepped up to the viewer table and stared into the depths of the image turning above it. 'Let us find this Magos Minoris Matthun Zentennigan Eight-Iota Zellik,' he said carefully. 'Let us find him and put him to the question.'

INSIDE THE BOARDING torpedo, the only light came from the sickly yellow-green glow of biolume sticks. Tethered to the pod's support stanchions with lines of wire, they drifted back and forth like dull leaves caught in a breeze. Rafen's occulobe implant had tightened the orbs of his eyes to allow him to see better in the near-darkness, but even so the interior was a landscape of greys and blocky shadows. He moved with care between the Space Marines in their acceleration webs, towards the bow. His enhanced hearing caught the peculiar low yowl that echoed into the capsule's hull from the tethers outside. Pulled like a lure on a line, the boarding torpedo moved in the shadow of the warship *Gabriel*, largely occluded by the vessel's mass. The cables snaked back to the cruiser through open space, servitors working the reels at their far ends in careful coordination; the machine-helots puppeted the capsule, they shifted and tacked it as waterborne sailors might do the same to a sail, helping it to maintain all of the precious velocity it had accrued since they had entered the system.

Rafen used a series of iron handholds welded to the inner hull, moving from ring to ring, hand over hand, drifting in the null gravity. Each ring had a rime of frost on it where ambient moisture in the air had chilled far below freezing, and every exhalation that escaped the Blood Angel's mouth emerged in a puff of vapour. The biting cold gathered on his bare face, stiffening the flesh over his cheekbones and his chin. The craft's internal heating mechanisms – in fact, practically all of the torpedo's energy-dependent systems – were inoperative. It was all another facet of the ruse, to cloak the capsule in the cold of space to make it appear like any one of a million other pieces of frozen, lifeless debris. It was the only way they could chance to launch a boarding operation against Zellik's Archeohort. Teleporters would not work; the construct was possessed of some kind of arcane dispersal field generator that would scramble any incoming matter signal into something unrecognisable. An approach towards any of the heavily defended airlocks, or docking bays bristling with autonomic guns, would be suicide. A forest of sensors turned mechanical eyes to all points of the aetheric compass. The only way in was the brute-force approach, and Rafen had seen the brief flash of relish in Noxx's dead eyes at the thought of that.

Arriving at the tapered prow of the capsule, Rafen pulled himself to one of the few windows in the torpedo's hull, a circular porthole little bigger than his clenched fist. He brushed away a layer of ice crystals and peered out into the dark.

What he saw there gave him pause. The Archeohort was rising above the bow of the *Gabriel*, and at last he understood the size of it. The construct was easily the mass of a city-sprawl, and the spider-like impression presented by the image viewer was cemented as he watched kilometre-long gantries cluster from the complex's main core around the drifting remnants of a slab-sided space hulk. They were closing the distance to the Archeohort with every passing second, and as the thing loomed, Rafen picked out bright sparkles of hard light along the places where the gantries brushed the derelict's hull.

'Zellik's savants are taking the wreck apart,' Noxx's voice reached him. 'Sifting it for anything of value.'

Briefly, Rafen wondered after the origin of the hulk. The diminishing shape didn't have the look of a warship about it. The craft had probably been some ancient colonial transport, perhaps set off from Terra

before the Age of Strife in search of new frontiers and
a better life. But now, whatever death had befallen it,
the old ship was suffering a second ignoble ending as
the Archeohort picked at its bones.

He turned away from the port and found Noxx's
shadowed form in front of him. 'This will be a challenge,' said the Flesh Tearer. 'Zellik's skitarii are
trained in the use of exotic weapons. I'll warrant we'll
get some exercise over there.'

Rafen accepted this and tapped his fingers on the
hilt of his sheathed power sword. 'I imagine so.'

Noxx studied him, and finally pointed to a circular
design etched into one of his armour plates. 'The Iron
Halo. I had wondered if they would give you an honour for what you did at the sepulchre.'

'I was told I had earned it. But I was only there at
the end. Others fought as hard as I, in other places, at
other times.'

The other man's flat, shallow smile flashed briefly
in the gloom. 'Such modesty. Only one as earnest as
you could carry that off and not seem false with it.'

Rafen's jaw stiffened. 'I speak what I feel. I do not
play at humility.'

'A commander never can,' came the reply. 'And
speaking of command. Before we are finally committed to this sortie, a point of protocol. We share
the same rank, but one of us has to have the final
word.'

'And you think you should be the one?'

'I am the senior battle-brother. It seems only
proper.'

'I may not have as many service studs in my brow as
you, Noxx…' It was the Blood Angel's turn to show a

dry smile. 'But this is *my* mission. Perhaps I should best you for the privilege?'

'Hardly the place, don't you think? And there's no guarantee it would go in your favour, as it did last time.' Noxx inclined his head. 'Very well, Rafen. I'll defer to you. For the moment.'

Around them, the torpedo shifted as the tethers were let out. 'Not long now.' He looked around and found Brother Mohl, his helmet still sealed, seated at a vox console. If not for the occasional twitch of his head, or a tic of motion from his servo-arm, the Techmarine could have been an empty suit of power armour. Enclosed in there, Mohl was conversing with the Archeohort's crew, laying the keel of the lie that would get them aboard. Rafen briefly switched to the comm-channel Mohl was using, but the strident noise in his ear bead made him wince. It was nothing but an atonal rattle of binary code.

He switched out again and sub-vocalised into the general vox. 'Brothers, be ready. Take your breaching stations.'

Turcio bent over an inert control console and spoke a prayer of activation, his thumb resting on the activation rune. 'On your command, sir,' he said.

'Moment of truth,' rumbled Puluo.

Rafen nodded, shrugging into his own restraint harness. Without the function of the mechanisms usually employed to maintain them, the disposition of the boarding torpedo's short-range thrusters was unknown. He glanced at the chronometer on the bulkhead, marking off the elapsed mission time. The capsule would be coming around now, the tethers playing out to turn it into a shot from a sling. The thrusters were supposed to double that speed, to bring them in too fast for the Archeohort's gunnery cogitators to react. If they failed to fire, the capsule would move slowly and the guns would mark their range in short order.

The chronometer's moving hand swept across the pinnacle of the clock face and Rafen dropped his hand like a blade.

Turcio stabbed the rune. A second ticked by, then another. Already, the pull of acceleration was tugging on all of them as the boarding torpedo was released. 'Perhaps–'

The Blood Angel never finished the thought; instead a thundering roar sounded from the aft of the capsule, and every warrior aboard was forced into his harness as gravity fell hard upon them.

Rafen struggled to spy through the small porthole, glimpsing only the shimmer of starlight off hull metal, but nothing he could define; then there were stark, silent lashes of colour blazing through the windows as lances of energy lit the void with their brilliance. Outside, the *Gabriel's* shipmaster had deployed his guns and fired on the Mechanicus construct at point-blank range. The boarding torpedo sailed among the unleashed maelstrom, masked once more by the salvoes as it made its terminal approach.

Mohl disconnected a mechadendrite from his helmet and spoke across the general vox channel. 'Zellik broke contact,' he reported. 'When the *Gabriel* refused to stand to and allow him to dispatch a lighter, he grew suspicious.'

A near-hit made the torpedo rock and the hull moaned. 'And that's not all,' muttered Puluo.

'The Archeohort has engaged the cruiser,' added the Techmarine.

'Clearly,' said Noxx. 'Now, if all goes to plan, the *Tycho* should be making its approach from the far side.' He glanced at Rafen. 'If your shipmaster is as good as you say, then Zellik will be too busy dealing with a pair of Astartes cruisers to direct his attention towards us.'

'*Tycho* will do its part,' said the sergeant.

Noxx was about to add something, but then the torpedo found its mark and struck the Archeohort's outer skin. With a resonant boom of metal on metal, the capsule made impact and began its work.

As WOLVES WOULD strike a bear, the two warships came close and circled the hulking Archeohort, making sweeping turns about the mass of the huge construct. Cannon fire, laser light and clouds of missiles flashed between the three combatants. The guns of Zellik's scavenger machine were not sluggish – they threw out hard pulses of x-ray radiation that lashed at the *Tycho* and the *Gabriel*, the backscatter of the attacks throwing sheets of colour into the void like an auroral display.

In return, the Blood Angels and Flesh Tearers cruisers gave their guns freedom to rake across the hull of the enemy. At this close a range, even a blind man could not have missed the target; but like the bear against the wolves, the Archeohort took the bites and claw-scratches, slow and heavy, returning with massive sweeps of fire that could crack hulls if they chanced a solid hit.

Now free of the derelict hulk it had been feasting upon, the construct's gantry-limbs began to coil inward, drawing to itself in a pattern of self-preservation.

THE ENTIRE FORWARD quarter of the boarding torpedo was a massive brass drill, hardened with a molecule-thin layer of cultured diamond and a sentanium tip. Spinning at furious speed, it chewed through the outer layers of carbide plating on the Archeohort's dorsal hull and ploughed inward. Tracks with spike-tipped teeth along the flank of the capsule pulled it through ripped splines of metal, plastic and wood, atmosphere and fluids outgassing around it into the vacuum. Great phlegmy boles of vac-sensitive gel vomited from pressurised canisters, racing to seal the breach made by the Astartes – and all too quickly the boarding torpedo's forward momentum was arrested.

Rafen was already tearing free of his restraints, his bolter in his hand. 'Deploy, deploy!' he snarled. 'Take the pace, brothers!'

Another of Noxx's Flesh Tearers was at the prow, and with a grunt of effort, he slammed down the heavy iron lever that released the drill mechanism. The conical bow splayed open into four segments, giving the Space Marines their exit. In quick, ordered lines, the two squads exited into Zellik's craft. Puluo, Kayne and a pair of Flesh Tearers were the last aboard, and Rafen glanced back at them in time to see the pod shake. The gelatinous matter ringing the capsule bubbled and spat, writhing as if it were alive; and then the torpedo jolted backwards.

'Get out!' shouted Ajir.

Puluo shoved Kayne hard in the back and the younger Astartes fell the remaining distance to the deck. The other warrior pivoted and jumped after him, one of the Flesh Tearers a heartbeat behind. The last man, slowed by the bulk of a heavy flamer, fared poorly. With a sudden belch of expelling air, the entire torpedo was ejected back the way it had come, the expanding wave of gel ballooning to form a wall before the atmosphere could go with it.

Noxx swore a gutter oath.

'A cultured bio-form,' said Mohl dispassionately, probing the hardening matter with a finger. 'Programmed to act like living tissue. Sealing wounds and ousting foreign bodies.'

'On a tyranid ship, perhaps,' said Turcio. 'But here?'

'Perhaps the stories of Zellik's contact with the xenos were not wrong after all.' Ajir made a sour face.

They were not given time to dwell on the question, however. A shout went up from the front ranks, a Flesh Tearer crying out over the concussion of his own bolter. 'Contact!'

'Engage!' replied Rafen. 'Sweep and clear!'

A spill of tech-guard troopers surged towards them from one branch of a curving corridor, in their haste the grey cloaks they wore flapping out behind them like the wings of raptor birds. A second rank of slow-moving gun-servitors followed on, lumbering along the wide passageway, weapons clicking as self-loaders spun up to speed.

The reaction time of Zellik's men was to be commended; on the ship of an ally, Rafen would have done just that, but here the matter became a minor impediment. A chorus of bolters crashed and met the guards with lethal force, the mass-reactive shells from the weapons opening them in red flashes. Bits of human meat and metal implants were flung about the walls. Enemy fire from the front rank came past in a wash of laser light, beams hissing across the surface of ceramite armour, cooking off layers of protective sheathing. The strangled crackle of split air molecules sounded around the Astartes, and the corridor was suddenly filled with the acrid tang of ozone.

The shambling gun-servitors, the bodies of men re-made with pistons for legs and great weapon tubes in place of arms, fired next, and Rafen ducked into the cover of a stanchion as Turcio took a glancing hit and spun to the deck. The machine-helots were all armed with close-range stubbers, fat ammo hoppers upon their bent backs feeding the weapons with frangible-tipped rounds. Close to the exterior hull of a starship, heavy bullet loads were a hazard – a single misplaced shot could breach a portal or even a wall, and cause an explosive decompression. Astartes, every one of them a marksman, did not concern themselves with such minor details.

Rafen heard the shattering of the bullet-tips as they rattled harmlessly off Space Marine armour and grinned. In their haste, Zellik's soldiers hadn't rearmed their guns, using the low-velocity, man-stopper shells more suited to dealing with pirates or common human foes. The candlepin-thick bolt shells of the Space Marines, on the other hand, were far more lethal, over-penetrating every target they hit. Turcio was already back up into a crouch, taking off the heads of gun-servitors with carefully aimed shots.

Noxx vaulted forward, and with a kick he put the last tech-guard down, clubbing him to the deck with his gun. The skitarii burbled something in machine-code, but the noise ceased when the Flesh Tearer stamped on its throat. 'That will do as a down payment for the man this cost me,' growled the veteran.

THE ARCHEOHORT BEGAN to rotate.

Slowly at first, moving with the lazy, inexorable pace of a moonrise, then gaining speed as the arrays of tiny thrusters hundredfold across its surface added power to the turn. Gun pods the size of habitat blocks spun and moved on thick brass rails that ringed the outer hull, pausing to reload at the maws of static ammo hoppers before sliding back to seek the Astartes ships and barrage them.

Tycho's shipmaster threaded his ship between a pair of towering gantries and let his forward tubes lay upon the closest of the gun-carriages. Spatial torpedoes leapt into the dark, crossing the distance on angry flares of thrust before transforming into fists of nuclear flame. Sheets of mobile armour plate raced to absorb the detonations and came too slow, some of them torn apart and tossed into the dark.

Above, the *Gabriel* supported its brother-ship with sheeting rains of superheavy las-bolts, burning away the brassy lustre that clad the hull of the Mechanicus construct.

Under the withering fire, the Archeohort turned, and as it did iris vents opened along its stern, disgorging engine bells woken from their dormancy.

Elsewhere, directed by cold machine anger, other hatches slid free to present new weapons to the fray.

'WE NEED TO locate and secure the command centre,' Rafen was saying, as the corridor opened out on to a vast open space in the middle of the Archeohort. 'Where is it?'

Mohl shot him a look. 'That will not be easy, lord.'

The Techmarine's commander gave him a hard stare. 'You told me you knew the configuration of this behemoth's interior!' said Noxx.

'I do,' Mohl continued. 'And that is why I know it will not be easy to find a single chamber in the middle of all… of this.'

Rafen stopped, and for a moment he felt a twinge of vertigo as his mind struggled to process the sight in front of him. Beyond the railed tier where the corridor had brought them out, the inside of the Archeohort was a hollow drum, and around it ran twisting ranges of staircases and ramps that defied gravity and sense, some inverted and connecting to one another in odd profusion, others looping like Möbius strips. And in the middle of this, shifting back and forward on complex systems of rails and vast, towering pulleys, massive wedges of decking as large as city blocks were constantly in motion. The noise was constant, a screeching of metal on metal, a hissing orchestra of working mechanisms as the wedges locked together, moved, unlocked, inverted, rotated and shifted. The motion was regular and fluid, lock-step-perfect.

'It's reconfiguring itself all the time,' said Ajir. 'How could you ever find your way around this thing? Enter one room here and a moment later you exit it on the other side of the complex!'

A slab of deck ground past them as Mohl located a skinny copper podium and bent over it. Rafen saw the thin, snake-fast movements of his mechadendrites as they probed outward and found interface ports on the podium's surface.

'Cover him,' he ordered, and brought his bolter to his shoulder. Aiming upward, through the weapon's targeting scope he picked out a flight of clockwork monitor birds as they broke off from a circular flight pattern and angled towards them.

Puluo braced himself and unleashed an arc of shell-fire into the air from his heavy bolter, the rounds killing most of the machine-proxies with murderous blowback.

Mohl shivered and stepped down. 'No maps for this place,' he coughed. 'There are wards in place and the Archeohort's machine-spirit is conflicted. But even as it will not show me some things, that too is a guide of sorts.'

'We go where it doesn't want us to go?' said Kayne.

'Aye,' replied the Techmarine. He tapped his helmet. 'I have computed a route. I have it here, but we must go now. If we tarry, the configuration will shift and it will be rendered meaningless.'

Another deck slab rotated into place, and Mohl made for it, the rest of them following him.

Rafen grimaced at the mad geometry all about him. 'How can we hope to find a way through this giant's puzzle?'

Noxx gestured towards his man. 'We make sure we keep Mohl alive.'

THE HARPOONS WERE taller than the statues atop Mount Seraph. Spinning, barbed things the length of a gun-cutter or system boat, they were ejected from the Archeohort's interior and ranged up and out through the hidden ports, probing after the *Gabriel* and the *Tycho*. The weapons had crews, after a fashion, if one were willing to give that name to a handful of limbless human torsos tanked in shock-resistant canisters of support fluid.

Chains with links that could loop a hundred men, double- and triple-threaded, rippled out behind the thruster-guided lances, screaming from helix rigs in the Archeohort's hull. The weapons spun and twirled, racing for the bodies of their enemies.

Cannons answering with death, the two warships veered from their courses, making stiff turns that sent grinding gravity shocks the length of their iron spines; but it was not enough.

'Quickly!' The deck parted beneath Kayne's boots, one planted on one side, one on the other, one section rising, the other dropping away. He felt strong hands take a grip on him as he reached out to take the hand of a Flesh Tearer. His fellow Astartes grunted with effort and Kayne pulled him up just as the deck they had been upon changed from horizontal to vertical orientation.

'This place is like the inside of an engine, all moving parts and grinding gears,' growled the Flesh Tearer. 'My thanks, cousin.'

'Kayne,' said the Blood Angel. 'And you?'

'Eigen,' came the reply. 'How these Mechanicus cog-boys can live in this and not be turned insane for looking at it, I cannot know.'

'Cogs are cogs,' shrugged the Astartes. 'They're mad enough already.'

Swift and low, the warriors threaded through ranks of quartz columns that reached away to support a vaulted roof overhead. Everywhere there were panes of glass that displayed streams of flashing machine-code, some hanging on suspensors, other chained to walls or the pillars themselves. The waterfalls of symbols cascading ever downward were utterly unintelligible to Kayne, but he knew that to someone like Mohl, these screens were filled with secrets. They were windows into the raw workings of the Archeohort and its machine-spirit, the mechanical equivalent of what he might see if he peered down a kinescope and into the swarming cells of his own blood.

Up ahead of the unit, Kayne heard Mohl call out directions; the Techmarine seemed to know where he was going, but so far each chamber they had passed through was one oddity after another. A tremor reached up through the floor and the metallic tiles beneath their boots shook.

Eigen frowned. 'Not the decking this time… That was an impact from outside.'

'Perhaps our ships are making headway against this thing,' Kayne replied. 'It'll count for little if we can't stop Zellik running for the warp, though.'

'Enemy!' The cry came from the middle of the formation – from the psyker Ceris, he noted – and in the same moment a wavering blue-white cloud phased into reality over their heads. Kayne raised his gun in time to see a face gain definition and form; a giant face coated in mirror-bright silver, shrouded by a red-trimmed hood.

'That's him…' said Eigen. 'It's some sort of hololithic image.' The Flesh Tearer looked around, searching for anything that resembled an emitter pod.

'Astartes!' The air around them vibrated into the sound of the Magos's voice. 'You have made a great error in attacking me! I stand with all of Mars at my side! Your Chapters dare to board my vessel without my permission, kill my helots? Have you gone mad?'

Up ahead, Brother-Sergeant Rafen skidded to a halt on the polished tiles and shouted back his defiance to the floating image. 'Surrender, Zellik. Present yourself to us now and I'll consider lenience. Your petty infractions of Mechanicus laws are of no importance to me. But you have information we want, and we will not leave without it.'

Zellik spluttered with amazement and ire, the sound like the clicking of switches. 'Your arrogance outstrips your idiocy, Blood Angel. Once I have left your warships behind, I will make your living bodies into cannon-bearers, and your Chapter Master will beg my forgiveness!'

'There!' Eigen pointed at a spherical pod floating high up in the shadows. 'The projector device. You see it?'

Kayne aimed. 'I see it, cousin.' He released half a breath and fired.

The sphere exploded in a flat bang of noise, and Zellik's face winked out.

'Good shot,' remarked Puluo. 'I'm already sick of him.'

The deck trembled again, and this time Kayne released a snarl of annoyance. 'Not a hit this time...'

'Contact!' Eigen called, pointed once more. The Flesh Tearer had sharp eyes, it could not be denied. More tech-guards were emerging from behind a quartz pillar across the way, charging at the Space Marines.

Kayne saw something arc through the air towards him, and recognised the shape of a grenade. 'To cover!' he yelled, shoving Eigen away and into the lee of another column, as gunfire erupted around them anew.

The grenade landed and detonated – but instead of an explosive discharge, a globe of emerald energy expanded out, at full size perhaps big enough to envelop a groundcar. When the glow dissipated, there was a perfect circle cut through the decking, the edges smooth and bright as if polished.

'Baal's blood! It must be a demat sphere!' said Ceris, firing off a burst as he approached. 'An archeotech weapon. Like a teleport, but everything inside the radius is disintegrated. I never thought to see such a relic in action…'

'I though those devices were a myth!' said Eigen.

'So did I,' the psyker said grimly. 'It would appear otherwise.'

Kayne saw a flicker of movement. 'Another one!' A second globe looped towards the assembled Space Marines, projected by a weapons-helot with a scaled-down trebuchet instead of an arm.

Kayne watched in amazement as Ceris jumped up into the air, to meet the demat sphere as it fell towards them. The psyker plucked the globe out of its arc and threw it as he dropped; it was a clumsy interception, but still effective. The sphere landed at the feet of the helot who had thrown it, and it triggered. The dissipation effect hummed and when it faded, there were only the odd, starkly severed parts of three gun-servitors remaining.

Ceris landed heavily and stumbled, drawing gunfire. Without hesitation, Kayne and Eigen ran from cover to aid him, and the three warriors broke into a dash, racing to close up with the rest of their comrades.

'Zellik must really want us dead,' ventured Turcio. 'Those spheres are worth a governor's ransom.'

'Then you should consider it a compliment, penitent,' said Ajir.

Mohl gestured towards a diamond-shaped door cut into the wall. 'We are wasting time. Zellik is trying to trap us. This way, quickly!'

Lasers snapping at their heels, the Astartes moved on, killing everything that dared to follow them.

TYCHO TOOK THE spear through the plough-shaped blades of its bow plate; *Gabriel* fared worse, the other harpoon entering the hull of the strike cruiser along its portside axis at an oblique angle. Both weapons buried themselves in the marrow of the warships and locked fast.

And then, even as the echo of the impacts resonated and faded, the huge chains of vacuum-forged alloy flexed and pulled taut. Deep inside the mechanism of Zellik's great construct, wheels began to turn, gears worked, and the lines drew home, reeling them in.

The shipmasters of the *Tycho* and the *Gabriel* had given their gunnery captains leave to fire with freedom, and so they did, punishing the Archeohort for such an attack, others training guns on the lines of chain, hoping to sever them.

On the other side of the construct, a hundred tiny suns flared into being, boles of fusion fire spilling out into the void. With increasing speed, the Archeohort dragged its attackers away, moving towards clear space free of the debris that clogged this zone.

Calculations were already being made, formulae computed, courses laid in. A leap to the warp would follow, and the ships now chained to the construct, like rabid dogs straining at their leashes, would be ripped apart by the flux of transition.

THE MELTA BOMB exploded and took down not only the armoured hatchway sealing off the command chamber, but also a few sections of wall to either side. The corpses of the heavy gun-servitors that had defended the entrance were ripped apart where they lay, the ammunition in their weapons cooking off in secondary blasts. Noxx led the charge with Puluo at his side, both Astartes shouldering in through the smoke-wreathed remains of the entrance with guns blazing. Skitarii went down in disarray, those that had not already been killed by the funnelled blast of the breaching charge.

Rafen followed them in, Turcio and Ajir at his flanks, delivering the Emperor's judgement with snapshot fire to the twitching, hooded figures sitting in the control pits before their command organs. The Blood Angels sergeant was only a few paces into the room when his keen Astartes senses, honed through the action of countless battles, rang a sour note in his mind. He halted suddenly. 'Wait…' he began, a creeping disquiet spreading through him.

Outside, holding the corridor with the other Space Marines, Brother Ceris made a growl in his throat – a sound of warning.

Ajir was deepest into the chamber, frowning at a seated adept. For all the sudden violence of their entrance, the crew at their stations had barely reacted. The warrior pushed the barrel of his bolter into the adept's back and gave it a hard shove. The figure rocked forward and the hood fell away.

There was no face beneath it, only an oddly featureless orb crafted to vaguely resemble a human head. It was a mannequin, little more than a body-proxy like those deployed on firing galleries. Rafen had destroyed thousands of them in target practice with his bolter and his sword.

Noxx ripped the cloak from another crew-serf, then another and another. All were identical automata, ghosting through the motions of a command crew. Only the handful of tech-guards that had been in the room appeared to be what they had seemed. 'What is this?' demanded the Flesh Tearer.

Mohl was behind him. 'This is the command centre...' he muttered. 'I am certain...'

'It's a *fake*,' said Turcio. 'Like a castle made of cloth and wood to fool a distant observer!'

Rafen glared at a console before him; it was nothing but a flat panel of blinking lights. 'Out!' he shouted.

The order came too late. Mohl flung himself away as a sheet of metal dropped like a guillotine blade across the ruined entranceway, cutting off any means of escape. Immediately, the deck began to shift as a crack opened in the floor beneath their feet. The false consoles yawned open like mouths to accept the mannequins, folding away into hidden spaces like some clever theatre trick. Stanchions and supports contracted into themselves, every handhold slowly retracting as the angle of the floor became steeper with every passing moment.

A belch of hot, dry air vented into the chamber and Rafen caught sight of a harsh orange glow beneath them. A long tray of molten metal, perhaps a conveyer barge from the foundry modules of the Archeohort's factorium, was sliding into place down there, ready to accept them when they lost their grip and fell.

As a trap, it was as elaborate and melodramatic as one might have expected from an arrogant Mechanicus tech-lord, and as Rafen looked up, he saw the ceiling overhead fold back to present a hanging gondola pod, and in it, behind glass and webs of brass, an adept and a bodyguard of skitarii. He saw no silver mask – it was not Zellik himself, then – but he could not miss the cluster of optical relays bristling from the bottom of the gondola. Wherever he was, the damned skulk was watching them inch towards death as if it were some kinema performance made for his amusement.

Boots scraping against the steepening floor, Rafen punched an armoured fist through the metal and made a temporary handhold for himself. He heard Puluo utter a curse as the Devastator Space Marine almost lost his grip before Noxx pulled him back.

They had moments before the strange folding room turned itself inside-out and deposited them all into the embrace of the molten iron. Even with their power armour, it would be questionable if the Space Marines could survive for more than a few seconds in such incredible temperatures.

'If we fall, he falls with us,' Rafen snarled, and with his free hand took aim at the gondola. His bolter crashed, and with it sounded shot and shell from his comrades as they joined in the attack. For a moment it seemed as if the defiant gesture would be in vain; but then the armoured glass webbed with fractures and splintered. Red and black fluid spurted through the shimmering air and a heavy tech-guard tumbled past them, falling soundlessly into the hot bath of liquid metal. The gondola began a desultory retreat along a dangling cable, but it was too late. By exposing themselves to watch the Space Marines die, the Mechanicus lackeys had placed themselves in the firing line.

With a stuttering wail of binary, the cloaked adept lost balance, stumbled into the air and fell, serpentine cyberlimbs whipping about, snatching at nothing.

Cursing the choice he was forced to make, Rafen let his precious bolter fall from his fingers to release his free hand. Extending as far as he dared, the Blood Angel lashed at the adept's robes and grabbed a handful of them. He grunted as the additional weight strained his one handhold, but did not release.

Beneath him, his weapon spiralled away into the glowing, sluggish liquid, melting into a string of hard, concussive blasts as the ammunition exploded with the heat.

The adept twisted about and came to rest dangling from the Space Marine's arm. He looked up, showing a face that was almost human; only his sapphire-blue augmetic eyes ruined the illusion. The Mechanicus tech-priest wore an expression of utter panic.

'That gun served me well,' Rafen snarled. 'Give me a reason why I should not send you to fetch it back!'

The adept's binary chatter warped and changed, becoming recognisable speech. 'Zero zero zero no no no no,' he rattled. 'Please no, zero, no! My orders… I did not–'

'Stop this death trap!' shouted the Blood Angel. 'Or I swear you'll perish screaming!'

'One one one yes yes yes!' The tech-priest stuttered out a reply, and from beneath his cloak came a viper's nest of mechadendrites. Manipulator tips reached for the walls, probing, flipping open seamless panels that Rafen had not even known were there. The adept gave a clicking sigh, and at once the floor reversed its motion. The contracting panels and columns were arrested, then began to telescope once more. In moments, the chamber was resetting itself, returning to its original form.

Rafen stood up, still holding the tech-priest in his grip, as the metal wall behind him rose in stutters. Heavy impact marks had distended it where Ceris and the others had tried to break through.

The psyker advanced warily into the false room. 'Lord?' he asked, the question in his hard eyes.

The sergeant did not answer; instead he drew his power sword from the scabbard across his backpack and pressed the glowing blade to his prisoner's chest. 'Where is Matthun Zellik?' he demanded.

The adept gulped air. Blood and oil dripped from his dangling limbs, pooling on the deck. 'Understand, Astartes, I could not stop him.'

'I did not ask you for an excuse,' Rafen growled. 'You came to capture the moments of our deaths for your master's pleasure. You have already forfeit your life to me. Answer, and it will end quickly.'

Noxx took a menacing step closer to the struggling tech-priest. 'More than he deserves,' snarled the Flesh Tearer. 'Give him to me, cousin. I'll make him speak.' The other sergeant drew his flaying knife, the wicked barbs along one edge glinting.

'I do not know where he is!' shouted the terrified adept. 'I, Logis Goel Beslian, swear on my oath to the Omnissiah that I do not know! Zellik's sanctum cube is in constant motion throughout the mechanism of the Archeohort. You cannot find him unless he wants you to!'

Rafen's lips thinned. 'Then, my esteemed Logis Beslian, you have no more value to us.' He turned the sword to present the tip to the adept's sternum.

'*I can bring him to you!*' Beslian bellowed at the top of his voice, the grating words filtering through a collar of speaker globes at his neck. 'Spare me and I will aid you!' The adept cast around, perhaps hoping to find a forgiving countenance among all the Astartes. He found nothing but cold anger.

With a sneer of disgust, Rafen released his grip on the prisoner and let him drop at the feet of one of Noxx's warriors, a sanguinary cleric named Gast. 'Keep this wretch breathing,' he ordered.

He stalked away, kneading the grip of his blade in annoyance at being forced to defer the kill. Noxx came to him.

'You believe this creature's lies?'

'If you have a better suggestion, I would hear it, cousin.' Rafen gave him a sideways look. 'This construct is like some vast logic puzzle… It confounded your brother Mohl as it confounds the rest of us.'

'I suspect a trap,' Noxx insisted. 'I always do. It's how I've managed to live so long.'

'And yet you entered the false chamber first.'

The Flesh Tearer gave a nod. 'True. But the best way to break a trap is to trip it.'

Rafen returned the nod. 'Then we shall do so. I will not waste time on this strutting Mechanicus fool Zel-lik when our real prey is still beyond our reach.'

FOUR

CLICKING AND GASPING, Beslian led the wary Astartes to a wide conveyor module that swiftly carried them up several levels of the Archeohort's shifting interior. Gast had bound the wounds the adept had taken from shrapnel hits, but not too well. Noxx wanted the tech-priest to suffer, and Rafen saw no reason to countermand the Flesh Tearer's order.

Techmarine Mohl positioned himself like a watchful hawk at Beslian's side, scrutinising the adept for any sign of obvious perfidy. Mohl's bolter was at a constant ready; if Beslian thought to cross them, he might conceivably act before a line Space Marine could follow what he was doing – but not Mohl. The quiet, precise warrior would kill the adept where he stood, and Beslian clearly knew it.

The conveyor arrived at a domed space somewhere near the top of the construct. A host of armed gun-servitors were there to meet them, but they had barely a moment to react before Beslian sang a binary code string that put them all into a stupor. Their weapons drooped to the deck and their heads lolled; whatever the adept had done, it robbed the machine-helots of all intent and motion.

The Space Marines deployed in a combat wheel, as Rafen took stock of the antechamber they stood in. Ahead, high glass doors patterned with gold etching like the tracks of a circuit board promised more beyond. Artificial light, tuned to resemble the ruddy hue of a Martian day, flowed from hidden lume arrays past the dome proper.

Rafen gestured to Noxx, indicating the somnolent gun-servitors. 'Brother-Sergeant, if you would?'

Noxx drew his knife once more and gave a curt nod. 'Just so.' He summoned a couple of kinsmen to assist him, and with quick, brutal actions, they moved among the silent helots, killing them one by one with vicious, slashing blows that tore open throats and veins. Rafen saw Kayne grimace and look away.

Beslian made a moaning sound. 'Astartes, there is no need to do that! They are in quietus! They can do you no harm!'

'So noted,' said Rafen, without interrupting Noxx's execution detail. 'Now tell me. Have you brought us to Zellik?'

'The next best thing,' said the adept. 'Behold…'

Beslian was breathless as he worked a spinning orb-lock on the end of a gimballed armature and, with the correct manipulation, the glass doors answered with a shudder of hidden workings. The entranceway slid back and the adept moved in on hissing piston-legs, his flat iron hooves clattering against a floor made of polished marble. Mohl followed, aiming his gun at Beslian's spine.

Rafen led the rest of the unit inside, and what he saw brought a tic of frustration to his lips. He had expected some sort of inner sanctum, perhaps the kind of opulent quarters a man who fancied himself superior might have – but not this.

There were perfect lines of glass cases ordered in row after row, most of a uniform size, the odd one here or there much larger so as to accommodate... *what*?

He peered at the cabinet closest to him and saw on pads of velvet, a dozen golden bowls, each the width of his spread hand, each with a regular circuit-pattern etched across them. They wore the tarnish of heavy age, but he made out a shimmer as the light caught them, tiny captured rainbows crawling across their surfaces. Looking still closer, he made out the glow of a stasis field screen enveloping the objects, and there in the corner of the case was a small data-slate. He tapped it and text appeared, but the words meant nothing to him.

'Those are precursor relics,' Beslian hissed from across the hall. 'Tens of thousands of years old, made on Terra before humans left their birth world.'

Understanding came to him then. He turned around and felt a kick of revulsion as he saw something he certainly *did* recognise; the severed skull and forearm of a necron warrior, corroded and age-worn, but still horribly distinctive. Other cases contained unintelligible bits of machinery, things that might have been human-made in eras beyond Rafen's reckoning. Some held objects that could only be weapons, his warrior's intuition immediately picking out shapes that suggested caged lethality.

'A museum,' said Puluo.

Mohl gave a slow nod. 'Zellik is a collector. These are his prizes.'

Ajir sneered. 'We did not come aboard this monstrosity to plunder it! These… relics are meaningless to our quest!'

Beslian gave a clicking gasp, exasperated. 'You do not understand. This is the Magos's relical! What you see here are artefacts beyond value, they are his greatest trophies! He values them more than a parent would their children.'

Rafen nodded, a plan forming in his thoughts. 'Then let us get his attention.' The Blood Angel strode back to the case containing the bowls, and with a sweep of his sword he cut the cabinet open, ripping through the stasis generator. The ancient objects were touched by the air of the outside world for what might have been the first time in recorded history; they rapidly discoloured, puckered and crumbled into particles of sparkling dust. Distantly, the Astartes registered the sound of a discordant alarm.

Beslian let out a screech and made an ill-advised motion towards the sergeant. His action was immediately arrested by the pressure of Mohl's bolter in the back of his neck.

Rafen destroyed the necron relics next, and allowed himself a grin at that; then another case, and another, precious bits of silicon and chromium-steel dashed to fragments that he ground into powder beneath his boots. Rafen did not once look upward, to the roosts he had noted upon entering the domed chamber, where doubtless more of Zellik's monitor birds were nesting.

Beslian was making a gibbering sound, halfway between a clock-tick and a sob. He held out his hands in entreaty.

Rafen glared back at him. 'You brought us here, adept. What did you expect us to do?' He glanced around at the other Space Marines. 'All of you,' he called, his voice rebounding from the dome. 'Take your weapons. Destroy everything in this room. Leave nothing intact.'

'*NO!*' The cry vibrated the air around them, and Rafen could not help but smile a little at it. A hololithic mist formed before them, the chrome face and the suggestion of a rust-red hood growing more distinct by the second. 'Savages!' it cried, 'Base fiends, animals! You have no understanding of the riches you trample upon! Every item in this chamber is a rarity, worth more than your lives a thousand times over!'

'Such a pity, then,' Rafen replied, swinging the sword again to cleave open an odd fluted thing that resembled a musical instrument.

Zellik cried out through the holo-image with such pain in his voice, that for a moment Rafen wondered if the tech-lord was somehow physically connected to the objects in the room. The Magos's ire turned on his adept. 'Beslian, you cur! After all that I gave you, and this is how you repay me? You betray the Omnissiah to these Astartes thugs?'

The adept shook his head. 'I... I warned you to stop, Matthun. I told you one day the Emperor's warriors would come looking for us. You said I was wrong, but I computed this long ago!' Beslian stood and shook a steel fist at the hololith. 'I will not be dragged down with you! You think you can defy Mars and Terra forever? How many logs have you falsified? How many lies have you told to our masters?' He shivered, clearly the effort of this new defiance hard upon his bent back. 'No longer! I will not be a party to it!'

Zellik's metallic face was a mix of anger and dismay. 'I trusted you!' he snarled.

Rafen aimed his sword at the ghostly image, taking charge of the situation once more. 'Magos Zellik. I care nothing for your toys and the falsehoods you tell your lords on Mars. But I will take this construct apart piece by piece until I find you, and I will commence by obliterating this gallery of relics... unless you are willing to submit to us.'

The Magos sneered. 'You threaten me? I will rip your ships apart! Every gun-servitor in the Archeohort is converging on your location...' He trailed off as Rafen walked towards a particular artefact displayed inside a cylindrical cabinet. 'What are you doing?' Zellik demanded, his panic rising.

There, hovering in mid air, floating on suspensors, was a nested set of turning rings, each one etched with tiny script, all of them constantly moving about one another. The device, whatever it was, gave the impression of incredible delicacy, as if it were made from spun glass. With languid care, Rafen drew back his power sword to the top of its sweep.

'*Stop!*' cried Zellik. 'Stop! Stop! No more! I beg you, no more!' He gasped. 'That object is millions of years old. It is the last of its kind in existence. Please, I beseech you, do not destroy it!'

Rafen held the sword up. 'You have only to surrender to me and I will do nothing more.'

Zellik's face faded away, and with it his defeated words hummed in the air. 'Very well.'

THE ARCHEOHORT WAS theirs. As battles went, it had been a comparatively bloodless one, but then Rafen recalled the doctrines drilled into him by his late mentor, Brother Koris. The old warhound had often reminded him that the victory taken with guile and not gunfire was all the sweeter – but by the same token a warrior was right to take care that such a victory did not dull the need to remain watchful.

The sergeant stood in a cloistered corridor on the outer face of Zellik's construct-ship; an enclosed highway for pneu-cars ranged away in both directions, lit by glow-globes and the illumination from the void, via hexagonal windows the size of a Land Raider. Grim-faced, he watched as motes of light swarmed around the massive chain tethering the *Tycho* to the Archeohort, a squadron of vacuum-resistant Mechanicus drone-helots burning through the links with beam-cutters. In the silence, he saw the chain shatter and fragment, the line of the lethal harpoon severed at last. Out of sight, on the other side of the Archeohort, another army of drones were doing the same to the *Gabriel*. The forward flight of Zellik's ship had been arrested before a warp gate could be opened, and now adrift in open space, the tech-lord's legions of servitors had been turned to the business of repairing the damage he had inflicted upon the Astartes cruisers.

Zellik had come to them as if he were still in command, ringed by a phalanx of his best tech-guards. Every one of the skitarii had been armed with weapons of arcane origin – laser fans, ornate bolt carbines, icefire guns capable of projecting streams of freezing flame, sonic mutes – and every one of them was killed before they could fire a shot. Noxx led his Flesh Tearers in their abrupt, fierce murders, taking the balance of the cost incurred by the earlier death of his luckless battle-brother and the *Gabriel* crewmen lost to the harpoon hit.

The tech-priest remained untouched by even the smallest splash of spilled blood or lubricant, standing all ashudder amid the carnage. Zellik was elsewhere now, in a bare storage chamber the Astartes had swiftly repurposed as a holding cell. Rafen ordered the Flesh Tearers Apothecary-Cleric Gast to attend to the Magos, using his tools to perform a surgery on Zellik that cut out the tech-priest's wireless machine-vox implant. Zellik's screams had taken on a strange tone, like the groaning of deck plates twisted out of shape by gravitic stressing. He would not speak to his ship or his minions again unless the Adeptus Astartes permitted it.

With Zellik's command terminated, mastery of the Archeohort was now in the hands of Beslian, and Rafen suspected that the nervous, oily logician had schemed for that all along. It concerned him that this opportunist cog might think himself able to use Space Marines as tools for own aggrandisement; but

for the moment it served the needs of the Blood
Angels to play along. In due time, all those who considered themselves above the rules of Holy Terra
would be shown the error of such assumptions.

Rafen turned at the sound of boots upon the deck
to find Mohl approaching him, a wheeled servitor
trundling at his heels. 'Lord,' began the Techmarine, 'a
moment?'

'What is it?'

'I took it upon myself to take a look over the catalogue of items in Zellik's collection. There is much of
value.'

'Of value to us, or to those who would hoard such
relics?'

Mohl inclined his head. 'Largely the latter, I admit.
But still, I have programmed some of the servitors to
sweep and reclaim any materials that should be
returned to the Adeptus Terra.'

'Good. Whatever Zellik has kept for himself is now
forfeit.'

Mohl nodded. 'Indeed. And so, I thought you
would want to see this, sir.' He snapped his fingers
and the servitor rolled forward. With spindly manipulator arms, it unfolded a stained muslin wrapping
from about a blunt, heavy object.

Rafen's eyes widened in surprise as he recognised
the shape of a thickset plasma gun. The weapon's
cowling was enamelled in blood red, and dressed
with a skull emblem in beaten gold.

'A twin-core design,' Mohl was saying, 'Dekker-
pattern. The rare Baal-variant model.'

Unbidden, Rafen ran a finger over the skull, tracing
the etching beneath it. '*Aryon*.' He spoke the hero's

name with reverence. 'This is the sidearm of Brother-Captain Aryon. He perished in battle at the Yennor Reach more than seven centuries ago… His remains were never found.'

'As your weapon was lost, I thought it would serve the mission to provide you with a replacement. Is this suitable?'

Rafen nodded, testing the gun's weight in his grip. 'It is. And now I have a fresh crime to add to those of the Magos Zellik. He was duty-bound to return this to my Chapter.'

'It is not the only Astartes relic in the museum,' added Mohl. 'Also, there are items of note belonging to the Adepta Sororitas and the Imperial Guard–'

'Continue your inventory. Take it all,' Rafen replied. 'In Aryon's memory, we will see every last piece go to the fate it deserves.'

'A fitting punishment for Zellik,' said the Flesh Tearer.

'And only the first,' Rafen noted. 'Have you been able to glean any data from the Archeohort's cogitators as yet?' He walked away, and the Techmarine trailed with him.

'Beslian has been surprisingly forthcoming, lord.'

'He knows his only chance to escape Zellik's fate is to cooperate with us in every way.'

'The name Haran Serpens was known to him. Beslian claims that Zellik has made several clandestine journeys into the Ghoul Stars region in order to meet with him. The most recent was only two solar months ago.'

Rafen halted. 'After Fabius fled Baal.'

'Aye.'

'The Ghoul Stars…' echoed the Blood Angel, his jaw drawing tight. 'It would seem, Brother Mohl, that we have the scent of our prey once more.'

The Flesh Tearer nodded. 'By the Emperor's grace.'

'I WOULD LIKE to see my relical,' coughed the tech-priest, twitching against the manacles that trailed thick cables from his many limbs – flesh and mechanical – to the rings set in the deck. 'If it pleases the Astartes.'

Brother-Sergeant Noxx rolled his flaying knife in his fingers, his lip curling at the barely-hidden contempt beneath the Magos's words. Even in this state, chained and disarmed, the scrawny cyborg dared to put on airs and graces. Noxx stalked forward, fanning the blade so it caught the light from the biolume pod on the ceiling of the holding chamber. 'Your precious collection? That is what you ask for? Perhaps your situation is unclear to you, priest. You are alive only on my sufferance. You are in no position to make demands.' He snorted. 'And in all honesty, you would be better served to consider your own fate than that of some stolen trinkets.'

'Idiot!' Zellik pulled at his bonds without success. 'Trinkets? My collection is without parallel! If you had a brain inside that thick skull of yours, you would comprehend that! But you are a barbarian! You know nothing!'

Noxx didn't look around as the hatch behind him opened; he knew who would be coming to join him.

'I cannot speak for my cousin,' said Rafen, drawing in, 'but I am no barbarian. I understand the majesty of great art. The glory of a great symphony. The perfection of fine craftsmanship.'

Zellik glared at him. 'Then you are worse than he,' spat the tech-lord. 'A Flesh Tearer, borderline feral and savage, he has an excuse! But you, Blood Angel? You should know better! And still, you were the first to raise a weapon to… to…' The Magos's voice became a weak moan. 'Oh, my cherished things. The Machine-God deliver me from this nightmare…'

Rafen continued as if the tech-priest had not spoken. 'I know the value of this, for example.' He raised the plasma gun, working the collimator dial with his other hand. 'Such a superior piece of work. Hand-crafted by Isherite artisans. Used with honour and care by a warrior of great character and nobility.' He took aim. 'Stolen from a war grave by a craven coward. Turned into a toy, a trophy for an arrogant fool.'

'I kept that weapon in trust!' spat Zellik, trying to flinch away but unable to move more than a few inches in the heavy restraints. 'It would have been lost or destroyed if not for me!'

'How selfless of you,' Rafen replied, and squeezed the trigger plate. On its finest setting, the humming accelerator coils atop the weapon glowed blue-white and discharged a thin rod of superheated plasmatic particles. The plasma bolt sliced into the top of a servo-arm waving from Zellik's spine, and turned it into a twist of slagged iron. After hundreds of years of inaction, the gun was hungry to fire on a new target.

The tech-priest screeched in binary and crashed to his knees, piston-legs chugging with the painful feedback.

Noxx made an appreciative noise in the back of his throat. 'Still works well, then. A fine weapon indeed.'

'I want my relical!' Zellik shouted. 'It is mine! You cannot take it from me! A dozen man-lifetimes it has taken me to gather it all–'

'But only a day to lose it,' Rafen broke in. 'Come now, Magos. Surely you expected this to happen? Beslian foresaw it, and he knew less than you. You know that death is the only coin paid to traitors.'

'Traitor?' The tech-priest shook his head. 'Perhaps I have interpreted the laws of my order with some laxity, yes, but I am no traitor! I am a staunch servant of the Machine-God! A devoted citizen of the Imperium of Mankind!'

Noxx tapped the flaying knife on his palm. 'Haran Serpens.' He sounded out the syllables of the name.

The name caught Zellik off-guard. 'What?'

'He's dead,' Rafen explained, working the plasma gun again. 'It appears he has been dead for at least three solar years, in point of fact.'

'Impossible,' snorted the tech-lord, but the denial seemed half-hearted. He was about to say more, but he halted, clearly fearful of incriminating himself still further.

'His identity was appropriated,' Rafen went on. The maw of the plasma gun was glowing white-hot, vapour seething from the emitter channels. 'Stolen by an agent of Chaos. A most foul and hated enemy of the Imperium you say you venerate. I'm sure you know the name Fabius Bile.'

The prisoner blurted out an exaggerated splutter of scorn, his silvery flesh wrinkling in dismay. 'Fabius Bile is a myth! A monster from the dark past created by over-zealous preachers in order to terrify the masses!' Zellik strained at the manacles as Rafen closed the distance to him. 'These accusations are lies. Lies spread by my enemies. Did the ordos send you, is that it? Were they so terrified to take me on themselves that they sent Space Marines to be their tools?'

'You are the one that has been used, Zellik,' said Noxx. 'Tainted, even.'

With slow care, Rafen reached out and gathered up a fistful of Zellik's robes. The tech-priest was shaking, his cyberlimbs rattling against the manacles. 'You will tell us about your dealings with the man who pretends to be Haran Serpens. You will tell us where he lurks within the Ghoul Stars.'

Zellik's clockwork eyes clicked and switched from Rafen to Noxx. The Flesh Tearer gave a thin smile. 'You must be very afraid to look to one like me for support. Do you really think you'll find it?'

Rafen held up Aryon's weapon, streamers of incredible heat coming off it in waves. 'I am not an inquisitor,' he said. 'I do not have an array of clever tools to induce you to speak truth to me. And I have neither patience, nor time. I am Astartes, and what I know best is how to kill. With speed... and without.' Rafen held the gun muzzle close to Zellik's flawless machine-face, and the chrome skin began to blister and darken. 'I will burn the answers I want from you. You will give them to me.'

He leaned closer, and the lowing screams began anew.

THE GAS-LENS VIEWER first sketched an orb, then filled it with lines of detail, one upon another, like the hand of a ghostly artist.

'The fifth world of the Dynikas system,' announced Mohl. 'Several parsecs out along the spinward edge of the Ghoul Stars. Our target.'

Rafen stood to one side of his squad, his arms folded across his chest. From the corner of his eye he saw Kayne glance at the plasma gun on his hip, and then at his face. The unspoken question was in his gaze, but his commander did not answer it.

Across the *Tycho's* tacticarium, Mohl went on, watched by Noxx and the rest of his fellow Flesh Tearers. 'From what we have been able to determine with data drawn from the Archeohort's cogitator arrays, Tech-Lord Zellik supplied equipment and materiel of a scientific and manufactory nature to this world.'

'Enough for someone to build a laboratory,' added Noxx.

Mohl nodded. 'The extant census records on Dynikas V are poorly drawn. The most detailed is that from a passing long-range scrying, by a vessel of the Imperial Navy engaged in a fleet action against the Cythor Fiends. The planet is determined here to be an ocean world with a few small island landmasses.' The hololith took on the blurry, lurid tones of a false-colour sensor image. 'A high content of metals was recorded, along with an apparent abundance of aquatic life forms. Ministorum adjuncts to this report indicate that the planet was classed as suitable for agricultural exploitation. A commerce flotilla was apparently dispatched, but records past this point were lost during the 9th Black Crusade.'

'That's all we know?' asked Eigen, frowning.

'There is more,' Mohl explained. 'This next data set was drawn from Zellik's personal stacks.' The image flickered and shifted. Now the patches of colour in Dynikas V's oceans were dead and hollow, flat expanses of white and grey instead of the riot of reds and oranges on the original scan. 'This is a more recent long-range scan. Zellik sealed this datum and prevented its upload to the Mechanicus codex-network.'

'It looks dead,' said Ajir. 'If it was teeming with enough fish for the explorators to set up a farming colony there, then what happened to it?'

'No radiological returns, no signs of planetary bombardment,' noted Kayne.

'Bio-weapon,' suggested Puluo.

'In a manner of speaking,' offered the Techmarine. 'Zellik's data also revealed this pict-relay of debris in high orbit of the planet.'

A new pane of imagery opened, dropping like a curtain. The flat display picked out a thick halo of dust and particulate matter collected into a sheer accretion disc.

'That wasn't there in the Navy's scry-scan,' said Eigen.

Mohl glanced at his battle-brother. 'No. It's the remains of a later destructive event. Zellik's hypothesis is that it is the residue of a battle between the notably territorial Cythor Fiends and a tyranid hive fleet splinter.'

'Tyranids?' Gast spat the name like a curse. 'But those xenos freaks are unknown in this sector.'

Turcio peered at the display. 'The evidence would suggest otherwise.'

'If you're willing to trust the word of that lying cog.'

Rafen considered what he was hearing. 'It would explain the ravaging of the planet's ecosystem. And the silence from the explorator flotilla.'

'Another question occurs, cousin,' said Noxx. 'Are the tyranids still there? Hive ships often eject spores towards the nearest planetary atmosphere at the moment of their destruction. Are we to believe that the renegade has built a bolt hole on an infested world?'

'Even Fabius Bile would not lay his head amid a pit of Fire Scorpions,' said Kayne. 'It would mean death for any being to venture down there, even for a champion of the Ruinous Powers.'

'There is only one way to be certain,' Rafen moved from where he stood. 'Have the navigators aboard our ships commune with those of the Archeohort. A course will be computed. Once repairs are complete, we will make space for the Dynikas system.'

'Do you really believe that the renegade is there, sir?' Kayne fixed him with a questioning look.

Rafen nodded once. 'The God-Emperor shows us the way, brother. We take the fight to this monster and we make him pay for what he has stolen from us.'

IN THE ARMING chamber, the Blood Angel completed the ritual of reconsecration with a final act. He cut his palm with his combat blade, and before the Larraman cells in his bloodstream could act to clot and knit shut the shallow wound, he wiped a smear of his vitae across the golden skull on the breech of the plasma gun.

With that, the machine-spirit of Captain Aryon's weapon was appeased, and the weapon's stewardship was now Rafen's. Perhaps it would be taken from him when he returned to Baal, if others judged that a more senior Space Marine was deserving of such a relic, but until that time, the sergeant would give it the liberation it deserved.

Rafen stood up in his arming chamber, the light of kolla tallow candles flickering over his power armour where it rested upon its racks. He pulled back the hood of his robes and glanced over his shoulder. 'You're slipping. I heard you coming this time.'

Ceris's lip curled. 'I beg to differ, lord. You only heard me because your thoughts were not clouded on this occasion. You have the clarity you sought.'

Did he detect some sense of accusation in the words? Rafen faced the Codicier with a level glare. 'Once again, you come to me with something to say, Ceris. Will this be a habit? I tell you now, if so my patience will quickly grow thin. I want warriors in my squad who will follow my orders and lend me their skills, not those who lurk and second-guess me at each turn.'

'Is that what you think I am doing?'

Rafen's eyes narrowed in annoyance. 'And I tolerate those who dissemble my words even less.'

'Because of who you are and what you have done, you should not be surprised that your conduct is being watched, brother-sergeant,' Ceris said mildly. 'Some say my Lord Mephiston is gatekeeper for the soul of our Chapter. His interest spans all who are a part of it.'

For a moment, the warrior considered a rebuke; but then he snorted and turned away. 'Say what you want to say and then leave me. I am in no mood for semantics and obfuscation.'

'There is word from the prize crew aboard the Archeohort. Magos Zellik will survive. The medicae serfs managed to keep him alive after your... interview.'

'Some might consider that a waste of effort and good narthecia.' He ran a finger over the casing of the plasma gun.

'Some? Like Brother-Sergeant Noxx?'

Rafen blew out an exasperated breath. 'What are you implying, psyker? That I have adopted the ways of the Flesh Tearers in order to gather information?'

'I did not say those words.' Ceris inclined his head. 'You did.'

Rafen glared at him. 'We do not shrink from the difficult choices, brother. That is why we were made. To do the things that mortal men cannot, to transcend what others might see as the lines of morality, in the name of a larger power.'

'Indeed? It is said we Blood Angels are the most noble of the Adeptus Astartes. But to torture a man to within an inch of his life, even a criminal... Is there nobility in that, sir?'

'You think I could have found another way, is that it? Perhaps you feel I did not give all due respect to the esteemed Magos, despite his dalliance with Chaos!'

'Zellik is no servant of the Dark Gods, we both know that. For all his genius, his greed and his conceit blind him to the reality of his misdemeanours. He believes he is loyal to Mars and Terra with every fibre of his being, even as he lies to them to swell his coffers.'

'Self-deception is a common trait of the weak,' Rafen retorted.

'And often of the strong as well,' Ceris countered.

'I feel no guilt for what I did to Zellik,' said the sergeant. 'I would do so again a hundred times over, if my service required it. Do not presume to judge me, psyker. You do not have the right.'

'I would never be so bold, my lord,' came the neutral reply. 'I only wanted to hear you say those words.' He turned to go, then hesitated. 'You will cross many lines, Brother Rafen, before this duty is brought to its end. These are just the first.'

The sergeant turned his back, ministering to his weapons. 'When you have something of substance to tell me, Brother Ceris, I will hear it willingly. But until then, keep your riddles to yourself. My tolerance is finite and you would do well to remember that.'

Rafen expected an answer, and when it did not come, he glanced over his shoulder. He was alone in the chamber.

FIVE

THE MIRROR MOVED through the darkness, bending about it the ghost-glows from far distant stars and the soft rains of radiation soaking the vacuum. A vast, curved kite shield of metals forged by long-forgotten science, the mirror told lies to the void around it, hiding its truth behind layers of energy-shunt circuitry, malleable lakes of superfluid surfactants and long, arching ribs of impossibly thin metals.

The mirror told the void that nothing was here. It lied by drawing in the wavelengths of visible and invisible energies all about, computed them and gently projected back returns that even the most advanced suites of scrying gear would read as little more than a few stray molecules of free hydrogen.

At its thickest point it was barely the width of a human hair, and yet it could withstand a lascannon hit if one were set towards it. The mirror was another of Zellik's great and secret treasures, a device that had enabled him many times to move the Archeohort's great mass by stealth, right under the noses of his enemies. On the far side of the curved kite, at its midpoint, the Mechanicus construct moved on inertia, thrusters silent and cowled ever since it had entered the Dynikas system. Flanking the Archeohort like pilot fish swimming with a whale, the warships *Tycho* and *Gabriel* kept in tight, exacting formation. The flight was straining their commanders to the limit, as all the crew-serfs knew that a single error of motion could send their cruisers outside the protective halo of the mirror – which would mark the end of both their clandestine approach and any chance of the mission's success.

Power systems across all three vessels were set as low as they dared; it was the same tactic the Space Marines had used to approach the Archeohort via boarding torpedo, but writ large. It had worked then; it would work now, if the grace of the God-Emperor favoured them.

The planet had two moons, both bulbous, misshapen asteroids captured by Dynikas V's gravity well. The far side of the larger was the flotilla's destination, baked by the sunlight of the hard orange-white sun. The primary moon was big enough to conceal all three vessels from any observers on the planet below. Dropping out of sight behind it, the mirror shroud began to fold away in a complex dance of shifting matter and clever machinery.

THE ARCHEOHORT'S ACTUAL command deck bore no resemblance to the fake that the ship's machine-spirit had attempted to trap them in. Ajir had been aboard many naval vessels and seen their bridges – the ornate stages for officers and ranged pits below filled with junior ratings and servitors, the windows that looked out from control towers across the prows of battle-ready warcraft. This was nothing of the like. The command space was a series of square terraces, balconied and cornered rings ranged one atop another, each smaller in dimension than the last. The effect was one of a pyramid turned inside out, the steps of a ziggurat falling down to a dais several levels below. Each terrace was lined with consoles of profuse complexity, and minor engineers and lexmechanics worked at them, heads buried under hoods or wired in via festoons of wafting mechadendrites. Some of the terraces were fitted with rails that the tech-priests rode on rollered feet, endlessly circling around and around.

The smell of ozone and electricity was sharp in the air, and a constant rattling rush of whispered machine code assailed the Blood Angel from every side. He stood behind Rafen, along with a few of his battle-brothers – as ever, the penitent Turcio among them – and the Logis Beslian, atop a hexagonal platform balanced between a pair of robot arms. The platform walked down the levels of the command pit by fixing itself with one limb, then swinging the opposite to another anchor point, then repeating the function anew. Beslian seemed to control its movements without any outward sign of direction.

'This is, to use an organic metaphor, the beating heart of the Archeohort,' said the tech-priest. The saggy flesh elements of his face showed slight disgust at his own terms. 'From here we may read data from any of the construct's systemry.'

'Your passive auspex sensors have analysed returns from the planet,' Noxx said curtly. 'What do they reveal?'

Beslian rolled his hooded head on his piston neck and the platform arrested its movement, shouldering over to the corner of a nearby terrace. 'Observe,' he began, beckoning a pict-screen on one wall to extend out towards them on a gimbal.

The display buzzed and displayed a flickering rune-prayer before reforming into a grainy real-time image of Dynikas V. Indicator overlays projected on to lenses swung around into position. Hot lines of red appeared, dots of varying size and lividity scattering themselves over the planet's dayside.

'Thermal blooms, lords,' explained Beslian. 'Trace patterns of waste gases ejected into the air through bio-processes. Feeding, and the decay of corpses, I would warrant.'

'I thought this planet was dead,' growled Sove, another of Noxx's Space Marines.

'*It* is,' said Mohl. 'What we are seeing is evidence of xenos, brother. Tyranids, marooned on this world, living off each other after their hive was destroyed.'

Rafen was grim. 'They must have eaten everything else.'

'I do not understand,' said Kayne. 'Is it not the tyranid way to gut a living world, then build new bio-ships and move on to the next? If Dynikas V is bereft of all native life, then why are these monstrosities still here?'

Beslian inclined his head, favouring Kayne with a nod. 'The Blood Angel is correct. But this behaviour is not uncommon. It has been seen before, when a nest is denied the governance of one of their command organisms.'

'You speak of a hive tyrant,' said Turcio.

Ajir's lips thinned. That much was obvious.

'Correct,' said Mohl. 'I hypothesise that there is no such beast on the planet below. As such, the extant tyranid warrior-organisms resident there revert back to their base natures. Killing and reproducing. Given a dozen generations, if this new ecosystem was not interfered with, it would probably eat itself into extinction.'

'And we are to believe that Fabius Bile resides among that morass of fangs and claws?' Kayne folded his arms across his chest, shaking his head. 'It cannot be.'

'No?' said Rafen. 'Explain that, then.' He pointed at a regular cluster of heat signatures on a crescent-shaped atoll in the southern hemisphere. 'That pattern is too coherent for an organic form.'

'Good eye, my lord,' said Beslian. He flipped another lens over the screen and turned it with his servo-arm. 'You are quite correct to suspect this locale. Solar albedo returns correlate with manufactured materials down there. Ferrocrete and metal alloys.'

'A building,' noted Puluo.

Noxx leaned in. 'Enlarge that image. Show us more.'

Beslian frowned. 'Without use of active sensors, I cannot provide the best resolution…' He worked the lenses irritably, expanding on the blurs of colour and reflection. 'Ah…'

Ajir made out the distinctive shapes of bunkers and revetments, wards around an open landing zone and what could have been a keep. 'He has himself a fortress, in the middle of a xenos breeding ground.'

'How is that possible?' said Turcio. The penitent leaned in. 'See, the island around the buildings. Every other scrap of land has evidence of tyranid spoil pools, spore chimneys or killing grounds. But not this one. How is Fabius keeping them at bay?'

'Sorcery,' muttered Sove darkly.

Puluo studied the image. 'Those look like embedded lance batteries, there and there,' he noted. 'Heavy gauge. Capable of reaching low orbit, I'd warrant.'

'Correct. I have determined that those weapons were among the items my former master traded in this quadrant. They are the secondary line of defence,' continued Beslian. 'The primary is closer to hand. Look here, Astartes.' The tech-priest beckoned one of his lexmechanics, and the hooded figure released another mobile screen to them. Still images captured from near-orbital space flicked past like pages from a book.

Rafen recognised them first. 'Gunskulls.'

There were orbs floating in the dark, kilometres up over the surface of Dynikas V, each of them clustered with engine nozzles and arrow-tipped spines. Even in the indistinct imagery taken in passing by the Archeohort's watch-scopes, the screaming mouths worked into their surfaces were clearly visible, as were the complex strings of text in forbidden tongues carved into the metal. Some of them dragged lines of chain with them, others were dressed with fans of solar panelling. No two were alike, but every one of them had a face. Ajir had once heard that the sculpted iron was modelled upon the aspects of certain champions of the Chaos Gods, as some form of veneration. He could see where superheavy laser cannons and the tips of melta torpedoes protruded from gaping, crack-toothed maws and blank eye sockets. Each one of these killer satellites had at its heart the flesh of a crippled madman, wired in and entombed in a sheath of steel, never sleeping, forever awake and desperate to unleash death upon the enemies of the Ruinous Powers. There were hundreds of them, all with their backs to the planet and cannons aimed outward, hundreds of frozen, howling faces and screaming skulls.

'I'm no shipmaster,' said Noxx, 'but I'd say those things bring poor odds.'

Mohl nodded. 'The satellites are intermediate range weapons, but more than capable of matching the guns of two strike cruisers. Anything less than a passing engagement would go in the favour of the defenders.'

'What about this hulk?' demanded Kayne.

Beslian took the insult with a sharp chug of air. 'The *Archeohort* is not a warship! It is not built for sustained military actions.' He looked away peevishly.

Rafen ignored the outburst. 'Fabius has dug himself in deep, that cannot be denied. But we've not come this far to be dissuaded at the very gates of our foe's redoubt.'

'A frontal attack will be a wasteful endeavour,' Beslian said airily. 'At best, you might be able to close to heavy weapons range and release an orbital bombardment upon Bile's facility. And even then, as the gunskulls swarmed your ships, you would not live to tell of it. Not to mention that it is highly likely that the traitor has hardened his base to well beyond–'

'Your insights are appreciated,' snapped the sergeant, iron in his tone, 'but matters of tactics are not yours to decide.'

Beslian pressed on, clearly concerned for the fate of the Archeohort now it was his. 'I would respectfully suggest you call in reinforcements from your Chapter starfleet, brother-sergeant. A massed force of ships could obliterate Dynikas V with a sustained cyclonic torpedo barrage and suffer only a few losses in return.'

Sove snorted, his scarred face wrinkling. 'It could take weeks to gather more ships.'

'The cousin is right,' Ajir threw the Flesh Tearer a nod. 'And even then, even if we had the time to wait, how can we be sure that Bile will not simply spirit himself away as he did when he fled from Baal?'

For a moment, Rafen was silent, perhaps recalling the memory of a dim corridor beneath the Vitalis Citadel, and the brimstone stink of a spent warp gate. 'The kill must be made close at hand. From high orbit, hiding behind guns... That will not suffice. Our honour demands more.'

'Logic–' Beslian barely got the word out before Noxx was at his side, a finger pressing on his sunken chest.

'You heard the Blood Angel,' he said. 'This is a matter of retribution, not your precious logic.'

The logis's optics whined as they blinked. 'As you wish...' He backed away, almost to the edge of the mobile platform. 'But... but what other means of attack is there?'

'Thunderhawks and drop-pods will be obliterated before they even cut atmosphere,' said Ceris.

'Teleporters won't work. There are wards in place to prevent their operation.' He tapped his temple. 'I see them.'

Ajir watched Rafen fold his arms. 'So all we have are impossibilities. It seems that every step we have taken along this road brings us more of them.' He glared at the image. 'I am done. I no longer care to hear what we cannot do, and how we will not succeed.' The sergeant turned around, his ire burning in his eyes, his gaze raking them all. 'We were not given this mission in order to fail it! The Emperor's hand is at our backs, and we will not disappoint Him! We have been entrusted with the honour of our Chapter...' Rafen caught Ajir's gaze. 'The honour of our primarch! So we *will* find a way!'

In the silence that followed, Mohl slowly raised his hand. 'If it pleases the brother-sergeant,' said the Techmarine, 'I have a suggestion.'

AT FIRST GLANCE, it resembled a bomb, but larger than any Rafen had ever seen, greater even than the huge Atlas-class weapons deployed by the Imperial Navy against hardened ground targets. Suspended on chains from a gantry over the heads of the Space Marines, it projected an air of menace, its black iron flanks curving up and away.

'It's a ship?' demanded Noxx.

'Of a sort,' Mohl replied.

Eigen bent his neck to take the whole thing in. 'I've never seen the like before.'

Rafen spotted hatches along the smoothly rounded prow of the object that lay perfectly flush with the hull metal, and at the opposite end, the strange vessel tapered to a teardrop stern. An 'X' of stubby winglets emerged there, and in the light from the flickering welding torches of servitors, he made out the low mound of a turret on the dorsal surface.

'My lords, allow me to present to you the *Neimos*. According to the dedication plaque within, it was built during the Great Crusade for the service of the Imperial Army. Zellik's relic hunters appropriated it for him several years ago, from a space hulk in the Drache Sector.'

'The streamlining...' began Turcio. 'It's an atmosphere boat.'

'No,' said Rafen, understanding coming to him. 'This craft is built for oceans, not air.'

Mohl nodded. 'Correct, brother-sergeant. The *Neimos* is a combat submersible, designed for deployment on ocean worlds. I came across a mention of it in the Magos's inventory.'

Kayne snorted. 'And how does this relic help us get to Bile? What do you propose we do, Flesh Tearer? Drop it on him?'

'The hull of the *Neimos* is constructed from a spun sentanium-ceramite mix. It is a solid piece, extremely durable and flexible. In addition, there are extra layers of ablative armour sheathing its length. While the craft was built for a crew of common sailors, I believe it can be quickly refitted to operate with a handful of Astartes and a contingent of servitors.'

'You're suggesting we sail this thing under the seas of Dynikas V, right up to the front door of Bile's fortress?' Noxx gave a chuckle that wasn't reflected in his cold eyes. 'Let us ignore the dangers of such a journey for a moment and concentrate on the boy's question.' He nodded towards Kayne. 'Or did you forget Beslian's little show? I ask you, what possible value is there for a boat in space?'

'The *Neimos* is orbit descent-capable, lord,' Mohl replied. 'Shunt-field systems and armour will protect it from the trauma of atmospheric interface. Ballute arrays will slow the fall.'

'I was right,' Kayne said, in disbelief. 'You *do* want to drop it on him.'

In spite of himself, Rafen found a sudden bark of dry laughter bubbling up inside him. 'I confess, Brother Noxx, I am not certain if your Techmarine has lost his reason or gained genius.'

'I feel the same way,' said the Flesh Tearer, glaring at his warrior. 'Is such a thing really possible?'

Mohl nodded. 'Craft of this class have been deployed in combat many times. The survival rate is not exemplary, however.'

'I'd ask you a number for that rate,' said Rafen, 'but I fear I would regret knowing the answer.'

'I fail to see the point of this,' said Ajir. 'If we could close to such range as to launch this… this curiosity… then why not a storm of drop-pods instead?'

'With the *Neimos*, we can deploy the craft into the ocean on the far side of Dynikas V from the target atoll, where the fortress's emplaced guns are over the horizon and unable to reach us. In addition, the coverage of the defence satellites is thinner in that area. Once we dive beneath the surface, the gunskulls will not be able to track us.' Mohl gestured at the submarine. 'We will be free to proceed in stealth.'

'But how do we get it to launch position?' Kayne insisted.

'It will require sacrifice,' said the Techmarine, after a moment.

A slow smile formed on Rafen's lips as Mohl's meaning became clear to him. 'Yes, I think it will.' He paused, musing. 'How long to ready the *Neimos* for the drop?'

'I have already begun the preparations, lord. A matter of hours.'

Rafen nodded to himself, voicing his thoughts. 'Two squads of men, infiltrated on to the planet, delivered by this vessel to the enemy's fortress. We go in under cover of fire and stealth, and hit the target.'

'We're doing this, then?' Noxx asked. 'Well. As plans go, it has audacity...'

'Will that count for anything if we die of it?' grated Eigen.

Rafen glanced around. 'Gather your wargear. Prepare yourselves for the coming battle.'

Kayne's face was sallow. 'And may we take the time to pray? I fear we will need all the blessings we can gather to us.'

The sergeant nodded. 'You're right. But know this – the God-Emperor is always watching, and He favours the bold.'

BESLIAN CAME UP to meet them on his mobile platform, the mechanism clanking up the levels of the command pit. Rafen turned from the relay helot conveying his orders to the internal and external vox-channels, giving the Mechanicus priest the briefest of looks.

'Brother Rafen!' snapped the logis. 'What is going on?' He pointed a spindly servo-arm at Mohl. 'The

Archeohort's control code protocols have been changed. This battle-brother did so, without consulting me! What is the meaning of this?'

Rafen ignored him, concentrating on his task at hand. The helot had plugged itself into the construct's machine-call web, and now the Blood Angel's words to it were being broadcast simultaneously to the Astartes upon the bridges of the *Gabriel* and the *Tycho*. 'Shipmasters,' he was saying. 'You know your orders. You have five solar days. If we fail in our mission, or if contact is not made using the correct cipher protocols, execute a maximum strike bombardment of the fortress. By the command of our Chapter Masters, you are to do whatever is required to turn that island into slag... To the forfeiture of your vessels and crews, and beyond. *Ave Imperator.*' The commanders of the two warships echoed his words and cut the channel.

'We are ready to begin,' said Mohl.

'Do so,' Rafen told him, before finally giving his attention to the adept.

'I believed we had built up a measure of trust!' Beslian grated. 'Instead I find my code strings severed, and intruder data impinging on the function of my ship's systems! This will not stand!'

'No?' Rafen took a heavy step towards him. 'Is it necessary for me to remind you how it is you came to be wearing this icon?' The Blood Angel prodded him in the chest with an armoured finger, pressing the master's sigil around Beslian's neck into the folds of his rust-coloured robes. 'Know this, my esteemed logis. You command the Archeohort in name only. This vessel belonged to the Sons of Sanguinius the moment we declared it so.'

'Mohl is a Techmarine!' The priest blurted out the title with mild disgust. 'And a Flesh Tearer into the bargain. You understand! He is not fit to take mastery of a fine craft like this, even in your primarch's name… The Techmarines come to Mars to be trained, but they do not truly excel! They never know the perfection of the machine as a member of the Adeptus Mechanicus does!'

'And yet, despite my apparent lesser status, I was able to lock you from your own codex-system,' said Mohl, with deceptive mildness.

Beslian ignored the jibe. 'Techmarines are brutish, crude and unsophisticated! And Mohl is all the more so for his Chapter and breeding!'

The Flesh Tearer's plain face suddenly twisted in annoyance, but Rafen stepped up before he could move towards the adept. 'What do you say to me?' the Blood Angel said coldly. 'That you are more loyal to my mission than a battle-brother from a kindred Chapter? Do you take me for a fool?' His fist unclenched and he backhanded the adept to the deck. The blow was as light as he could make it – he did not wish to kill the man – but still Beslian went stumbling down in a clatter of metal. 'If I learn that you again speak ill of an Astartes, of any Son of Sanguinius, I'll have you cut up for servitor spares. You will obey Mohl as you would the word of the God-Emperor of Mankind!'

Beslian made a wounded, sobbing noise, but his head bobbed and he tried to right himself with whatever scraps of dignity he still possessed. 'I… I only wish to know why! What have I done to displease you?'

Rafen eyed him. 'You think yourself superior to us, and you think us so inferior that we would not know it. That is enough.'

The iris hatch to the command deck rattled open, and Beslian saw the figure framed in the open doorway. Immediately, his words with the Space Marine were forgotten and he threw up his arms, organic and mechanical alike, in a gesture of self-protection. 'No!' he cried, his implanted vocoder resonating with static-filled feedback. 'Why is *he* here? No! Take him away!'

With Brother Sove to his right, a bolter held at his silver skull, and an ever-watchful Brother Ceris to his left, the former Magos Matthun Zellik shambled into the chamber, dripping with restraint cables and detention cuffs. The machine eyes in his scarred metal face were hard with hate as they found Beslian. 'Turn-coat!' snarled Zellik. Immediately he began a chattering hymnal of harsh binary code, but before he could speak more than a few phrases, Ceris yanked on his tethers, and the magos was choked into silence.

'What was that noise?' said Rafen.

'Meme code,' said Mohl, with a grimace. 'Clogs the mental functions of those who absorb it.'

'If he does that again, kill him,' the sergeant told the other Flesh Tearer. Sove nodded and as an after-thought, tore a length of cloth from the prisoner's garb, quickly fashioning a gag from it.

Beslian followed Rafen, deliberately keeping the Blood Angel between him and his former master. 'Why have you brought him here?' he bleated. 'He should be on the dungeon decks, or executed!'

'Zellik will perform a final duty for the Imperium,' said Ceris. 'As a lesson for the weak.' He shoved the ex-magos towards the helm podium that overlooked the command pit. A largely ceremonial construction, the podium was used by Mechanicus rune priests to awaken the engines of a vessel at the start of a voyage or before a mission of great import. There, they would appease the machine-spirit of the craft in the Emperor's name, all the better to see it perform its function. It was the helm in ritual only; in actuality, the steering of the Archeohort was done by mindless servitor drones down in the lower levels of the pit.

Ceris took Zellik's tethers and secured him to the podium. The cables keened as they tightened and became rigid. Zellik rebelled against this new indignity, but Sove held him down with no visible effort. The ex-magos roared behind his gag, froth escaping his bound lips to trickle off his tarnished metal chin.

Rafen studied the prisoner for a long moment. 'All those who turn their backs upon the God-Emperor, through the embrace of the alien, the mutant or the traitor… For greed. For their own glory. In ignorance. In fear… All of them must pay for that crime.' He shot a glare at Beslian. '*All*, adept.'

'It's done,' said Sove. 'The rest of the squads are boarding the *Neimos*. We're ready, Brother-Sergeant.'

Beslian balked at the mention of the submersible's name. 'What… are you doing with that craft? It's just a relic! An engineering novelty…'

Ceris turned a penetrating stare on the tech-priest. 'For your sake, you had best be wrong about that.'

'Take the logis below,' said Rafen. 'Tell Sergeant Noxx to start the count.'

Beslian went towards the hatch, his iron hooves scraping as he moved with reluctance. 'I don't understand...'

'You will, soon enough,' Ceris noted. The psyker paused and threw his commander a nod. 'Don't fear, sir. We won't go without you.' He showed something like a smile, but Rafen felt chilled at the sight of it.

He turned away and found Mohl watching him. The Techmarine had extended a length of mechadendrites into brass sockets along the command console. 'Ready,' said the Flesh Tearer.

'You're certain you have full control of the Archeohort?'

Mohl nodded jerkily, as if he was distracted. 'Aye.' Rafen could only imagine the torrent of machine code filtering into the warrior's mind through the cables, the flood of binary babble from hundreds of chattering functionaries and cogitators.

Zellik howled something unintelligible behind his gag, straining at his tether. Rafen ignored the traitor's protests, shoving him back to the deck. 'There can be no errors. A single hesitation, any act of rebellion by one of the crew—'

'There will be none,' Mohl said, with finality. 'The commands are hard-coded. It would take a millennium to unlock them. This helot crew will do as they are ordered to, and they will not be permitted to question. *I* will not allow it.' With care, the Techmarine set down his bolter on the deck and dropped to one knee, as if he were about to pray.

Rafen felt a moment of confusion. 'Mohl, what are you doing? We must away.'

The Flesh Tearer shook his head. 'Not I,' he replied. 'I must remain to steward the Archeohort.' Mohl smiled ruefully. 'I did say this would require sacrifice.'

For a long moment, the Blood Angel weighed the words of the other Astartes, the full understanding of Mohl's choice becoming clear. At last he spoke. 'There is no other way?'

'None, lord, and it is to my regret. I would like to be there when you find the renegade. To see him pay.' He frowned in concentration. 'Time draws short. The engines are coming to power, sir. You must go.'

Rafen nodded, and placed a hand on Mohl's shoulder. 'You will be remembered, cousin.'

Mohl did not look up. 'That is all I ask.'

ON RODS OF blazing fusion fire, the massive bulk of the Archeohort rose over the surface of the primary moon, the derrick-limbs pulled in tight. Torpedo turrets and weapon batteries spun up to full power, turning to bear on the looming disc of Dynikas V. With the mirror-shield folded away and the drives open to full, the inferno of energy returns lit the scrying sensors of the orbiting gunskulls like dawn breaking the night.

The satellites turned on manoeuvring thrusters, puffs of gas orienting them towards the intruder, even as quick sensor engines examined the silhouette of the vessel. They compared it to ships of all known types within their knowledge banks, and the answers they found brought only a mass of confusion to the chained organic minds at the heart of each orbiter. The whole process took only fractions of a second, and garbled machine speech back and forth via low-power laser beams swiftly led to a consensus. The web of gun-skulls sent a vox code down through the turbulent, wind-swept atmosphere of Dynikas V – a question demanding an immediate answer, to kill or not to kill.

Any ship intending to slow into a parking orbit over the ocean world would have required a scheme of careful thrust-gravity-mass formulae to avoid over-shooting or unwarranted atmospheric interface. The *Archeohort* reached the point of transition and did not lose pace; if anything, with the pull of Dynikas V now upon it, the massive Mechanicus construct was accelerating.

Aboard the vessel, the first querulous, frightened messages began to trickle in to the command centre's vox buffer from the minor adepts and more sentient of the ship's servitors. Each one was snubbed by Mohl's firm denials and hard, uncompromising orders.

The *Archeohort* continued to close on the planet.

THE NEIMOS WAS already moving as Rafen sprinted into the cavernous departure bay. Now upon a long, low cradle that rode on steel rails, the full shape of the craft was visible to him. A childhood spent on a world of deserts meant that oceans and the beasts that dwelled within them were alien to him, but on some level he understood the aspects of hunter cetaceans, with their fins and streamlined bodies. The *Neimos* resembled them, but in Rafen's eyes it was easier for him to equate the craft with the shape of a weapon. The submersible reminded him of a cudgel, heavy and dangerous – a brute-force device ready to bludgeon an enemy into submission.

In swift, loping steps, he mounted the cradle, scattering crew-serfs too slow to get out of his way, and clambered to the hatch on the dorsal fin. Rafen's boots clicked over a layer of curved lamellar tiles, the extra ablative armour that would be the ship's heat shield through atmospheric interface. He glanced back down towards the stern, past the X-planes to the ring where the thrusters would be; for now, they were folded into the submarine's hull, only to be deployed once they were in the sea.

Rafen squeezed into the open hatch and pulled it closed behind him. New weld marks and gobs of sealant marked the places where the airlock had been widened to accommodate the bulk of armoured Space Marines. As the lock cycled, he spoke the litany to weapons with brisk intention.

Inside, the dimensions of the *Neimos* were close and confined. Built for men of normal stature, the corridors and chambers of the vessel would have been cramped even for them; for an Adeptus Astartes, and one in full power armour at that, it made the coffin-like space of a drop-pod seem roomy by comparison.

'Watch your head, sir,' said Turcio, beckoning him down an accessway. 'It's a snug fit, that's for certain.'

The sergeant followed, noting the places where bright metal showed, indicating the spots where panels had been cut away or decks removed to accommodate the girth of a Space Marine. They were quick and dirty fixes, but if this mission had revealed anything to Rafen, it was that the most expedient course of action was rarely the cleanest.

He entered the control room and found a crew of servitors at the stations, with the rest of the Astartes crowded around a raised island in the middle of the chamber. He spied Kayne watching the two helots at the helm station; nothing but a wall of blank screens and inert dials lay before them. The whole vessel rocked as the transport cradle shifted over points and swung wide.

'Where's Brother Mohl?' said Sove, his bearded face tightening.

Noxx shared a look with Rafen. The other sergeant must have known the intentions of his squad-mate from the outset, but said nothing of it. 'Mohl has his work to do. We have ours.'

Sove glared at Rafen, as if the Techmarine's absence was his fault, and then looked away.

'The ship is sealed,' said Ajir. 'For better or worse, this antique will be our saviour or our coffin.'

'Status?' Rafen put the question to Noxx.

The Flesh Tearer's dead eyes met his. 'We have twenty helots aboard, the best of Zellik's bunch, at all the crew stations. I'm afraid the honourable Logis Beslian became hysterical when he figured out what our gambit was.'

Rafen looked around; there was no sign of the Mechanicus adept. 'And how did you deal with that?'

'He's in one of the descent racks,' said Noxx. 'Gast put him out with a sedative from the *Neimos's* infirmary. I thought better there than running about the boat like a panicked grox.' Off Rafen's nod, he gestured around. 'The prize crew have returned to the *Tycho*. We're all that's left.' He frowned. 'Not counting Mohl, of course…'

The Blood Angel took in the faces of the warriors before him; there, a knot of crimson and gold,

Battle-Brothers Kayne, Turcio and Ajir, and the Devastator Space Marine Puluo, the psyker Ceris
standing out in his indigo wargear. To the other side,
in their black-chased, wine-dark armour, Sergeant
Noxx and the remainder of his squad, Brothers
Eigen and Sove, and the cleric Gast. Ten warriors, ten
Sons of Sanguinius ranged against a world teeming
with rapacious xenos beasts and a heartless scion of
Chaos Undivided.

A smile crossed his lips, and Rafen's fangs flashed.
'Our victory is down there, brothers. We have only to
reach out and take it.'

Another shock rumbled up through the deck of the
Neimos.

'It's starting,' said Ceris.

Zellik was screaming behind his gag, his augmetic
eyes wide and rolling. His entire body vibrated with
furious shock, and he pulled at his restraints with all
the strength of madness and desperation. His
implanted antennae – the ones deep in his muscle tissue and bone marrow, the ones the clumsy Astartes
had not discovered and excised – picked up the short-
range radio wave speech bursts between the minor
servitors working the closest console ranges.

What Zellik heard there he quickly pieced together
with the behaviour of the Blood Angel and the
blighted Flesh Tearer Techmarine; the sum of that
datum was enough to cause a spike of actual, genuine
emotion deep inside the tech-lord's mind. It had
been a long time since he felt true, real *fear*. Other
emotional states, ones like greed or desire, hate and
envy, those he indulged in with frequency. Matthun

Zellik had never been one to eschew the whole emotive experience, unlike many of his Mars-born kindred; where they held to the belief that only in cold logic could perfection be found, Zellik believed that emotions, just like any abstract system, could be reduced to knowable equations if only one had the time and the intellect to find them. He used emotions as toys, turned them on and off to enhance his pleasure at every acquisition he made, used them to sharpen his mind when he was in conflict.

Already, he had almost been swamped in loathing after discovering that Beslian had betrayed him to the Astartes; but that had faded quickly with the realisation that, had circumstances been reversed, he would have done the same to that irritating little null unit. That had been replaced, first by hot, blazing anger. The rage at being forced to do nothing while these ham-fisted fools smashed about his precious Archeohort and laid waste to it. But he had not regretted his decision to surrender to them, at least not at first. On some level, he understood – *he had always understood* – that the collection down in the holds was more important than any individual life, more important than his life, even. Zellik made his peace with that; he would happily let himself perish if the collection survived. There would be others to take on his great task of gathering the tech-relics of the past. Each find had taken him closer to the Machine-God, and he regretted nothing.

But now that was taken from him, and there was such great and transcendent woe in his clockwork heart. He listened with his antennae and he heard the orders, he understood the horrible thing that the

Astartes were doing. He pulled at his tethers, screaming and screaming, but the Techmarine Mohl, only a few spans away from him there on the deck, ignored him utterly.

It was then a new voice joined the others. A vox signal, filtering up from the planet below, bearing ciphers that labelled it for Zellik's attention. Broadcast in the clear, the voice of Haran Serpens issued out from bell-mouthed speaker horns.

'My dear Matthun,' it boomed. 'You've impressed me. How you managed to venture so close without being detected… I always knew you were a man of great cleverness.' There came a metered sigh, and as he listened to it, Zellik was wondering after the words of the Blood Angel, the mad claim the warrior Rafen had made.

Haran Serpens could not be dead, it was impossible! And more so, that someone like Zellik could be duped by an agent of Chaos into thinking him still alive. He would have scoffed had his mouth not been stuffed with a ragged cloth. *Fabius Bile, indeed!* The very idea was the pinnacle of idiocy!

'Will you not answer me, Matthun?' asked the voice. 'No? Your ship comes closer, and you do not announce yourself to me. What am I to think? Have we not had a mutually beneficial relationship? Or is it that the seeds of covetousness I always saw in you are now bearing fruit? Yes. I think that is what it is.'

'*No! No!*' With effort, Zellik forced the tiny manipulator arrays in his mouth cavity to finally cut through his gag and allow him to shout. He projected the bellowed cry on every frequency he could, but static jamming rebounded in on him. The tech-lord glared at Mohl, who still had not moved, not reacted one single iota as the Archeohort drove in towards the planet at greater and greater velocity. 'Haran!' cried Zellik. 'This is not my doing! Hear me!' His words went no further than the walls around him.

Then the greatest insult of all came to pass. Zellik detected machine code streaming out from the Archeohort's transmitters, directed down at the planet. The data strings were mimics of the tech-lord's own proprietary vox protocols, hyper-complex packets of information that flashed past in split-second bursts. They were perfect emulations of Zellik's own coding patterns, the digital renditions of a gifted imitator. He glared at Mohl, affronted by this intrusion. Then the fear returned to him as he parsed the content of the faked signals; they were brusque, sneering strings of code, demands for surrender and declarations of combat, all directed at Haran Serpens.

A dark, throaty chuckle sounded through the ether. 'I'm sad it has come to this,' said the voice, and by turns it began to shift and alter. 'I see that you are more the fool than I thought you were. A pity, Zellik. But I suppose I should have expected no better. You are like all the rest of them. Limited. Weak. Serving your Corpse-God blindly.' Zellik's machine heart hammered against iron ribs and he felt the fear again. 'Such a waste. Such a terrible, foolish waste...'

New data flowed invisibly to the tech-lord; on the planet below and the gunskulls in close orbit, weapon discharges bloomed, throwing fire into the path of the Archeohort.

* * *

THE MECHANICUS CONSTRUCT cut a wide arc across the dayside of Dynikas V, retro-thrusters stabbing out tongues of nuclear flame, the cannon batteries atop its derricks and ringing its rail-nets aiming out in twenty different directions, seeking targets on the surface and amid the swarm of gunskulls.

The orbit it had entered was not a stable one; the course it projected dipped low and into the edge of the atmosphere, passing through the day-night terminator zone and into the gloom of the planet's dark side. But before it reached that point, there was a gauntlet of lances and missiles to run, a hard rain of particle beams, radiation and guided warheads. Nothing short of a battle-barge would have been able to weather such concentrated fire and survive – but still the Archeohort came on, every intelligent system aboard it blinkered and forbidden from dwelling on the fate before them, controlled by the iron will of Techmarine Mohl.

The gunskulls were in rapture. Every shot they fired, every blazing ejection of energy, each one lit sparks of pleasure in their hobbled minds. Jars filled with cuts of human brain matter bubbled and frothed, filled with the joy of attack.

Missile hits grew into spheres of flame expanding out to consume the brass limbs of the construct, entire derricks tearing apart, some severed and set tumbling away. Ragged cuts bled electricity and streamers of gas. Cannons howled in the darkness, the shock of their release echoing through the decks of the Archeohort, their silent payloads smashing gunskulls to fragments; but there were so many more of the satellites, and now they were jetting in from other orbits like starving carrion birds drawn to a fresh corpse.

Zellik's great ship began to shed parts of itself, cutting a line of shredded metal and spilled fluids across the sky. This was a vain, arrogant attack that only the most foolhardy, the most overconfident of commanders would ever think to undertake – that, or one with a death wish. The slow, ponderous guns down on the surface tracked and fired, fired and tracked, and each shot they released was a palpable hit. A smaller, more nimble ship might have managed to veer off; not the Archeohort. The construct's path became confused, showing panic. The drive bells glowed bright, frantic to push the mass of the vessel away from the engagement zone; but as they worked, to the mad joy of the gunskulls, laser fire threaded across the void. Where it touched the hull of the Mechanicus construct, force field envelopes buckled and faded, allowing raking hits to cleave through armour and into the decks below. The corpses of vacuum-suffocated servitors followed the rest of the ejecta into space, bloated cyborg bodies adrift as their machine implants continued to work mindlessly at nothing.

Falling and falling, the Archeohort's main hull split open and imploded. In moments, even as the autonomic guns about its mass continued to fire back, the great construct entered its death throes. No longer a ship, now a collection of slow-dying wreckage as large as a city, the craft tumbled deeper into the gravity well of Dynikas V, towards the oxide-thick oceans that would be its grave.

SIX

ACROSS THE COMMAND lectern, strings of indicator lumes snapped from red to blue, each accompanied by the hollow chime of a long bell. The heavy, grinding echo of metal sealing tight against metal worked its way through the hull plates, and glass-faced dials buried their indicator needles at the active stop.

'All decks report ready,' droned a servitor, oblivious to the vibrations thrumming through the plates beneath it. 'Craft is sealed. *In nomine Imperator, aegis Terra.*'

Suspended from the low ceiling, masks made of cracked ceramic, fashioned after the fat faces of cherubs, piped crackling hymnals from their open mouths. The chorus from their lips was just at the edge of hearing, the moaning and creaking of the *Neimos* a far more strident and powerful orchestra.

Rafen's eyes scanned the bridge of the vessel; each of the machine-slaves had dutifully wired themselves to their assigned command stations, the active webs of restraining harnesses tying them into place. The Blood Angel had briefly glimpsed a schematic of the *Neimos*, and knew that the bridge was one of a few compartments inside the submersible mounted on shock-resistant mechanisms, enveloped with arcane energy-shunt technology that would allow the crew to survive impacts that would otherwise turn a body into wet paste. The system was not powerful enough to encompass the whole of the craft, however.

'Brothers, to your drop stations,' Rafen ordered, turning to the line of Space Marines ranged close by. 'We have only one chance at this. Make no mistake, a single error will be enough to kill us all.'

'Our lives are in *their* hands?' Sove jutted his chin at the servitors. 'The bond-servants of a criminal conspirator?'

'Try not to let it worry you,' Turcio replied.

Puluo gave both Astartes a sharp look, and spoke for the rest of them. 'We're ready.'

Rafen accepted this with a nod. 'This is the point of no return, brothers. This day we venture into the realm of the unknown, down to a world teeming with aliens, a world blackened by the Mark of Chaos. Look to your battle-brothers, to your wargear, and you will prevail.'

Noxx raised his helm up upon his fist. 'For the Emperor and Sanguinius.' The Flesh Tearer's words were a hard bark of fury.

'Aye!' chorused the warriors.

Rafen closed his eyes, and formed a silent prayer in his thoughts. *Let us live, Great Angel,* he said silently. *Let us live so we can bring our quest to the end it deserves.*

THE ARCHEOHORT CAME apart in blinding flashes of light. Severed conduits channelling rivers of electrothermal energy spat great gouts of colour as they vented. Whole decks made of stained glass, rescued from worlds razed to rock, were shattered into powder. Objects from thousands of planets and hundreds of histories were torn apart with the construct's slow, agonising death throes. Storehouses of items never catalogued, things that were alien in origin or just alien in nature, were crushed under the weight of collapsing metal. Centuries of papers fuelled the fires that boiled bio-fluid meme-stores and cracked the delicate lattices of record crystals. Libraries of junk and bric-a-brac mixed with valuables and undocumented treasures were destroyed alongside one another. This great monument to one man's greed and obsessive covetousness bled out into space, leaving a slick of shattered antiquities behind it. The lighter debris would slowly be gathered in by the planet's gravitational field, drawn to a fiery death; the large fragments fell faster.

They loomed large and hot against the dark of the void, thermal signatures burning brightly before the synthetic senses of the gunskulls. The weapons satellites poured more kill power into them, smashing the remains into smaller and smaller pieces.

At the heart of this tumbling madness, the fractured core of the Archeohort, the single biggest shard of wreckage, continued its fall. At the leading edge of the jagged scrap of hull, panels blew free on explosive bolts. Behind them, a shape like a cudgel emerged, riding on a launch cradle, inching towards flight.

MATTHUN ZELLIK FELT his ship dying around him, and he would have wept bitter tears for it if he could have; but the pieces of his flesh that served that purpose had been cut out of him one hundred and fifty-seven point two years earlier, during an enhancement of self at the Morite Thane conclave. Instead, he allowed small loops of emotive emulation subroutines to turn around and around within a partition of his thoughts. Isolating his grief in this fashion allowed him to concentrate the rest of his intentions on freeing himself from his confinement.

The Techmarine Mohl looked into nothingness, the manifold mechadendrites falling from the connector implants along his neck waving and writhing. His single servo-arm was twitching, stuttering.

Zellik's metallic lip curled in disgust. In the privacy of his own thoughts, he so often ridiculed these Astartes half-breeds for their foolish behaviour. Space Marines – the whole and full variety – they were impressive tools to be sure, and to be respected in much the same way a common man would respect a vicious attack dog. But these so-called 'Techmarines'... What were they? Abhumans playing at being adepts? Their Chapters sent them to Mars to learn the mysteries of the machine, but could they really ever hope to come anywhere near such a thing? Only the Mars-born could truly understand the scope of the Machine-God. Only the true bearers of the cog could dare to know the majesty of the Omnissiah.

Zellik bent, affronted at the indecorous nature of what he was being forced to do, and let the micro-mandibles concealed in his mouth cut at the bond tying him to the Archeohort's helm. He blotted out the screams of tortured metal and spitting fire, afraid to listen fully for fear he would learn just how wounded his precious vessel was. Instead, he concentrated on the cutting, filling his thought buffer with his dislike of Mohl. The Techmarine was clearly no scion of the Great Binary Lord; if he had been, he would have ignored Rafen's insane orders to place the Archeohort on a suicide course. A true child of the Mechanicus would have placed his loyalty with Zellik...

But even as that thought formed in his mind, Matthun Zellik experienced a moment of despair. Beslian was as Martian as he, and still his subordinate had put himself before the fate of the Archeohort and her precious relics. Zellik grimaced. *No matter*. This day's events had revealed a truth to him. These fools thought themselves better than he, better than those whose sacred duty was to safeguard the lost technology of mankind, the mislaid future of humanity – without which they would surely perish!

As it came to Zellik that these would be his dying moments, he formed the plan for what he would do. At last the tethers were cut, and with a grind of foot-gears, the tech-priest tore free, standing splay-legged on the trembling deck plates.

For a moment, he was afraid the Astartes Mohl would turn and kill him; but Mohl's eyes were blank and stared past, unseeing. Zellik knew that look – it was the great rapture of the network. Mohl was pushing himself to directly impose his will upon the myriad of servitors and thinking engines aboard the Archeohort, forcing them to obey his suicidal command. It was a task that even a tech-lord would have found taxing; Zellik's nose wrinkled as his olfactory sensors picked up the rank odour of human sweat emanating from the Flesh Tearer's exertions.

Marshalling all his pistons and aligning his rod-like limbs, Zellik coiled and then sprang at the Astartes. Close to the armoured warrior, the hulking slab of a boltgun lay on the deck. The adept's clawed fingers grabbed at the weapon and pulled. The bolter was heavier than he expected, and the weight of it was strangely balanced. He managed to drag it up into some pretence of a firing stance, steadying it against the frame of his carbon-steel hips. Zellik could hardly hold on to it, and was already regretting his rash action, even as his spindly digits reached for the trigger.

'What are you doing, priest?' Amid the rumble and the madness of the destruction, Mohl's voice was strangely loud. His words came slow and thick; the Astartes was trying to disengage from the Archeohort's web of controls, but it was not a process one could manage swiftly. The servo-arm snapped at him.

'You will pay for this,' Zellik spluttered. 'I'll make every one of you pay!'

'No–' Mohl began; but then there was a massive, thunderous detonation of noise and light, and suddenly the tech-priest was on the deck several metres away, squealing with pain, a wracking ache making his limbs twitch.

Zellik's face was wet and the sensor-tongue in his mouth cavity flicked out, sampling the warm matter dotting his face. His internal scanners told him it was blood and brain material. Wiping himself clean with an arm from his servo-harness, Zellik looked back along the quaking deck plates and found Mohl's body lying at an angle. Where the head had been, there was now a red ruin that was part of a jawbone; nearby, the big shape of the bolter sat upended, the muzzle smoking. He heard a gurgling sound that sickened him.

Zellik looked at his clawed hands, rewinding the data-spools in his skull cavity. It had happened so fast. The weapon, the trigger… He had not been aware of placing so much pressure on it. Had his body not been so greatly improved and reinforced by the works of the Magos, he would never have been able to hold the great gun, much less actually fire it; even so, the recoil of the act had caused him great pain.

The priest expected the fear to come back to him; instead there was a peculiar sense of elation. He had killed an Adeptus Astartes! Granted, one distracted and severely hobbled by his interface to the ship, but still…

'I said I would make you pay,' he told Mohl's corpse. 'You dismissed me! But I won't stop here!'

A strange hysteria threatened to overcome him, and Zellik damped it down once more, walling off his emotional responses behind partitions of cold logic. He made it to the corridor beyond the bridge and hesitated. Only a short distance away, to the starboard, lay a compartment where a half-dozen saviour pods were nestled. He could make it there in moments, get away from the wreck before it was lost forever…

'But why?' he asked the smoky air. 'Why?'

The Archeohort was dying around him, and suddenly it seemed churlish for him to outlive it, this grand monument to Zellik's personal quest for glory. His place was here, with the collection. He had lived for it; it was right he died for it.

'Not yet,' he snarled, his final scheme ringing clear and true in his thoughts. 'Not yet!' Zellik shouted, racing away as fast as his piston-legs would allow, towards a hidden sanctum of his private museum – and the forbidden alien devices that lay within.

THE DESCENT RACKS were arranged along the spinal corridor of the *Neimos*, resting on hydraulic rams and pressure cradles that would absorb the shock of a fall from orbit. Their usual functionality allowed them to contain three humans, but in this case each Astartes had a capsule to themselves. Two at a time, quickly and evenly, the Blood Angels and Flesh Tearers entered the pods and sealed themselves within. Rafen watched a claw-footed machine-slave connect bulbous pipes at each closed hatch, the tubes flexing and chugging as they pumped shock-absorbing bio-gels into the racks. The semi-solid matter would dampen the impact effects still further; the Space Marines, already cocooned inside the ceramite and plasteel cowls of their power armour, would know nothing until the drop cycle completed itself.

The sergeant bent to peer through a glass portal into one of the pods. He made out a shape floating in the thick murk, robes open in the gel-mass, the clasping hand of an oxy-mask over a face. Beslian, like a fly trapped in amber.

'If we perish, he'll never know it,' ventured Noxx.

Rafen looked up to see that he and the other sergeant were the last two remaining. Stepping carefully over the shuddering deck, the Blood Angel reached up and secured his helmet.

'We will make it down alive,' he told Noxx. 'I trust Brother Mohl's judgement.'

'Why?'

It seemed an odd question; but then Rafen had learned by now that Brother-Sergeant Noxx sought challenge in everything. He gestured upward, as if towards the Archeohort's bridge. 'I trust him, because of what he has given up to see we finish the mission.'

Noxx looked up and met Rafen's gaze; for a moment there was a flicker of dark rage in eyes that were so often lifeless and hollow. 'I'll cut his name into a score of enemies and not think it too many. That will be a fitting tribute.' He climbed into his rack and pulled on the cowling. 'See you in hell, Blood Angel.'

Rafen stood alone on the deck and listened to the rumble all around him. Any moment now, the *Neimos* would break free and the fall would begin. Any moment now, and then their destiny would be in the hands of the fates. The mission at the mercy of powers greater than anything the Astartes could summon. He considered uttering another prayer, perhaps a litany of protection before entering the pod, and then dismissed the thought. No more words needed to be said. The Emperor was watching, Rafen could feel it. He closed his eyes and stepped into the rack, shutting himself inside.

As the clamshell door locked into place, he closed his eyes; and so, he did not witness the sudden, brief fit that overtook the nearby servitor. The machine-slave twitched and frothed at the mouth, manipulators clenching and unclenching, thought-pattern indicators glowing brightly.

In the next moment, the clanking spasm passed and the helot went back to its duties as if nothing had happened.

AT LAST, THE Archeohort ended.

The rain of fire from the gunskulls enveloped the spinning fragments of the construct and turned them into a storm of metal and glass, wood and meat, gas and plasma. Spread out over a thousand kilometres of stratosphere, crossing into the dark, heavy night of Dynikas V, the remains of the ship clawed into the atmosphere, pieces of the Mechanicus vessel consumed in the fires of re-entry, others surviving long enough to punch into the upper reaches of the planet's thin cloud layers. These fists of torn iron, these jagged spears of wreckage, they were scattering themselves over the vast tracts of featureless rust-orange oceans. Some would be large enough to create tidal shockwaves that would be felt on the other side of the world. Others would sink quickly into the abyssal depths of the Dynikan seas, and some few hammered at infrequent coral islands and atoll strings, letting the leaden oceans rise up and fill the craters they left behind.

Hiding in the blaze of crashing wreckage, the shape and form of it lost in the roaring heat and fury of the fallout, the *Neimos* spun in towards the waiting waters.

At first, incredible heat buffeted the bullet-prow of the vessel, in seconds burning through the sheaths of lamellar armour protecting the leading edges. Beneath, energy-siphon technology invented twenty thousand years ago, its functioning and nature lost to time, worked to bleed off the intense glow. It fed on the friction, suckling on the heat to power itself, turning the energy back against its origins.

Invisible cloaks of ionised particles flared around the craft, visible only to the enhanced cyber-sense organs of the machine-slave crew. Over and over, sonic booms crackled across the night side of Dynikas V as falling debris shattered the speed of sound. In the apex of one such compression wave, the *Neimos* came down trailing fire, a single burning arrow amid a hundred others.

Sensor returns tripped switches in the vessel's control systems, causing stubby dual-function winglets to emerge from the hull. At the same time, great grey-blue cones of untearable synthsilk billowed from the aft of the *Neimos*, filling quickly with a mix of spent gases from the engine core and the local atmosphere. The wide ballutes stiffened and gave the ship a moment's stability. Still concealed beneath an umbrella of tumbling wreckage, the *Neimos* veered into a series of slow turns, the fins bending air this way and that, bleeding off the terminal velocity of descent. Without the remnants of the Archeohort to blind them, the sensors of the orbital gunskulls would have picked out the craft in moments; but for now all they could detect was a field of conflicting, corrupted returns. To discover the *Neimos* among such wild disorder would be akin to finding one single torch amid an inferno.

Then; the impact.

The churning ocean waters rose and fell beneath a sky cut by streaks of fire, and from that flame-lit darkness the *Neimos* came like the hammer of a war god. Flicker-fast gravity displacement fields, fed on the energy converted from the heat of atmospheric interface, haloed the submersible as it touched the wave tops. An invisible bowl of force ballooned outwards, displacing kinetic power, cutting a channel into the murky sea.

The vessel howled as it passed through a storm of dynamic stress more powerful than anything it had experienced so far, and the back-shock discharged a sharp thermal flashover, oily water boiling instantly into a greasy fog of superheated steam.

All this happened in seconds, before a thunderclap of displacement sounded loud as the *Neimos* vanished beneath the surface, the descent ballutes torn away, the guide fins crumpled and discarded.

The craft was down and sinking, as the rain of wreckage continued all around it.

IN THE WARM silence of the liquid-filled capsule, Brother Ceris allowed himself to use the brief moments of quiet as respite. It was only a matter of fine concentration to draw in his preternatural senses, to wall off the rushing ebb and flow of psychic input pressing in from his battle-brothers. Some of them were afraid, although they would never show it; others angry, all of them tense with the sublimated urge for combat. The mingling of emotion-colours was strong to him. Warriors of the Adeptus Astartes were not known for their metered natures – they were bold and potent, and that character informed every single aspect of their beings. But what drew the psyker's thin lips into a cool smile was the realisation of a clear truth. For all the outward dissimilarity between the noble Blood Angels and the savage Flesh Tearers, in their hearts and minds they were alike. At the core, no different.

Ceris felt a brief swell of certainty; they would win. Fabius Bile would die a death and the sacred blood would be preserved. He felt this so keenly that it almost seemed like precognition – and when a voice in the back of his thoughts suggested that he only believed what he wanted to, he silenced it. Failure would not be accommodated. They would succeed; they *had* to. To return to Baal with empty hands would be the greatest shame Ceris could imagine.

He drifted on the edge of dreams as the fall took its course, the shocks through the hull distant and vague. Had the *Neimos* been manned by a human crew, he might have felt the mists of their anxieties, but the mind-wiped servitors working the vessel's systems had no such emotions to give. Dimly, he sensed the deaths of two of them as the force of the drop damaged minor systems in different compartments, but they perished with all the circumstance of a candle being snuffed out.

The fall passed quickly, or so it seemed, the sus-an membrane in his grey matter lulling him into a demi-sleep for a brief time. Not quite the full oblivion of suspension, but enough to rest his body for the coming fight. Then, as quickly as it had begun, it was over, and he felt the fleeting torpor bleed away.

Ceris became aware of the shock fluid draining into the rack's exit vents, and presently the oval hatch before him rose up. Shrugging off the slicks of gel that stuck to his armour, he climbed out and allowed a servitor to blast him clean with an air jet. The rest of the squad were ministering to one another; there had been only minor injuries, contusions and bruising from the roughness of the descent. With their enhanced healing factors, the slight damages experienced by the Space Marines would be forgotten within hours.

'Still with us then, witch-kin?' said Eigen, clearing sluggish fluid from the vanes of his breather grille. 'Did you enjoy the trip?'

'I dozed through it,' Ceris replied, in all honesty.

Turcio gave a wry chuckle. 'I should have thought of doing that. A warrior should take his rest whenever he can.'

Ceris nodded. 'I'll warrant none of us will find the time for respite from hereon.'

'Just try to stay awake when the enemy come calling,' Eigen retorted. Irritation hazed his aura, and Ceris suspected that the Flesh Tearer had felt the sharp bite of every second of the drop from orbit.

A glimmer at the edge of his thoughts drew up his attention and the psyker glanced across the deck to where Noxx and Rafen stood in conversation. One of the bridge servitors was with them, and from its mouth drooled a spool of data-tapers. 'That moment may be closer to hand than you might wish,' said Ceris, seeing the tension in the gait of the two sergeants. Without waiting for Eigen to reply, he walked away, approaching his commander.

Rafen was fingering the end of the tape, studying it intently. 'There is no margin for error?'

'None,' clattered the servitor.

'So quickly?' Noxx frowned. 'Tell me that the element of surprise has not been lost to us already!'

'I think not,' said Rafen. 'We would be under fire already if that were so.' He looked up at Ceris. 'Codicier. Have we been touched by witch-sight?'

The psyker shook his head. 'No, lord. I would have felt the passage of it.'

'There are surface vessels in the area,' Noxx said by way of explanation, raising his voice so all the Astartes could hear him. 'Barges and a fast cutter, if the sound of them rings true. Too close for comfort.'

With a gurgling hiss, the last of the descent racks cracked open, and a bedraggled figure stumbled out, collapsing to the deck. The Logis Beslian gave a metallic choke, and spurts of liquid escaped from gill-vents hidden beneath his sodden cloak. He emitted a low, wet moan that drew the cleric Gast to his side. The rest of the Space Marines ignored him.

'We've barely made planetfall,' Ajir grated. 'How could these Chaos whelps know we are here?'

'They must have already been nearby,' offered Turcio. 'A patrol, perhaps?'

'On the other side of the planet from Bile's stronghold?' Ajir shook his head. 'For what purpose?'

Turcio ignored the barbed tone in the other Blood Angel's tone. 'There is still much we do not know about the traitor's work on this world.'

Rafen was nodding. 'Fabius is shrewd. He sends these vessels to investigate the wreckage... Likely to recover what he can, knowing the value of Zellik's Archeohort.'

'Do we engage them?' said Sove.

'Curb your impatience, Flesh Tearer,' Kayne folded his arms, glaring at the other Astartes. 'We do that and we lose the only advantage we have!'

'You would rather we hide in the shadows?' Sove took a step towards the young Space Marine.

'That will suffice,' snarled Noxx. 'There will be blood enough to sate all of us when the fight comes. But until that moment, we hold.' He shot a hard look at Sove. 'Clear?'

The Flesh Tearer nodded once. 'Clear, brother-sergeant.'

Ceris watched the interchange, and then cleared his throat. 'With all due respect, I must point out that there is a third option. Neither to attack nor to lie dormant.'

Rafen eyed him. 'Go on.'

'We are in the lair of the enemy, and yet as Brother Turcio noted, we move with only our wits and our courage to guide us. We should gather our strength, learn what we can about these vessels and the men Fabius crews them with.'

'Fair point,' said Puluo. 'But we're Astartes. Not spies.'

Eigen nodded in agreement. 'We're bred for attack, not to observe.'

'True,' admitted Rafen. 'But some aboard this vessel *are*.' He studied Beslian as the adept got shakily to his feet.

With a racking cough, the Mechanicus tech-priest grimaced at his own sorry state, before slowly becoming aware that every Space Marine in the room was staring at him. He flinched as if he had been struck, and backed away from Gast. 'Oh no,' he husked. 'What do you want of me now? Have you not taken enough?'

'Our duty to the Golden Throne never ends, adept,' said Gast.

THE NEIMOS HAD survived the fall from space with only minor damage, and there was a quiet exchange of amazement between some of the Space Marines. Rafen was certain that Gast and Eigen had placed a wager on some fatal occurrence taking place, and his brow furrowed at the idea of betting on something that might have killed them all. The crude humour of it escaped him.

At his command, with Beslian parsing the orders for the servitor crew, the submersible was brought up to sensor depth, hovering below the surface. The Mechanicus tech-priest was reluctant to obey at first, citing numerous reasons why raising the ship would be dangerous; but a combination of Noxx's barely-veiled threats and a small amount of flattery on Rafen's part brought the adept around to the idea.

Tethered by a long cable, a scrying pod sheathed in low-visibility, detection-resistant materials was released from a cowling in the dorsal tower. It rose slowly, silently breaking into the turbulent waves.

Up above, under the glowering, windswept Dynikan night, constant winds lashed across the ocean, ripping at the swell. The heavy, oxide-laden waters seethed and churned, the impacts of wreckage from the Archeohort still echoing on. Parts of the construct would continue to rain down on the planet for several hours, and the atmospheric distortions and contact shocks made it difficult to get clean scan returns. But the problem cut both ways; while the *Neimos* could not clearly read the distant flotilla, neither could the enemy be certain of detecting the submarine. A spread of light wreckage floated on the writhing surf, and the *Neimos* moved into its shadow.

In the command centre, Rafen stood with Noxx and Ceris, watching the complex play of the sensor returns. The rest of the Space Marines were elsewhere, preparing their wargear in a cargo bay the servitors had converted into an arming chamber.

Beslian leaned in to study a pict-screen. 'I believe I have a match.' He tapped the panel with a servo-arm. 'See here. The Standard Template Pattern of this barge is known to me. It is a Kappa-Rho-Six ocean transit freighter, Lapidas pattern.'

Rafen saw a grainy pict overlaid by the glowing lines of a schematic stencil. The large ship lay low in the water, and the basic slab-sided shape of it was disfigured by fluted additions that resembled castle donjons.

'Retrofitted weapon emplacements, perhaps,' suggested Noxx, thinking along the same lines as the Blood Angel.

'Aye. But these…' Rafen pointed out the vanes of a peculiar crystalline antenna and a bulbous sphere riddled with holes. 'What function do they have?'

Beslian didn't attempt to supply an answer to that question, and continued on a different tack. 'Records indicate that several ocean-going craft were deployed with the explorator fleet sent to set up an agri-works on this planet. That vessel would appear to be one of them.'

'Fabius probably salvaged whatever the tyranid attack had not destroyed,' said Noxx. 'Efficient use of materials. This world is far off any conventional trade axis or warp route. Doubtless the traitor would have found it hard to ship in a large amount of new hardware.'

'He uses what he has to hand,' agreed Rafen. 'His fortress is likely to be a repurposed facility left over from the farming colony. That could work in our favour.' The sergeant filed that thought away for later consideration.

Noxx's blank eyes narrowed and he gestured at a secondary scrying relay. It was a sweep display, green-on-green, and each time the hands looped around, dots of luminescence appeared and then faded. 'This is not the flotilla,' he stated.

Beslian shifted uncomfortably. 'It is not. These are... *biological* returns.'

Rafen sucked in a breath. The ecosphere of Dynikas V was bereft of any native life, which meant any living thing they encountered that wasn't connected with Bile's operations could only be of one origin. 'Tyranids? Did you not deem it important to inform us of their proximity?'

The adept flinched, as if fearful of being struck for his misdeed. 'They are not a threat... Not yet, lord. They are too distant.'

Noxx nodded. 'They're closer to Bile's ships. If they attack, they'll attack them before us.'

'No,' Ceris intoned. The Codicier had not taken his gaze from the pict-screen, remaining intent on the peculiar constructs Rafen had indicated. 'They do not see the flotilla. The xenos are blind to it.'

'How is that possible?' Noxx frowned, and pointed at the sweep scan. 'Those scaly bastards are so close they could rise up and spit at those boats.'

Ceris shook his head. 'They will pass.'

Rafen watched the progression of the scan. The staggered dots of the tyranid shoal were crossing near to the barges, which had cut their engines and started to drift. 'How can you know that?' he asked the psyker.

'Because I see the ships...' He tapped his psychic hood. 'But I do not *see* them.'

'The antenna?'

Ceris nodded. 'Perhaps a psionic dampener. When I reach out to sense the minds of the beings aboard those craft, there is nothing but a wall of white noise.'

'The tyranids are animals but they're not blind,' said Noxx. 'That can't be all there is to it.'

'You are correct,' said Beslian, turning back from a chattering cogitator. 'The sensor pod has been sampling the atmosphere of the planet to determine hazard protocols.' He held up a fan of printed parchment. 'These readings suggest a large amount of a particular tyranid pheromonal deposit in the air. Several parts per million, far more than I would expect.'

'Spores?' Rafen's lip curled as he said the word. He had witnessed the work of the xenos spores on the flesh of men, and been disgusted by their loathsome virulence.

'Negative,' replied the adept. 'I will need to cross-check to be certain, but we appear to detect a prevalence of death-indicator pheromones.'

The tech-priest quickly elucidated; in tyranid hives, just as in those of common communal insect life, information was passed via pheromone scent-markers. Thus, something that was toxic would be marked as *not-food*, something to be denatured and rendered in conversion pools would be marked as *consumable*, and should a hive member die, their corpses would secrete a pheromone that labelled them as *dead*, attracting workers to recover and recycle their biomatter.

Confronted by such scent-markers, the warrior creatures would simply ignore something their primitive brains considered to be dead, as long as it remained inert and did nothing to confuse that understanding. The subterfuge would never work on higher-order tyranids, those capable of intelligent reasoning approaching that of a human being – but on Dynikas V, there was no apparent evidence of high-level clades such as norn queens or hive tyrants; only warrior forms adapted to the planet's ocean environment.

'The bulb array on the barge,' concluded Beslian, nodding to himself. 'It is a dispersal mechanism for the pheromones.'

'Bile's fortress must possess the same technology,' said Rafen. 'The tyranids do not attack him because they cannot sense him.'

Noxx jutted his chin at the screen. 'But they *do* sense us. See?'

The alien shoal was changing course, veering towards the coordinates where the *Neimos* hid among the floating wreckage.

Rafen glanced at Beslian and saw what flesh there was on the adept's face go pale. In the next second, Beslian moved with a jerk towards the helm console.

'We have to flee!' he piped. 'Bring the drives on-line, make for maximum speed–'

'Belay that order!' snapped Rafen. 'Thruster discharges will show on the scrying grids of those barges. You'll bring them to us as surely as if you sent up a mag-flare.'

'But the creatures…' The adept controlled himself with a visible effort.

'They'll attack us if we remain close to the surface,' said Ceris.

'They are tyranids,' snorted Noxx. 'They'll attack us wherever we are.'

'We do not have the benefit of Bile's protective devices! We cannot simply lie dormant and pray that they leave us be!' Beslian's metallic fingers knitted. 'If the *Neimos* cannot run from them, neither can we stand and fight!'

Rafen glanced at Ceris. 'There's always a third way.' He stepped up and addressed the crew servitors. 'Bring back the pod and take us down. Leave the thrusters off-line. Fill the ballast tanks and let us sink into the depths.'

'That won't stop them coming for us,' said Noxx.

The Blood Angel nodded. 'I know. But the deeper we go, the lower the chance that any engagement will be detected by the enemy.'

The other sergeant shook his head. 'You're risking us all.'

Rafen let out a bark of laughter at that. 'Of course I am! But risk is our meat and drink!' He glared at Beslian. 'Now carry out my orders.'

The adept gave a shaky nod and began to speak in machine-code. The servitors stuttered and jerked into action, working their control lecterns.

'And what commands do you have for us?' said Ceris, his brow furrowed.

'Alert the squad. The order is… stand by to repel boarders.'

THE HUNTER-PREDATOR forms had eyes, but they were poor things, vestigial orbs that could only penetrate the oily murk close at hand. Instead, they felt their way through the oceans of Dynikas V through networks of electroreceptor nerves in their bony skulls and feeler barbels that writhed about lipless mouths ringed with teeth. They tasted and smelled their way through the thick waters, riding on sonic vibrations that showed landscapes of sound and pitch.

Once, when their hive had first deposited its spoor upon this world, they had been something close to the genus of tyranid that humans called a lictor; but a rapacious evolutionary cycle and a physiology based on an infinitely malleable octo-helix DNA had tailored them to fit the new environment where they found themselves. Now the lictors bore only the most basic resemblance to their more common kindred. These creatures were sleeker, skinned with sheer microspines, sporting flat fans of talons that doubled as steering vanes. Powerful legs slick with secreted mucus thrashed hard against the ocean, propelling them forward.

Their animal minds reacted to the object they sensed before them, the metallic mass falling away into the gloom. The returns from their sonic barks were garbled and confusing; the lictors were made furious by this. There were no scent receptors in the murk, nothing to warn them off from something that might have been part of their kind. The object was alien to them; it carried the taste of other worlds with it and a warmth that was out of place in the cold seas.

Coming closer, slowing to match pace, the tyranids unfurled their claws from the flesh pockets where they lay and raked them along the hull of the *Neimos*. Looking for purchase, for a way in.

KAYNE DIPPED A finger in the oil of anointing and traced it around the muzzle of his bolter as Brother-Sergeant Rafen spoke. 'Watch your fire,' he was saying. 'Single shots only. Close quarter weapons. Any collateral damage could make this hulk our grave, so be circumspect.' His commander brandished a plasma gun, the coils turned to their tightest beam setting.

Kayne looked around, still uncertain as to why Rafen had assembled them in this chamber. It was a slope-floored bay along the ventral surface of the submersible, towards the aft but clear of the steering vanes. The deck disappeared away at a steep angle, while a grid-floored balcony ringed it along the plane of the main deck. It reminded the Astartes of a Thunderhawk's drop bay, but wider.

The deck of the *Neimos* trembled as something rebounded off the portside hull, drawing everyone's attention. Kayne heard another sound seconds later – a high-pitched screeching, like blades scraping against blades.

At his side, the Flesh Tearer called Sove cocked his head and scowled. 'Talons,' he said sombrely, making a claw of his hand to demonstrate.

'We're tinned meat to them in this iron coffin,' muttered Ajir. 'They'll be sick of their diet of traitors and each other... They'll be hungry for something new.'

'The xenos will find only death,' retorted Eigen.

Rafen turned to Puluo, who stood near a control podium. 'Flood it,' he ordered.

Puluo nodded gravely and worked a dial; immediately, sluggish laps of seawater began to fill the lower level. The sloping floor vanished beneath them, and Kayne realised he had been correct; the deck beneath the gantry was a single piece, a massive hinged drop-ramp. Above him, set in secure racks, there were blocky capsules with fins and propellers – auxiliary craft of some kind, he imagined, that could be manoeuvred over the ramp and then released.

An unpleasant thought occurred to him. 'We're going out there?'

'Not yet,' said Rafen, a wolfish smile playing about his lips. 'Remember your tactical studies, brother. Choose your battlefield, lest the enemy choose it for you.'

'Outside, we're at a disadvantage,' added Puluo. 'We'd need tethers, boot magnets...'

'You want to bring those things in here?' Noxx's voice was low.

'Aye,' nodded Rafen. 'We'll take them and move on.' He was in the process of removing his right gauntlet.

Noxx approached him. 'Did you strike your head upon the deck during our drop from orbit, Blood Angel? That's not a bold plan, it's a foolish one!'

'The tyranids will tear their way into this vessel if we do not stop them. Better we face them head on, on our terms, than let them hole the *Neimos*.' Rafen stowed the armoured glove and drew his combat blade. He glanced at the others. 'Weapons up. Prepare to meet the enemy.'

Kayne moved towards a cargo container, already figuring lines of fire from the partial cover, when the Flesh Tearer sergeant spoke again.

'Hold!' snapped Noxx, raising his hand to the other Astartes.

Rafen eyed him. 'You countermand me? Did you not agree to follow my orders?'

'I said I would obey you *for now.*'

'You mean, until you took issue with one of my commands?' Rafen closed his bare hand around the knife's naked blade, drawing blood. 'I'll discuss mutiny with you if you wish, cousin. But not here.' He stepped down the ramp until the brackish seawater was lapping over his boots. 'First we deal with the xenos.'

Kayne watched Rafen extend his hand, curled in a fist; blood from the shallow gash pooled and dripped into the water.

'Gather yourselves,' said the sergeant. 'They'll come to us now.'

Noxx growled in the back of his throat and shot his Flesh Tearers a sharp look; in turn, the warriors in red and black went to the ready.

Close by, Ceris unsheathed his force mace. He aimed it towards the deepest part of the now-flooded bay. 'There!'

Kayne saw movement in the murky waters, shapes that were slick and fast, shifting like smoke. He had once heard that some ocean predators were capable of scenting a single drop of human blood in the water from more than a kilometre's distance; if that were true, then he imagined that the tyranids swarming about the *Neimos* could not help but be drawn in.

The pool's surface suddenly grew turbulent, and in the next moment night-black forms exploded out from the water.

Kayne opened fire, even though he had but a vague impression of the shape of his target. He glimpsed a torso, barbed curves of claw and snapping flukes. Bolt rounds crashed from his sidearm, and a surge of harsh scents crashed over him; saline, old rust, the rot of decayed fish-meat and something foul and acidic. He grimaced; the creatures could exude a chemical trail that, left unchecked, would attract every tyranid for hundreds of kilometres.

A bright spear of plasma roared through the air and blasted one of the tyranids back into the water, bolt shells following to rip through its torso.

'Lictors!' snarled Sove, snapping off shots from behind a reel of cable. 'But different... like Cretacia's selachians...'

'Adapted,' said Kayne, through gritted teeth. 'They killed the top predators on Dynikas and then became them!'

Five of the creatures had emerged from the pool; one already lay shaking and dying. The rest let out shrieks pitched so high that Kayne felt needles of pain in his skull.

'Nothing lives!' Rafen shouted, leading with the plasma gun in his fist. 'Kill them quickly, before they can summon more of their kind!'

Ceris leapt boldly from behind cover to strike at one of the lictor-shark hybrids, bringing down his force mace in a humming arc of white light. Where the weapon struck the beast, the psyker projected a bolt of telepathic power through the brief instant of contact, and the tyranid screamed again – this time, in agony. Kayne turned, aiming down the iron sights of his bolter, lingering for a split-second over where to place his shot; he fired at the corpse-flesh wattles around the throat of the beast and hit his mark. The lictor's feeder tendrils thrashed and it vomited up black blood from its lamprey mouth.

The psyker bellowed a war cry and beat the xenos again and again with the mace, the spikes of psy-force cleaving open the bony exoskeleton of the lictor's head.

A hot wave of burned air from plasma fire gusted past Kayne as he shot twice more into Ceris's target, all the better to be certain of the kill. More alien screams drew his attention as a second tyranid stumbled into the water, one massive scything talon melted and cracked like wax from a candle. Ejected shells clattering off the gridded deck at his feet, Brother Puluo ended the wounded, bellowing beast by marching shot after shot from his heavy bolter up the line of the alien's torso.

Kayne felt his lips draw back from his fangs, felt the rumble of his blood in his ears. The taste of battle was in his mouth, sweet and strong.

Ajir was caught on the backswing of another lictor's fin-tail, and he tumbled over the deck and into the water, landing in the shallows with an angry shout. As he splashed back up the ramp to rejoin the fight, Gast and Eigen harried the beast with shots to its face. Noxx had gone in close with his chainsword, carving great jagged slashes in its chest-armour. A muscle spasm racked the lictor, and it fired a fan of flesh hooks at the sergeant. Noxx parried the attack and caught the sinewy chords trailing the hooks in the teeth of his weapon, ripping them out with a growl of spinning blades. Turcio lent his weapon to the Flesh Tearers, his bionic arm absorbing every iota of recoil as he fired one-handed at the tyranid's legs. Driven to the deck, Noxx snarled and buried his chainsword in the soft underbelly of the lictor, his weight behind it to force the chattering weapon into the vital organs within.

One more. Kayne swung about as Rafen called out his name in a warning. He ducked, and the hum of air buffeted him as a massive crescent talon tore past; a moment's delay, and the alien's heavy blow would have connected with his head. He released two snap-shot rounds as he let himself continue the turn, the bolter tucked low. Kayne heard the distinctive *crunch-crack* of the mass-reactive shells as they impacted on the lictor's chitinous torso plates. It lowed in pain, but it did not halt its attack.

A bony fin-limb, barbed at every joint, scraped across the deck at him like a trailing whip, gobs of stringy mucus looping from it. He fired at it, but there was nowhere else for him to go; caught in the rush of the battle he had let himself be forced into a corner, blocked in by cargo containers and the far wall. Splaying open with a wet hiss, the talons rose before him–

–and then the lictor-shark was staggering backwards, hooting in pain. A halo of smouldering plasma fire wreathed its back and it spun in a circle, wild with distress. Kayne saw Sove leap up and try for a point-blank kill, but the xenos flailed, clipping him and knocking the Flesh Tearer's gun from his grip. Undaunted, the snarling Space Marine pressed his attack. A massive push-dagger, a long and slender triangle of polished, fractal-edged steel, flicked out from a snap-rig on Sove's vambrace. Leaning into the blow, he put the wicked tip of the weapon into a point between two thick ribs and pushed it down to the hilt, twisting the dagger to widen the wound.

Kayne fired at the creature, and was dimly aware of other shots streaking in from other quarters, each Astartes careful to nip at the tyranid's limbs for fear of striking their comrade.

The lictor hooted and lashed out. Kayne saw the attack in all its bloody glory. The beast ripping at itself to tear out the blade in its gut. Sove's weapon, and his hand and right arm with it, torn away and discarded in a welter of blood. The Flesh Tearer, his shoulder jetting crimson, batted away like an afterthought by the swing of a talon-fluke.

Sove was flung into a collection of storage bins and vanished into the clutter. The last of the lictors, blood an oily black river from its torn abdomen, became the centre of a hail of bolt shells and plasma fire. The creature's death screams beat at the walls before becoming the thin, fading hiss of flash-boiled fluids.

Rafen walked to the corpse and kicked it into the flooded section of the bay, the meat-smoke and spent cordite in the air drifting about him. His face was scratched and bleeding. 'Vent this to the ocean. Let their kindred feast on their corpses.'

Kayne moved towards the mess of fallen containers where Sove had landed, but Noxx was already there, with the Apothecary-Cleric Gast a step behind. The sergeant tore savagely at the debris and dragged his injured man from the deck. Sove had lost his helmet in the fall, and his bearded face was pale.

Rafen began to speak. 'Is he–'

'Alive,' grated Noxx. The Flesh Tearer hesitated on the verge of something unspoken, and finally added '*for now*.' Before Kayne's commander could say more, Noxx issued terse orders to Gast, and the cleric bore Sove away towards the *Neimos's* upper decks.

After a long moment, Kayne saw Rafen secure his weapon and study the slick of dark fluids across the pool of seawater. 'We have consecrated this world with our blood and that of the enemy,' he said to the air, his gaze distant. 'And if we must, we will choke these seas with their dead.'

UP ABOVE, ON the surface, the world turned towards the weak glow of a distant, oncoming dawn. Light crossed the wave tops, turning them to beaten silver.

But beneath, where the sun never reached, in the endless grey gloom of the abyssal reaches, the *Neimos* went deep. Alien corpse-meat twisted in the vessel's wake, mute witness to the fury of the Astartes. A ripper shoal found the remains and dwelled a few moments, considering the feast; but they stayed away, the animal sense of the tyranid forms aware of something far larger – and more lethal – drifting nearby. Something watching, measuring itself against the new intruders in its realm.

Beneath, where the sun never reached, a dark and sinuous mass followed the *Neimos* into the depths.

SEVEN

GOEL BESLIAN WALKED with care, listening.

On the keel deck, in the lowermost section of the *Neimos's* engine compartments, the sound of the humming drive trains was a rhapsody of machines. Finely tuned mechanisms, gears and rods and cogs married up with one another in a flawless execution of function; all of it made more incredible by the great age of the system in question. The submersible's drives were based on a design philosophy laid down in the ages before humankind had left the cradle of Holy Terra – although like some in the service of the Adeptus Mechanicus, Beslian was one of those who secretly believed that humans had actually evolved on Mars first, and cast off to her neighbour planet before the rise of the Emperor, and not as some insisted, the other way around. Mars had always been the seat of genius, the cradle of mankind's greatest minds.

At a different time, in a different place, Beslian might have been able to stop and enjoy the beauty of this great machine and marvel at its works; but that was denied to him. As much as he wanted the noise and power of the engines to soothe him, all it did was grind the gears of his thoughts still further. He could find no respite.

Finally, he stopped at the reactor control chamber, ignoring the trio of servitors working silently at their consoles, and stared at the fan of indicator lamps on the core monitor lectern. All was well, for the moment. His augmented eyes whined, losing focus, as his gaze turned inward.

Goel Beslian was very much afraid, and his fear was so strong that he imagined it like a stench of spent spindle oil, trailing him wherever he went. He was certain that those Astartes brutes could smell his terror on him; like animal predators, they sensed it every time he was close to them.

He looked down at the brass manipulators that were his hands. Fine pieces of work, they were, laser-cut and polished by forge-slaves. Careworn ratchets of metal, cable and ceramic, far more dextrous and faceted than any human digits could ever be… but still they trembled. He had tried many times to adjust the feedback gain and the subtle function of his limbs, but the twitches never quite went away. When the fear came, they were there. It was a horribly human, disconcertingly *fleshy* thing to behold. It betrayed Beslian's imperfections, showed him how far he was from the majesty and flawlessness of the Machine-God.

Unbidden, a question formed in the logic spools of his enhanced brain. *How did I get here?* With the question came a stark jolt of self-knowledge.

'Because I am afraid,' he told the servitors. They ignored him; unless he gave them a direct command prefaced with the correct data-phrase, they would behave as if he was invisible.

Beslian watched them work, and felt a stab of anger so strong it surprised him. He hadn't thought himself still capable of such emotional potency. He almost envied the machine-slaves; their higher brain functions lobotomised, the personas of the men and women they once had been excised, they were never afraid. Never angry. Never hobbled by the weight of their own cowardice. They moved back and forth, whispering the lines of their command strings to themselves, muttering order memes and operating codes. They were content with their lot, and unafraid.

The logis was damned by his own failings. No matter how much of him he replaced with the precision of the machine, he was still Goel Beslian at his core. Still weak.

He thought of the others, those who had come up through the training regimens of the collegia at the same time as him. They had since attained ranks far above his. He thought of his crèche-mate Lytton, who was now Lord Magos of the Mondasia Forges, of the elegant, waspish Defra who had gone on to take command of explorators, and all the others he had known. Beslian was the least of them all.

Someone with his talents and a measure of self-confidence could have risen to become the master of a tech-guard division, or even placed in charge of his own elite cadre of archeotechnologists; but instead Beslian had worked in the shadow of greater men, hanging on the tails of their robes. He had always taken the option of lowest risk, the path of least resistance.

His solid, if unremarkable career in the Adeptus Mechanicus had brought him into the orbit of Matthun Zellik. Perhaps Beslian's character had been the very reason Zellik had recruited him – perhaps because he needed a second who would not question when his conduct veered outside the rules of the Mechanicus, someone who would never have the strength to dare challenge him.

And now, after so long, after Goel Beslian had finally drawn together the dregs of his courage, defying Zellik to side with these Astartes... After that monumental effort to show some kind of spine, what was his reward? Did the Machine-God smile on him and grant him the dream he had never been able to voice, of being master of the Archeohort?

Negative. Instead he had been damned. Each new indignity followed the last. The Archeohort had been shattered and destroyed. Beslian's skills were mocked and denigrated; and now his life was squarely in harm's way, dragged along on this insane, suicidal mission.

He shuddered, thinking of the images he had seen of the Space Marines on the internal monitoria, watching the Blood Angels and Flesh Tearers fighting the lictors with mad abandon. Beslian had always suspected that all Space Marines were psychotic on some level. He had seen nothing yet to dissuade him.

He took a deep breath. This was where his cowardice had brought him, to this madness where the threat of death was all around him. The adept shrank inside his robes, drawing them in as a feeble gesture of self-protection. All he could hope to do now was to survive this. To live another day, and perhaps, if the Omnissiah was willing to turn a measure of His radiance on him, not to be forsaken.

'Traitor.'

Beslian's head snapped up from his musings at the sound of the word. He glanced around, searching for the source of the voice. 'Who said that?'

The three servitors ignored him. He moved towards the closest of them, a former male, now an engineering helot, third class. It was listing thrust tolerance percentages in a breathy, sub-vocal whisper. Beslian frowned at it. Perhaps it was an artefact of his reverie. His aural processing centres had been mistaken–

'Traitor.'

A woman's voice this time, he was certain of it. Beslian stalked across to the lone machine-slave built from a female donor; it was a reactor monitor, babbling to itself about fluid temperatures and reciting stanzas from the litany of nuclei.

This time he addressed it with the correct interrogative codes. 'Did you speak to me?' he demanded.

'Negative, Logis.' The response was cursory. He was turning away when it spoke again. 'You traitor. Beslian.'

The adept grabbed the servitor and shook it. 'What did you say?' he shouted. 'Who told you to say that? Answer me!'

'Traitor. Traitor.' He heard the echo of the words again, this time from all three of the machine-slaves at once. He let go of the female and backed away. The three helots began to twitch and spasm. Beslian had seen malfunctions like this before, often at the end of servitors' life cycles when their mental functions had decayed beyond repair and they had to be put down – but this was different.

Flecks of spittle marked the lips of the helots. 'Traitor,' they chorused. 'Traitor. *Traitor!*' An identical cast of anger flooded faces that had been slack and inanimate. The threefold voice thickened and deepened, taking on a familiar cast and meter. 'You loathsome, weakling turncoat, Beslian! This is how you repay me?'

'Matthun?' he gasped the name in shocked recognition. It was then that the adept understood; what he had considered to be *fear* was not in fact the deepest expression of that state, not at all. What came upon him now was a far greater, far darker measure. The adept cried out.

As one, the three servitors reached into the pockets of their gear aprons, each producing a single tool – a sanctified wrench, a cutter blade, a notation stylus – before stabbing, bludgeoning and finally beating the Logis Goel Beslian into silence, there amid the thrumming noise of the reactor control chamber.

When it was done, their faces returned to a neutral, blank cast. With care, the servitors paused to clean off their tools before returning them to their pockets. Then, once more isolated in their own small worlds of duty, task and function, the machine-slaves went back to work.

Beslian lay inert on the deck between them, sprawled and bloody. They behaved as if he were invisible.

ON THE SECOND deck of the *Neimos*, the lights burned low. Bunk compartments lined the corridor that ran the length of the submersible's spine, all of them locked down and unused, built for human crewmen on long-duration missions. Neither the servitors nor the Astartes aboard the vessel needed the conventions of sleep required by common crew, however. The empty spaces echoed dully with the report of ceramite boots on deck plates as a red-armoured figure walked towards the bow of the craft, lost in thought.

'Rafen.' The figure stopped at the sound of his name, and turned.

Behind the Blood Angel, Brother-Sergeant Noxx almost filled the breadth of the corridor, his head scarcely a hand's span from the snarl of pipes above, his arms tense at his sides as his heavy shoulders blocked the light spilling from the gantryway beyond.

There was fresh blood on the Flesh Tearer's battle armour; Astartes blood.

Rafen's expression was carefully neutral. 'Noxx. What is Brother Sove's condition?'

Noxx's dark eyes glittered in the dimness. 'Gast is ministering to him. He lies in the infirmary, pumped full of anti-shock philtres and counter-venoms. He will live.'

'Good.'

'But he will not fight. And now I am three brothers down,' Noxx went on, without acknowledging Rafen's reply.

'*We* are three brothers down,' Rafen said firmly. 'This is a joint action, cousin, do not forget. You own Chapter Master demanded it be so.'

'He told me to hunt and kill a traitor, Blood Angel. He did not bid me to use my brothers as cannon fodder.'

'If that is a suggestion that I have allowed your kinsmen to take the greater risks, then you would do well to reconsider it. We are all in harm's way.' Rafen folded his arms, a grimace forming on his lips. 'Shall we cut to the heart of this?' he snapped. 'I have no time for barbs or sly criticism. Say what you think, Noxx. Let me hear you say the words.' He glared at the Flesh Tearer. 'You believe you could do better than I have done.'

'You seem sure of yourself,' said Noxx, 'but answer me this; do you even have a plan, Rafen? Or are you just making this up as you go?'

The Blood Angel felt a surge of annoyance. 'You've fought longer than I have against the Emperor's enemies. Tell me, how many times have you been forced to go into battle with only your wits and the blessing of Holy Terra?'

'Don't throw dogma at me, boy,' retorted the other warrior. 'Those things alone are not enough! The commander who enters combat without a strategy is a dead man walking.'

'And you would do well not to presume to teach me tactics,' Rafen shot back. 'How often must you test me? I bested you once in the arena on Baal... Do you wish me to fight you again, here and now? Do you want to challenge me for command of this mission?'

Noxx's body tensed, and for a moment Rafen thought the Flesh Tearer might strike him. 'Perhaps I should.'

'And what a fine example that would set,' Rafen sneered. 'At this time, when unity of purpose is what we need the most.'

'Aye!' said Noxx. 'And how can we have that if we do not have trust in our commander?' He took two quick steps forward. 'Make me believe, Rafen. Convince me why I should continue to follow you.'

'We *will* find the renegade who came to Baal, and we *will* destroy him,' said the Blood Angel. 'Doubt me if you must, but do not doubt that. The Emperor is with us.'

Noxx arched an eyebrow. 'Did the witch-kin tell you that? So tell me, will He step off the Golden Throne and come spear Fabius for us?' He snorted. 'Yes, I have fought in His name longer than you, and in that time I've learned He helps those who help themselves.'

'Watch your tongue,' snarled Rafen.

The Flesh Tearer glared back at him, paying no heed to the warning. 'So far you have made a poor showing, cousin. You let that cloud your thoughts. You are still fighting the battles you have lost, Rafen! Dwelling on every circumstance of Bile's escapes instead of preparing for the fight ahead! And I will not let my brothers die of it.'

Rafen turned away. 'You do not know my thoughts. If you did, you would not question me!'

Noxx's hand shot out and grabbed Rafen's vambrace. 'I know what you are thinking, Blood Angel! I know it because I think it as well!'

'Unhand me,' Rafen growled.

'What is he doing with the sacred blood?' Noxx threw the question at him.

Rafen felt ice in his veins, and he stiffened. The shadow of great horror, of a shame and repulsion as dark as old hate uncoiled in his thoughts.

That question dwelled at the back of his thoughts. It had done so since the moment Rafen had left the company of Lord Dante, after the Chapter Master gave him this mission.

'That question...' Noxx's hand fell away. 'It robs me of my sleep. Sometimes I wish I were ignorant of all this... If only for a moment's respite...' All the anger, the chained fury at the heart of the Flesh Tearer waned, and for a moment he seemed almost vulnerable.

Strangely, Rafen felt a sudden pang of sympathy for his comrade-in-arms. 'Aye,' he said. 'I hear the question in my own thoughts and I dread to know the answer to it.'

'We fear it,' Noxx replied. 'As well we should. This foul Chaos whoreson, his black sorcery and corrupt science have forged such grotesques. I have heard it said Bile once turned his hand to the creation of a replicae of the bastard-king Horus...' The warrior's face twisted in disgust, and he spat on the deck. 'If he would dare to recreate that lowest of traitors... Then in Terra's name, what more might he do?'

Rafen felt sickened. 'I cannot wonder.'

'But you must,' Noxx told him. 'You must dare to face that question, or else you go into this fight unready!' He paused. 'And if you do that, then you prove me right. No fit commander can turn his face from such dark and terrible uncertainties. It is a price for the laurel. If you want to lead us, you must be willing to lead us into a nightmare.'

'And do it with eyes open,' Rafen added, with a nod.

'Just so.' Noxx studied him. 'I will say this to you. I am a Flesh Tearer, a Son of the Great Sanguinius, an Adeptus Astartes. Loyal servant of the Golden Throne, and so on and so on. I could stand before you and trot out list after list of my victories and my pious, zealous deeds in the name of Holy Terra. I need not prove myself to you, nor any other man under the stars.'

Rafen eyed him. 'But yet you demand I must attest to you!'

'That too is a burden of command. You know this. Rise to it, Rafen, or stand down.' Noxx stood before him, waiting. 'What is it to be?'

After a long moment, the Blood Angel released a slow breath. 'I have no great scheme,' he admitted. 'Every plan we have employed against Fabius, every design to take him has turned to ashes in my hands. He is like no foe I have ever faced. Ten thousand years ago, he was a match for heroes and champions, and time has not dimmed his skills. This monster is a singular quarry, Flesh Tearer. Know that.'

'I do. We all know.'

Rafen's gaze fell to the deck. 'I have nothing left now but the blade of my hate, and the fury that propels it. We will close to his island fortress by stealth, and break its walls with our bare hands if need be. Whatever we find within will perish.'

'And the... the vial of sacred blood?'

'It will be liberated. In one way, or another.'

Noxx was silent for a moment. 'This mission will be the end to all of us, Blood Angel.'

'Perhaps.' Rafen glanced at him. 'Do you regret joining me now, cousin?'

Noxx shook his head. 'My only regret will be if we do not make that whoreson suffer before he dies.'

'I need only to get close,' Rafen went on, almost to himself. 'Just one strike, no more. Close enough for the kill.' He shook off the moment. 'Sove fought well in defence of his battle-brothers and the mission. It is a great pity he was so wounded.'

'He's not out of the game,' said Noxx. 'None of us are out of it yet.'

Rafen accepted this with a nod. 'So, brother-sergeant. Have I answered the question? Am I worthy of your loyalty? Will you follow me into the unknown, to the jaws of death?'

Noxx turned to walk away. 'Do you recall the words I said to you in the descent bay, just before the *Neimos* began the drop?'

'You said… *see you in hell, Blood Angel.*'

Noxx nodded grimly. 'Then you have your answer.'

Rafen hesitated; but anything else he would have added was waylaid by the chirp of the vox bead in his ear. He toggled the general channel. 'This is Sergeant Rafen. Report.'

He listened with growing alarm as Turcio described what he had discovered down on the engineering deck.

ASTERN OF THE submersible, a faint wake of distortion melted away into the current of the sluggish Dynikan sea. Slow and steady, with the cold, calculating intent of a true-born predator, a shadowed form followed on behind the vessel.

Faint phosphor dots, lined in trails along a body of jointed, flexible chitin, outlined the dimensions of the monstrous shape. In mass, it matched the size of the *Neimos*, and subtle flexions of its flukes and fins allowed it to keep pace with the human craft. The tyranid creature moved through the ocean unseen, unsensed; it instinctively understood the landscape of the waters. It shifted in and out of thermoclines, the great bands of current where waters of differing temperature lay across one another, where sound waves reflected back and away, further masking its careful approach.

It was perfectly adapted to its killing ground. Generations back down the line of its rapacious evolution, its ancestor-genotypes had torn their way through the life of Dynikas V's seas and in the process, absorbed what they consumed to emulate and ultimately exterminate it. Trace elements of heavy metals in the waters were expressed in the dull matt sheen of the creature's natural armour, in the tusks surrounding its oval mouth, and the rings of fangs surrounding every sucker along the manus of its tentacular clubs. It *flowed* more than it moved, riding the deep tides, inching closer to the intruder in its realm. Along its flanks, a plated eyelid rose to reveal a glassy lens, filled with a dark pupil. Optic matter evolved to sense thermal radiation drew upon the shape of the *Neimos*, tracking it. Delicate sensory palps that could detect perturbations in magnetic fields wafted on the end of wiry fronds.

In the slow, sullen pace of the creature's thoughts, it equated its prey with all the others it had fed upon. Some were organics, of meat and cartilage and genotype of tyranid origin; and sometimes there were others, things clad in hard cases of ceramite or drifting in iron shells that appeared atop the waves. Those it would reach up to, drag down, killing with the brutal pressures of the depths and its own whipcord embrace.

It had consumed the remains of the selachian-form lictors in a single motion, extending wide to draw in the corpses and strain them through grids of metallic baleen. Brain matter was siphoned away to a secondary stomach lined with omophageacic receptor cells and denatured. Chains of ribonucleic acid broke down as memory elements were soaked into the creature's own biosystems. The tyranid drew on the remnants of sensory input and pheromone recall from the dead, reassembling what it could. Through the eyes of corpses, it experienced their killings and some sense of the meat-life they had tried to devour. Abhumans, like the surface-things, but somehow different. The creature had briefly picked through some of the rain of strange wreckage that had entered its domain from high above; nothing it had found there had any meaning, however. But now it was gathering in an understanding.

The prey above had never dared to venture beneath the surface before. This was unknown to the tyranid; and in its ponderous mind, its constant hunger gained a new shade of emotion. Anticipation.

As the *Neimos* went deeper, so the creature went with it.

* * *

THE SMELL CAME to Rafen even before he reached the infirmary, down the steep steel stairs that led to the tertiary deck. It was thick with the heavy, rusted tang of spilled blood, but his senses picked out other odours in the mix; lubricants and ozone.

He moved at a pace, aware that his heavy boots dented the steps as he took them hard and fast, two at a time. The deck was at a shallow tilt, the *Neimos* turning gently to starboard, and he hauled himself on to the upper level with the help of an iron handhold welded to the curved wall. The hatch to the ship's sickbay was wide open, and hard yellow-white light spilled into the corridor. Turcio stood outside, his expression grave. His bolter dangled from the grip of his augmetic arm. Rafen automatically noted that the weapon's safety catch was disengaged.

'Lords,' began Turcio, nodding to Rafen, and again to Noxx as the Flesh Tearer came up after him. 'He's in there. Brother Gast is seeing to him.'

Noxx made a negative noise deep in his throat and spoke before Rafen could frame a question. 'You're certain of what happened? The adept was weak of spirit... perhaps he was attempting to take his own life.'

Turcio shook his head. 'There would be simpler ways for him to do it. Unfortunately, there is no data on the spools from the ship's internal security scopes. It appears there was a malfunction at the time. Granted, the *Neimos* is an antiquated vessel and its systems are elderly, but I believe that was no coincidence. This was a deliberate attack.'

'By whom?' said Rafen. 'The Adeptus Astartes may have little kinship with the Mechanicus, but Beslian has no enemies among us. We must assume we have an intruder on board.'

'Perhaps someone slipped on to the *Neimos* before we left the Archeohort,' offered Turcio. 'Another adept. If one of them had learned what Mohl intended to do…' He trailed off.

Noxx shook his head. 'Mohl would have known. He would have warned us.'

'It doesn't matter how,' Rafen broke in. 'All that matters is that we deal with this quickly.' Off Turcio's nod, he gestured at the gangway. 'Gather the brothers, begin a sweep of the ship from bow to stern.'

The Blood Angel nodded and moved past them to carry out the order, while Rafen entered the infirmary. Noxx hovered at the hatchway, brooding.

Inside the compartment, beneath the glow of a lume array, Brother Gast was busy inside the torso of the tech-priest. He had removed his gauntlets and vambraces, and thick, oily blood marked his hands where he worked in Beslian's wounds. Assisting him, a wiry machine-slave wearing a leather smock deployed a small laser quill, and it buzzed and sizzled as the helot used it to seal veins, wires and conduits.

Beslian himself had all the cast of a corpse, a piece of battlefield detritus. If not for the festoons of wires connecting him to the glass-dialled monitor frame above his pallet, and the slow chime of a life sensor, Rafen would have thought him long dead. He watched the Apothecary-Cleric's labour for a moment; on some detached, distant level, he was intrigued by the sight of the adept's internals. The warrior had always wondered what kind of heart beat inside the shrunken chest of these cogs.

On another nearby pallet, shrouded by a support collar, the heavy form of Brother Sove lay unmoving. The injured Flesh Tearer's breaths came in a low, rasping rhythm. Rafen spared him a brief look. The warrior was in a healing trance, the engines of his Astartes implants working to repair him. Sove seemed oddly disproportioned, however, with one entire limb missing from his body.

Gast applied a dermal stapler and a vac-tube of morphic glue to the incision in Beslian's side, and began to close him up. Without turning, he spoke to the other Astartes. 'The adept is lucky to be alive. Turcio found him before his bio-implants completely shut down from the physical shock. Blood loss was great. I doubt he will come to consciousness for several hours yet. There were many incisions across the torso, from more than one weapon.' He pointed out weeping, bloody lesions and areas of heavy tissue damage. 'Blunt trauma about the head and neck. Multiple planes of attack.'

'You are suggesting there was more than one assailant?' said Noxx.

Gast's head bobbed. 'Not a suggestion, brother-sergeant, but a statement of fact. And these were persons of reasonable strength, too. The violence behind these wounds was done in frenzy, with speed. Not, however, with much skill.'

'If it were an Astartes who did this, Beslian would have been killed with a single blow,' mused Rafen. 'Quickly and economically.' He pointed at the adept's throat, considering how he would have done such a thing. 'A sharp, crushing blow there. Or perhaps a blade into the braincase.'

'As I stated, the attack was inexpert,' continued Gast. 'Beslian survived it, for one thing.'

'Then we have a witness, after all,' said Rafen. 'Was there any neural damage to him?'

Gast moved away, letting the servitor finish the work of closing up his patient. He cleaned his hands with a sanctified cloth. 'Difficult to be certain. My learning stretches to battlefield medicine and the calling of the sanguinary priesthood, but no further.'

Rafen leaned in, studying the ashen face of the injured adept. 'Wake him.'

'Sir?' Gast stopped, and threw a questioning glance towards Noxx. 'Perhaps I was unclear about Beslian's physical state–'

'You were clear enough,' said Rafen. 'Now wake him.'

The servitor stepped away and slouched into a standby stance, its task completed. Gast reached for a narthecia pack and hesitated. 'If I do this, you understand it could end his life?'

'If there are intruders aboard this craft, that could end all our lives,' said Noxx. 'Do as the Blood Angel says.'

'As you wish.' Gast adjusted an injector tubule, drawing a measure of fluid into it. He paused over a nozzle visible in the meat of Beslian's neck. 'I would marshal your questions now, lords,' he told them. 'The adept may not be coherent... or alive... for long.'

The tubule hissed; the effect was almost instant.

Beslian's body went rigid, the mechadendrites and servo-arm sprouting from his spine flexing and whipping at the air. His back arched and he went into a harsh spasm, releasing a sound somewhere between a screech and a sob. The adept's eyes opened and fixed on Rafen. He began to prattle in machine code, the chattering noise rising with his panic.

'Logis!' Rafen snapped, demanding Beslian's attention. 'Who attacked you? Tell me!'

The adept tried to speak and raised a hand. A whirring noise issued from his lips. The sound wavered and changed; it was like listening to a vox open to a dead channel, the winds of static slowly giving way to the certainty of a comm-broadcast. From the rambling babble, Rafen caught a single clear word and his eyes narrowed.

'Zellik!'

Gast heard it too, and turned to the Blood Angel. 'The Magos? He died in space. Perhaps the adept's mind was damaged after all...'

Beslian was shaking, rocking back and forth. 'Zellik wants to kill me!' The words were heavy with distortion, warped and barely articulate. 'All of him! Revenge! Revenge–'

The tech-priest's writhing head slumped as he spoke, and for the first time it tilted towards the quiescent servitor standing by the monitor frame. Beslian's mouth opened wide, wider than any normal jaw should have allowed, and from his lips came a siren wail.

It happened so quickly that the motion was a blur; the servitor twitched once and launched itself at the Mechanicus adept. One hand, not a thing of flesh and blood but a medicae tool with scalpel fingers and jointed probes, stabbed out and plunged into Beslian's eyes. Steel digits buried themselves to the knuckle in his skull and tore.

Rafen reacted, lashing out with a punch at full force. The blow from his mailed fist stuck the murderous servitor in the base of the spine, where a set of iron piston-legs joined the nub of a human pelvic bone. Fluids jetted and the machine-slave fell to the deck. The shock of the impact seemed lost on it, however; it still scrambled towards the adept, fingers wet with optic jelly clawing desperately to inflict more damage.

He heard the helot mutter something as it fell. It sounded like the word 'traitor'. With a growl, he raised his boot and stamped the servitor's throat into the deck plate.

The attack had taken only seconds, but the sudden silence from the life sensor made it clear enough damage had been done. Rafen's face twisted in a grimace as Beslian's head lolled back, showing bloody, empty eye sockets.

'It appears you were correct,' said Gast, after a moment.

'It appears we were both correct,' Rafen replied.

Noxx crouched and turned over the corpse of the servitor. 'This was our attacker? Or one of them, at least?'

Gast shook his head. 'Not possible. That machine-slave is tether-tagged to the infirmary chamber. Its programming prevents it from leaving this compartment.'

'He said Zellik.' Rafen studied the dead man, thinking. 'Zellik wanted revenge.'

'Matthun Zellik is dead,' insisted Noxx. 'I am as certain of that as if I put an end to him myself.'

Rafen glared at the helot. 'There is dead, and then there is *dead*.' Inwardly, he chided himself; the warrior had not even thought to consider a machine-slave as a potential assailant.

The mindless servitors could barely be described as human. For the most part they were clone-stock, gene-formed replicae spawned in growth tanks beneath the mountains of Mars, or else the bodies of felons and heretics given over to the Cult Mechanicus for repurposing. Wired with implants, bionics, data-spools and tool pods, whatever scraps of a persona might exist in them were ruthlessly expunged by stringent rituals of conditioning. Some were programmed for combat operations, some for computing tasks in tandem with cogitators, but the helots aboard the *Neimos* were not nearly so advanced. They were technomats, capable of performing set regimens of duties and little else. They had no sentience, no more will of their own than a boltgun or an auspex.

At least, that was what Rafen had believed. 'The Magos reaches out from his grave,' said the Blood Angel. 'He hated Beslian for his part in our capture of the Archeohort. The servitors are the tools of his vengeance.'

'How is that possible?' said Gast.

'If the helots did this, then we must cull them,' added Noxx. 'We do not have one enemy aboard, we have a dozen!'

Rafen shot him a look. 'And how will we pilot this vessel without the servitors, cousin? How will we run its reactors, keep its machine-spirit in check?'

Gast gathered up the dead servitor and placed it on a work table. 'I do not understand. One helot, perhaps, prepared by Zellik for just such an occurrence, I could accept. But all of them?'

Rafen thought of something that Mohl had mentioned on the command deck of the Archeohort. 'Or more than that. An… *infection*.'

'A viral meme?' Gast's brow furrowed.

'Cut that thing open and find us some answers,' demanded Noxx.

The cleric nodded once, and reached for a bone saw.

CROSSING AN ABYSSAL trench, the *Neimos's* forward velocity slowed a degree as the ocean exerted tidal force across the plane of the submersible's course. Working to return the craft to its pre-programmed heading, small thruster modules hidden beneath anti-cavitation cowls came to life, nudging the vessel through the field of cross-currents.

Hiding in the thin lines of wake bubbles, the tyranid flattened its body into a planar shape, settling into the same pattern of motion. The sensor array on the tip of the *Neimos's* X-fin tail planes relayed a tiny return, twitching a needle on a gauge before the dull gaze of a tethered crew helot.

The servitor blinked and the datum did not register; behind those dead eyes, another process took place, as a very different kind of killer stalked the vessel.

'LET ME SEE if I can fathom this,' said Ajir, with scorn in his voice. 'We are hunting a killer hiding in the hollows of this hulk, sent by a man who was flashed to ashes as the Archeohort burned up on re-entry. A dead traitor whose cogs and gears are still raining down on this light-forsaken planet.'

'You seem to have the measure of it,' muttered Puluo.

Ceris watched Ajir rock off the curved wall of the cargo bay and stalk across the space that served as their makeshift arming chamber. 'Does the brother-sergeant think we do not have enough impossible tasks already?'

The psyker sensed a tic of annoyance in the aura of Turcio, who stood close by, examining a fan of tools in his hand. 'Would you rather we did nothing and risk the same fate as Beslian?'

'Don't be a fool,' Ajir replied. 'I can kill any servitor who tries to end me without a moment's thought.'

Eigen, the lone Flesh Tearer in the room, was staring at the floor, deep in thought. 'Not if that servitor unlocks the reactor's machine-spirit, or sends this ship past its crush depth.'

'He's right,' said Turcio. 'This isn't a problem we can solve with a bolt round.'

Ajir's eyes flashed, but he held his tongue. Ceris had sensed the fractious relationship between the two warriors under Rafen's command from the moment he had joined the squad. Turcio openly wore a penitent brand on his cheek, the mark burned into his skin in recognition of the rites of purification he had endured. The warrior had been one of those who followed the false angel Arkio, only to repent at the revelation of his pretence and return to the fold. A second mark, one only visible to someone with the witch-sight, coloured Turcio's aura – *regret*. The colour of the emotion marbled everything about him; even though Lord Dante himself had forgiven the transgression of the Blood Angels misled by Arkio, Turcio had not forgiven himself. Ajir, whose aura rarely strayed from the crimson tinge of fury, seemed to think it was his avowed purpose to remind Turcio of his penitent status at every juncture.

Ceris wondered why Ajir could not look past the brand. He sensed something there about the other Astartes, but far enough below the surface that he could not read it.

He put the matter aside as Kayne opened the hatch and stepped aside to allow Sergeant Rafen to enter with Noxx and Gast. The young Blood Angel stood astride the entrance, cradling his bolter. Puluo had ordered it so – it seemed prudent, given recent events aboard the *Neimos*.

Rafen wasted no time with preamble. 'Logis Beslian is dead.' He explained what had transpired in the infirmary with the medicae servitor.

Eigen frowned. 'If the machine-slave wanted to kill him, why did it not do the deed the moment Turcio brought him to the sickbay? It must have had the opportunity.'

Gast nodded. 'It only attacked after Beslian was awakened. After he mentioned Zellik's name.'

'A trigger word,' said Puluo. 'Hypnogoge assassins use the same technique to activate a servile.'

'It's more than that.' Rafen glanced at Noxx. 'Show them.'

The Flesh Tearer veteran had a bloodstained cloth in his hand, and with a gesture of disgust that twisted his scarred face, he unfolded it to reveal a faceted gemstone, a long emerald droplet webbed with fine golden threads. Ceris could make out a line of green glyphs along the surface of the object; something about the hue and the way it reflected light made him immediately erect his mental barriers.

'What is it?' said Noxx.

'*Xenos*,' added Rafen, with dour certainty.

'This object was buried in the base of the medicae servitor's cerebellum,' Gast explained, 'and the wires you see emerging from it were laced into elements of the helot's organic brain.'

Eigen grimaced at the gemstone. 'A control device?'

Rafen nodded. 'Or something of the like.'

'We know the Inquisition suspected Zellik of trading in alien materials. This, and what we saw in his museum, is confirmation.' Noxx held the gem as if he could barely stop himself from crushing it to powder.

Ceris came closer. The bauble was drawing him to it. He had to get a better look, see it more clearly.

Behind him, Turcio showed the tools in his hand. 'Blood traces on these implements, lord. I took them from a trio of servitors in the reactor control chamber where I found Beslian.'

'We should open the skulls of those three,' snapped Ajir. 'No doubt we'll find the same foul implant in them as well.'

'It's worse than that,' said Rafen. 'I asked Brother Gast to conduct an auspex scan of a random pick of servitors.'

'Once I knew what I was looking for, I found them easily.' Gast gave a heavy sigh. 'Brothers, cousins. Every machine-slave aboard the *Neimos* carries one of these jewels inside their skull. I suspect that Zellik implanted his entire helot crew with them.'

'We kill the crew – assuming one of them doesn't scuttle the ship before we can end them all – and we're dead in the water.' Noxx outlined the hard reality of the situation. 'We let them live, and there's no way to be sure that they won't turn on us at a moment's notice.'

'We can't trust any of them,' Turcio was saying, but Ceris's attention was elsewhere. He was reaching for the stone. He could feel the sense of it, even through his gauntlet. A strange cold heat, like the heart of a dead star.

'Let me see,' he said, and before Noxx could stop him, he took the xenos gem from the other man's palm.

IT SANG TO him; and it was not a pleasing melody.

A shouting, atonal chorus beat at Ceris's psionic senses. There were a hundred voices, and they were all one voice. All drowned in rage and pain and heart-stopping terror. All mad with the need for vengeance. All of them Matthun Zellik.

It was as if Ceris stood in a hall of broken mirrors, but in every shattered reflection he saw the Magos's scowling, screaming, weeping face. He could feel a piece of the man's soul, a shard of his mind and spirit enclosed in this tiny sliver of gemstone. The psyker steeled himself and dared to probe deeper, peeling back layers of the device.

Within its indigo depths he saw lines of quantum connectivity stabbing out in all directions, each ending in another gem buried in another mind. And dimly, he perceived the web that meshed the implants into one enclosed system. Reaching out, he felt his psy-senses rebound off walls of alien symbology, preventing him from seeing more. Ceris felt the edges of a broken, furious mind out in the web-mesh, moving from point to point, and he knew its name.

* * *

'ZELLIK!' THE PSYKER choked out the word and recoiled from the gemstone as if it had bitten him.

'You looked into it…' said Noxx. 'What did you see, witch-kin?'

Rafen came to the Codicier's side and spared him a measuring look. 'That was foolish, brother. That thing could have burned out your soul!'

Ceris shook his head, colour returning to his cheeks. 'I… felt compelled. It was the right thing to do.' He glanced around at the other warriors. 'Zellik is dead, of that you may be certain, but he is still plaguing us.' The psyker pointed at the implant gem. 'This is, as Sergeant Rafen said, of alien origin. A psi device, capable of storing part of a living consciousness.'

Eigen's expression was incredulous. 'You're saying that Zellik somehow… *copied* himself into a machine-slave?'

'Not one,' said Ceris, '*all* of them. He splintered his mind and spread it out among them, parsed like the chapters of a book.' He paused, thinking. 'Perhaps, with enough intact elements, he might have been able to reconstitute his psyche at a later time… and cheat death.'

'If Zellik's mind controls these servitors, then why are we still alive?' demanded Kayne, shooting a tense glance over his shoulder into the corridor.

'It's not control,' said Ceris. 'He did this as a desperate act. There are only fragments of him left, perhaps enough to draw together briefly, but not enough to fully manifest.'

'Not *yet*,' said Puluo.

Rafen's lips thinned. 'If Zellik exists in these… fragments… then perhaps we can expunge him, erase him like a toxic data-meme.'

Ceris nodded. 'There's a core of intent, out in the web of connections between the implants. That's the strongest aspect of his persona. If we can isolate it, kill the servitor hosting that fragment of him…'

'Then he'll die a second time…' Noxx nodded to himself.

Rafen studied the psyker. 'You can do this?'

Ceris nodded. 'I can.'

'Then put an end to him–'

Without warning, the deck beneath them echoed as if it had been struck by the hammer of a giant.

Loose items scattered and crashed to the floor, and the lume rods over their heads flickered and sparked. A long, lowing groan sounded, the torsion of an ancient hull tightened under sudden, lethal pressure.

Rafen staggered and grasped at a stanchion. 'Something struck us!'

'Zellik?' said Kayne.

Eigen shook his head. 'That came from outside the hull.'

Noxx reached for his gun. 'Those lictor-hybrids, back for more!'

Another blow resonated, and the *Neimos* listed sharply to port, robbing them of their balance once again.

'We're too deep for them,' Rafen told him. 'It's something else.'

EIGHT

A WRITHING, FLEXING impulse shocked down the length of the tyranid and it shot forward through the stygian sea, barbed tentacles exploding outward in a grasping motion.

The bony armour across its torso scraped along the starboard flank of the *Neimos*, and the creature's chromatophores flashed redly, declaring its attack colours. The alien's probing limbs looped around the hull and scraped the anechoic plating, scoring deep grooves. Chemo-sense glands in the tips of the tentacles led them towards sealed vents and hatches. The tyranid wanted to open the vessel to the ocean, rip it inside out and feed on what was hidden within.

Steely coils tightening, the predator-form cemented its embrace of the submersible, acidic venom gels secreting from its body where metallic tusks snapped at the curved hull. The *Neimos* rocked and twisted, the skeleton of the ship flexing against itself as the tyranid pulled and pushed.

THE DECK TILTED wildly as Rafen raced down the narrow corridor, and he slammed into the wall, the plate of his shoulder pauldron smashing an inert screen. Sparks glittered from a damaged junction box near his head and he ignored the dazzling flares, pressing on. Through the gridded flooring beneath his boots he heard voices, angry and sharp, calling out in the guttural snarls of battle-language. The Blood Angel took another two steps and heard a creaking howl above. He threw up his arms in time to catch a broken length of pipe as it swung down, allowing a trickle of waste water to drip free. Shoving it aside, he pressed on, striding through the aft hatch of the command chamber.

A small fire had taken hold inside one of the control consoles, and a servitor was pouring retardants into the machine's innards; elsewhere running lights flickered ominously and the chamber shook as another glancing blow caressed the *Neimos*. Warning clarions rang a constant underscore.

'Report!' he cried, drawing the attention of another helot. All of the machine-slaves seemed irritatingly unruffled by the vessel's condition, their expressions as blank as they would be on a cruise through millpond-calm waters.

'Working,' said the servitor, chattering out a punch-card from a cavity in its chest. 'Alert condition. The *Neimos* has made contact with a xenos biological.'

'Is that so?' said Noxx, arriving a few steps behind him. 'I'd hardly noticed.'

Once more, the ship rang like a struck bell. The rest of the battle-brothers followed Noxx into the chamber, all of them chafing at this indignity.

'Observe,' the servitor was saying. Rafen studied it, wondering about the xenos gem buried in its grey matter. Was some fraction of Matthun Zellik's mind in there right now, watching this interchange? He frowned and dismissed the thought. *One problem at a time.*

The helot worked a set of carved wooden keys and a flickering hololith sprang up over the chart table. It dropped in and out, but the ghostly image was stable enough for the Astartes to get an understanding of what they were facing. The holographic display showed a resonance-scan model of the *Neimos*, and wrapped around it like some obscene lover was a thing of tentacles and barbs, a bullet-shaped form covered with quills.

'Throne and blood,' muttered Eigen. 'It's a kraken.'

'Not like those from the home world,' said Noxx. 'It's tyranid. It cannot be anything else.'

Rafen nodded. 'Another ocean-evolved form, like the lictor-sharks.'

'Can we shake it off?' asked Turcio. 'Go even deeper? Perhaps it won't follow us down.'

Kayne shook his head, and pointed to a large needle-dial on the far bulkhead. The pointer was crossing a band of yellow, making slow progress towards a red stop. 'Depth gauge,' he explained. 'Much less ocean beneath our keel and we'll be crushed like a spent shell case.'

'Look at those bone plates,' added Gast, nodding at the image. 'I'll warrant that behemoth could survive the depths far better than we could.'

'The other way, then,' Turcio replied. 'Raise the ship. If it's a deep-dweller, when we make for the surface, it might lose interest–'

Twin impacts off the port bow jerked the *Neimos* sideways, the torsion popping rivets from the inner hull. Puluo swore beneath his breath as a panel near to him coughed out a shower of sparks and died. 'Beastie doesn't seem like one to be easily discouraged.'

Rafen sniffed, and caught the smells of baking wires and stale seawater wafting in from the corridor. 'It'll tear us apart if we don't stop it.'

'The *Neimos* is armed with lascannon turrets,' ventured Eigen. 'Mohl mentioned it before...' He swallowed and went on. 'Blue-green frequency lasers, tuned for use underwater.'

'No good,' Noxx replied. 'That thing is directly upon us, inside point-blank range.'

'We'll need to deal with this in a more direct manner,' Rafen agreed. 'Look it in the eye.'

'Out there?' Eigen blinked.

The Blood Angel sergeant nodded. 'Out there.'

Noxx folded his arms. 'A blunt way of doing it. I almost approve.' He leaned in '*Almost*. But what about Zellik and these "fragments"? We can't ignore what the psyker said. If some ghost of that unctuous fool is stalking this ship, we leave ourselves open to a knife in the back!'

'Indeed,' Rafen agreed. 'That's why you will take Brother Kayne and Codicier Ceris into the lower decks of the *Neimos*, and find the host where Zellik's mind is hiding. Kill it and be done.' He turned away before the Flesh Tearer could respond. 'Gast, Turcio.

You two will remain here and maintain an open vox link. Keep this chamber secure at all costs.'

The others nodded.

Rafen's gaze swept the other Astartes; Ajir, Eigen and Puluo. 'The rest of us are going to get our feet wet.'

KAYNE TOOK POINT, leading the way down the canted ladder well, past the secondary level and into the engineering spaces. Reaching the reactor level, he stepped off and braced himself as the submersible shivered again. The impacts on the hull were coming thick and fast now, and he felt a mist of fluid raining down from a pinhole rent in the ceiling. The stream had a rusted, heavy smell to it; somewhere the outer hull had been breached and the *Neimos* was taking on water. He moved onward; wasting concentration on a problem he could not solve would sap his focus.

The warrior glanced over his shoulder and into the hooded eyes of the psyker. Ceris seemed to look straight through him, the crystal matrix of his psionic hood glowing faintly in the wet dimness.

Behind him, the Flesh Tearer Noxx was a shadow outlined by a flickering safety lume. 'Look sharp,' said the sergeant. 'This Mechanicus freak has dogged us for long enough, and I want him dead properly this time.'

'Aye,' said Kayne, with feeling.

Ceris spoke quietly, working the bloodstained alien jewel in his hand. 'He's close,' he whispered. 'Can't stop me from seeing into the web of connections. He's killed, and liked it. Not just Beslian.'

'Mohl?' Noxx ground out the name.

'Yes,' said Ceris distantly. 'He suborned your battle-brother's sacrifice. Took him while he could not fight back.'

Even concealed behind the solid planes of his power armour, Kayne saw Noxx go rigid as the psyker spoke. He saw cold fury on the Flesh Tearer's face, a strange kind of rage that never reached the man's dead eyes.

'This way,' added Ceris, pointing past Kayne into a shadowed corridor.

Noxx nodded once. 'When we find the core of this man,' he told them, 'the killing blow is mine alone, understand?'

Neither of the Blood Angels disputed the order. Kayne stepped forward, and led the way into the gloom.

AJIR WAS THE last of the four to reach the antechamber at the submersible's forward lock. The kraken-creature had latched on to the stern of the *Neimos* and wrapped many of its feelers around the dorsal sail, making the hatch there unusable. Similarly, the bay where they had fought the lictors was a risk; opening the ramp to the sea would let the tyranid monster slip its tentacles inside and rend the craft from within.

Rafen was walking from man to man, checking the joints of their wargear. 'Make certain the closures of your armour are locked tight,' he said. 'A single leak out there will be like a knifepoint to your flesh. You may lose a limb before you can stem the flow.'

Eigen was in a crouch, busying himself with his combat helmet. He ran a layer of sealant around the ring of his gorget. 'We'll need to stay on internal atmosphere,' he noted. 'The waters outside are too noxious for our multi-lung implants to draw oxygen from.'

'Won't be out there long enough to suffocate,' Puluo noted, working at his heavy bolter. 'More likely to drown.'

Ajir considered that for a moment and fought off a shudder of revulsion. He had battled in hostile environments before, on airless moons and worlds where the atmosphere was a toxic soup that even an Astartes could not endure; but never in the ocean depths. He imagined how it might feel, to have one's armour fill with the brackish, acidic seawater, to fall into those abyssal depths trapped in a flooded ceramite coffin. He grimaced and turned his concentration to his weapons.

His bolter was a Godwyn-pattern variant, the standard iteration of the gun found in the hands of thousands of Space Marines across the galaxy. That said, each warrior's weapon was unique in its own small ways. Many of them were centuries old, and some had been passed down from Astartes to Astartes over the life of a Chapter. Ajir's gun was the shade of onyx, patterned with whorls of dark colour like traces of burned oil. Hundreds of names, of brothers and battles, were etched into the breech and slide mechanism, along with lines of combat prayer and holy sacrament. He checked the ammunition loads in the sickle magazine; the mass-reactive rounds were less a bullet, more a miniature rocket, and each one contained within its casing a measure of oxygenated igniter compound. Thus, even in stark vacuum or, as now, in a fluid environment, the boltgun could still deliver its lethal load.

He worked quickly, adjusting the iron sights and the muzzle brake; the waters would attenuate the velocity and range of the weapon by a large degree, and he would need to compensate. The floor was constantly shaking now, like the deck of a Thunderhawk in full flight. Ajir kept his focus, ignoring the moans of the hull-metal. They were close to the exterior of the *Neimos* here, with only a few layers of plasteel and ceramite between them and the dense ocean.

'As soon as we clear the outer lock, activate your magno-plates.' Rafen tapped the knee of his boot, and it gave a dull ring. 'They'll keep you on the hull, but you'll be slow with it.' He reached into the open air-lock and returned with a steel cable. 'Tether yourselves and check all your battle-brothers. If one of us does chance to leave the deck, we'll be able to reel you back in.' The sergeant drew his power sword and gave it an experimental swing.

Puluo brought forward a hexagonal case and peeled back the lid, offering it to them as if the contents were some delicacy. 'Hull-breakers. Enough here for us to make chum out of that monster.'

Ajir reached in and took one of the charges; they were a modified version of the more typical krak grenades, shaped detonators designed to be applied directly to the hull of an enemy ship. When he looked up, the other warriors were waiting, their helmets in their hands.

The hull wall vibrated again, the tremors reaching up through the base of Ajir's boots and into his bones.

Rafen looked at each of them, one after another. 'Keep your heads. Don't fight the drag of the water, it will only tire you.' He raised his helm with one hand and locked it into place. 'Measure your shots,' continued the sergeant, his voice reaching them through the vox. 'Make every round count.'

Ajir and the others followed suit and stepped into the lock chamber. Eigen was the last in, and drew the heavy inner hatch closed behind him.

Rafen gave a nod to Puluo, and the Devastator Space Marine slapped at an ornate red switch. Then a deluge like a thousand hammer blows struck them as the sea thundered in to fill the chamber.

GAST LOOKED AWAY from the glowing red rune on the etched brass indicator board. 'Forward lock reads open.'

Turcio blew out a breath, his fingers kneading the grip of his bolter. 'Activate the automatic cycle. Close it as soon as they're out of the ship.'

'Is that wise?' said the Flesh Tearer. 'What if they need to fall back?'

'Any hatch we leave open is another way in for that horror,' replied the other warrior. 'They know that.'

Gast frowned; the Blood Angel was right. He turned back to the panel and manually activated the remote hatch control – but he stopped short of venting the water-filled airlock.

Turcio glowered into the shimmering green frame of the hololithic display. He traced the lines of the tyranid's probing limbs and his brow furrowed. Distant thudding impacts sounded from the aft of the vessel. 'The kraken… it's pushed tentacles into the thruster ring. I think it's trying to choke the propellers.'

The cleric-warrior came to his side. 'It must be drawn by the vibrations...' He trailed off as an unpleasant thought occurred to him. 'Or perhaps by deliberate intent.'

'Tyranids are xenos animals,' retorted Turcio. 'Cunning, yes, but still beasts.'

Gast shook his head. 'Can you be certain? What if the beast out there is sentient?'

'Why would you believe such a thing?'

The Astartes watched the scans of the writhing cephalopod. 'I cannot shake the sense that this monster is toying with us.'

PULUO STRODE FORWARD from the airlock and the plane of his perception switched; he went from the level of the *Neimos's* horizontal interior decks to the side-on surface of the exterior hull. The murk out here was thicker than he had expected, the soupy rust-coloured ocean reducing his visibility to close combat range. Needle-lights at the temples of his battle helmet snapped on, casting hazy cones of illumination out before him, but they did little to improve the situation.

His boots thudded dully on the black and grey hull; the surface curved away from him to the right and the left, vanishing towards a hidden horizon. Puluo could feel the motion of the vessel through the waters; he was facing aft and the pressure of the headway current was pushing insistently at his back. Without the magno-plates in the soles of his boots, he would have already been coasting sternward, his tether playing out behind him. He took another step, feeling the drag on every motion he made. The

Astartes could hear the sea all around him, a slow and steady rumble like the rushing of blood in his ears. For a moment, he felt utterly isolated; then his vox bead crackled and Rafen spoke. 'There, to the stern! Do you see it?'

The optics in Puluo's helmet worked to enhance the view and abruptly, he *did* see it. Only the vague impression of the thing, a huge, hulking shadow in the middle distance. It had gathered itself along the lines of the submersible's fins, and although he could make out no fine details of it, the Blood Angel could gauge its size. The kraken loomed like a faraway thunderhead, and Puluo dragged his heavy bolter upward. Distances were deceiving out here – the thing looked as if it could have been kilometres away. He concentrated on the tiny particles of waterborne debris drifting around him, using their passage to gauge the range.

Something glowing a dull cherry-red, like forge-fired metal, moved towards them.

'I think it sees us,' said Eigen.

The shape drew close, defining into a splayed cobra-head leading a serpentine coil of thick, sinewy flesh. In the light from the helmet lamps it was corpse-white and lined with sucker rings bigger than a man's head. The red glow came from a fluorescing spot across the tip of the vast tentacle.

Puluo's grip tightened on his trigger-bar and he fired a three-round burst from the hip. The gun's languid recoil pressed him into the current, as lines of squealing compression fanned out behind the bolt shells. Everything seemed to move in slow motion – everything but the massive whipping limb of the kraken. Two out of three of the shots missed the mark, but the third hit hard and the tentacle shuddered with pain. Eigen and Ajir fired into it, following Puluo's lead.

'Advance!' called the sergeant, his power sword's active blade wreathed in a halo of frothing bubbles. 'Move in and engage all targets of opportunity!'

Puluo needed no more encouragement. Quickly, taking the measure of this new, strange field of combat, he moved with steady, exact steps. He fired as he went, and first blood was earned as the flexing feeler tore apart along its length. Inky vitae billowed and twisted from the wound.

A low, hollow moan vibrated through the water, the pitch of it so deep Puluo felt it through the bones of his ribcage.

'You have its attention, brother,' said Ajir.

Puluo gave a slow nod, as a scattering of red discs grew brighter and more distinct in the murk. The colour strengthened as the moaning peaked, and more pieces of the larger shadow seemed to break off and move closer.

'Here they come!' called Eigen.

It was easy to think of the attack as many foes, not one; whip-fast cables of muscle came racing towards them, each one seemingly unconnected to the others. Lost in the shadows, the main mass of the kraken's body seemed cut off, out of reach. It was a dangerous line of thought to take; Puluo reminded himself that each limb was only one facet of a larger foe, all of them working together at the bidding of a single predator mind.

The firing began again, bolt rounds moving with agonising slowness. The Astartes saw the glimmer of

Rafen's sword on a falling swing, cutting a glancing blow across a tentacle that left a slick of dark blood swelling out behind it.

Then for the first time, the sergeant raised his plasma gun and fired it; for a brief moment the area around the warriors was illuminated with a stark, hard glow that threw jumping shadows. A streak of burning white plasmatic matter lanced through the water, boiling a channel towards its target, and for a split-second Rafen vanished in a shroud of churning froth as the gun's heat-displacement backwashed across him.

Another tentacle shrank away, the tip withered and molten, and the kraken let out another sub-frequency howl.

'Press the attack!' snarled his commander.

OTHER THAN THE command centre two decks above, the enginarium was where the largest concentration of machine-slaves were located, and it was little wonder. In the middle of the *Neimos*, sheathed with far greater protection than any other section of the vessel, the submersible's heart and soul lurked within a massive armoured sphere.

Ceris chanced a look up at the module, briefly entranced by the trains of light moving up and down the coolant columns that surrounded it. A fusion reactor; behind those plates of titanium and hyperdense alloy, an ember of blazing fire churned. It was an infant star, shackled there to give power to the *Neimos's* drives and internal systems. The reactor should have been tended by a drive-gang of enginseers, but the circumstance of this mission had meant that only servitors crewed this compartment.

The psyker's hard gaze crossed the slack and vacant faces of the machine-slaves as they went about their tasks, apparently ignorant of the fact that the vessel was under attack. Now and then, a tremor through the hull sent one of the helots off-balance and sprawling to the deck in a heap of robes; but they simply righted themselves and continued on.

At his shoulder, Noxx spoke over his raised boltgun. 'Is he here?'

Ceris glanced down at the xenos psi-gem in his hand. Was that a flicker of emerald there behind the runes, or just the play of wan light upon the object? He couldn't be certain. But he was certain of something.

'He is,' nodded the psyker. 'I smell the spoor of his mind. It leaves a trail.' The whispers of the stone had drawn him, like towards like, to this place.

Kayne ratcheted the slide on his bolter. 'Which one?' He panned the weapon around, drawing beads on the mumbling servitors.

There were several of them. Ceris sensed weak glimmers of thought-energy from the machine-slaves, small flickers of mind that barely registered unless he turned his full focus on them. Zellik's broken psyche had stained them all, the taint of the xenos implant shadowy and visible to his preternatural senses, like oil moving over water.

Before he could reply, Noxx gave an answer of his own. 'We'll kill them all. Take no chances.'

Ceris shook his head. 'No, sir. You cannot shoot them all at once. Kill the wrong one and it will give Zellik's essence the moment it needs to relocate to another host-mind.' An alarm began to keen as a fountainhead of liquid jetted from an overloaded valve, and a handful of servitors rushed to see to the problem. 'His psyche is barely coherent. He has lost so much of himself. All the Magos has left now is his hate and his need for revenge... but we must be certain we end the helot where his spirit is hiding. Otherwise, he flees to another servitor through the implant and our search begins again from scratch.'

'Then find him, and be sure of it,' Noxx grated. 'A death is owed, and by Seth, blood payment will be taken!'

The psyker drew up the gem in front of him and stared into its depths. The cloying telepathic miasma that shrouded the xenos device made his skin crawl, and he vowed that once this matter was dealt with – if they survived the predations of the tyranid kraken, he amended – he would take a moment to conduct a ritual of purgation and cleanse his mind of exposure to the xenos stone. How a human being, even a half-cyborg Mechanicus like Matthun Zellik, could have willingly allowed his mind to become part of this alien thing was beyond him. The Magos's fear of death had clearly overcome any piety he might once have had. For all his oaths, the fear of death had made him into a heretic. As well as damning himself for eternity in the eyes of the God-Emperor, Zellik had damned his helot legion into the bargain. Another matter to be dealt with later, he mused; all the servitors would have to be put to death once the mission was over.

For now, though, he had a coward to find. Steeling himself, Ceris pushed a blade of mental force into the psi-gem and once more he glimpsed the web of connections between the flicker-minds of the technomat slaves.

The sense of Zellik was immediate. He lingered in the air, a coil of his thought-trace hanging smoke-thick, invisible to all without the witch-sight. What remained of the Magos's ragged psyche was made of rage and terror.

And it was stronger than Ceris had expected. Even as he realised his error, cursed his arrogance, he felt the shift in the psionic tempo of the chamber.

'Which of them is he?' Noxx hissed, growing impatient.

Every helot in the chamber – those at the leaking pipeway, those at the reactor consoles, the rune-watchers and the rod-runners – all at once their minds dimmed and allowed themselves to be written over by a sketch of Matthun Zellik's thoughts.

'Hate you,' whispered one of them, gripping a carved iron spanner with menace. 'Hate you.' Lips moved, and each of them joined in a chorus of muttering, breathy loathing.

Ceris shot a look at Noxx. 'All of them,' he said.

A machine-slave with bulbous loading arms of fluted steel stumbled forward at Kayne, chattering louder and louder.

The Space Marine put a shot into its chest and it wavered, but did not halt; then all the helots were moving and shouting.

IT WAS AS if a switch had been thrown; one moment, Turcio and Gast stood across from one another, either side of the chart table display, the servitors busy at their stations. The next, the command deck exploded into a riot of noise and motion.

Every machine-slave, at every station and console stopped their work and turned to stare at the Space Marines – and then they were shouting, raising their hands and manipulators, crying out.

'Hate you. Hate you hate you hate you *hate you hate you*–'

Their blank expressions, normally masks of bland vacancy, were twisting in inchoate rage as they crashed about, surging towards the two Astartes.

Turcio knew the look of murder-lust well. He had seen it many times on the faces of his foes. He brought up his bolter, the pistons of his bionic arm locking reflexively into a firing position – and he hesitated. Elsewhere aboard the ship, he would have discharged the shot without a moment's thought, but here in the command chamber they were surrounded by vital systems at every turn, the cogitators and calculating engines that ran every element of the *Neimos's* functions. Even if he scored a direct hit, a bolt round would over-penetrate the torso of a helot and go on to wreak further damage.

At the last second, he reversed his grip on the firearm and slammed the butt of the gun into the face of the nearest member of the maddened horde. Bone and silver cracked, blood spurting from the nostrils of the servitor in a crimson fan. It sank to the deck, killed the instant a shard of skull cut into its brain matter.

Across the table, Gast brought up his gauntlet and punched down a technomat grasping at his arms. The blade-sharp reductor protruding from the armoured glove's underside pierced the chest of the servitor and it gave a strangled cough, choking out pink foam.

Gast batted it away, drawing his serrated flaying knife with a flourish. 'Blood's oath!' growled the sanguinary cleric. 'It's a revolt!'

Turcio let his bolter swing away on its shoulder strap and mirrored the Flesh Tearer's actions, bringing up his own combat blade. 'We can't kill them... the ship...' Mumbling its anger, another helot lashed out, and the Blood Angel knocked it away with the pommel of his weapon.

'They may not give us the choice!' said Gast, shouting to be heard over the choir of murderous cries.

The servitors were massing before them, forming into ordered ranks, leaving their duties behind. Turcio stepped back, unsure of how to proceed, and felt a stanchion at his back. The helots were backing them into a corner.

Gast pointed. 'The rudder!'

With no hands on the steering yoke, the controls moved freely, and Turcio watched the tiller jerk and tilt as the *Neimos* was buffeted by the kraken. The deck took on an angle, growing steeper every moment. The Astartes looked up and saw the depth gauge dial twitch and shift. Ungoverned, the submersible entered a shallow, turning descent.

EIGEN FELT THE change in aspect immediately as the current washed over him. 'The ship... We're changing course.'

He heard Ajir call out on the general vox channel. 'Turcio, respond. What's going on in there? Turcio? Gast?'

Over the open comm, the Astartes caught the clatter of steel on steel and the faint sound of sirens.

'We can't go back,' Rafen's voice cut through everything. 'Trust your battle-brothers to keep the ship secure. We have our target. We cannot tarry!'

The Flesh Tearer looked up the line of the hull and found the silhouette of the Blood Angel sergeant beckoning him forward. The blazing arc of his power sword left a sparkling pennant of froth trailing from the blade.

'Move!' snapped Puluo, underscoring his commander's orders.

Eigen gritted his teeth and did as he was told to. Each footstep was difficult, and he felt his muscles tensing against it. He had trained to fight in many conditions, sparring in the swamps of Cretacia with weights tied to his legs, engaging in close combat in spaces without air or gravity. This was no different. He remembered the words of Amit, first Master of his Chapter, drilled into him as an initiate; *There is no battlefield that can defy us. We are masters of all wars.* The maxim gave him focus and he pushed on.

Fighting on the hull, in the dense grip of the ocean, was like nothing he had ever done, however. Strange echoes of subsonic sound caught in the hard current of the waters came to him, and it was difficult to draw a bead. They were closing in on the main mass of the kraken now, and the large tentacle arms still lashed back and forth over their heads, beating at the hull of the *Neimos*.

He could see the humped body of the tyranid monster, lit in split-second flashes as Rafen fired boiling bolts of plasma at the creature, and Puluo tossed hullbreakers into the fast-moving tide, letting the ocean carry the explosives into the beast. What he had thought were deeper threads of polluted murk were actually slicks of alien blood trailing away from burn wounds in the kraken's thick-armoured flanks.

Smaller limbs reached from the creature's torso, and these were more akin to great bone talons. They sliced through the waters leaving lines of shimmering photoplankton in their wakes.

The crashing echo of gunfire resonated towards him, and from the corner of his visor he saw Puluo firing a burst of heavy bolts into a questing serpent-limb that flicked up behind them. The warrior's shots were true – he was getting the range now, as were they all – and the limb blew apart in a sphere of concussion.

'How do we kill this freak?' Ajir was saying, breathing hard.

'We get closer,' Rafen told him, the fury of battle thick in the other man's words. 'Blind it, choke it, shoot it until it dies, whatever we must! Our mission will not end because of this xenos abortion!'

Eigen nodded. 'Aye!' He took heavy steps forward, his boots ringing on the hull, leading with his bolter. He aimed for the phosphor spots on the kraken's hide, and it reacted with a shiver and a subsonic screech as he fired.

'To your right!' came a shout. Eigen heard Ajir call out his name in warning and he pivoted at the waist in time to see a line of barbs rip towards him over the curvature of the *Neimos's* hull. The splayed talons tore a ragged channel through the grey-black sheath of anechoic tiles and Eigen reacted, dodging away; but his reflex to tuck and roll was the wrong one, and his magno-clamped boots resisted. Too late, he tried to turn, but the spinning fanged club at the end of the tentacle caught him. Barbs ripped into ceramite and punctured layers of plasteel and flexmetals. Locked in place, Eigen fell back under the force of the blow but did not fall, his arms spinning like windmills. With a shout of effort, he pushed himself back to a standing stance, but the kraken's lethal limb was already snaking back and away.

It was then his breath was struck from him as he felt an icy fist at his gut, and with it a growing chill that spread quickly across his torso. For a moment he feared it was shock from a penetrating wound, perhaps even some kind of venom injected into him by the glancing attack – but then he saw the streamer of bubbles issuing from the rent in his chest plate. He smelled rust and stale salt; his armour was flooding with seawater.

'THEY KEEP COMING!' shouted Kayne, blowing the head from the shoulders of a rod-runner. Gunfire echoed around the engine deck. 'You have to stop this!'

Ceris struck out and punched a technomat with a pincer-claw arm to the deck. The blow staggered the helot and left it shaking, but it rocked back and swiped at him again. Blood and bone fragments bloomed in a lethal burst as a round cleaved into it from behind, killing it instantly.

Noxx raised his smoking bolter, holding away a wild servitor at arm's length with his free hand. 'You heard the boy!' said the veteran. 'If this is happening all over the ship–'

'It will be done!' retorted the psyker.

Kayne wondered exactly how it would be done; but then again, he did not want to know. The strange magicks of the warp disquieted him, and he found it hard to mind his ease with someone only steps away from a sorcerer wearing the armour of a Space Marine. Ceris's eye-line crossed his and, for a moment, the Blood Angel wondered if the other man had read his thoughts.

Ceris's mailed fist closed around the alien gem Gast had cut from the brain of the dead servitor, and he gasped. Immediately, eldritch viridian light spilled from the gaps between his fingers, and the crystals lining the Codicier's psychic hood flashed blue-white with power.

'Hate you,' cried the marching machine-slaves. 'Hate you. Hate you. Hate–'

Silence fell like an axe blow, sudden and without warning. For a long second, all Kayne could hear were the faint clarions of warning sirens on the upper decks and the constant rumble and moan of the tortured hull.

Ceris took a step deeper into the chamber, pushing through the statue-still helots. They stood in place, trapped and twitching as if rebelling against the paralysis forced upon them. Kayne saw sweat film the psyker's brow, his eyes narrowing. A greasy, electric tingle filled the air, setting the warrior's teeth on edge; the overspill of telepathic energy clouded the room.

With effort, Ceris raised the hand gripping the glowing gem and held it out, pointing with his fist. 'I feel him. He is there.'

A lone servitor, an overseer model constructed to serve as gang-master for the rod-runner helots, stumbled and staggered. It moved as if it were wading through thick oil, unable to drag itself free. The machine-slave tottered towards Ceris with its hands curled into talons, moaning and snarling. Kayne fancied he saw a greenish glimmer deep in the sightless eyes of the helot. The meat of its face twisted and distorted, and for a moment it took on the cast of the silver mask he had seen floating in the holoprojection aboard the Archeohort.

In a stuttering, punch card chatter, the servitor's head tilted back and it spoke. 'You will pay for this!' The voice was crackling and broken, like a fouled recording spool. 'I'll make every one of you pay!'

'He's trying to flee...' Ceris bit out the words. 'Shift to... another host...' The glowing stone throbbed and pulsed. 'Take him now!'

Kayne aimed his bolter, but what he saw made him pause. Wreathing the head of the howling servitor was a ghost, a faint tracery of Magos Zellik's screaming face shimmering like an auroral discharge. As he watched, tiny fireflies of green melted out of the air and merged with the phantom; they were the fragments of Zellik's shattered psyche coming together, perhaps in a last desperate effort to resist the psyker's will.

'Now!' cried Ceris.

'*Make... You... Pay!*' cried the strangled voice; but before it could speak again, a figure stepped out of the gloom behind the helot and bright steel flashed.

A toothed knife, trimmed with wicked barbs the length of its blade, burst from the open mouth of the servitor. Brother-Sergeant Noxx leaned in, pushing his weapon in through the back of the machine-slave's skull. Kayne heard the sickening crack of breaking bone, and then a second sharp report, like glass breaking.

The helot coughed out black blood and pieces of broken gemstone, the screaming ghost about it releasing one final howl before it discorporated and became nothing. With a savage jerk of his wrist, Noxx tore his blade from his kill and spat upon the corpse at his feet. 'For Mohl and Sove and all the others,' he grated. 'This time you stay dead, you worthless maggot.'

Ceris gave a slow nod, and dropped the psi-gem to the deck. Still panting from the effort, he brought down his boot on the emerald stone and ground it into powder beneath his heel. Kayne thought he heard a distant scream, but then it was gone.

All around them, the servitors turned about and ambled back to their workstations, ignoring the Astartes as if they were not there.

RAFEN SAW EIGEN take the hit from the kraken and cursed as the Flesh Tearer recoiled. He saw a dim red shape moving towards the other man across the hull – the murk was too thick to be sure if it was Ajir or Puluo – and the sergeant forged forward, knowing that his battle-brothers would aid the injured warrior.

He was at the twitching flanks of the tyranid monster, and the sea-beast's thick cilia lashed out at him like a storm made of lashes. The plasma gun in its holster for the moment, he concentrated on batting the attack away with the furious blade of his power sword, parrying and slashing at the nest of probing limbs, turning them to ribbons of pasty meat. Vibrations from the kraken's throat canal rumbled out to him, the sound of the alien's pain drawing a wolfish grin across his lips.

A sickle-sharp talon hummed through the water, on a downward arc that would have punched through his helmet and through into his chest had he not shifted at the last moment. In the bubbling wake of the attack, he felt a hard tug on his waist that threatened to pull him off-balance, and the warrior staggered against it. Suddenly the drag vanished and he stumbled back across the hull plates, his boots clanking. Something long and ragged spun past in the corner of his vision and he snatched at it. His glove briefly closed around a frond of severed cable, the end splayed open and frayed; *his tether*.

'No matter,' he said aloud, and threw the broken cable away.

The creature moved, the length of it sliding past him. He spied a place where Puluo's bolt salvos had carved out a divot of armoured hide, and beneath Rafen saw pallid flesh. Without a moment's hesitation, the Blood Angel pushed in with a heavy upward slash, cutting deep into the kraken. Even as the monster bellowed in pain, Rafen tore a hull-cutter from his belt and jammed the device into the slippery open wound.

The kraken rolled and writhed, still turning. A concussion echoed, and a huge sphere of red-black foam blossomed above Rafen's head. The hydrostatic shock buffeted him, but he weathered it, reaching to unlimber the plasma gun once again.

The monster recoiled, the upper length of its body rising off the hull, its massive tentacles starting to uncoil.

For the first time, Rafen saw the mouth of the tyranid fiend, a black chasm ringed with hundreds of rapier-like tusks that flexed and clattered against one another. Streamers of blubber and meat-matter were clogged in its multiple gumlines, the remnants of its last meal. The behemoth loomed in the twin pools of light cast by his helmet lamps, and suddenly the dark death-tunnel was expanding to fill his vision. It could consume him whole in a single snap of those gargantuan jaw-parts, swallow him down into its gullet where virulent acids and grinding bone would break the Space Marine apart.

An armoured plate as large as the hatch on a Rhino slid up off the flank of the kraken as it fell at him; behind it Rafen saw a glassy lens and a single eye filled with hateful alien menace.

In the space between the beats of his hearts he understood; *it wanted to see him*. The xenos wanted to watch as it chewed into the man-prey that had dared to defy it.

'Not today,' he told the beast, raising the plasma gun.

The weapon discharged with a thundering gurgle of superheated fluids; the seawater around the muzzle was instantly turned into fat orbs of gas as the plasma stream speared out and blinded the kraken's eye.

A hot backwash of xenos blood and boiling liquid flooded over Rafen, followed by a moaning scream so deep in the subsonic range, it made his bones vibrate and his gut twist. Mad with new agony, the tyranid reflexively released its hold upon the *Neimos* and became a spinning nest of flailing tentacles and talon-limbs. Angled claws and fanged feelers stabbed and lashed at nothing.

Rafen heard someone call out; it sounded like Puluo, the dour warhound's stern, hard voice cracking in his ears, warning him.

It was not enough. A tentacle as thick as a Thunderhawk hull struck Rafen on the backswing as the kraken retreated. The impact broke ceramite, smashed seals and fractured bone.

The Blood Angel knew pain, the impact of a godhammer slamming into his spine, crushing the systems inside his backpack. Agony lit wheels of colour and flares of light behind his eyes, robbing him of the breath in his lungs.

He tasted the heavy copper of blood in his mouth, felt the blades of broken ribs clawing at his chest. Then he realised he could no longer feel the hull beneath his feet. He could not see, thick fluids gumming shut his eyes. He was falling, tumbling.

Rafen tried to summon the strength to speak, but he could utter no words. The effort was immense, and it forced him to a rumbling dark nothingness, where light could not follow.

NOXX SPRINTED TO the corridor outside the infirmary, and he was immediately assailed by the stench of stale seawater. Washes of the tainted liquid sloshed around his boots, draining away through the gridded deck plates. He saw Puluo, the Blood Angel resting heavily against one wall with his helmet off. He was breathing hard, glaring at the floor.

'Eigen?' said the Flesh Tearer.

'He lives.' The dark-skinned Astartes called Ajir approached, his lank black curls spilling out over his neck ring. 'Thank the Throne.'

Noxx glanced at Puluo. 'Zellik is no more. You drove off the creature?'

The warrior gave a nod. 'Aye. At a cost.'

The sergeant took a breath, glancing around. 'Rafen…'

Puluo nodded grimly. 'Beastie took him. Saw it happen. Tore the lad right off the deck, threw him into the murk. Gone.'

'He does not answer the vox,' said Ajir quietly. 'Auspex read is null. In those currents out there, even if the cursed xenos didn't devour him…' The Blood Angel trailed off, his gaze turning inward.

They were silent for a long moment. Noxx glared at the deck, examining the sudden kernel of regret the he felt in his chest. *Another brother lost…* 'Damn this duty,' he muttered.

When he looked up, Noxx found Puluo and Ajir watching him intently. 'Command of the mission now falls to you, lord,' said the Devastator Space Marine. 'What are your orders?'

Noxx told them.

NINE

TIME WAS BROKEN and bleeding; it had that in common with Rafen.

He was aware of the passage of moments, not in a linear manner, but in fits and starts that lanced into his thoughts. Each elapse was a jagged shard of pain and awareness piercing the blood-warm veil that had engulfed him.

His body was feverish with heat, the outward manifestation of his enhanced Astartes physiology as it worked to repair him. Bones were knitting, fluids clotting and wounds drawing closed all over his body, but Rafen's mind struggled to hold on to any sense of it.

Dislocated from the real world, he bobbed upon the turbulent surface of consciousness like a cork, dropping into the troughs of towering waves and vanishing into the black depths. Now and then he would surface, become aware, only to sink back again.

He tried to draw the pieces together into some kind of cogent chain of events.

The spindrift fall through the dark abyss of the waves; yes, that had happened to him. In the moments after the pain of the kraken's parting attack, he had been lost. The agony of the impact, so great and so breathtaking, seemed a distant thing to him now. *How quickly the flesh forgets*, he thought.

Breaking the surface; that too was real... wasn't it? His helmet filmed with oily seawater, cradled in the leeward surge of a low, fast breaker. The battle armour's simple machine-spirit reacting, trying to keep him alive. The icy cold at his back from the broken cryo-pods of the microfusion reactor. The shapes of the mud-coloured wave tops ranging away beneath a rusty, weeping sky. Something out there in the distance, regular in shape, glittering dully. *Rescue*? He dared not hold on to the ideal, for fear it would disintegrate in his thoughts.

The little creatures in the water; eel-like things with bony plates across their heads like arrow tips. Probing at him, looking for new wounds in his armour. Tyranid things, yes. The biomechanical striations clear as he grabbed one and crushed it in his armoured fingers. Some phylum of refuse-consuming animal, perhaps, seeing the Blood Angel as little more than organic mass in need of denaturing.

The dark waters again. Fathomless deeps, burning with blood, thundering with the sound of life. Was that real? Did that exist outside his skull, or was it a torpid fever-dream?

Fingers finding the chains around his wrists, the lanyards trailing to his weapons. The gun and the sword not lost to him. A flash of elation. *Good*. The looming abyss of this alien ocean was denied his weapons. To perish unarmed seemed somehow wrong, as if meeting the veil of death stripped bare and weak.

The shape again, coming closer. Shadows framed against dimming clouds. *A ship?* A tall, blade-sharp prow. The heavy, rotting scent of tyranid pheromones, a haze of foetid mist descending. The air greasy and acid.

Dark and light. Dark and light. Dark...

The light–

THE BLUNT, BRUTISH lines of the patrol craft rode high in the sluggish swell, solar vanes creaking in the constant wind. Searingly bright illumination from questing spotlamps turned the waters around the drifting body into lines of stark, jumping shadows. The crimson-armoured figure stood out like a livid brand, and in moments webber guns had been deployed, projecting nets of sticky matter out into the sea. The figure made weak attempts to push away, but to no avail. The mesh of cultured biofibres wrapped around the limbs of their target and stiffened; immediately the retractor mechanisms inside the webbers chugged into life, dragging in their catch across the lowered trawl deck at the aft of the vessel.

There were splices down there, eyes wide with interest as this strange new captive rolled out of the waves towards them. They exchanged twitchy glances, scratching at the implants protruding from the grossly inflated muscle mass of their arms. The larger of the two, a male modificate spliced with arachnoid DNA, turned its eight-eyed head towards the arrival and ventured closer to it.

This was unexpected. The ships had been diverted off their usual patrol-and-trawl missions by an urgent summons from Cheyne, the Master's subaltern. The command had forced them to dump the entire xenos harvest from that week's gatherings and make full speed to a region near the Oxide Banks. The splices were confused, but they knew better than to disobey Cheyne's orders, which carried the weight of the Primogenitor himself.

Soon it became clear why they had been sent, however. The sky lit with the death of a starship, and soon a rain of wreckage came upon them. They had not stopped since, sifting the fall of debris for useful materials, throwing what they could not use over the side and packing out the hold with the choice pieces. Like their master, the splices were adept at taking whatever was at hand and turning it to new purposes. Every piece of salvage had a use.

But they had found nothing living; not until now.

The arachkin-modificate closed in on the figure in the nets and saw a man-thing in power armour, close to its own mass. Using its vestigial extra arms, it peeled away the lines of webbing, flicking its spindly fingers to dislodge the gooey adhesives that matted it. The tall, distended head nodded to itself. It recognised this. It knew a servant of the Corpse-God when it saw one.

The arachkin turned back to speak to the other modificate, a canine-splice with a glistening snout and constant snarl about its lips. '*Astartes*,' it said, the word thick with sibilance from a mouth crowded with mandibles.

The canine barked a curse word; it became a yelp of surprise as the Space Marine abruptly jerked from where he lay upon the greasy, shifting deck, swinging a sword. The weapon seemed to have come from nowhere, doubtless lost in the folds of the thick netting, now freed by the arachkin's thoughtless interest.

The power sword stuttered, the energy vanes within it misfiring, but still the blade was heavy and lethal. The weapon took the modificate's head from its neck in a welter of blood, and suddenly the Astartes was coming to his feet, staggering.

The other splice smelled pain on the Space Marine, and knew instinctively that the abhuman was badly injured; yet still deadly, as the headless corpse of the arachkin demonstrated. The dead modificate's remains slid off the deck and into the ocean as the ship rose into another swell.

Another strangled bark, this time pitched high for panic and need. In answer, the other modificates came running, and they brought more webbers and the crackling lengths of electromag halberds.

They wasted no time and set about the wounded Space Marine, all of them understanding that what little advantage they had would be lost if they dallied. In the end, it took every splice on the crew to fell the Astartes, and even then he killed two more, turning them to screaming torches before the plasma gun could be struck from his grip.

When the warrior in crimson armour stumbled and fell, all of them came in and took a turn with the halberds, beating and shocking him into pain-wracked unconsciousness.

The dark–

The kills seemed faraway, dreamy and incoherent incidents that could have been the creation of a fevered mind. Rafen felt an icy cold upon his bare skin and it was with that shock that he strained open his rheumy eyes, forced a focus upon his hands. They floated before him, indistinct and grimed with muck and caked blood. His chest shocked him with razor-blade stabs each time he dared to take a breath, and he became aware of more and more sites of pain scattered across the map of him. There was wetness seeping through his garb of micropore weave, and with this understanding Rafen's sluggish thoughts at last caught up to his predicament.

His power armour was gone; he had been stripped without care or attention, as the torsion marks and cuts on his legs and arms attested. Clad only in a rough set of threadbare prison garments, Rafen was lying in a reeking metal cell, damp with patches of grey mould and orange rust. Cables as thick as his wrist disappeared away into the gloom, extending out from heavy iron collars about his neck, his forearms and ankles. The fetters were arranged so that he could not stand, could not move more than a few steps from where his captors had left him.

His captors…

With an effort, Rafen cleared the fog in his mind and tried to think back. He gathered in the pieces of the past few hours, sifted them for meaning and nuance. It came back to him in shards of recall. The agony of the shock-staves upon him, and the blessed embrace of nothingness. The sense of losing something... yes, the moment when they sullied the holy armour of his Chapter, tearing it from him, bearing it away. His gun and sword taken, his helm ripped from his head.

'The voice...' He spoke without thinking as another piece of memory resurfaced. In the moments before a fall into silence and darkness, he had seen something. A shimmering ghost made of light, a towering figure in a coat of screaming faces.

'Fabius...'

The traitor had been speaking in low tones, communicating with one of the bestial mutants that attacked him. Rafen struggled to gather back what he had heard, but his memory failed him, clouded by pain. All he remembered was the holograph of Bile, peering through the bars of his cage and smiling thinly, nodding to the mutant. Then speaking, the words lost to Rafen's ears, but the movements of his lips clear enough to read.

'Bring him to me.'

The Blood Angel nodded to himself, thinking back to the words that Ceris had said to him in the chapel aboard the *Tycho*. Was this some machination of the God-Emperor, he wondered? Did the Master of Mankind hold the skeins of Rafen's life so tightly that He himself had brought these events to pass? Every step along this path had been to bring Rafen face to face once more with the creature that called itself Fabius Bile – but now fate had torn him from his battle-brothers, ripped apart the careful plans he had drawn against this traitor, deposited him here. Alone and unarmed.

He closed his eyes and let himself seek the edges of a healing trance, drawing into himself. Through the roll and motion of the cell floor, he was certain the ship he was aboard travelled at high speed – doubtless back to Bile and his fortress, to the very place Rafen wanted to be.

The Blood Angel sat in silence and let his body repair itself, marshalling himself, making ready. If the Emperor brought him to this, then it was right and true; and if it were nothing more than capricious fate, then fate would be *damned*.

He was unarmed; but no Astartes was ever truly without a weapon as long as he could draw another breath.

He was alone; but no Astartes was ever truly alone, not with his battle-brothers and warrior kindred still there in the deeps, the mission still in their hearts.

In the darkness, he prayed silently for guidance.

THE DESULTORY LIGHT of the Dynikas star cast shafts through the fast-moving tier of cloud ranging over the curved archipelago, the wind hard and constant across the waves. The sand-seared shapes of the rocky island chain rose up from the turbulent, ruddy waters. Smoothed by the action of millions of years of typhoons, the outcrops of stone – rare atolls that were the very tips of colossal undersea mountains – resembled great growths of coral or fungus, sculpted into curves and even lines that belied organic forms where none actually existed. Like all else on Dynikas V, the island chains had been scoured clean of life by the tyranid splinters marooned on the planet. In this place, that had meant human life as well as native

flora and fauna. An agri-colony, built to farm the rich-
ness teeming in the Dynikan oceans, had been the
first to fall to the rapacious devourers. Buildings and
structures cut from the rock or assembled by Imperial
hands were made into ghost sites, every man, woman
and child taken and consumed by the hive.

This place, this monument to human ill-fate, was
where Fabius Bile had come to craft a bolt hole for
himself. Upon the empty ruins, on a world no sane
being would ever dare to visit, in a region dead and
forgotten to the galaxy at large, the twisted genetor
had built his fortress.

The patrol craft roared into the bay along the main
island's southern coast, engines dying with a howl as
the wave-surge brought the vessel in to the crumbling
ferrocrete docks. Derelict pilings hung at crooked
angles, the last remnants of a complex that had been
built for dozens of trawlers. Only one small section of
the dock was maintained; the rest had been forgotten
and allowed to fall into disrepair.

Chugging greasy smoke into the air from its
exhausts, a defiled Atlas recovery tank grumbled into
place, the crane extending from its rear spooling out
lines of heavy black chain. The vehicle had once served
the Imperial Guard in the Emperor's name; now it was
despoiled with the iconography of the Eightfold Path,
and stripped down to its iron frame. A snarling, hooting avian modificate capered on the prow of the
vehicle as its chains dropped through a hatch in the
trawler's deck. Sounds of violence issued out from
within, flashes of hard electric discharge following
them. The chains went taut and the crane pulled back.

* * *

DANGLING FROM HIS manacles, Rafen rose into the light. He struggled against the iron restraints, but he could find no purchase. Each move he made only sent him twisting, the chains cording around his limbs.

The mutant freaks on the boat snarled at those on the dock, the animal noises evidently some kind of language; in turn, the Atlas rolled away, and Rafen found himself dragged up over a crest of bone-white stone, swinging this way and that as the crane bounced in its mountings.

He struggled to twist into a position where he could observe, blinking away the purple after-images on his retina from the kiss of the trawler crew's shock-staves.

They passed a steep cliff angled away from him, rising to a sharp point. Etched into the rock was a blackened design that resembled a monstrous wing and a claw – the mark of the warriors of Fulgrim and Fabius Bile's former Legion, the Emperor's Children.

A low, thickset tower emerged first, rising up over the line of the island. Sheer, angled sides with few portals fell away from a ziggurat roof. He spotted what might have been communicator vanes up there, flexing in the constant winds, and other antennae that seemed alien in form and function, crystals at their tips glowing a sullen blue-white.

The tank rolled around a curving roadway, on one side leading down into a wide beach of shale and algae-slicked rocks. Stubby pillars emerged from the beach at regular intervals, stretching away in a line that vanished around the arc of the atoll. To the other side of the road was what at first glance resembled a vast impact crater; but as Rafen tugged on his chains to steady himself, he took a second look. Inside the crater on the far side he could see levels cut into the walls, one atop another, extending downward out of his sight, with balconies of skeletal metal impact-bonded to the stone.

Everywhere there were metal tubes growing out of the ground, sprouting like steel trees. Each of them ended in a sphere made of iron mesh, and from them came that foul stink of tyranid pheromones. The entire island was awash with it, a pall hanging over everything.

Rafen became aware of a siren honking somewhere down in the crater. He heard the sizzle of laser fire and the tank came to an abrupt, grinding halt. Seizing the moment, the Blood Angel gathered in handfuls of chain and moved, hand over hand, up towards the spool of the crane. He was close to the top when a figure swathed in ragged, hooded robes threw itself over the lip of the crater and sprinted across the roadway, making for the beach.

Rafen hesitated, expecting the mutants inside the Atlas's cab to take a shot at the runner; but they did nothing. He could not see any detail of the figure, only that it was humanoid and larger than a normal man. As large, he realised, as an Astartes.

The hooded escapee scrambled down the steep cliff and on to the shale. As his blackened, bare feet touched the beach, a new siren sounded. This was a four-tone clarion, a trumpet-call that brayed from the line of pillars. Rafen watched as the upper sections of the two closest columns cracked into quarters and slowly fanned open.

The runner slowed; Rafen had expected him to bolt for the water, but he did nothing of the kind. There was no fatigue about the robed man – only a strange air of resignation.

A voice crackled out from hidden vox relays. 'Don't be a fool.' Rafen's lip curled as he recognised Bile's silken, metered tones, and for a split-second he thought the words were directed at him; but they were for the running man. 'Turn back. Return, and this will be forgotten.'

With care, the figure dropped to his haunches and went down upon the stony beach. Rafen heard the grinding of gears, and to his dismay he watched a pair of sentry cannons extrude from the open tops of the pillars. The alarm clarion sounded again, each iteration quicker and quicker.

The man knelt on one knee, and the Blood Angel's breath caught in his throat as the robed figure bowed his head and crossed his hands over his chest. He heard the distinct murmur of a prayer; the Litany of the Aquila, the age-old entreaty to the God-Emperor for deliverance from evil. Rafen knew what would happen next. He cried out and struggled against his bindings, snapping one of the chains. The robed man did not react.

'So be it, then,' said the voice from the speakers. In the next moment the cannons tracked, locked and fired. A brief storm of energy shrieked across the beach and tore the runner – *the Astartes* – apart. A slick of bloody mist and glass-fused sand were all that was left behind.

Cursing, thrashing in his manacles, Rafen tried to break free; but then the Atlas started up and rolled on. The mutant crew, he realised, had known all along what would happen; they had paused because they wanted to watch.

Rafen felt as if he had been plunged into ice. To see a battle-brother perish on the field of conflict was one thing – and he was certain now that the one he saw die was without doubt a Space Marine of some stripe – but to witness one perish in so ignoble a fashion made him angry and heartsick in equal measure. He tried to comprehend what he had seen and could find no reason for it.

The Atlas swerved and spun to a halt upon a wind-scoured ferrocrete apron surrounded by fortress walls on three sides. The chains unlocked and he tumbled to the ground, landing poorly. Rafen pulled himself up as the vehicle rolled away, scanning the area.

Immediately he saw more of the strange bestial mutants gathered in guard posts and cupolas behind the barrels of autocannons and flame-throwers. But what caught his attention were the *others*. He could only see two of them, watching indolently from an arched gallery, but they were Astartes-tall and broad with it, men seemingly cut from planes of meat like those in a butcher's shop window. At first he wondered if they were Traitor Marines, but he dismissed the idea. They wore odd mixes of combat gear but they were not clad in the corrupted versions of power armour favoured by the legions of the archenemy. Despite the mark he had seen upon the cliff-face, he saw no recognisable turncoat sigils, only the eight-point star of the Ruinous Powers. If anything, the men reminded Rafen of Fabius himself, towering figures that radiated menace.

The sound of a rusted gate made him turn around. A saw-toothed portal opened and from it came a man in robes like those of the suicide. A hand, wiry of

muscle with skin like old leather, reached up to draw
back the hood. 'If you wish to die now, cousin, the
animals will accommodate you. Otherwise, I'd say
best not to make any sudden moves.'

Lank hair that would have been grey-white, if not
for the grime in it, framed an old, scarred face heavy
with a ragged beard. The grizzled newcomer had no
eyes; there was only a thickness of molten, waxy tissue
over the orbits in his skull. Sable lines of ink were visible on his sunken cheeks and the cords of his neck,
forming sharp-angled letters in a tongue Rafen could
not read. Still, the warrior knew the pattern of them
well enough to recognise the runes of the tribes of
Fenris. The old man showed teeth, yellowed fangs visible against his lips. 'Name your liege,' he demanded.

'You're a Son of Russ. A Space Wolf.' Rafen found it
hard to believe. A Space Marine, even an old, blind
veteran without weapons or armour, was the last
thing he had expected to see here.

'But you are not,' said the sightless warrior, with a
long sniff. 'I'd know it if you had any ice in your
veins. And you'd not have waited to try killing me. So
I ask again. Name your liege.'

Rafen saw little reason to make a secret of his lineage; had the Space Wolf eyes with which to see, the
winged teardrop design branded into the meat of his
shoulder would have told him the answer. 'I am a Son
of Sanguinius, of the IX Chapter Astartes.'

'Heh.' The veteran gave a mirthless grin. 'A Blood
Angel. Of course. I can smell how pretty you are from
here.'

Rafen took an angry step towards the Space Wolf.
'Don't mock me, old man. Perhaps I should do as you

say and kill you! For I cannot think of any reason why an Astartes would be here, in this fortress of the arch-enemy, unless he was a traitor!'

The smile dropped off the other man's face, and he bared his fangs. 'Whelp! You know nothing of me or this place!' He nodded bleakly. 'But you will. Oh yes, you'll know.' He beckoned him with a brusque gesture. 'Follow me, or don't. The splices will use you for gunnery practice if you stand still too long.'

Grudgingly, Rafen fell into step behind the Space Wolf, trailing him in through the entranceway. 'Splices…' he echoed. 'Those mutants?'

'It's what *he* calls them,' said the veteran, pausing to cough out a gobbet of phlegm. 'They were common men once, until Bile decided he could gain something from their torment.'

'Fabius Bile. Where is he?' said Rafen.

'Pray you never have the misfortune to find out,' came the warning. The gate closed slowly behind them until the tunnel they walked through was in pitch-blackness. Rafen's occulobe implant contracted to give him a muddy cast of vision, but the blind Space Wolf walked with surety, as if his sight were perfect.

The Blood Angel frowned and stopped. The other warrior kept walking. 'I am a prisoner of a Chaos renegade,' said Rafen. 'What does that make you?'

'The same. But much longer in the tooth. Much, much longer.'

'Is that why you're his servant, then? Fetching me for him like an obedient dog? Did he break you?'

'You know nothing, boy.' The old man halted.

'I know that men say the Sons of Russ are indomitable, fighters of endless courage and stone will. Yet I look at you and the lie is put to those words!'

The Space Wolf gave a savage growl and spun to face him, his hands coming up in claws; but he hesitated, and his arms fell to his sides. Even in the gloom, Rafen could see the expression on his face. Not anger, but something else… resignation. 'There is no escape from this place,' said the veteran. 'No way out, save the one you witnessed.' He nodded in the direction of the doorway. 'Ask yourself why one of us would willingly take death instead of life in this place. Ask that and think on the answer, Blood Angel.'

'There are more Astartes here? From other Chapters?'

'*Ja*. And all of them thought as you do now.' The old man sighed and came closer, his voice falling low. 'I have had this conversation with new arrivals many times, and it is always the same. They ask why I am here. They ask why I do not resist.'

'We are Astartes,' Rafen snapped, his ire building slow and cold. 'We never capitulate. We were made for challenge!'

'What is your name, Blood Angel?'

'Rafen, son of Axan. Sergeant.'

'I am Nurhünn Vetcha, Long Fang. Do you know my name?'

He shook his head. 'I do not.'

'That is because I am dead, like every cousin and kinsman here. We resist, Rafen, as well as we can. We resist by staying alive as long as possible, by making every breath we take an act of defiance!'

'How many of those mutant freaks can there be?' Rafen demanded. 'Are you all without hope? Has no man ever drawn enough courage to take this place and raze it?'

'Many have tried.'

'They tried and failed?'

'They tried and *died*,' Vetcha said firmly. He turned a stoic face to the Blood Angel. 'I resist by believing, boy. Each day I ask Russ and the Emperor to witness what happens in this place and give me the strength to endure it. I do this because I know one day I will have my opportunity!' A stir of fury laced the old man's words. 'I wait, Rafen. I wait for the day. For the moment I know is coming. Even a knife made of lead is sharp enough for a single cut.'

'And in the meantime, Fabius Bile lives on and continues his crimes against the galaxy.' Rafen shook his head.

The Space Wolf walked away. 'When you have been here as long as I have, Blood Angel, you will understand. Now, come. They flush this channel with promethium to kill any rippers that may make it past the pheromone shield. You would not wish to be here when that happens.'

AT THE FAR end of the dark tunnel, another set of gates retracted into the ground and Rafen hissed as needles of pain lanced his dark-adapted eyes. Blinking quickly, he found himself standing on the lip of a spiral stone ramp that descended into the vast pit he had glimpsed from the Atlas. What he had thought were distinct levels were in fact all part of one single inclined slope that wound around and around the inside of the crater, descending towards an oval enclosure far below. Hundreds of uniform cargo containers lay in rows along the slope, the standard rectangular boxes of iron like those used on thousands of starships. They were fixed in place with fat gobs of hardened ferrocrete, reinforced with sheets of steel that looked like they had been cut from trawler hulls. Strings of lumes hung over the spaces between the walls and the containers, dark now but placed so they would throw illumination in every corner when the sun set. Abhorrent scrawls of blasphemous text decorated the stone bulwarks, and small altars protruded from the sides of the stockade at regular intervals; the little platforms were soaked in blood so thickly caked it was as black as ink, and grotesque swarms of flies hummed in the air. Rafen looked away, disgusted.

More of the mutants – the 'splices' – ambled back and forth over the tops of the containers, all of them armed with electromag weapons. Rafen saw beings that were closer to apes than men, others that had bovine or serpent-like attributes. It chilled him to think that these devolved horrors might once have been innocent men.

'This way,' said Vetcha.

Rafen followed him warily, conscious of the heavy shapes of bat-like things that circled through the air below the lip of the crater, riding on thermal updrafts. He couldn't see them clearly enough to determine if they were mechanical constructs or more splices; but he could see the shapes of heavy lascannons dangling from their claws. He glanced up at the sheer walls of the crater, gauging distances and looking for handholds. There was no cover and the odds were poor; he had no doubt the bats were some kind of sentinel, constantly circling, waiting for someone to make an attempt to flee. Here and there he saw blackened pockmarks on the stone where rock had been turned to obsidian from a beam strike.

The Blood Angel weighed his chances for escape, considering. Was it worth it? He estimated he had a fair probability of making it to the crater lip up above, but even if he did, where could he go? The sentry guns ringed the island, and beyond them lay an ocean full of tyranid bioforms. In this place, so it seemed, freedom was a death sentence.

And then there was the mission. Fabius Bile was here, and working his horrors. The sacred blood he had stolen could not be far from the renegade's hand. Rafen thought on Vetcha's words in the tunnel, considering them against his own circumstances. For now, so it seemed, the Blood Angel would follow along, eyes open and ready; he had to trust that Noxx and the others aboard the *Neimos* were still on their way. When they came, he would need to know as much as possible about this place.

'Where are we going?' he asked.

'Cheyne has summoned you,' said the Space Wolf. 'Bile's second-in-command.'

Rafen gestured at a hissing snake-man that glowered down at him from an overhead gantry. 'One of these freaks?'

Vetcha shook his head. 'No. Cheyne is something worse.'

The Blood Angel had another question, but he forgot it as he passed in front of a heavy hatch leading into one of the cargo containers. A diamond window cut into the door showed the scene within; Rafen recognised the yellowish cast of armourglass. The material was technology from the Dark Ages, harder than steel, clear from the obverse side but opaque from the reverse. A dozen strikes from bolt shells would be needed to shatter it.

Beyond the glass, he saw an Astartes bent in prayer on the floor of a dingy cell. The warrior did not seem to be aware of him, instead lost in the depth of his meditation. The other man's ebon skin was dull with a sheen of sweat.

Rafen took a step towards the cell and the serpent-splice skittered forward, raising its weapon. The warrior felt a tug on his arm, and turned to find Vetcha holding him back. 'Don't give them an excuse,' said the Space Wolf in a low voice.

'In there...' he said. 'A brother of the Salamanders Chapter?'

Vetcha nodded and pointed to another container some distance away. 'Raven Guard.' He pointed to another, and another. 'Tauran. Tiger Argent. And more.'

'How many?' Rafen snapped.

The veteran gestured towards another hatch set in the wall, and it creaked open on automatic pistons. 'There are deaths all the time,' said Vetcha. 'The count... is low.'

THE BLOOD ANGEL crossed the threshold and into darkness again. Before he could adjust his vision once more, the hatch slammed shut behind him and locked, separating him from the Space Wolf.

Rafen banged on the metal. 'Vetcha! Vetcha, what is this?'

Then he heard the sound of a breath, and a grim, humourless snort. 'Don't make a friend of him, cousin. He's the worst of them all.'

At the far end of the container, he defined a figure sitting against the wall; another Astartes, stocky but slump-shouldered. 'Rafen, of the Blood Angels,' he offered.

The other man shot him a doleful look. He was dusky-skinned and drawn. 'Tarikus. Doom Eagles. Not that those names have any meaning in this place.' Misery laced every word.

'How long have you been here?' Rafen asked, coming closer.

'I think three years. Perhaps five. The passage of time here is difficult to reckon.'

'Five years?' The Blood Angel was shocked.

Tarikus looked away. 'Others have been here longer. Vetcha claims he has been a prisoner for more than a decade, but I give no credence to anything he says.'

Rafen shook his head. 'Impossible. These brothers... if they were all missing, it would have been noted. Your Chapters would come looking...'

The Doom Eagle looked back, and this time with cold anger. 'Do they remember us, cousin?' He scrambled to his feet, suddenly animated, stabbing his finger at the ceiling, pointing towards the sky. 'Do they remember? *No*! Because we are all dead!'

Rafen stood his ground. 'I do not understand. Why would that accursed traitor do this? Why gather battle-brothers as if they were tokens in a game of regicide?'

'Now you are dead too.' Tarikus ignored his question, turning his back, stalking into the deep shadows. 'You have fallen into this light-forsaken hell with the rest of us.'

Rafen frowned. Tarikus's Chapter were known for their dour and melancholy outlook on the universe, but even that ingrained character was beyond what he showed now. The man seemed drawn and haggard in a way that no battle could have wearied him. 'What is Bile doing here?' Rafen insisted. 'You, Vetcha, all the other Astartes… What does he want with you?'

'To do what he does best,' grated the other man, reaching up to scratch at his shoulder. 'To bring pain.' Rafen glimpsed a livid, deep burn on the warrior's chest, wet with fluids. 'We are his playthings. The raw fodder for his *experiments*.' He spat the last word with venom.

'Tarikus, I must know,' he said. 'Cousin, help me.' Rafen offered his hand. 'If we are to share this cell–'

Tarikus snorted. 'This isn't a cell, Blood Angel.'

There was a grinding noise from beneath their feet, and suddenly the floor fell away and they were tumbling into blackness.

HE SNAPPED BACK to awareness at the sound of the Doom Eagle screaming. Rafen tried to push forward, but gravity itself was turned against him. He lay sprawled against a canted platform, the humming murmur of a g-field generator whirring behind him.

The Blood Angel blinked to clear his vision. He saw a space that was half cavern, half abattoir, lines of blood-slick chains hanging from a curved ceiling, tiles across the floor slick with jets of water sluicing remains down into drain gutters. He turned his head with effort and found Tarikus on another platform, three figures crowded around him. Two of them he knew – the strange hulking men that he had spotted as he arrived. The third was of the same mass and build, but oddly proportioned. It turned to him and he felt confusion.

The face that looked at him was strangely beautiful, almost womanly, but with a cruelly masculine cast that could not be fully hidden. The androgyne moved its hand away from Tarikus's chest, over the place where Rafen had glimpsed the bloody burn. A horrible thought occurred to him; the Doom Eagle's wound had been *self-inflicted*.

He blinked, unsure of the flash of something maggot-white he saw vanishing beneath Tarikus's flesh. The other Astartes screamed again and tried to move, but like Rafen he too was pressed fast against a gravity frame, the power of a hundred times Terra-standard g-forces holding him like a butterfly pinned to a board.

The androgyne came towards him, and it smiled. 'I am Cheyne,' it told him. Its voice was high and musical, incongruous from such a towering figure. 'I welcome you.'

Another of the figures returned from a shadow cradling a squealing, doughy mass in his hands. The size of his fist, the thing resembled a mutant larva, one end a mouth of questing cilia ringed with black eye-spots, the undulating body wet with clear slime.

Cheyne flicked its wrist and a wide push-dagger emerged from a slide holster. 'This gift,' it said, 'this is for all our guests.' The androgyne glanced at Tarikus. 'You may think you can divest yourself of it. You are mistaken.'

Rafen pressed with all of his might, struggling to push away. Cheyne seemed amused by the strain upon his face, and ripped open the Space Marine's undershirt, enough to reveal the flesh of his breast. It drew a curved blade and spun it about playfully.

'Welcome,' Cheyne repeated, and slashed a deep cut down the Blood Angel's chest. Before he could react to the shock of pain, the other hulking man rammed the maggot's head into the new wound and let it wriggle into the incision.

Rafen felt the thing burrowing into his flesh and cried out, echoing the Doom Eagle before him.

TEN

SWEAT DRENCHED RAFEN's body and he reached up, pushing matted, slick threads of hair away from his face. The inside of his cell reeked with perspiration and stale seawater. Outside, night had fallen and the constant, chilling winds were howling around the prison complex, but in here, the air was thick and heavy from Rafen's exhalations.

In the gloom, he gingerly probed the great scab across the wound on his chest where the maggot-thing had dug deep; the shock of pain that hit back at him struck the breath from his lungs and made him dizzy. It was a searing agony, but it was an improvement. After Cheyne's thugs had thrown him into this iron box, he had tried to dig the parasite out, finding bundles of milk-white threads already worming into his chest and towards his primary heart. He pulled at them and then remembered nothing. So great was the pain that came in the wake of that action, it hammered him into a daze.

The thing moved beneath his skin and the feel of it made the Blood Angel retch. This violation sickened him beyond words, and all he wanted was a blade, even a dull sliver of metal, something, *anything* to cut it from him.

Panting, he took in a shuddering breath. He wanted to believe that the powerful Larraman cells coursing through his bloodstream from his bio-implants would reject the parasitic organism, but he did not expect the agents of Fabius Bile to be so easily thwarted by such a well-documented factor of Astartes physiology. Bile had been an Apothecary of high rank to the Emperor's Children in the age of the Great Crusade, long before the heresy of the arch-traitor Horus; what he knew of the intricacies of the gene stock of Space Marines could doubtless fill libraries.

Rafen felt cold, even in this heat. His captors had given him shapeless, rough-hewn robes, and now he gathered them in. The warrior had stripped lines of cloth from them to fashion bindings for his feet and hands. The hooded mantle smelled of other men's deaths.

A sound reached him. A tapping, metal upon metal, issuing out from the plasteel mesh bonded over the vent channel in the corner of the cell that served as a waste channel. Rafen slid closer to it, his nose wrinkling at the stink, and listened. After a few moments he recognised the pattern of the noise. A regular series of short and long reports, like the ancient Orsköde battle language. Some Chapters still used the cipher, and it was known to him. He tapped out a return, and presently a low voice threaded out to him.

'Still alive, Blood Angel?' Rafen had to strain his ears to capture the whispered words beneath the sombre howl of the winds outside.

'Tarikus?' He hadn't seen the Doom Eagle after Cheyne's warriors had dragged him away into the darkness. 'Where are you?'

'A few cells down. The waste feeds drain into a common channel. Too small for anything larger than a rodent, but enough to carry a voice.'

Rafen settled to the floor, resting against the wall. He felt as if the parasite was sapping all his energy. It seemed an effort just to stand on two feet. 'No prison can hold an Astartes…' he said, with more bravado than he felt.

Tarikus was silent for a moment. 'And now you will ask me how I plan to escape, is that it?' The Doom Eagle snorted. 'Does Bile think that because we shared a little pain, we can now be confidantes?'

'I do not doubt that there is a machination to every deed done by that traitor scum. Everything I have seen since I came to this island has likely been some kind of lesson for me.' He winced as the maggot shifted in his breast.

'I won't trust you!' Tarikus snapped, the sentiment coming out of nowhere. 'Kelleth escapes and perishes on the rocks, and you arrive to take his place only moments later? Does Bile think us all fools?'

'Kelleth…' Rafen weighed the name. 'He was the one who died under the sentry guns?'

'A battle-brother of the Stone Hearts,' came the reply. 'Shattered now.'

'I am no spy.' Rafen bristled at the insult. 'Believe me, Doom Eagle, there is no man in this blighted place who wishes that bastard Fabius dead more than I!'

The other Astartes fell silent again, and after a while Rafen began to think that Tarikus had no more to say; but then he spoke again. 'How did they take you?'

Rafen hesitated. Fabius had to be listening to every word they said. He was a thorough and calculating man, and even though this makeshift prison was built from salvage and ruins, the Blood Angel did not question that the so-called Primogenitor would have wired it with scrying tools and monitors of every kind. Then there was the chance, a notion so loathsome that he hated to even consider it, that there *was* an insider secreted in the prisoner populace – and worse still, that the turncoat could be Tarikus. He sighed; he had been here less than a day and already the place was bleeding the trust from him.

He picked his next words with care. 'I was aboard a ship of the Adeptus Mechanicus. I had infiltrated it by stealth… I knew the vessel's master had dealings with Bile, but I did not reckon on his folly. The ship was destroyed attempting to attack the planet. I escaped in a saviour pod, and the splices dragged me from the ocean.'

'You came here deliberately?' Tarikus asked.

Rafen nodded. 'For my sins. And you?'

'I was captured in the void. A medicae cutter was taking me back to my Chapter's throne world,

Gathis... I had been injured fighting the Necrontyr. The ship was snared and obliterated.'

The Blood Angel thought about the Doom Eagle's earlier words. 'Your Chapter believe that you were lost with the cutter.'

'Aye.' Tarikus sighed. 'Every man here has a story of a similar stripe. Bile's agents picked us off: the injured, the lost, the isolated. Brought us here, and made certain that no one knew of it. We are the vanished, Rafen. The forgotten. The dead still awaiting death.'

The maggot moved again, and Rafen hissed in pain. 'Rot this thing! Is it some slow murder, this parasite?'

'No.' Tarikus seemed weary as he explained. 'Kelleth believed they are a kind of xenos, or perhaps even a minor phylum of warp-creature. Bile and his New Men use them to regulate us. There is no greater fetter than the one that lives within a man's flesh.'

'New Men...' Rafen echoed the term. 'I have heard that name before.'

'Cheyne and the others,' said the Doom Eagle. 'The results of more of Bile's unbound experimentation on human beings. Imagine the inverse of the noble ideals that created we Astartes. Bile's monstrosities are psychotics with prowess and strength that rival ours. But they are our antithesis, gene-adapted killers without souls, without conscience or morality...' Tarikus paused again. 'You asked a question in the chamber, do you remember? You asked what the renegade is doing here.'

Rafen crouched down, speaking in muted tones. 'You know the answer?'

'I have an idea,' came the reply. 'You must have seen the tower, up above the ridge. Inside that building there are... chambers. Places of such horror and pain.' Tarikus's voice took on a dire timbre. 'Some of us taken from the cells never return. Others are tortured for days at a time and are brought back as shadows of their former selves. As warnings to the rest of us.' He took a slow breath. 'Imagine a gifted child studying the complex weave of a tapestry. He wants to both know it and destroy it. He takes it apart, thread by thread. This is Bile's game with us, Blood Angel. He dismantles men as if they were puzzles made for his amusement.'

Rafen's hands tightened into fists. 'If he is there, then I will find my way to him. We have unfinished business.'

'Pray that you do not,' Tarikus retorted. 'Slow death and debasement are all that await you.'

Rafen glanced at his dirt-streaked fingers, thinking of the crystal vial. 'I have no choice,' he whispered.

The other Space Marine continued, voicing his thoughts. 'We are kept isolated from one another. Months can pass and we never see the face of another Astartes. Bile knows that keeping us apart prevents us from plotting... But I think he may allow us to talk just so he can mock us from his aerie.' He sighed. 'No man has ever escaped from this place.'

'I do not seek escape–' began the Blood Angel; but then, in the distance, Rafen heard an abrupt rattle of bone on metal. It was coming closer.

'The guardians approach,' hissed Tarikus. 'If they catch us speaking to one another, they will flood our cells with rot-bane and scour our lungs.' The chemical gas was potent and could kill a Space Marine in large enough doses.

The Doom Eagle spoke quickly, suddenly intense. 'Listen to me, Blood Angel. You must not sleep! Do not allow yourself to dream! They peer into your mind and forge nightmares... Bile has servants cursed by witch-sight. They exert their will upon us as we rest. Do not dream!' Tarikus's voice began to fade. 'And the food... Cheyne laces it with potent, insidious drugs that soften the will! Find protein elsewhere... The lichen on the iron walls. Some even take the meat of a servitor if desperation comes–'

The sound of clawed footsteps clattering over the tops of the cells echoed loudly, and Tarikus said no more. Moving quickly, Rafen slid across to the flat panel of a sleeping pallet that was the chamber's only furniture. He drew himself upon it as capering shadows moved past the armourglass window, dwelling for a moment to glare at him before moving on. He could make out only shadows.

Then there was only the howl of the wind, rattling loose rivets in the walls and pushing scours of gritty sand through the passages of the gaol. With effort, Rafen worked to push his thoughts away from the burning, unremitting pain in his breast and tried to find a moment of focus; but he could not.

His mind remained clouded with a churn of emotions, at once eager to find his prey, but sickened by what he had experienced and tormented by the hollow eyes of the others imprisoned with him.

THEY GATHERED IN the makeshift arming chamber, the hull of the *Neimos* creaking gently as it knifed through the waters of the sea. They all went unhooded, but only Eigen was without the rest of his wargear; the injured Flesh Tearer was stripped to the waist, his torso wrapped in diagonal bands of bio-active bandages. An auto-doser clung to his bare right arm like a fat brass tick, slowly administering supplemental anti-venoms to counteract the effect of toxins left in his system by the talons of the tyranid kraken. He sat upon an ammunition crate, his gaze scanning the rest of the Astartes.

'This has not become a democracy,' Brother-Sergeant Noxx was saying, addressing the psyker Ceris. 'We are not a petty council of civilians arguing over every tiny decision. This is an order. I am in command, and so will it be.'

Ceris's face was set in a grimace. 'I respectfully offer an alternative.'

The cleric-medic Gast shook his head. 'Did you do so when Rafen was commander of this mission? I saw no questioning of orders when a Blood Angel called the shots. Now it is a Flesh Tearer at our lead, you are unhappy?'

Ceris shot Gast a hard look. 'Just because you did not see me sound out Sergeant Rafen does not mean I did not challenge him.' He looked away. 'This mission is too important to be prosecuted with high emotion. Choices must be made with cold logic, or else we will fail.'

On the other side of the room, Ajir gave a sullen nod. 'If I have learned anything about my witch-kin brother, it is that Ceris would say these things even if the Lord Sanguinius himself were to command us.'

'I don't doubt it,' said Noxx. 'And I welcome your input.' He said it in a way that seemed casual, and yet a threat all at the same time. 'But I choose not to listen.'

Puluo, the burly, taciturn warrior with the heavy bolter across his back, spoke for the first time since they had gathered. 'You are certain he is dead?'

None of them spoke for a long moment. Then Ceris let out a slow breath. 'Certain... is not the word I would use. The ways of the warp do not often lend themselves to certainties. It is the nature of the immaterial realm to forever be in flux.'

'Then what *are* you certain of, psyker?' demanded Kayne. The younger Space Marine came forward in two angry steps, ignoring Turcio as the other Blood Angel reached out a hand to stop him. 'Tell us!'

Ceris met Kayne's fuming glare. 'I sense no hint of Brother-Sergeant Rafen's mind-trace. In the wake of the kraken's attack, there was pain and anguish from the animal, and there was confusion after the destruction of Zellik's psi-gem... When the mists cleared and I had a moment to focus, I could not sense him. Rafen may be outside the range of my awareness, or he may...' Ceris paused. 'The oceans may have taken him to the deeps.' He gestured at the air. 'I have tried to spread my senses thinner, wider, but beyond there is only a telepathic thicket. The closer we get to the fortress, the more clouded the warp becomes.'

'Bile's island is protected from the tyranids by more than material means,' said Turcio darkly.

'Nothing new is brought to this,' said Noxx, his irritation showing through. 'We talk in circles.'

Ceris shook his head. 'You must listen to me, sir. Our options close to us. We must contact the *Tycho* and the *Gabriel* and advance the kill order. Dynikas V must die. There is no other way open to us now. We cannot risk failure.'

Eigen felt a surge of annoyance. 'I can still fight! Sove can do the same, if we wake him from his healing trance!'

Gast frowned, uncomfortable at the suggestion. 'Possibly…'

'Brother Ceris is not talking about numbers of warriors,' said Puluo. 'He's talking about the mission being compromised.'

'Explain!' snapped Kayne.

After the Astartes had driven off the kraken, the *Neimos* had ventured into a network of canyons along the seabed, masking the submersible's course at the cost of speed and time; a tactic made necessary by the movement of surface vessels in the area. 'There's a chance Rafen could have been captured. A slim one. But still a possibility we should not ignore.'

Kayne's expression tightened. 'Brother, do you suggest that the sergeant would be broken so quickly by Bile and his men? You think he would spill his guts to them?' The Space Marine's lip curled. 'He would die first!'

'This is Fabius Bile we speak of,' ventured Gast. 'The master of a million horrors and a high champion of Chaos. We cannot know what dire methods he has at his fingertips.'

'Our target may know we are coming,' said Ceris.

Noxx folded his arms. 'Bile defiled a holy relic of all Sons of Sanguinius and fled Baal after killing our kinsmen. *Of course* he knows we are coming! Such a crime could never go unanswered. But what if he does? What if he drained Rafen dry of all he knows? It does not matter. Our mission does not change. We must find Bile and kill him, to the cost of all our lives if the need is such. Sergeant Rafen gave that order. I still hold to it.'

'I do not disagree,' said the psyker, 'I only question the means. If this planet is bombarded with cyclonic torpedoes, nothing will survive.'

'Including us,' said Ajir. 'So we perish either way. But if we succeed in a ground strike, then the crews of those two ships will not need to follow us to hell.'

Eigen nodded. If the *Gabriel* and the *Tycho* closed to deliver their lethal payloads, both vessels would be ripped apart by the orbital gunskull flotillas and the multiple remote guns dotted across the other island chains. 'And if we do not, they will bombard the planet anyway.'

Ceris looked in his direction. 'By then it may be too late. Every moment we delay, we give Bile the chance to prepare an escape. A hidden ship, perhaps, or a warp-gate like the one he used to flee the Vitalis Citadel. We all know the enemy will flee if the chance is given to him. He does not have the stomach for a toe-to-toe fight.'

Noxx walked to the centre of the bay. 'The coward thief who stole the sacred blood must die, he *will* die. But this cannot be a sanction taken from three hundred kilometres up, with the push of a button from the far end of a torpedo launcher!' He raised his gauntlet and slowly clenched the fingers. 'We send in the ships and that will be warning enough for the whoreson.

No, the enemy must be seen to be killed by one of us. The vial recovered or denied to the foe. We must do this. Our honour demands no less.' He looked at all of them in turn, his cold eyes boring deep. 'If we do not do this, then everything we have gone through, the defeats and the setbacks, the oaths we swore, the brothers we have lost, the warriors crippled and killed along the way... all of it means *nothing!*'

'And honour is more important than life.' Ceris pitched his words evenly.

'Are you making a statement, brother?' asked Turcio. 'Or is it a question that you ask us?

'The order has been given.' Ceris did not look at him, resignation in his tone. 'Does it matter?'

Noxx turned away, the expression on his face making it clear that the conversation was at an end. He glanced at Kayne. 'How far now?'

'A day, no more,' said the Blood Angel. 'Our course through the undersea trenches will bring us out close to the location of the enemy's island fortress. With the blessing of the Emperor and Sanguinius, we will be able to bring the *Neimos* in upon them before any perimeter defences are triggered.'

The Flesh Tearer's head bobbed. 'Then, kinsmen, I suggest we all employ the time remaining to us wisely. Prepare your wargear and yourselves. Look to the rites of battle. Be ready.'

Gast's eyes narrowed. 'And Sove? You want him able to fight? He still needs to heal, lord.'

'I know,' said Noxx. 'But we are close to the end of this now, and if I allowed him to sleep through it, he would curse me from here to the Eye of Terror. We need every man, every sword and gun.'

'*Ave Imperator,*' intoned Puluo.

The rest of the squad repeated the words; Ceris was the last to speak.

THE WORDS OF Tarikus fresh in his mind, Rafen let the catalepsean node implanted in his brain tissue allow him to skate along the borderline between sleep and wakefulness; the effect was strange, but known to him. Time seemed to pass at accelerated rates, hours compacting into moments. Cast through what seemed to be a bullet hole in the high roof of his cell, a shaft of cold moonlight advanced doggedly across the metal floor of the cramped compartment, and the Blood Angel watched it. Behind the moon that reflected that light, hidden from detection, were the strike cruisers of his Chapter and their Flesh Tearer allies. In less than twenty solar minutes they could move from concealment and attack this place from high orbit. He wondered if that would be his fate now, to hear the whistling screams of falling warheads and be consumed in a fusion inferno.

Rafen shrugged off the gloomy thought, momentarily cursing the Doom Eagle as if Tarikus's morose mien had somehow crossed over to him. The burning pain of the parasite had fallen to a dull background ache now, the throbbing of the maggot-thing's heartbeat a rattle against the cage of his ribs. He vowed that he would tear it from his own flesh with knife, laser or flamer if that was what it took.

The shaft of moonlight faded away as the cold ebbed from the metal walls and the first weak glow of dawn began to appear. With care, Rafen took himself through the series of mental cues and disciplines that lulled the catalepsean node back into its dormant state, and retuned his brain activity to normal. At its full function, the node implant allowed an Astartes to eschew normal sleep; the organ could partition a human brain in quadrants, resting some elements of the grey matter while others remained active. He felt his body return from the torpor of the not-quite-sleep; the sensation was like rising up through water to the surface, and he gave an involuntary grimace as he recalled his ordeal in the ocean.

Rafen got to his feet and crossed to the centre of the cell. He paused there, breathing silently, listening.

After he had been thrown into this cage and sealed within, the Blood Angel had spent several hours scouring every fraction of its surface; it had been a good way to occupy his mind and ignore the pain of the parasite. Rafen examined every shadowed corner, each weld and rivet joint, each patch of rust and cor-roded bolt-head, learning the exact dimensions of his confinement and probing it for weaknesses. But the outward appearance of the construction belied a deeper truth. The cells here in the pit were built from cargo pods that were space-hardened, canisters designed to be able to survive the destruction of any carrier vessel, and the extremes of heat and cold in the deep void. The oxide-red slashes of corrosion were only surface blemishes, enough to fool the eye at first glance, perhaps even lull the hasty into false hopes. Rafen wondered if such a thing were deliberately engineered on the part of Fabius Bile. Had he chosen to make these cells seem ramshackle and ill-fit for purpose, just to make the brothers incarcerated inside waste their energy and effort on fruitless escape attempts? The Blood Angel imagined the prison complex like some vast game board and the prisoners within it pieces in play for Bile's twisted amusement.

He heard movement. Iron feet, thudding along the stone ramp. Pausing. The hiss of pressure and fluid gurgles. Rafen smiled to himself and moved towards the hatchway.

Set into the metallic wall at waist height was a short length of iron pipe. A crust of stale matter caked the open end, and below it there was a discoloured patch on the floor. It was a feed channel, little different from those used to introduce nutrient gruel into stables for grox or equines. Rafen remembered Tarikus's warning about the drug-laced victuals provided by the splices; but he didn't intend to partake.

During his rest in the cradle of node-sleep, Rafen had also set another of his bio-implants working. The Betcher glands in his mouth were slightly swollen with venom; like the poison sacs of some reptiles, the glands could secrete a toxic fluid that would work like acid. The process of the glands was not a swift one, but in the right circumstances the acid could be spat into the face of an enemy at close quarters or disgorged on to restraints to burn through metal. The implant's use was not common in his Chapter – there was a perception among his battle-brothers that to deploy it in single combat was somehow beneath them – but it had its uses in the right circumstances.

Rafen knew he had to use the glands now; his body's reserves would quickly be spent trying to reject the parasite maggot, and he would not be able to fill them again. The toxin would not be effective upon the locking mechanism of the hatch or the armourglass – but it could loosen the fitting of the pipe through the wall. The Blood Angel retched and spat upon the welded joint, and was rewarded by a sizzle of melting metal.

The clanking steps were coming closer. He estimated that it was a single servitor unit toting a heavy drum of gruel, with three splices guarding it. Wisps of acrid smoke rose from the pipe joint and Rafen tested it. The tube rattled and shifted; this would work.

Shadows passed in front of the hatch, and there was the hiss of a pressure hose connecting to the other end of the feed tube outside the cell. Immediately, thick coils of a grey and stale-smelling paste oozed out, spattering on the floor. The implication was that the prisoner should debase themselves and eat like an animal, denied even the most simple dignity.

Rafen gripped the tube with both hands and gave it a savage jerk, twisting it towards him. The pipe resisted, then gave. Outside he heard a clatter of confusion and guttural howls. The Blood Angel tensed, and shoved the pipe hard, forcing the length of it back through the weld-joint. It slowed as it punctured something doughy, and he twisted it again. The flow of paste coughed and choked, quickly replaced by spurts of blood and machine oil. Satisfied. Rafen dragged on the tube and pulled it back into the cell, this time all the way. The last half-metre of the pipe was livid with gore where it had punched into meat and bone.

The hatch was unlocking. Rafen spun the tube around like a fighting staff and stamped the far end flat, forcing the tip into a makeshift blade edge. The doorway rotated up and away, and through the entrance came three splices; a canine, a horned mino-tal and an ape-like simian. Each had a crackling electro-scythe, and they raised them in attack.

Rafen gave them no time to take the offensive. Holding the far end of the pipe, he spun it up from the ground and used the sharpened end to slash a deep wound across the face of the simian. The splice shrieked as it lost an eye, clapping hands to its face as blood gouted.

The bull-like minotal bellowed and came at him at a rush, lowering its head to present a set of gnarled horns. He was actually disappointed; such a tactic was an obvious one, and hardly a challenge for the Space Marine. Ducking low, he swept the pipe about and slammed it into the second splice's gut. The tube buckled and broke with the force of the impact, throwing the minotal off its feet and into a crumpled, panting heap.

Rafen discarded what was left of his improvised weapon, dodged a humming scythe-swipe from his periphery and lurched forward, stamping on the bull-man's throat with his heel so it would not rise again. He contemplated falling into a drop in order to gather up the minotal's weapon, but he felt strange, light-headed. The parasite was putting him off his stride, trying to slow him by injecting fatigue poisons into his bloodstream. He shook it off and met the last of the three, the canine, as it barked and snapped at him. The dog-thing was almost as big as an Astartes, and it had a wolf's jaws filled with dagger teeth. It roared and connected with its weapon.

The Blood Angel snarled in pain as a massive surge of voltage rippled through his torso, and he felt the parasite keen in response. The canine opened its mouth wide, coming in to bite out a hank of flesh from his shoulder. Rafen pivoted, thrusting out his hands, and his fingertips caught the beast's jaws, holding them open. Using the splice's own momentum against it, he pivoted and ripped the creature's head open. Flesh parted with a jagged tearing sound, blood fountaining.

By the time the simian had recovered enough to try an attack, Rafen had an electro-weapon in each hand. He parried high and closed the distance, shoving the ape-man back out through the cell door and on to the stone pathway outside. Nearby lay the cooling corpse of a servitor, in a puddle of blood and paste.

No sooner were the two combatants out than laser fire sparked around them, lancing down from overhead. Rafen was aware of one of the bat-like sentinels circling, and with a hard flick of his wrist he threw one of the curved scythe blades, striking it in the chest. Without losing a second, he spun on the simian and punched it to death with flurry of brutal blows to the head.

The creature dropped to the dirt and Rafen stood there, wet with gore and winded. He was unusually short of breath; the parasite again. He would have to compensate for the drag it was placing on his performance – against common thugs like the splices he would still have the advantage even if he fought blindfold, but there were larger threats here. Rafen looked around and got his bearings; the whole complex seemed oddly silent. There were no sirens, no cries of alarm. Only the steady moan of the winds.

He sought and found the top of the tower, the place Tarikus had seemed so fearful of, just visible over the lip of the crater. He nodded to himself. That was his target. The Blood Angel broke into a sprint, weaving through shadows as he went.

A REAL FOE stood waiting for him at the rise of the slope, just in front of a heavy iron portcullis guarding a tunnel into the hillside. The figure shrugged off a robe of dun-coloured material and kicked it away. Beneath, there was nothing that could be considered clothing as such; instead, the enemy was wrapped in what appeared to be a single long strip of black leather that looped around and around sinuous limbs and a lithe, wiry torso that seemed almost eldar in form. Belts of chain mail and pins made from red steel held the costume together. Webbing hung with small pistols and razor-edged fans dangled across the figure's chest.

'Cheyne.' Rafen slowed and approached carefully. 'Your prison cannot hold me.'

The androgynous warrior laughed. 'Your kind are so predictable, Astartes. You all say the same things, and come to regret them. Tell me, is there a special schola during your training that teaches you how to parse such utterances?' The sexless figure cocked its head. 'Do your mentors teach you all the ways to sound pompous and portentous?'

'It's a gift,' Rafen replied, with a sneer. 'And it seems I have tired of your voice as quickly as you tire of mine.'

'Oh, good,' said Cheyne. 'Less talk, then. More fight.' The androgyne spun in a pirouette and discarded the weapons vest, presenting Rafen with the palms of its hands. It nodded at him. 'No weapons. Just for the sport of it.'

The Blood Angel's eyes narrowed. In the centre of Cheyne's hands there were vertical slits like some strange stigmata. He was still processing this when the wounds abruptly opened and disgorged long, wet daggers of grey bone. Cheyne attacked with slashing, downward swoops and Rafen dodged, hearing the bony awls whistle through the air. He threw out a sweeping kick that Cheyne easily escaped, and the androgyne gave a little gasp of pleasure. It seemed to think this was some sort of game.

'Enjoy this while you can, freak,' Rafen spat.

Cheyne pantomimed a hurt expression. 'Such harsh words. You cut me deeply.'

'I intend to.' Rafen stabbed out with his remaining electro-scythe and missed by the slightest of margins. The shock-nimbus creased Cheyne's shoulder and the warrior wriggled as the charge passed through it. The voltage was high, but the androgyne took it with a hiss.

'You think you're a cut above,' Cheyne said, dancing about him, careful to keep beyond close combat range. 'But the truth is, your kind is old, Space Marine. I am the new, dear Rafen. I am a New Man.'

'Man?' echoed the Blood Angel. 'That's open to debate.'

'I thought your Chapter understood beauty. Don't abhor me because I am so exquisite,' it retorted, with a cackle. 'It cheapens everything.'

Cheyne attacked again and Rafen managed to avoid taking cuts across his torso and arms; but the hafts of the extruded bone blades still slammed into his head, and the impact almost dazed him. The maggot turned in Rafen's chest, and he resisted the urge to strike at it. The parasite seemed to sense the Chaos champion's proximity.

'Your design is outmoded,' Cheyne goaded. 'In ten thousand years, the pattern of the Adeptus Astartes has not been improved upon. I, on the other hand, am the product of genius. Not just the next generation, much more than that.' It gasped again as it threw a strike at Rafen's legs, the tip of a blade slashing skin. 'A step up. *Astartes Novus Superior*. New and improved.'

'So you say,' Rafen replied, catching one of the bone-blades in his hand. He punched it with the pommel of the scythe weapon and the bony matter snapped along the midline, eliciting a chug of pain from the androgyne. 'Not so improved, by my lights.' He eyed the portcullis; Cheyne was keeping him from it, holding him off. He guessed there were more of these New Men on the way, and realised that this fight had to be finished quickly so he could proceed.

Cheyne's porcelain-white face was studded with beads of sweat. The broken blade retreated into the palm and the androgyne spun, presenting the other bone-weapon in a duellist's approach. 'You are strong,' it told him, 'but you're weak inside.' It tapped its head, eyes wide and wild. 'In here. Hollow. You follow empty dogma and the worthless mythos thrown up around a corpse on a throne, because you have nothing left.' Cheyne tittered. 'Your world is static, Blood Angel. Derelict and decaying. But mine? Mine looks forward, it grows and evolves. This is the gift of the Master Fabius! He has seen the past and now he builds the future.'

Rafen's battle rage churned inside him at the affront of this creature. 'Still you prattle, despite your earlier words. Is that all you can do?' A prickling fire was building in his chest, spreading from the infection site.

'Do I anger you?' Cheyne retorted. 'It would appear so! If only you could be like me, and fight with a smile upon your lips–'

Ignoring the dull pain, Rafen feinted right and then at the last moment, reversed. He stepped inside Cheyne's guard and struck. The androgyne reacted, swiftly enough to stop the Blood Angel's killing blow from reaching its conclusion; but still it was a palpable hit, and the tip of the scythe blade ripped across the New Man's cheek, opening it wide.

'You are right,' Rafen retorted, over Cheyne's howl of pain. 'I could never smile so broadly as you do.' Taking the moment, he advanced and struck at his opponent, slamming it to the ground.

The Blood Angel bent and grabbed a length of the leather wrapping, dragging Cheyne up. They were close to the edge of the ramp, and there was a good distance to the bottom. At the very least, throwing the androgyne off would break many bones, even if it were as hardy as an Astartes. Cheyne tried to stab him, and he caught the other blade, holding it away. Blood flowed where his fingers held on tightly.

Then Cheyne's cries shifted and became something else. *Laughter*.

Rafen's ire returned at the sound of the creature's mocking tones. 'You are amused? Make it last, freak! Your future ends here!'

'Oh,' gasped Cheyne, 'I think not.' When Bile's warrior spoke again, it was a sound so unholy that Rafen felt sickened to his core. It was, if such a word could be used to describe so abhorrent a noise, a *prayer* of sorts. A summoning, an entreaty, a litany; but not one to the vile gods that this creature worshipped.

The mantra was for the parasite. At the sound, the maggot erupted into violent life, and suddenly Rafen's blood turned to fire. Every nerve ending in his body screamed at once, plunging him into the embrace of an agony that shredded all will. He released his grip on Cheyne, everything else forgotten. There was so much pain, such a galaxy of it within him, that Rafen could do nothing but stand in the core of it and try to endure.

He heard howling, and knew that he was the first in the chorus.

ELEVEN

THE HULKING NEW Men dragged the Blood Angel into the tiered room through a heavy airlock door, and threw him hard to the floor. The hatch slammed closed behind them with a hissing whine and the Space Marine gasped in a breath as his eyes focused. The first thing he saw were the eldritch symbols etched into the grey tiles that spread out all around him, the curse-glyphs, warding runes and eight-point stars. He recoiled from them reflexively, disgust welling up in him, and the New Men laughed to see it.

Rafen tried to moderate his breathing, but it was difficult. The action of the maggot in his chest was turning his enhanced Astartes physiology against him; the functions of the implants in his body warred with his base human biology. He fought to hold off the shaking in his hands caused by cell imbalances in his blood chemistry, blinked and tried to keep himself steady even as his normally perfect equilibrium was disrupted. The thing was pumping poison into him with every heartbeat. He glared at Cheyne, who returned the look with malice, the Chaos champion twitching with pain as the servitor trailing at its heels used bio-wire to stitch the cut sections of its face back together.

Cheyne had done this to him, called the parasite to full potency with that strange mnemonic it had spoken. The pain ebbed and flowed, but only in small increments. Rafen now understood fully the insidious purpose of the implanted larva; it made chains and fetters obsolete. Any prisoner so tainted with one of these things was on an invisible leash; only a word need be spoken, and untold agony was let loose.

'You wanted to come here, didn't you?' slurred the New Man, flecks of blood and spittle issuing from the androgyne's ruined mouth. 'Do you like what you see?'

Rafen glanced around, uncertain of why he had been brought into the tower after Cheyne had seemingly done so much to prevent his entry. He was immediately struck by the similarity between this room and the co-opted hospital his squad had found aboard the tau asteroid; there was more light in here, though, and on some level Rafen wished it was otherwise.

Benches and worktables were arranged in neat rows, surrounded on all sides by circular tanks of murky fluids. Objects moved inside the tanks, and Rafen hesitated to peer too closely at them. Where the place of cruelty inside the tau colony had seemed abandoned and disordered, this laboratory was regimented and careful in aspect. A pair of servitors, their faces blank and sealed things with only eyes still open, moved around the edges of the room, performing tasks that Rafen could only guess at.

Light struck from harsh biolume strips set into the ceiling, yellow colour falling upon the tiled floor and the metal-sheathed walls. The illumination glittered on cowled trays of bladed implements that were more wicked than any fighting knife. The warrior wondered if he would be able to make it to them before the pain came again.

Overhead, racks made of clawed iron talons held polymer bags filled with splashes of liquid and matter that could only be human meat. On many of the operation tables, more plastic shrouds hid lumpy shapes made of pasty flesh. The smell of blood was constant; not the stench of a killing field, but the half-masked stink of a sanatorium, a place where death was brushed away as inconsequential.

Rafen shook his head to dispel the dizzy sensation in his skull. His thoughts were like mud, thick and slow. He took a few steps and became aware of a glass disc set into the floor beneath him. He looked down and his gut twisted in response. Through the thick lens, he could see into a misted nest of stringy, mucal matter; dozens of maggots of varying sizes writhed blindly over the top of one another, cilia grasping at nothing. He turned away in disgust, feeling the weight of his own unwanted passenger upon him. Rafen wondered if the parasite was gaining mass or if it were just his misperception. He felt a stab of dread;

would it grow to consume him from the inside out? Or would it do something far worse, make his flesh its own?

He forced himself to look again, and this time he saw something else. Down, under the wriggling carpet of maggots, drenched in wet ropes of gel... Something made of bone armour and pasty flesh, coiled in on itself, horribly bloated.

'A tyranid zoanthrope,' said a dark, rich voice. 'At least, it was at the beginning, before I took it, married its flesh with a biovore archetype, altered it to better serve my ends. Now it is both less and more than it was.'

Rafen knew that voice. Knew it and *hated* it.

He looked up to see a figure stride into the chamber through another hatch on the far side of the laboratory. As tall as any warrior-born of the Adeptus Astartes, the new arrival dominated the room with a black presence that was the very antithesis to warriors of noble character, such as Rafen's master Commander Dante. The man – although in truth he had long since given up any claim to that appellation – wore a voluminous long coat that hung upon him like a cloak. Leathery and cracked, it was a patchwork thing sutured together from the flesh of the dead. The Blood Angel saw the still-screaming faces of Astartes stitched into the cut of the coat, flesh cut from men who had perished at this killer's hands thousands of years before Rafen was born.

This mantle was drawn tight over heavy power armour in the style of the aged Maximus pattern, but reforged and remade into something unholy. Once the armour had shown the colours of brilliant gold and imperial purple, but now the tarnished shell was the tint of dark wine, the ceramite sheath soaked in such tides of shed blood that the porous surface had taken on their shade.

At his back, the hulking figure's silhouette was unbalanced by a large brass construct that clung to him like a giant, predatory scarab beetle. Its claws and talons were hidden away, retracted, but atop it bulbous pipes and glassy tubes arrayed with skulls worked quietly, pumping resinous ichor with wet and breathy murmurs. With a solemn, heavy tread, the new arrival advanced into the light, showing a hard face of deep-set eyes to the Space Marine. White, wiry hair framed an expression of indolent interest.

'What have we here?' he said.

This man, this traitor, had once walked the stars as a soldier of the Emperor's Children, but like the rest of his dishonoured Legion he had taken the coin of the heretic warmaster Horus and embraced the riot of the Chaos Gods. Some held that he had already been on that road even before Fulgrim's warriors had broken their covenant with Terra, experimenting on his fellow Astartes during his service as an Apothecary. Once freed of any moral codes, those foul deeds had quickly spread wider, as he tormented and experimented on anyone luckless enough to cross his path; and then, even as Horus was defeated and Fulgrim hounded into the Eye of Terror, this twisted genius earned the traitor's brand a second time, divorcing himself from the corrupted Emperor's Children to go renegade – and all so he could delve ever deeper into the perverse possibilities of his dark flesh-arts. His catalogue of atrocities touched beings on thousands of worlds.

The pain of the parasite seized at Rafen's chest, but he ignored it as his rage threatened to ripple over the bulwarks of his self-control. If it had been possible to kill with the venom of words alone, then Rafen would have spat death. 'Fabius Bile,' he growled, 'by the God-Emperor, I name you traitor!'

'Of course you do,' Bile replied, unruffled by the sheer force of odium that welled up from the Space Marine. 'You and so many others. It's tiresome. I sometimes hope one of you will say something different to me.' He showed a mouth of tombstone-grey teeth, amused at himself. 'After a hundred centuries, I yearn for a break in the monotony.'

Rafen took a step towards the tray of medical blades, but Cheyne was suddenly there, blocking his path, licking its lips in eagerness for another combat. Blood was still seeping from the gash on its cheek. The Astartes was aware of the other New Men behind him, taking up battle stances.

Bile studied his minion and nodded. 'You did that to him, eh? Even with the leech in you. Such fortitude.'

'I'll be more than happy to demonstrate my skill to you, turncoat.'

Cheyne giggled at the idea of that, but Bile shook his head. 'No fighting in here. Not today.' The twisted scientist stepped down, coming closer. 'Not yet, at least. Not before my questions are answered.'

'I will give you nothing,' Rafen spat. 'nothing but your ending! You will not escape this time!'

Bile examined him. 'This time?' His brow furrowed. 'Have we met before, whelp? I confess I do not recall.'

'I was there when you fled Baal, like the coward you are!' snarled the Blood Angel. 'You did not even have the courage to face us in combat!'

The renegade showed no sign of recognition, and gave an arch sniff. 'I have not lived so long by taking on fights I cannot win, not when another avenue is open to me. Your kind, on the other hand, seem to make it a point to engage in battles that are beyond you.' He gestured around. 'Hence your internment here, yes?'

'Send your dogs away, traitor, and we will see who is beyond who.' Rafen's eyes flashed, the muscles in his hands tensing.

Bile ignored the retort, glancing at Cheyne. 'This is the one dragged from the ocean. Such a gift, but I am unwilling to accept it without due consideration. Where did he come from?'

The New Man glared at Rafen. 'Answer the Master's question, or there will be pain, Blood Angel.'

Rafen returned the angry look. 'Don't pretend you don't already know.'

'Perhaps,' admitted Cheyne, with a laugh. 'But I want you to say it.'

'I came from Baal,' Rafen replied. 'I came here to kill all of you.' He looked back at Bile. 'To give you the punishment you so richly deserve for your insult to my Chapter.'

'He said he came alone,' added Cheyne. 'Aboard the ship of that fool Zellik.'

The Blood Angel said nothing; the androgyne had confirmed what he had known, every word spoken in the prison complex was heard by Cheyne's spies.

'Did he?' Bile mused. 'A lone Astartes on a quest for vengeance, out to avenge an affront.' He drifted away, towards another lock-hatch. 'What could he be so upset about?' The renegade spoke a whispered code-word and the hatchway ground open. Bile stepped through, gesturing languidly to his second. 'Bring him.'

Rafen felt a sharp impact in his back and turned to see the other two New Men, halberds with multiple blade-heads raised and pressing into his flesh.

Cheyne followed his master, beckoning Rafen. 'Come, come. I promise you, Space Marine, there are sights to see here that you would not wish to over-look.'

As much as he hated to admit it, the Blood Angel's interest was piqued. More than anything, he wanted to release the fires of his Chapter's gene-curse, the dark berserker potential of the Red Thirst; he wanted to let himself become a whirlwind of death and tear this place apart. But there were the other voices in his mind, the remembrance of words from his trusted mentor Koris and his liege lord Dante. He could not unchain his rage, not yet. There was the mission first.

Grim-faced, he followed Cheyne through the hatchway.

'YOU ARE CERTAIN?' Noxx's voice was pitched low so that it would not carry across the command deck of the *Neimos*. The Flesh Tearer leaned in and peered over the Blood Angel's shoulder at the ornately-framed pict-screen.

Puluo nodded gravely. 'Wouldn't speak up if I wasn't. See for yourself.'

Noxx's eyes narrowed as he scrutinised the display; the image was of a zone of ocean in the wake of the submersible, a pie-wedge shape filled with rippling lines of grey and black static. It was a sonaric scope, a device that could scry though water using hyper-sensitive audial sensors that listened for minute changes in the thermocline of the surrounding sea. 'I don't see it.'

'Wait,' said Puluo. He pointed at a blank sector of the display. 'Look here.'

After a moment, the screen flickered, and for a split-second, Noxx saw the ghost of a streamlined shape – something like a bullet trailing lines of wire. He froze the image and looked up at the other Astartes. 'It came back?'

'It came back,' Puluo said, with a grim nod.

'I thought you killed that thing out there.'

Puluo shook his head once. 'Drove it off. Thought that would be enough.'

Noxx examined the rangefinder dial next to the screen. 'It's far behind. Moving slower. Injured.'

'Not *that* far behind,' added Puluo. 'According to the cogitators, the kraken is more or less matching our speed. If we drop a cog for any reason, it'll be on us in minutes.'

'All the more reason for haste, then.' Noxx went to move away, but Puluo grabbed his arm. 'What now?' The sergeant was irritated.

The Blood Angel frowned and tapped the pict-screen. 'Not done yet. Keep watching.' He tapped the control tab and the playback went on.

There was a glimmer on the display, this time on the far side of the wedge, and Noxx raised an eyebrow.

How had the tyranid moved from one side of the screen to the other so quickly?

The image fuzzed with static and reset itself for another loop of passive scans; and this time the scope presented not one, but five distinct returns. Each the same bullet-shell profile, each trailing streamers of distortion out behind it.

'It came back,' repeated Puluo once more, 'and it's brought some friends.'

Noxx smiled thinly. 'Perhaps we ought to be flattered. The bloody horror has to gang up on us just to make a dent.' He paused, thinking. 'Tell the servitors to push this tub up to maximum velocity. We need every second ahead of those things we can get, because we'll have to slow the moment we reach the island.'

'If we don't get out of the water quick enough, they'll be on us,' said the Blood Angel.

'Oh, I don't doubt it,' Noxx replied. 'All the more reason for us to take the pace, cousin.'

Puluo nodded again. 'As if we needed another thing to motivate us.'

HE HAD EXPECTED to look upon another chamber of horrors; and in a way, it was exactly that.

Pressed in by the angry shoves of Cheyne's thugs, Rafen walked on behind the androgyne and its servitor into a long chamber that was more a gallery than it was a room. Set on racks lining the walls or hanging from chains that dangled from the low ceiling, there were trophies upon trophies.

Pieces of ceramite armour, chest plates and pauldrons, gauntlets and helmets, all of them lay mute and broken like so much battlefield debris. On an upper tier, out of reach, there was an armoury of weapons, swords and guns.

What struck Rafen dumb was the fact that everything here was Astartes-issue hardware. It was Bile's prize room, the spoils stripped from every prisoner he had brought to this secret hell.

He saw the red gauntlet of a Crimson Fist, knuckles cracked and broken; the skull-helm of a Space Wolf; shoulder pauldrons bearing the crests of the Black Dragons, the Salamanders, the Soul Drinkers, and more.

'This is a lesson,' said Bile airily, walking towards a bubbling tank of fluid at the far end of the chamber. 'I like to keep these relics close to hand to remind me of my steps along the road to success.'

Cheyne eyed the Blood Angel. 'He's wondering how long this has been going on for. That's always the first question.' The androgyne cocked its head. 'Would it shock you to know that *decades* have passed since my Master began his work here?' Cheyne made an amused noise. 'Now think, abhuman. How many battle-brothers have been declared missing presumed dead in the last ten, twenty, thirty years, hmm? Interesting to consider how many of them might have ended up here, don't you think?' It traced long fingers over the cracked, bloodstained brow of an Ultramarines helm.

Rafen tried to find his voice, but he could not. His eyes were locked on a red torso plate that lay as if discarded upon one of the racks. On it, there were wings of gold surrounding a ruby droplet. He moved to it, held it in his hands. For a moment, Rafen had thought the armour was part of his wargear – he imagined everything the splices had stripped from him on the boat had ended up in here somewhere – but cold shock ran through him as he realised this item did not belong to him. With reverence, he turned the plate over and found the roll of honour inscribed on the inverse face. The last among the lists of combat records and warriors who had worn this armour was smudged with soot.

Rafen rubbed the dirt away with his thumb. 'Brother Kear,' he husked, reading the name aloud. He did not know the man, but still his anger flared brightly to think that a Chapter kinsman had died in this place before him, alone and forgotten. 'One more to add to the butcher's bill,' he whispered, hoping that his dead comrade's spirit might still linger to hear him. 'On my oath, you will be avenged.' He turned and met Fabius's sullen stare, his eyes aflame.

'Look at him,' Bile said to his lieutenant. 'So furious, so consumed with rage that he can barely restrain it.'

'The Blood Angels are known for their reserve,' Cheyne replied, as if discussing the flavour of a fine wine. 'Or perhaps it is just a reluctance to fight?'

Rafen drew in a slow and steady breath, imagining the sound the androgyne would make when he strangled the life from it; but still he resisted the urge to attack with tooth and claw. He knew the character of these Chaos-kin; they adored their own arrogance, their convoluted schemes and their inflated sense of superiority. They could not be content with silence or letting their deeds speak for them. Men like Fabius Bile loved to gloat, to twist the knife before the final strike; and as much as he hated to stand here and endure insult after insult, Rafen knew he must if he were to learn the truth behind this hideous place. He quietly added each slur to the tally he would take.

'I should thank you, Blood Angel,' said the Primogenitor. 'You and your foolish kindred. You have helped me advance one of my greatest works by leaps and bounds, and all through the arrogance of one of your battle-brothers.'

'Caecus…' The name slipped from his lips before he could stop himself from uttering it.

Bile nodded. 'A desperate man. Fearful for the future of his Chapter, but proud enough to believe that he alone could save it. Instead, he opened your secrets to me.' He smiled thinly. 'He deserves your pity.'

'He is dead,' Rafen snarled. 'Dead by my hand. In the end, he understood the errors he had made. He died accepting that responsibility.'

'How noble,' Cheyne tittered.

I will be damned for my hubris. The Apothecae Caecus had said those words. Rafen remembered the weight of his bolter in his hand as he had pronounced a sentence of death upon his kinsman, and the echo of the single gunshot. The Blood Angel wanted to feel hate for the dead man, but he did not. Bile, rot his soul, was right; instead he felt pity for Caecus. In a vain attempt to bolster the numbers of the Blood Angels in the aftermath of the Arkio crisis, the senior Apothecary had dared to dabble in the arcane art of cloning. His failures ultimately led him to make a pact with a biologian who called himself Haran Serpens – fatally unaware that this identity had been usurped by Fabius Bile.

Rafen's voice was steady but loaded with menace. 'You stole from us, traitor. You took a piece of our heart. I have come to reclaim it and see you pay for your crimes.'

Bile laughed, and it was an ugly, grating sound. 'My crimes? They are so many that you would perish of old age before you could list them all. And yet you, a mewling whelp suckling at your Corpse-God's wizened teat, have the temerity to think you can judge me?' The scientist's face stiffened, his eyes glittering like dark gems. 'Tell me, is this what you seek, warrior?'

A mechanical arm extruded itself from the tarnished brass exo-frame on Bile's back, and dipped into the churn of the fluid-filled tank. When it returned there was a crystalline phial clasped in the manipulator claw at its tip.

Rafen gasped; *the sacred blood!* He could almost see the crimson liquid within the tube, the measure of preserved vitae from the Lord Primarch kept alive by the sanguinary priests of his Chapter. His hand came up to reach for it before he could stop himself.

Bile sniffed, and dropped the phial back into the tank, as if it meant nothing. 'So much value ascribed to something that is, when all is considered, a trivial collection of protein chains, hydrocarbons and base molecular compounds. And yet, in the correct combination, a priceless thing.' He stepped back and with the sweep of his coat, the rest of the tank's contents were revealed.

Small knots of flesh hung in suspension, drifting in the sluggish flow. A faint haze of dilute blood marbled the liquid medium, and it was with building horror that Rafen recognised the shapes of the strange organs.

'You know what these are, yes?' asked Bile.

Rafen had come to this blighted world believing that the renegade was working some foul plan connected to his Chapter's genetic legacy; but now he began to understand that the Blood Angels were not alone in this. The objects in the tank were harvested progenoid glands.

Each Space Marine, regardless of Chapter or origin, carried such implants within them after their ascension to full brotherhood. Over time, the progenoids absorbed genetic matter and matured. New gene-seed grown within the organs could then be harvested and reintroduced to a Chapter's genetic stock, to begin the cycle anew. The progenoids were the very lifeblood of the Adeptus Astartes, the raw material of generations of warriors to come. Some said they were the most precious of treasures, beyond holy relics and sacred lore, because they represented the future.

And here stood Fabius Bile, smugly exhibiting a collection of these priceless elements that he had ripped from the corpses of the warriors he had murdered.

'I have gathered these for many years,' he was saying, smiling at the sound of his own voice. 'At first I stole them or bartered for them from the warriors of the legions that had broken with the Emperor to follow the eightfold path... But I could salvage little. The power of our new gods is so strong that it altered the nature of the Emperor's Children, the Death Guard, the Night Lords, Word Bearers and all the others–'

'It corrupted you!' Rafen spat. 'Poisoned you!'

'If you wish,' continued the scientist. 'For what I had conceived, admittedly, you might be correct. I needed to find a more... stable source of genetic material. Something closer to the source.'

'We've been collecting for a very long time,' sighed Cheyne.

Bile went on, in the manner of a teacher addressing a student. 'It isn't an easy prospect.' He walked back towards Rafen, bearing down on him. 'It's difficult to appreciate the amount of effort I have put into this work.'

A sickened, horrified sensation built up inside the Blood Angel. Part of him wanted to remain ignorant, to never know the scope of whatever scheme Bile had designed; but this was why he was here, to know the truth. The renegade was enjoying this moment, knowing what Rafen needed to ask even as the question appalled him. 'What... work?'

'I have made so many great things,' Bile said, inclining his head towards Cheyne and the other New Men. In turn, Cheyne made a winsome face that seemed oddly feminine. 'You were on Baal. You saw my Bloodfiends.'

Rafen shuddered to recall the monstrous vampiric beasts rendered out of Astartes gene-matter. The business of killing the creatures had been hard-fought and bloody. 'I did. All of those vile abortions were destroyed. We burned every one of them.'

Bile's nostrils flared with annoyance. 'Great art so often fails to find an audience with the intellect to appreciate it. Sometimes I am filled with woe to think that no one in this blighted millennium has the wit to see the scope of my brilliance.' He advanced towards the Blood Angel. 'I am the Lord of Life, Astartes. Primogenitor and master of the flesh. Not like your silent Emperor, dead-alive behind his army of lesser men, all of them picking at the decayed carcass of the galaxy.'

'You are less than nothing compared to Him!' Rafen snapped. 'You would be ashes and dust if not for His touch upon you! The Emperor made your turncoat Chapter along with all the rest, from the raw stuff of His own flesh!'

'I have done the same,' Bile said, his mood shifting again. 'Built life from fractions into living, breathing magnificence. I brought back the greatest warrior of all time from thousands of years of death...'

Cheyne gave a breathy sigh. 'Great Horus...'

Bile nodded. 'I made him anew. Gave life to our warmaster once again–'

Rafen had heard the dark rumours of the Reborn Horus during his time as a Scout Marine, but he had always thought them to be propaganda stories seeded by the archenemy. It seemed he had been mistaken. 'You created an abomination! A monstrosity so foul that even your own allies could not stomach it to live!'

'It is a regrettable truth,' agreed the renegade. 'That ungrateful thug Abaddon should have welcomed my replicae with open arms... But instead he sent his Black Legion lapdogs to kill it and raze my laboratoria to the ground. He called it "blasphemy", as if such a thing can exist.' Bile snorted. 'Codes, morality, principles, ethics, call them what you will. These things are only abstract constructs invented by weaker men who do not have the courage to forge their own path!'

The Blood Angel turned slightly, stiffening. The renegade was close to him now. He felt a tingling in his fingers as a very real possibility became clear. *I can attack him. Another step closer, and Cheyne will not be able to stop me in time.* Rafen licked his lips, and his tongue touched the tips of his fangs. What would this fiend's blood taste like, he wondered?

'I have known many weak men,' Bile continued. 'Many men who believed they had vision, but who were limited by the petty bonds they put upon themselves, of so-called virtue… Your Emperor was one of them.'

'You have no right to speak of Him!' Rafen could not help himself; it was impossible for the Astartes to hear his god disparaged and say nothing.

'No?' Bile studied him. 'Unlike you, whelp, I once walked the same ground as your idol. I breathed the same air as him. And I tell you this, without lie or artifice. He never wanted to become what you have made him! He did not wish to be your god-thing. He abhorred such ideals! The slavery of your crippled, blind Imperium would sicken him, if he had eyes to see it.' He folded his arms across his barrel chest. 'You may call me traitor, and be right in it, but I have never betrayed what I know to be true. I have never betrayed *myself*. You, Astartes, and all your kin, betray your Emperor with every moment of your worthless lives!'

'Your words are worthless to me,' said the Blood Angel.

Bile continued as if he had not spoken. 'And yet… He taught me a lesson that for many years I did not understand. In a way, Abaddon brought it back to me.' The renegade seemed as if he were thinking aloud, almost as if he were alone in the room, voicing his musings to empty air. 'The lesson is this. The only real crime for those of superlative intellect and great prowess is to allow one's self to become shackled by mediocrity. The crime is to let your grasp be less than your reach.' He nodded to himself. 'To aim low.'

Something in Bile's tone made Rafen hesitate. 'What in the name of Terra are you talking about?'

'I am a patient being. I have worked long and hard, and I know the hardest toil is yet to come, but I embrace it. I know it will be worth the struggle. When I made my New Men, I duplicated the works of Chapter Masters and Primarchs.' He looked at Cheyne once again. 'But it was not enough, and so I sought to go beyond that, to clone Horus Lupercal, to echo the work of your Emperor and create a Primarch.' Bile smiled. 'But even in that, I was wrong. For, I realised, my destiny is not simply to rise to the level of the Emperor's skill and duplicate his works, oh no…' He took a step towards Rafen, and the Astartes could smell rust and the fetor of old, decayed flesh. 'My destiny is to *eclipse* him.'

The sheer conceit of the scientist's words bared Rafen's teeth in a sneer. 'Your hubris is vast enough to shroud the sky! And your madness dwarfs even that!'

'You don't understand. Of course you don't. You are limited and without vision!' He tapped his brow. 'Think, Space Marine, think! If I could hold the skeins of DNA from an entire Chapter in my hands and mould them like clay, what could I create? A Primarch? Now imagine what I could do with the genetic legacy of not just one, but hundreds of Chapters!'

'No...' The beginnings of comprehension crowded into the edges of Rafen's thought, and he gasped, for the enormity of the ideal was so vast and so horribly monstrous that he could scarcely contain it. '*No!*'

'Oh, but *yes!*' Bile roared, grinning as wide as his wolfish mouth would allow. 'I am assembling the disparate genetic strains of every single Adeptus Astartes, teasing out the threads of inherited gene-matter that tie them to their Primarchs, and their Primarchs to their creator! The greatest puzzle of them all, Blood Angel! I am going to reassemble the genetic code sequence of the ur-source for all Space Marines! The progenitor of our kind, the father of us all!'

'The Emperor...' The atrocity of Bile's scheme defied dimension. 'You will build a replicae... of Him?'

'Can you imagine that?' Cheyne offered. 'The most powerful human psychic in history, reborn under the allegiance of the Ruinous Powers!' The androgyne's eyes were shining with tears of joy.

'And you have helped me prepare, Blood Angel,' said Bile. 'There are a great many voids in my map of the Imperial genome, but the pure blood of a direct-line son of the Emperor... say, that of the Primarch Sanguinius... will go a long way towards correcting those errors.' He laughed to himself. 'And one day soon, when I have gathered enough progenoids and tortured enough of your errant kindred, a child will take its first teetering steps from out of a gene-engine tank, and call me father! A child who will remake the galaxy! A Prince-Emperor free to rule, not hobbled and confined—'

The dazzling magnitude of this horror seemed to dislocate Rafen from the here and now; he felt as if his mind were being pulled away, sucked into the undertow of this gargantuan, hideous concept. The shock of it was almost too much to conceive, as if he were trying to imagine the size of the universe. *Could such a thing be done?* He had seen much in his service to the Golden Throne, horrors and spectacles of near-infinite scale. Cold crept into his veins as it came to him that of all the minds in the galaxy who might be capable of this sacrilege, Fabius Bile was foremost among them.

The far-distant part of his reeling mind understood this; the more base, animal will within him reacted in a manner in keeping with its nature.

Moving without conscious thought, Rafen leapt at the renegade and slammed into him with such impact that Bile crashed bodily into one of the trophy racks, scattering relics across the metallic decking. Fuelled by a rage as primal as it was potent, the Astartes tore into his enemy, shredding open his skin-coat.

Bile's hands came up, and the metallic claws of the arcane device on his back exploded outward; but Rafen was already upon his bared throat, his jaws wide. The Blood Angel sank his fangs into the leathery flesh of the renegade's neck and bit down hard, ripping skin, puncturing veins, crushing cartilage.

A torrent of oil-thick liquid jetted outward in a spray, and Bile's cry of shocked alarm was a wet, strangling gurgle.

Limbs of flesh and metal stabbed and punched at Rafen's torso, but he blotted out the pain; all he wanted was the kill, the blood – as foul-tasting and polluted as he had expected it to be – washing down

over his chin and his chest. Bile tried to cry out, but
his throat was a collapsed ruin.

The New Men were on him now, electro-halberds
spitting blue fire that surged agony along his every
nerve-ending, but still he ripped at his foe, feeling the
meat of Bile's throat shred to rags in his teeth. The
twisted scientist stumbled and lost his footing, crashing to the floor, and still Rafen did not release,
slashing and tearing. It was only when Cheyne began
to sing the pain-prayer once more that the Blood
Angel's frenzied attack ceased.

The parasite turned over and over, pouring boiling
hot agony into Rafen's chest. Drenched with blood,
he screamed and fell away from his prey, doubling up
in pain. All the other injuries and hurts topped the
dam of his will and flooded in to follow. Rafen reeled
and gasped, clinging to the edge of awareness.

'Get him out of here!' Cheyne was screaming, its
voice pitched high and shrill. 'Don't let the whelp
perish! He will live to pay for this! Take him away!'

Darkness closed in on Rafen, billowing out from
the shadowed corners around him, colour leaching
from everything in his vision as his wounds sang with
agony. The last image he carried with him into the
black was of Fabius Bile twitching and dying, blood
still emerging in arcs of brown-red fluids as his ruined
throat lay open to the air.

With one last effort, he swilled a mouthful of foul
matter and spat it from his lips, ejecting it across the
faces of the New Men. The exertion drained him, and
he lost his grip, the light breaking into shards that
faded like smoke.

TWELVE

A WAVE OF brackish, icy water brought Rafen reeling back to wakefulness, and he spat and flailed, his fists coming up to fight off any attack. Blinking, he could make out only dim shapes. His face was swollen from impact and blood gummed one of his eyes shut.

The mist over his vision began to dissipate, and he determined he was in another of the metal cells, shafts of dull yellow daylight slicing in through vertical gaps in the walls. There were no exits other than a heavy steel door on thick hinges.

'On your feet, boy,' said a gruff voice. He heard the clank of an empty bucket as a slump-shouldered figure discarded the container.

'Vetcha,' said Rafen, wiping back his unkempt, blood-matted hair. When he looked at his fingers they came away a dirty red. 'I expected to wake up dead.'

The old Space Wolf gave a wheezing laugh. 'Thought you'd see the Emperor's face next, did you? Find yourself in Elysium?' Vetcha spat. 'You don't have the luck, Blood Angel. No man here does. Too easy a way out.' The blind veteran reached out a gnarled hand and helped him stand. Vetcha's fingers were bony but strong like rods of iron.

Rafen looked around, his brow furrowing. He could hear a noise coming from beyond the walls of the metal cell; a clashing, banging rhythm of impact after impact. 'Where have you brought me now, Wolf?'

'Not I,' said Vetcha, moving into the shadows to stoop down for something. 'The New Men dragged you here.' He chuckled again. 'My, but you must have angered them to a great degree. I've rarely seen them take such delight in kicking a man while he could not fight back.'

'Aye,' Rafen replied, hawking up a gobbet of phlegm and blood. He coughed and heard a tinny ping of sound; a broken piece of tooth had gone with it. 'Did they bring a herd of grox in to trample me?' He took stock of himself, feeling down his arms and legs with care. Everywhere he laid his hands, Rafen winced with pain from deep, heavy bruising. 'Why did they not simply slit my throat?'

'You still do not understand the way of this place, do you?' Vetcha shook his head, returning with a heavy object wrapped in oil-cloth. 'No deaths occur on this Light-forsaken island unless they are in order to serve the will or the whim of Fabius Bile.'

'Fabius...' Rafen licked his dry, cracked lips, remembering the foul taste of the primogenitor's blood in his mouth. 'He has met his end.'

'Oh?' The Space Wolf paused. 'I've heard that said more than once, and by men in better shape than you, boy. If I were you, I'd concentrate on staying alive for the next few minutes.' Outside, the rattling percussion was picking up speed. 'Just make it to the table first. You'll know what to do when you get there.'

'Table? What table?' Rafen was confused, and the pounding from his head was doing little to dilute the uncertainty.

'Pay attention!' snapped the veteran. 'Listen to me if you want to live!'

Rafen eyed him. 'You're my wolf-guide, is that it? But I've heard others cast doubt on your motivations, old man.'

'You are ignorant,' came the reply. 'Your edges all sharp, still not worn down... But that will come! Mark my words, that will come to you, if you don't perish first!'

'Is that what happened to you?' Rafen challenged. 'Did you weaken? One has to wonder how it is you move so freely in this place.'

'Damn you, I am not free!' snarled the other Space Marine. 'Fenris's Blood, you ungrateful mongrel! I am trying to help you!' He thrust the cloth-wrapped item into Rafen's hands with a growl. 'Here! Take it and be gone!'

The Blood Angel tugged the cover and it fluttered away to reveal a long-handled mass hammer; Rafen knew this kind of implement. It had a specially densified head upon it that could shatter boulders in the right hands – but it was a thing for Chapter serfs and servitors, a tool, not a weapon fit for an Astartes. In his grip, it seemed slight, undersized. 'What am I supposed to do with this?'

'Try not to get killed!' Vetcha reached into the shadows and yanked at a rusted crank handle; with a groan of metal, the front section of the cell parted and opened out on its hinges.

Rafen's eyes jabbed him with darts of pain as they adjusted to the sudden influx of light. The Dynikas sun was high in the sky, shining directly down upon him, and he smelled the chemical stink of promethium fluid. The rattling cacophony rose to a peak, and the Astartes saw its origin.

He was on the lowest level of the crater, the curves of the ramped walls rising up around him. On the higher levels, he could see the profiles of the metal cell-chambers ranged like viewing boxes in an amphitheatre. The walls of the cells vibrated in the heat of the day, and he could see window slits open in every one of them. He had an audience of his kinsmen.

But they were not cheering; the clattering sound came from ranks of modificates and New Men lining the floor of the crater all around him. They were beating armoured fists or drawn weapons against their chest plates, the pulse of noise quickening with each passing moment.

He took a careful step forward; in front of the cell was a raised platform made of welded iron plates, and it ended in the chains and cables of a narrow suspensionway – a swinging bridge with barely enough width for him to pass down it. Beyond that, he could see little more than a concrete bunker, its roof torn down and missing.

The stink of stale, decayed fish-flesh was everywhere. This place, he reasoned, must have been part of the old agri-colony's infrastructure, a section of processing plant involved in the harvest of Dynikas V's rich bounty; at least, until the tyranid splinter had come and scoured the planet.

He heard a clanking noise and spun to see Vetcha being winched up behind him, dragged away by a crane arm. 'Don't wait,' he called out. 'The guns are already on you.'

Overhead, the winged sentinels circled, and for the first time Rafen noticed the bright red dots of laser designators moving to and fro across the metal at his feet, tracing up over his legs and torso from the cannons they carried in their claws.

He glanced around, looking for options even as he knew there would be none. There was only one way off the platform – along the bridge. Promethium fires burned around all other avenues of escape, searing blue flames jetting from tank clusters beneath the holding cells. Even if he did make it off, below him was nothing but a crowd of angry mutants. He would take many with him, but in his condition he would not live to take them all.

It was then Rafen noticed another iron cell, another suspended bridge, set off to his right. An identical path, paralleling his. A roar went up as the other cell's doors opened, and a heavy figure shrouded in robes walked forward with steady, dogged purpose.

'Now we have some sport,' said a voice, broadcast in hard echoes across the width of the crater. The words pealed from hundreds of vox horns wired to the misting pillars scattered about the complex.

Rafen spun in place, turning towards the source of the voice, and found another crane-array, this one with a massive iron shovel that had been converted into a mobile viewing platform. Cheyne stood there, the androgyne's scarred face now forever pulled up in a tight grin, leaning indolently on a double-headed heat axe; but Rafen's attention was on the figure who stood beside him, laughing with callous amusement.

'Yes, indeed,' Fabius Bile leered into a vox relay, 'now we will have our sport.'

The renegade's aspect was virtually untouched, the same coat and the hulking shape of the Chaos-forged chirurgeon device upon his back, the same insouciant and superior grin. His throat was shrouded in dark cloth, preventing Rafen from seeing any signs of the wounds he had inflicted, but *in the Emperor's name!* How could he still be alive?

The Blood Angel had torn the traitor's throat open, ripped into him with such violence that another blow might have taken his head from his neck. The vitae he had spilled was enough to drown a man, and yet there Fabius stood, laughing it off. How was it possible? Rafen wondered what foul magicks the renegade had at his command that he could undo such a mortal blow. His fingers tightened on the haft of the mass hammer, remembering the words of his Oath of Moment. He would survive this, and if fate demanded it, he would kill Fabius Bile as many times as it took.

'Begin!' shouted Cheyne, and the splices hooted their approval. Rafen saw a flash of motion in the corner of his eye, as the hooded figure on the other platform broke into a run and sprinted on to the swinging bridge.

The Blood Angel threw a look up and saw the sentinels overhead drawing a bead upon him. He grimaced and rocked off his heels, surging off onto the shaking gangway.

The metal bridge swayed and creaked ominously, leaking rains of rusty flakes beneath his heavy footfalls that scattered over the baying audience below him. Rafen was almost at the halfway mark when he felt the cables twang and go taut as extra weight was applied to them. He shot a glance over his shoulder to see a big simian scrambling up after him; and then, the bridge bowed again as two more splices were boosted up by their comrades, tossed high so they could claw over to land ahead of him. The other two resembled some hybrid of man and rodent, pointed rat-like snouts sniffing in his direction. Spindly and thin, they each had forked katar punch-daggers in their clawed hands.

It was not just a race he had to win, then. Without losing an iota of his forward momentum, Rafen spun the mass hammer into a reversed grip and brought it up in a sweeping arc. The heavy head of the tool collided with the base of the first rat-thing's jaw, smashing it with a wet noise. It stumbled and the Astartes shoved it aside. The assailant tumbled back over the line of the gangway and fell back into the crowd. The second rodentine ducked low and thrust forward the katar in its fist with a sharp hiss. Rafen brought down the haft of the hammer like a baton, striking it hard on the snout. Blood gushed from the splice's mouth; still moving, the warrior caught the creature's neck in the crook of his weapon arm and trapped it, dragging it off its feet.

Rafen jerked his elbow closed and snapped the rat-thing's neck. He slowed a step or so to discard it, and that was enough for the big simian to bound into grappling range.

The crowd roared their approval as the mutant drew him into a bone-crushing embrace, and Rafen's bruises sang with pain as the pressure came upon him. He felt the simian's hot, stinking breath on the back of his neck; the thing was easily the size of a Terminator in full battle armour, and the bridge moaned under the weight of the beast's exertions. Rafen leaned forward, then slammed his head backward, butting his skull into the ape-thing's face. It cried out and the vice-like grip around him slackened for an instant. It was all the time he needed.

The Blood Angel lurched forward, straining against one side of the swinging gangway, then pushed off in the opposite direction. The suspended bridge flexed and twisted, the footing beneath the simian's boots suddenly unsteady. Rafen hooked the head of the hammer into a loop of cable and repeated his action; this time it was enough to flip the bridge on its side, and he kicked out, hard.

The ape-thing's mass did the rest of the work for him. It panicked, surrendering its grip on the Space Marine in order to try and save itself from a fall. Rafen kicked out again, his heel connecting with the impact point of his previous attack. The simian roared with pain and lost balance; in the next moment it too was flailing away, into the furious crowd.

Rafen recovered, clinging to the thick cables, as the bridge rebounded. He sprinted across the rest of the gangway and slid down a shallow, slippery incline, into the derelict blockhouse beyond.

He looked around. He could see no sign of the other runner – his opponent? – but an open hatch on the far side of the bunker was a clear indication of where he was supposed to go. The Astartes moved, and heard the clicks and snaps of oiled metal. A rush of air creased his bare cheek and Rafen instinctively ducked. An armature tipped with a bouquet of spinning blades lashed out and wove patterns in the air where he had been standing. He spun, dodging a second and then a third cutting tool, as rotary blades emerged from slots in the stone walls. Knives cut close, snagging on his dirty tunic; he reeled away before they could slice into his flesh. Jets of fire lashed out from hidden nozzles, the heat threatening to crisp his skin.

He realised he was standing atop a floor of fine mesh, the metal dark and greasy. Beneath there was a channel choked with stagnant fluids, a brown slurry of fatty deposits; a wide blood gutter. Nearby he spied corroded rollers and the remains of a conveyer mechanism; the blockhouse had been another part of the agri-facility, for the flensing and cutting of the day's catch. The stench of flammable chemicals was even stronger here, tasting sour on his tongue.

Rafen put the hammer to the blades and struck hard, bending them so the retractors would not work, the gears behind them popping off their tarnished guides. He smashed a path through and broke out, feet skidding over the slick decking and out through the far hatch. Next, the race put him through the spinning interior of a massive tumbler array, the curved walls turning and turning. He ran full-tilt, bouncing from frame to frame, his impetus keeping him from falling into the rolling grinders revolving below. Using the hammer like a climber's pick, he swung it into a vent in the chamber and used it to lever himself up.

The shouting and braying of the crowd met him as he emerged at last from the far side of the block-house. A makeshift ramp led up a steep incline to another raised platform; on it, there was a table.

Rafen hazarded a glance to his right. The hooded fig-ure was ahead of him, already sprinting hard up the parallel ramp. The Blood Angel discarded the mass hammer and threw himself forward, his muscles tight with a hundred aches, and raced the last few metres to the top of the ascent. He could feel the parasite flexing inside his chest, excited by the exertions of his heart.

His blood thumped in his ears as Rafen paced his rival and then overtook him. His rag-swaddled feet slammed against the platform as he hauled himself on to it, and there before him on the low bench he saw a scattering of heavy steel components that were as familiar to him as the cast of his own face.

Receiver; barrel; mainspring; magazine. The disas-sembled parts of a discoloured, ill-cared for Godwyn-pattern bolt pistol lay there in front of him, and to the side stood a single round of ammunition, resting on its base. Schola-trained reflexes made him reach for the weapon parts, even as he looked up to see his opponent across the way doing the same thing. The splices were thrashing their limbs against their chest plates in frenzy now; the race was at its final moment.

Quickly, with care and control, Rafen's hands bus-
ied themselves rebuilding the pistol, each part fitting
into the next, the action sliding together, the magazine clicking home. He had done this so many times
that the deed required almost no conscious thought
on his part; his fingers did the work though ingrained
muscle memory.

Rafen was aware of the hooded man, watching him
finish the deadly task almost at the same moment.
Bolt shells slipped into breeches, slides locked and
hammers cocked in the mirror of each other; and
then the two of them were aiming across the gap
between the parallel platforms, each drawing a bead
upon the other.

This was how the race was to end; to the fastest, the
kill. To the slowest, the killing.

As he turned, for the first time the other man's
hood dropped back off his head, and Rafen saw a
familiar, mournful face watching him from behind
the muzzle of the gun.

'Tarikus?'

THE NEIMOS ROSE from the dark ranges of the abyssal
depths, the prow of the submersible angling upward
as if seeking the pale glow of weak sunlight that penetrated the upper reaches of the Dynikan Ocean.

The vessel slowed, following the wreck-strewn
seabed, weaving over the remains of scuttled trawler
craft and the bones of long-dead cetaceans starved by
the extinction of their prey or killed by tyranid
carcharodon-forms. To the ship's stern, a distance
behind now shortening with every passing moment,
the shoal of kraken came on, driven by hunger and a

shared, almost bio-chemical sense of hatred that burned in their xenos blood.

Every system aboard the *Neimos* that could be silenced was made quiet; and deep inside the hull of the Mechanicus craft, a group of warriors armed themselves and made rituals of combat, counting off the moments until they would face their enemy.

RAFEN HESITATED, HIS finger locked on the trigger. At this range, an Astartes could not miss his intended target.

The Doom Eagle's eyes narrowed, but the other warrior did not fire. His fingers flexed about the pistol's grip, uneasy and tormented. Down below, the splices hooted for death, angry that they were being robbed of the promise of bloodshed.

'Do it,' Tarikus called out, his words carrying. 'Kill me! I have nothing... I am damned and forgotten! Shoot, Blood Angel! It will be a kindness... *Do it!*'

'No...' Rafen began, the pistol wavering in his hand.

'If you do not, I will kill you!' Tarikus spat the words at him with venom. 'I have nothing left to lose!'

The crowd were screaming and chanting, the noise so loud it was like the lashing of storm waves across a shoreline. Rafen blotted them out, and shook his head.

'I cannot, kinsman. There is no honour in it–'

'Honour?' Tarikus shouted the word back at him. 'We have been robbed of that, can't you see? Must I beg you to end this for me? We are in hell, Blood Angel! No one will come for us.' He punched at his chest, where his parasite was coiled. 'We are tainted! Death is the only release.' The Doom Eagle's face fell, and he seemed to age years in the space of a single breath. 'I desire only the Emperor's Peace,' he husked.

It shocked Rafen to see a fellow Astartes laid so low, his will on the verge of breaking. A memory rose to the surface of his thoughts, something he had once heard his mentor Koris say. *Every man has his breaking point, even one of us. Those who say they do not are fools and liars. The trick is to know that truth and to know your-self, and be ready if the day should ever come.*

Tarikus's day, so it seemed, was here. Rafen felt the weight of the bolt pistol in his hand. It was an easy shot; he could put the round right through the mid-dle of the Doom Eagle's eyes, end him instantly in a blaze of white agony. End the pain of a brother war-rior who had been tortured beyond his limits in this hellish prison.

But what would that make him? What line would Rafen have crossed to deal out death to one of his own? It felt like a betrayal – not just of his own moral code, but of his Chapter and his nature, and of Tarikus, who needed brotherhood more than he needed death.

'Listen to me,' he called. 'I will never lie to a battle-brother! And I tell you this, Tarikus of the Doom Eagles. We have not been abandoned! We are not for-gotten!' He held up his free hand. 'That is the defeat our enemies crave!' Rafen stabbed a finger towards Fabius and Cheyne, on the far side of the starting platforms. 'That is the victory you will give to them! We will not break today, you and I!' He shouted as loud as he could. 'Trust me!'

When Tarikus looked up and met his gaze once more, for a moment there was something in the Doom Eagle's eyes that could have been hope. Then he nodded.

Rafen heard the beating of leathery wings, and overhead the shapes of the bat-winged creatures passed in front of the sun, casting swift, sharp-edged shadows. The crowd wanted their blood, and if Rafen and Tarikus would not provide it for them, the flying sentinels would burn down the Space Marines where they stood with laser fire.

Two; they were two, with a weapon and a single round each. Not enough to dispatch a horde of modificates and a flight of sentinels. Would the bolt pistols even fire? Rafen would not have been surprised to discover the whole race was no more than the preamble to a sick joke for Bile's amusement.

'Time to find out,' he said to himself, and turned, coming low, falling into an aiming crouch. He was aware of Tarikus doing the same, following his lead.

The wind had changed direction, and Rafen scented the chemical tang of fuel in the air. The top of a stubby promethium tank was visible just over the lip of the broken-down blockhouse.

Rafen pulled the trigger, and the pistol barked, Tarikus doing the same an instant later. He saw sparks of bright colour as the mass-reactive rounds tore through the container's protective cowling; and then there was a huge sphere of rippling orange fire, expanding outward, ripping into the ranks of the splices.

A wash of heat-shock slammed into the Blood Angel and it threw him from the platform. Rafen went with it, curling into a ball to ride out the blast.

THE DOOM EAGLE hit the ground in a crouch, still gripping the empty bolt pistol in his hand as if it were some kind of talisman – and perhaps it was, the inert weapon a small reminder of the things he had once taken for granted, the trappings of his life as a warrior of the Adeptus Astartes. He turned it over in his grip, examining the scratched, pitted surface of the gun in the dancing orange light from the fires. The weapon was ruined; if he had presented such a thing to the armoria adepts on his home world, they would have cursed him for such poor treatment of the bolter's machine-spirit. But still, damaged though it was, it had performed its given function.

'I will do the same,' Tarikus said to himself, listening to the animalistic screams of the panicking beast-men. He said the words with more assurance than he felt.

A shadow came through the thick, choking wall of smoke that was rapidly filling the lower level of the crater. The Blood Angel Rafen emerged and nodded to him, offering his hand. 'Come,' he said. 'Bile was foolish enough to think we would not be a difficulty to him. He allowed himself to grow lax in this place, but that advantage is now lost to us.'

Tarikus accepted the other warrior's help and got to his feet. He frowned. 'What you said, up there on the platform… they were good words.'

Rafen shook his head. 'I told you only what you already knew.'

'No,' said Tarikus. 'You told me what *you* believe. And perhaps, a fraction of me wants to believe it too. But you need to understand. I am dead, Blood Angel. It matters little if you pulled the trigger or if you did not. I am already dead.'

The other man snorted. 'You're a cheerless one, aren't you? Well, you may speak for yourself, Doom Eagle, for I am very much alive, and I intend to remain that way for a long time to come.'

He turned to move off, but Tarikus stopped him. 'Tell me what you meant when you said that we were not forgotten. Were those just the words you wanted me to hear, or were they something more?'

Rafen paused, then leaned closer, speaking in low tones. 'Know this. I am not alone, Tarikus. A cohort of my brother warriors even now makes its way here through the oceans, aboard a vessel called the *Neimos*. They will be here soon, I'm certain of it. And when they come, I want this place to be a burning beacon to them.'

'You came from this ship?' asked the other Astartes. 'But how can you know if they are still out there?' He grimaced. 'Dynikas V is a death world. The hazards out in the deeps are lethal, monstrous things. You have no way of knowing if your kinsmen will make it.'

'*I know*,' Rafen insisted. 'I have my faith in them, and that is unshakeable.' He studied his fellow warrior. 'You remember *faith*, don't you? You must have had it once, for Bile and his torturers to have taken it away.'

Tarikus's expression hardened. 'I remember. I have not lost it.'

Rafen seized on his words. 'Then help me remind all the rest of the brothers here as well!' He swept his hand around, indicating the ranks of cells up above them. 'Bile likes to have an audience for his games, doesn't he? The braggart can only find his pleasure in inflicting pain upon others and then basking in the glow of it. But now we can turn that on him.' The Blood Angel's bruised, smoke-smeared face split in a thin smile. 'Every battle-brother held prisoner in this place was made to watch this cruel little race. Forced to observe because Bile thought to make us another of his "lessons".' He took a breath. 'I know many battle-brothers have fought back before me, and failed. But I won't. *We* won't.'

'How can you be so certain?'

'Because every single Astartes in this place is going to join us. Mark my words, Doom Eagle. Together, we will rally these kindred.'

'They are no longer the warriors you think they are, Rafen! They have been broken by years of unspeakable torture, or else convinced they are forsaken!'

'Like you?' Rafen asked. The smile became a feral grin. 'Come. We need to raise our army, if we are to put this place to the torch.'

In the mayhem that followed the promethium explosion, the splices were in chaos. Some lay dead, consumed in the blast set off by the bolt shells, and more were caught unawares by the swift fires that lashed across the lower levels of the prison complex, propelled by the constant winds.

Of their master, there was no sign, and unknown to them, in a fit of fury, Fabius Bile left his minions to fend for themselves, having ordered his second Cheyne to let the flames run their course and burn out untended. The Primogenitor reasoned that the splices too slow to escape on their own would be stark reminders to those who did flee the fire, reminders that when Bile demanded blood and death, he would not accept anything else.

But still the beast-men were pathetically loyal. Whatever remained of their human identities was long gone, subsumed by a cocktail of genetic reorientation drugs and irrepression surgery. Bile had taken each one and caused dormant strains of animal DNA to reassert themselves; what emerged at the end of such a process was either dead or utterly inhuman.

Their bestial minds were in thrall to their creator, and so it was that in his name groups of them swept through the still-burning, smoke-wreathed wreckage, looking for the inmates who had dared to show defiance.

It was an error they would not live to regret.

ALONG ONE SHEER wall of the crater, fires burned and gave off tarry smoke where a service channel filled with oily fluids had been ignited by a stray piece of white-hot wreckage. The smoke enveloped a work-shack raised up on iron pilings; webbed into the network of pylons ringing the arena-like space, it was the centre of a nexus of old, corroded cables looping away towards the bell-mouthed vox horns.

Nearby, the ape-splice that had survived being thrown from the bridge by the Blood Angel led a pair of stocky ophidians as they stalked through the grey-black haze.

The simian was the first to perish, as Rafen decided to correct his earlier lenience in leaving the mutant alive. The Astartes burst from behind cover and clubbed the splice hard in the base of the spine with his inert bolter. It reeled and tried to spin around, its huge hands grasping at the air – but the blow was so hard it snapped spinal bone and tore nerves. Even as the simian tried to snarl out its anger, pain threaded through it as it lost all feeling below the waist. The beast went to the ground and Rafen followed through by falling hard on his enemy's throat. A sickening crack, a wet gasp, and it was done.

The serpent-like ophidians panicked and fell back, straight into the path of the other Astartes. Tarikus punched the closest of them to the ground, taking care to pull the blow – they needed one of them alive – then spun and disarmed the second, wrenching a curved short-sword from its grip.

Rafen crossed to the second ophidian, and without a moment's pause, he gathered up the stocky reptilian and threw it into the burning fluid channel. Soaked in the flammable muck, it screamed and boiled.

Tarikus pointed the stolen sword at the splice he had knocked to the ground. 'That will also be your fate unless you do as we command.'

The ophidian's head bobbed on its long neck, yellow eyes wide with fear.

Rafen gestured at the workshack. 'The vox network runs through there. You will activate it for us.'

The splice broke into a spasm of nodding, and scrambled towards the shack, eager to do whatever it could to preserve itself. Its comrade had stopped screaming, and now a new stench – of sweet, burned meat – joined the others in the air.

WHEN IT WAS done, Tarikus gave the ophidian-splice the gift of a quick and painless death, slicing its throat with a quick pass from the blade. It looked at him as it bled out, a betrayed look in its dull eyes; as if there was any chance they would allow it to live.

Rafen leaned forward over the blinking lights and chiming clockwork of the workshack's console. Perhaps in another life, this compartment had been a control centre of sorts, but now it was a retrofitted nexus for cabling and conduits that defied the Blood Angel's understanding. They snaked across the walls and the floor in bunches, coiled over one another like the roots of a giant plant. He wondered what damage might be wrought with a single krak grenade in a place like this; but the point was moot. Even with a blade, one could hack at the cables around them for hours and never cut into anything vital.

He dismissed the thought and found what he was looking for; a honeycomb-shaped vox pickup dangling at the end of a collapsible armature. Rafen saw the power lumes glowing where the ophidian had dutifully activated them. He tapped at the vox and a dull thud sounded out beyond the workshack, resonating out of the speaker horns.

He glanced at Tarikus, who stood watching at the doorway. The Doom Eagle gave him a nod.

Rafen took a deep breath, and began to speak.

SO OFTEN, THE VOX horns were used to broadcast sonic tortures, execution commands or the damning sermon-like orations of Fabius Bile himself. Today, they carried different words, in a voice that was strong and clear. Every Astartes in the compound halted, held their breath, strained to listen to the sound of it.

'Brothers,' began Rafen. 'Kinsmen, cousins, Astartes all. Hear me. I have much to say but little time to say it, so I will not waste breath on tricks of oratory or rhetoric.' Angry shouts sounded from the splices as they understood what was going on; but the voice from the vox was louder than all of them. 'This place was built to destroy something precious to us, something each of us shares, no matter which Primarch or Chapter we call our own. I speak of *brotherhood.*'

The Blood Angel's hand clenched, and he remembered the feel of a slip of parchment between his fingers, an oath-paper lined with words in thin ink-script. 'Bile has isolated us, severed all but the most cursory of contacts. He sows distrust and suspicion, wears you down with the slow grind of mindless days and tormented nights. The bastard wants you to believe you are forgotten. He lies. I am here to tell you that he lies and lies!' Rafen's voice rose, finding its strength. 'Look within yourselves, brothers, and you will understand. You have been waiting for this day, even if you did not know it. This day, when you are reminded of who you are. My purpose here is the same as yours, to serve the God-Emperor and Holy Terra! Know that each of you is the harbinger of your own freedom!'

From the corner of his eye he saw Tarikus react to something outside; and in the distance he could hear the shouting of his enraged enemies, coming closer.

He could not stop now. 'I say to you all that this day, we are not Blood Angels, Doom Eagles, Space Wolves, Taurans, Salamanders, Crimson Fists… We are one great legion, one heart and one mind! We are the Adeptus Astartes, the Space Marines, the war gods and terrible swift sword of our Emperor! We are His will, and we have always been so!' Gunfire was rattling off the walls of the workshack now, shells ripping chunks from the walls and blowing out machinery in fat plugs of sparks. 'You have nothing to lose, Sons of Mankind, and honour to be gained! Even if you doubt all that I have said,' he shouted, his words coming in a rush, 'know this single truth! Alone, you are lost. United, we are unstoppable–'

His voice was lost in the screech of an incoming rocket motor. Rafen threw himself away from the console as the short-range missile screamed in on a trail of orange smoke and impacted the workshack with a thunderous detonation.

THE FLIMSY STILT-CONSTRUCTION folded as if it were made of paper, the support pillars snapping and the cables strung to the vox horns ripping free to lash at the air like errant whips.

Cheyne stalked forward, into the heaped, smouldering rubble, cursing the New Men who stood around him, hesitating. 'Find those whoresons! I'll bite out the hearts of any one of you that fails me!'

A thick-necked New Man in a tattered leather cloak waded into the debris and used his sword to sift through the wreckage. 'Here!' he began.

He did not speak again, as his throat was opened. Tarikus exploded out from under a heap of rubble, leading with the curved blade he had stolen from the ophidian, and tore into the New Man, stabbing him over and over in a frenzied, vicious assault. Close by, Rafen staggered up, shouldering aside a flat panel of cracked sheetrock. He was bleeding from dozens of small wounds where chips of broken glass were embedded in his face, but he was panting and high with battle-anger. The Blood Angel shook off a sheen of dust and steadied himself, glaring around for something he could use as a weapon.

'I wanted to execute you the moment I laid eyes on you,' spat Cheyne. 'My master wants you to toy with, but I think I will defy him just this once.' The androgyne raised a wicked-looking bolt pistol, the muzzle shrouded by a blossom of mirror-sharp knife blades. 'Your rousing little speech was wasted on these worthless fools, whelp. Don't you understand? They're defanged, they have no will to fight. Fabius struck it from them! You Astartes are no better than common men, at the core. In the end, you all break just the same.' Cheyne's torn cheek rippled. 'I will drag your carcass up the ramps for all your blighted brethren to see.'

'Your error,' Rafen said, spitting out a mouthful of dust, 'is that you think your words are as pretty as your face. But neither is true.'

'Enough talk, then.' Cheyne aimed. 'When you see your Corpse-God, be sure to tell him how you failed.'

'Not today!' A grey-haired figure rushed from the smoke and shadows, slamming into Cheyne and knocking him off-balance. Rafen saw a rusted length of metal press into the flesh of the New Man's throat.

'Vetcha...' muttered Tarikus, disbelief clear in his voice.

'Aye,' said the Long Fang veteran. He ground the improvised blade into Cheyne's neck. 'Have your freaks stand down, then put up that gun of yours. And if you even think about speaking a word of that damned agony prayer, I'll gut you like a rock eel.'

The androgyne forced a crooked smile as blood pooled in the hollow of its neck. 'What's this? The blind old Space Wolf has finally gone senile?'

'I've never needed to see you to find you, creature,' spat the Astartes. 'I can smell you! Now do as I command, or I'll bleed you here and now!'

Cheyne glared at the two other New Men, and they let their guns fall to the ground. 'What has come over you, Vetcha?' The androgyne changed tack, speaking in a warm, calm tone. 'I thought you had reached an understanding about this place, yes?'

'What you *thought* was that I was your lapdog! What you thought was that I could never be a danger to you!' snapped the Space Wolf. He grunted in annoyance. 'Throw the pistol to Rafen! Do it now!'

Cheyne gave a theatrical sigh and tossed the gun, but deliberately so, landing it beyond the Blood Angel's immediate reach. As Rafen bent carefully towards it, Cheyne kept talking. 'You know it's useless to fight us, Vetcha. You learned that lesson. Now you're throwing away your life just because this arrogant idiot tried to rouse a rabble?' He chuckled. 'What have you done?'

'You know *nothing!*' snarled the Space Wolf. 'If one single Astartes defies the enemies of man, then we *all* defy them! If you had not been grown in some vat of chemicals, you might understand that…'

'How human of you,' said the androgyne. 'I'm so disappointed.' With a sudden jerk of the wrist, Cheyne's hand flicked up and the lengthy bone blade whispered out of the hidden sheath in his palm. The New Man spun and gashed Vetcha across the throat and torso, trying to find an angle to pierce flesh and find the old warrior's heart. The Space Wolf hissed in agony, and jerked his own weapon forward. The blunt, rusted blade went in through the androgyne's ribcage and burst from its back in a welter of crimson. Vetcha shoved again and pushed the makeshift knife deeper.

Boltfire rang out as Rafen fired a salvo of shots at the other New Men, and Tarikus went in to finish off Bile's thugs with his blood-smeared blade.

Cheyne staggered and collapsed, falling to the sandy ground in spasming jerks. Breathing hard, Vetcha hawked up phlegm and spat in the androgyne's face.

'I will not lie,' Rafen told the veteran. 'I wasn't expecting you.'

'Neither were they,' Vetcha replied.

The Blood Angel eyed the old man's wound. It was deep and running dark. 'Are you all right, Long Fang?'

'It is nothing,' he was told. 'I'll mend.' Vetcha pulled his ragged prison robe closer about him. 'Now give me a weapon.'

'Why the change of heart?' said the Doom Eagle. 'You've been here for years, old man. The Emperor knows how many times you must have had that chance, to kill Cheyne or Bile, and yet you did not take it. Why now, all of a sudden?'

'He doesn't trust me,' Vetcha said to Rafen.

'Can you blame him?' came the reply. 'So, answer his question.'

Vetcha turned and glowered at Tarikus. 'I did it because... *Because this is the day I have been waiting for.*'

The Doom Eagle said nothing for a long moment, then gave a slow nod. 'Good enough, old man.' Tarikus pressed a sword into the veteran's grasp and the Space Wolf grinned as he ran his thumb down its length.

Rafen took a moment to loot the dead for weapons; he came away with skinning knives, bolt pistols and several clips of ammunition. 'This will do for a start.'

Vetcha made practise swipes with the sword. 'You meant what you said.' It was not a question. 'Are you ready to take those words and make them actions?'

'This place will be a charnel house by nightfall,' said the Blood Angel. 'In the name of Sanguinius, I swear it.' He hesitated, drawing a device from a pouch on Cheyne's cooling corpse. It resembled an Astartes auspex, but carved from bone and slivers of crystal.

'What is that?' said Tarikus. 'A control device?'

Rafen gave a nod. 'For the cells, I'd warrant. A master key...'

'If you open the cells, Bile will know we have escaped,' warned Vetcha. 'He'll reverse anything you do...'

'We'll see,' Rafen replied, and crushed the device in his fist.

THIRTEEN

In their current state, the warriors three – Rafen, Tarikus and Vetcha – resembled anything but the noble ideal of the Adeptus Astartes. Robbed of their armour and Emperor-blessed weapons, clad in rags and torn robes, stained with dirt and smeared with blood, an observer would have thought them to be hellish death-dealers from the heart of some nightmarish battlefield, choosers of the slain drawn up from ancient myth to bring murder to all that lay in their path.

Only in the set of their jaw, the intention of their swift gait, did they reveal themselves for what they were. Warriors of single purpose, joined for a common goal. The Blood Angel, the Doom Eagle and the Space Wolf ran swiftly along the ascending ramp of stone and hard-packed dirt, climbing the spiralling levels towards the lip of the crater-prison.

They came upon the iron cell chambers ranged up around them in unkempt piles. The containers creaked and rocked in the endless winds, unsecured hatches caught in the gale banging open. The sun passed behind a wall of heavy cloud and pits of deep shadow grew in the spaces between the cells.

Rafen slowed and carefully peered into one of the open chambers. He fingered the magnetolocks on the doorjamb; they were set in the open position. 'Well now. It looks like Cheyne's toy worked.'

Tarikus came closer, sniffing the air. He made a sour face. 'These cells were not occupied, Blood Angel. I doubt they've been used in years.' The Doom Eagle glanced around. 'Much of this infernal place lies derelict and empty.'

Rafen considered that for a moment. Had Bile's fortress once been filled with Astartes prisoners? And if so, where were they now? From what he had gathered from the old Space Wolf, the interned population of the retrofitted complex had to be less than a dozen lost Space Marines. 'If the locks have been deactivated, then there may be battle-brothers walking free on the upper levels–'

Vetcha sucked air in through his cracked teeth and shouted over Rafen's words, raising the scimitar-like sword in his hand. 'Warriors,' he snarled, 'I smell company!'

Rafen heard the heavy clatter of dozens of clawed and cloven feet over the tops of the metal containers. He brought up the boltgun he had stolen from Cheyne and panned it around, waiting for a target to reveal itself.

'Behind us, too!' called Tarikus. He had a bolt pistol in each hand, aiming them in different directions.

Above, there were the canyon walls made of cells, and below, the curve of the rocky slope. Rising up the latter, bearing weapons and stinking of spent promethium, came a cluster of cloaked New Men.

'Come to succeed where Cheyne failed, no doubt,' said Rafen. He fired off a trio of shots, breaking up the line of the Bile's gene-thugs.

'Splices incoming!' shouted Vetcha.

Rafen's gaze snapped back in time to see a wave of beast-things boil over the edge of the cell towers and drop towards them. Once-men with aspects torn from insects, felines, bats, reptiles, canines and simians came rushing down; it was a true menagerie of horrors.

The blind veteran bellowed the name of his primarch in a raucous war cry and became a whirl of violence, swinging the scimitar blade in lethal circuits, wading into the mass of the enemy without a moment's pause. Rafen heard the old man laughing darkly as he took heads and cleaved bodies; the ill-trained splices had come down bunched up tightly, and Vetcha could smell their odours so clearly he had no need to look upon them to make his kills.

Tarikus opened fire with the bolt pistols, firing both weapons at once. Rafen saw an orange-furred, ropey-limbed simian blown backward with a fist-sized hole punched in its chest, a minotal at its side killed by a round that blasted through its eye socket.

The New Men were closing the gate, however. Rafen eschewed cover and dropped to one knee. A spindly arachkin that made it to him reared up; in return he slashed with the cluster of blades along the muzzle of Cheyne's bolter and opened the creature's gut, spilling ropes of steaming entrails across the dirt floor. Kicking the dying splice away, he fired into the advancing party.

Vetcha howled as a canine took a bite from his arm; in turn the Space Wolf cut the dog-thing apart. 'How many?' he called out.

'More than enough,' Tarikus retorted, gunning down a pair of rat-men. He staggered back, ejecting spent ammunition clips from his pistols, reloading on the move. 'Has every one of them in this hell-hole come to fight us?'

'It would seem so...' Rafen offered, then grimaced as the gun in his hand locked on a fouled round. Cursing the ill-maintained condition of the purloined weapon, he worked the slide as the New Men charged. Ejecting the misfire, he slammed a fresh round into the chamber, but Bile's gene-formed warriors moved like lightning. Shots went wild as the biggest of them – a man-mountain of flesh in a long mantle of leather rags – struck the Blood Angel with a heavy mace.

Rafen rolled with the impact, letting it knock him off his feet. He landed hard and wheezed. The effort to get back up was burdensome, suddenly twice as difficult as it should have been. He felt the now familiar, unsettling spasm against his ribcage. The parasite was moving, awakening.

'Mistake,' said the cloaked warrior, its voice rumbling like an engine. 'Nothing but pain for you now. Nothing but *pain*.'

Rafen raised the gun and his finger tightened on the trigger; but the New Man was already speaking, whispering the parasite's cantrip. Cheyne, so it seemed, was not the only one who knew the words of the agony prayer.

The Blood Angel tried not to scream, but the exhalation burst from him uncontrolled; white-hot jags of torture lashed through his nerves and he stumbled, dropping the gun. Every muscle in his body was aflame, his flesh aching with searing, burning pain. The core of the fire inside him was the roiling, writhing maggot, thrashing within the meat of his chest. He tried to frame a litany of strength, an entreaty to Sanguinius to grant him fortitude, but every iota of his self was given over to the agony. He was an empty vessel, slowly filling with suffering.

The hulking figure's voice grew louder and louder, the sound reaching Vetcha and Tarikus. They too fell, weapons silenced, as their bodies rebelled against them.

THE NEW MAN drew in a deep breath, preparing to speak the terminal stanza of the pain-prayer. These words would stimulate the daemonic parasites within earshot into a fatal frenzy, climaxing in an eruption through flesh and bone that would kill their hosts.

He did not begin. A spear of rusty iron, hastily fashioned from a length of gantry, whistled out from the shadows beyond the cells and impaled the New Man through the throat, silencing him. The rod lodged there and blood burst from the entry and exit wounds in a red tide.

From the shadows came figures in torn robes, warriors who resembled anything but what they were. Some were scarred and beaten, others dazed or hollow of eye as if they moved through a dream; but all of them brought death as their companion. The freed Astartes rushed forward in a tide of fury, ripping apart the splices and storming straight into the lines of the New Men. Every throat that could be cut was cut, every voice of the enemy silenced before a single word of the pain-prayer could be uttered.

The agony abated, withdrawing from his body, and strong hands hauled Rafen to his feet. He lurched unsteadily and shuddered, as if uncomfortable in his own flesh, as if it had become ill-fitting on him. 'Warp take this thing,' he grated. 'Someone give me a blade and I'll cut it out of myself right now!'

'That would be a mistake, kinsman.' Rafen looked up into a craggy, frost-grey face lined with a cross-hatching of deep, livid scars. 'They know when you're trying to kill them. The cursed things bleed a poison so potent it can shrivel your hearts to cinders.'

'I... I am Rafen, of the—'

The pale-faced Astartes waved away his words. 'Blood Angels, yes. We know who you are, Son of Sanguinius. I am Kilan of the Raven Guard.'

'Well met, Kilan.' Rafen panted, feeling his flesh retaking control of itself. 'You heeded my call.'

Kilan looked around at the rest of the unkempt handful of warriors as they performed confirmation kills on the enemy survivors. 'You opened the doors.'

'In more ways than one,' said another Astartes, his tone heavy and weary as he approached. 'How did you do it?' The swarthy, shaggy-haired warrior had a bull's head icon branded into the meat of his arm that marked him as a brother of the Taurans Chapter.

'Luck,' said Rafen, 'luck and the Emperor's grace.'

'*Ave Imperator,*' said Kilan, bowing his head. When he looked up, he had a feral grin on his lips. 'I tell you, Rafen, I am almost giddy. So many attempts at escape we have made, so many failures... When the cell doors opened, many of us refused to leave.'

'They thought it was another of Bile's mind games,' said the Tauran. 'More of his bloody tricks of the brain.'

'No game,' said Tarikus, coming closer. 'Not this time.'

Kilan studied Rafen, the deep red of his eyes boring into him. 'Those were fine words you spoke, Blood Angel. They stirred a fire in all of us.'

'I did nothing,' he replied. 'I only reminded you of what you already know.'

'He has a way of doing that, *ja,*' said Vetcha, his breathing laboured. The Space Wolf's words got a hard look from Kilan and the other escapees.

'Why is this relic still drawing breath?' spat the Tauran. 'He's a collaborator. He should be corpse flesh!'

'You dare?' growled the old veteran. 'Try if you will, runt!'

'He helped us,' Tarikus insisted. 'The androgyne died by his hand.'

'Indeed?' said Kilan, his grin widening. 'Then it appears you chose your moment well, Long Fang. I don't think I've ever heard of a Space Wolf showing such slow cunning and restraint.'

Vetcha's lip curled. '*Ja.* Well. Live a decade inside an iron cell and you have plenty of time to discover a more... careful method.'

'We have to move,' said the Tauran. Rafen sensed the man was unconvinced, but he knew that alacrity was more important. 'Matters of reproach and culpability can be considered after the fact. The fires are burning out. Soon the smoke will dissipate and the sentinels will over fly the cells. We can't be caught in the open.'

'The others, the Astartes still up there,' Tarikus insisted, gesturing at the ramp. 'No man will be left behind. Today we either burn this place and leave it behind, or it becomes our grave.'

'Rafen, what say you?' Kilan turned to the Blood Angel, but the other man was staring into space, as if listening to a voice only he could hear. 'Rafen? Do you hear me?'

Do you hear me?

The thought-question billowed into telepathic vapour and faded. Ceris blotted out everything around him; the thudding rumble of the *Neimos's* engines, the pitch and roll of the submersible's deck as it rose up through the ocean, the chatter and movement of the crew-servitors at their control stations. He was dimly aware of the others nearby, the Blood Angels and Flesh Tearers gathering their weapons for one final check before they took to the battle.

The Codicier had already prepared himself in a moment of quiet contemplation, finding an empty crew cabin where he could consecrate his force mace with a measure of sanctified oil, blessed by the High Chaplain Argastes himself. The weapon hung at his hip, ready for use, and his bolt pistol, duly cleaned and newly affixed with fresh purity seals, nestled in his holster. Ceris was upon one armoured knee, head bowed and his helmet at his feet. The soft sapphire glow of his psychic hood cast a cold light around him, and he sensed the air of unease it created in his battle-brothers. They kept a distance from him as he worked his magick; even among his kindred, the ways of his psionic arts were forever viewed with distrust.

He pushed out again. Out past the sparks of thought that were his comrades; Noxx, the warrior's feelings marbled by streaks of darkness and duty; Kayne, fighting down his self-doubts as if they were monsters to be slain; Ajir, unable to let go of the conflicts inside him; Gast, clear and strong like ice; Sove, struggling to hide the pain of his injuries lest he be thought unfit to fight; Eigen, proud and ready; Puluo, caught between nursing his hate and hoping to see his commander again; and Turcio, repeating the litany of weapons, seeking focus in the name of his primarch.

Ceris pushed out, out past the hull of the *Neimos*, ignoring the flashes of feral xenos hate at the edges of his sensorium, looking, seeking. Finding knots of fear and hope, all tied around one another. Finding… Rafen. He felt a moment of pride to know that his kinsman was not dead.

Do you hear me? Stand fast, brother. We are coming for you.

THE SQUAD OF canine modificates standing guardian over the dock were skittish and nervous. All of them were given to making low yowls and they constantly fingered their lasguns, their attention being drawn back time after time, away from the featureless ocean they were commanded to watch and over their shoulders to the fortress proper. A ribbon of black smoke emerged from behind the ridgeline, growing slowly into the sullen clouds overhead. Their sensitive ears picked out the noise of gunfire, but no word reached them from the tower. No new orders came, and with every minute that passed, the canines were losing their focus. It was a failing with this breed of human-splice; without a commanding influence on them, they fell into simple action-reaction patterns.

They were unprepared for the invasion from the sea. Breaching the surface like the massive sifter-whales that once thrived in the oceans of Dynikas V, the submersible *Neimos* arrived in an explosion of spray and churned foam. The bullet bow of the vessel pushed a shock front ahead of it, the wave lashing up to wash over the patrol cutter tethered to the corroded dock pilings. The impulse-drive propellers concealed in fairings along the stern of the *Neimos* thrashed at the rusty water, hydrojet systems pushing the craft forward at its maximum surface velocity. The stubby central sail rose like a raised axe head, streams of seawater sluicing across striations of still-fresh damage; in places, the broken tips of kraken talons were still embedded in the rubbery anechoic skin of the submarine.

The canines scattered, running in halting loops, then stopping, then running back, unsure of what to do next. Finally, one of the modificates – a splice that had been an Imperial Guardsman in its old life – raised a laser rifle and fired on the oncoming vessel. The rest of the dog-things began to snarl, and they too opened fire. Drawn by the shrieking concussion of the beam weapons, further up on the rocky shore the silent ferrocrete pilings twitched and folded open, the auto-guns within awakening.

Any ship wanting to make dock would have slowed; the *Neimos* did not. Atop the dorsal sail, a cupola extended from beneath a sealed cowling, presenting a tubular lens array made of etched brass. The weapon was modelled on the shape of an extinct form of Terran selachian, its toothy mouth the muzzle of the energy cannon. Sharp blue-green light lashed out, bursting canines unlucky enough to be caught in its nimbus.

The *Neimos* rammed the stern of the cutter and a swell of seawater flooded into the open deck of the converted trawler craft as it wallowed. The vessel tilted and shifted to starboard, sinking. Now with only a few feet beneath its keel, the submersible ploughed on, losing a steering vane on a bent curl of iron reaching up from the derelict dock. The last of the canines lost their will and ran for the shoreline, but the invader was already upon them. The craft cleaved through the supports and decking of the ramshackle quay, collapsing it into the churn along with the rest of the guards.

Laser fire, red like hate, lashed out from the autoguns on the beach, burning great craters in the hull of the *Neimos*. The vessel would not stop; in answer, the blue-green ray from the top of the sail cast around like a lighthouse beam, scorching a line over the rocky shore, fusing stone and gritty sand into black glass before finding the target. Pulses of emerald lightning flashed and the auto-guns were obliterated in fans of detonation, the servitor brains within boiled alive in their nutrient tanks.

At last the submarine's thrusters died, but the swell it rode drove it on, up the apron of the coast and on to the rough seashore.

With a shuddering moan of tortured metal, the *Neimos* came to a halt on a rise of displaced gravel, listing a few degrees to port as the craft settled. Conformal hatches blew open on explosive bolts and spun away. From the interior of the craft came nine figures in armour all shades of crimson, and they raced up the beach in loping steps, making for the site of the smoke plume.

A KILOMETRE OR SO offshore, the surface of the ocean appeared to boil. In the shallow waters, a cluster of tentacled, furious beasts swam around and about in angry confusion. Cilia beat the water and hooked beaks of chitin gnashed. The prey had vanished into a fog of chaos, merged into a strange barrier of pheromone stench and telepathic anathema that forced the krakens away even as they tried to swim into it. The tyranids were driven back with shuddering force, repulsed like magnetic poles; beyond that, so powerful was the genetic compulsion within them that their own flesh failed to obey the hunger brimming in their thoughts.

Some of the smaller, younger krakens attacked one another in annoyance, their food-need and anger finding expression elsewhere. The older and larger xenos, and the dominant male that had led them here, whipped at the younglings to quiet them. Their simple, bestial predator brains were bewildered, but they were patient hunters. They drew in their tentacles, sleek bodies bobbing in the slow current, and waited.

* * *

'RAFEN!'

Vetcha heard the tone in the Raven Guard's voice and he tensed. The Long Fang felt a tingle along the hairs of his forearms and tasted something greasy and metallic in the back of his throat. He knew that ethereal spoor of old, and his lip curled to be within reach of it. There was witchery afoot, and it was close by. He focused his thoughts on that idea for the moment, using his ingrained loathing of all such sorcery to drag his attention away from the still-burning pain of the wound Cheyne's knife had inflicted upon him.

'What is wrong with him?' asked Tarikus.

The silent Blood Angel gave a sudden gasp and grunted in pain. 'Ceris...' he muttered.

'Who?' The Space Wolf didn't know the name.

'One of my battle-brothers, a psyker...'

Vetcha spat, his suspicions confirmed. 'A weirdling, you mean...'

'My brothers are coming for us. Blood Angels and Flesh Tearers. They're going to attack the fortress.' The warrior's voice took on a new strength. 'The Emperor turns His face towards our endeavours, kinsmen. The time for revenge is upon us.'

'This... Ceris...' said the wary Tauran. 'He spoke with you? In your thoughts?'

Vetcha sensed the nod in Rafen's words. 'Aye. With his talents at our command, we will be unstoppable.'

The Space Wolf made a negative noise. 'Perhaps so, as much as I hate to admit it. In all the years I have been in this place, Bile has never held a psyker hostage here.'

'How could he?' said Kilan. 'There are no walls nor barred gates for a mindspeaker. We can use Rafen's witch-kin to tip the balance for us!'

'We must take the fight to the traitor,' said the Blood Angel, quickening with the pace of the moment. 'We need to gather the rest of the detainees…'

'I'll do that,' said Tarikus. 'Kilan, if you will lend me your aid?'

'Gladly, Doom Eagle.'

Rafen smiled. 'Find the assault team.'

'And then?' The veteran noted how Tarikus and the others had immediately deferred to the Blood Angel's leadership; the lad had a way about him, all right.

'Then,' said the Raven Guard, 'we'll bring the wrath of Holy Terra down upon this place.'

'Indeed,' said Rafen. 'Vetcha, if you will lead the way, we will enter the tower and deny Fabius Bile any chance of escape.'

'Gladly–' The Space Wolf's voice died in his throat as he began to speak. The fire from the blade cut was growing in power, and he clenched his hand, feeling the sensation in it as if it were a distant thing. 'Gladly,' he repeated, this time with more force. 'Follow me, you pups, if you think you can keep up.' Before any of them could question his momentary lapse, he was moving away, the senses of sound and tread guiding him towards the heavy doors that led to Bile's inner sanctum.

His face turned from Rafen and the others, the old man's lips moved in a rare moment of prayer. Vetcha mouthed a silent plea to the God-Emperor and mighty Russ. He asked them for a measure of strength. Not for long. Just long enough to see the day to its end. The veteran fought off a shudder. All he needed was enough strength to stave off the warp-venom that had coated Cheyne's blade.

THE APPROACH TO the fortress was a maze of gunfire. Las-rounds and bolt shells criss-crossed in the air as Noxx and his strike team pushed forward along the dirt road. Resistance was lighter than they had expected, but still stiff enough to trouble them. Sove laid down a line of krak grenades, showing that even with one arm he could still provide a lethal addition to any assault. Eigen and the Blood Angel Turcio were in cover behind a stalled vehicle, sniping at the shadowy figures appearing in the gun-slots of the bunker.

Noxx fired off a salvo of shots and ducked back behind a stone pillar. The psyker was close by, his crimson helmet wreathed with tiny jags of lightning. 'Care to conjure a hellbolt for us?' said the sergeant. 'We're in danger of losing our momentum here.'

'I am afraid my attention is elsewhere.' The Codicier seemed distant, distracted. 'Sensing... I am sensing the dimensions of this place. There is a very strong warp energy signature...' He pointed in the direction of the tower. 'In there.'

The Flesh Tearer cursed. 'Tell me you're not talking about another warp gate! I'll not blast down the doors to this place to find the stink of Fabius Bile and nothing else!'

Stray lasers chopped chunks from the rock near Ceris's head, but he appeared not to notice. 'I cannot be sure. Lord Mephiston gave me a telepathic imprint of the transit-magick Bile used to flee from Baal... This is not the same, but–'

'Enough!' Noxx cut him off. 'If we cannot get to the source of this energy, then perhaps Rafen can. Send to him, guide him to it. Tell my errant cousin that Bile will slip our grasp if he cannot neutralise it.'

Ceris didn't answer; instead he bowed his head low, and the crystal matrix of his psychic hood glowed brighter.

Noxx chanced a look around the pillar, and a storm of laser fire lanced towards him. He swore again and ducked back, his eyes finding Brother Puluo across the way.

The other Space Marine's voice clicked in the vox bead in his ear. 'There's a high-gauge lascannon in the fire slot, lower right quadrant.'

'I'm acquainted with it,' Noxx replied, considering a carbon score-mark across his power armour's right shoulder pauldron.

'All units, give me cover,' continued Puluo. 'I'm going to kill it.'

Noxx nodded in agreement. 'Do as he says.'

Puluo hefted the weighty form of his heavy bolter up in front of himself, then broke into a full-tilt run. The second he left his cover, red streaks of coherent light stabbed out at him. Noxx revealed himself as well, firing from the shoulder, and he saw Ajir, Kayne and Gast do the same, all of them giving the enemy gunners a sudden feast of targets to choose from.

An Astartes behind that gun would have concentrated their fire on Puluo, the largest extant threat; but instead there was a moment of hesitation, then sporadic, reflexive fire towards the other battle-brothers.

It was enough for Puluo to close the distance. He swung down the heavy bolter as he ran and squeezed the trigger bar. The gun crashed, the reports from the muzzle echoing off the walls of the enemy stronghold. Too late, the laser cannon traversed back towards Puluo, but the Blood Angel was nimble for his size, and he weathered glancing hits across his armour to come all the way in to point blank range.

Fuelled by battle anger, Puluo leapt up and jammed the barrel of the heavy bolter into the firing slit where the lascannon gunner was hiding. He released a wild burst of automatic fire into the chamber beyond, riding the big gun's recoil, ranging it around to be sure that everything inside would be killed.

With the lascannon out of operation, the rest of the squad moved up, taking down the remainder of the defenders. Ajir used hull cutters to blow open the portcullis, and together the Space Marines crossed into Bile's fortress, wreathed in cordite smoke.

THE DOUR TAURAN – he called himself Nisos – moved quickly, but he seemed to be always a step behind Rafen as they moved through the corridors of the lower tower, along stone passages laser-cut from the living rock. The Blood Angel paused in the lee of a support and glanced at him. Nisos was watching him carefully.

'You have something to say to me?' Rafen pitched his voice in a whisper.

The Tauran tapped his head. 'You say you hear a voice in your thoughts. This Brother Ceris you spoke of.'

'Not so much a voice,' Rafen admitted. 'More a sense of the man…' He frowned. 'It is difficult to put into words. But he is guiding me. *Us.*'

Nisos kneaded the grip of a lasgun he had stolen from a dead guardian. 'That does not sit well with me. How do you know it is your battle-brother? What if that presence in your thoughts is some trick of Bile's? What if–'

Rafen extended a hand and placed it on the Tauran's shoulder. The edge of fear in the other man's voice was troubling, and he wondered how long Nisos had been in this prison, and what manner of torments he might have endured to so unsettle him. 'You must trust me, my friend. Trust that I trust the psyker.'

'The ways of the warp are the maze of damnation,' Nisos said quietly. 'I have seen men touched by the power of the immaterium, good men, and watched them burn in daemonfire.'

'It is Fabius Bile who will burn this day,' snapped Layko, a wiry, malnourished Crimson Fist who had joined them on Kilan's recommendation. He brandished a pair of wicked combat blades. 'I am eager to give him a taste of my revenge. Why do we delay?'

'Move with care, Son of Dorn,' said Vetcha, slipping back towards them. 'New Men are close by. I smell the foe, all sweat and rotting meat.'

Rafen nodded, half-hearing the old man. He fell silent, allowing himself to lose focus for a moment. Immediately, he sensed Ceris's presence. The psyker was almost there in the corridor with him, like a ghost at his shoulder. Without words, the witch-kin pressed him onward. A pressure, an ethereal hand at his back, turned him to the right. He peered around the curve of another support and saw two of Bile's New Men guarding a heavy circular hatch.

Retreating, he turned back to the other Astartes. 'In there,' he began. 'A psionic energy source, likely the power for our target's arcane warp-sorcery. It must be neutralised.'

Nisos shivered. 'I feel it in the air. A taint, slick on my skin.'

Rafen nodded. He could feel it too, the telltale greasy texture in the atmosphere, the sense of lurking power like the precursor to an oncoming storm.

'Two guards,' noted Vetcha. 'I expected more.'

Nisos gestured around at the walls; a distant alert klaxon had been sounding for some time. 'The others have probably been drawn off to deal with the escape, or Rafen's friends.'

'We go, then?' said Layko, battle-need written large across his drawn features.

'Oh, indeed, we go,' Rafen replied.

THEY CHARGED AROUND the corner in a tight wedge, Rafen leading from the front with the barbed bolter screaming. The closest of the New Men was hit and fell, injured but still alive. The second dodged away, sending laser flashes back towards them.

Nisos returned fire with his captured lasgun and scored hits on the second New Man; the gene-freak's cloak smouldered and caught fire.

Layko came in shouting and beheaded the downed guardian as he tried to rise again. The body fell to the deck, but the Crimson Fist continued to hack at it, shredding flesh and bone into an unrecognisable mess.

With Vetcha covering their rear, Rafen and Nisos sprinted past the massive hatch and bore down on the last guard. The enemy released a fan of laser fire, and had he been clad in his battle armour, Rafen would have dared to wade straight into it and let the ceramite shunt away the lethal flashes of hard light; but he was wounded, ill-prepared, poorly-armed and slowed by the parasite, and such brute-force tactics now would have ended him.

Instead, he threw himself forward, low and close to the ground. Rafen fell into a tuck and roll as Nisos harried the New Man with return fire, and the Blood Angel came up close to the guard, leading with the bolter. He stabbed the blade-wreathed muzzle of the gun into the meat of his enemy's thigh, and before the New Man could react, he fired. At point-blank range, Cheyne's gun blasted a massive divot of flesh from the creature and sent it howling to the ground. Nisos swept in, and fired another laser blast through the New Man's eye; the energy bolt instantly flashed the guard's brain matter to steam and his skull exploded in a cloud of pinkish-grey mist.

Rafen kicked the corpse away and returned to the hatch. Vetcha had pulled Layko away from his kill; the emaciated Astartes was covered in splashes of blood, his fists as crimson as his Chapter's sigil. Layko's face was set in a rictus grin.

Acting quickly, the Blood Angel found the series of iron levers set into an alcove along one of the walls. In moments, the heavy hatch began to groan open, swinging out in thick hinges.

New gales of the psyker-stink gusted out at them as the doorway widened, and with it came another, horribly familiar smell – the battery-acid stench of tyranid pheromones, heavy and cloying in their nostrils.

Rafen cleared his throat with difficulty and took a shallow breath as he moved to cross the threshold; and suddenly, the docile parasite awoke once again. His hand went to his chest, expecting another surge of pain, but this was different. The maggot-thing seemed to be trembling, vibrating inside his flesh. The sensation was nauseating and he felt revolted to his core by it.

The Blood Angel looked up to survey the chamber beyond the hatch and the disgust churning inside him grew tenfold.

Nisos was next, Vetcha and Layko following. All were silent, all sharing the same horror at the sight before them.

The chamber was spherical, and shrouded with metal walls, although these were hardly visible beneath the layers of oozing, gelatinous matter coating every surface. High overhead, above a raised gantry, light seeped in from a circular window. With a flash of understanding, Rafen recognised it as the viewing port he had seen in the floor of Fabius's laboratory.

The wan illumination cast shadows everywhere, but was not so merciful as to hide the full scope of the monstrosity that dominated the room. Hanging in mucus-encrusted chains from a cruciform support frame was the distended and diseased form of a limb-less tyranid beast, shrouded by the softly glowing planes of crystalline psi-baffles.

'A zoanthrope,' grated Layko. 'Throne and blood, it's alive…'

'Bile's pet,' said Vetcha, with a nod.

Rafen studied the beast coldly. Distended and horribly warped by its massive brain, nearly half the mass of the hydrocephalic tyranid psyker-creature was made up by its huge head, a hammer-shaped mass of blackened chitin armour over pulsating pink matter. A drooling mouth of yellowed fangs hung open, serpent tongues lolling out and dripping thin fluids. Rheumy eye-pits glared back at him from beneath a bony cowl, and even in the alien expression, the Blood Angel could sense a palpable, ready hatred. Beneath the bloated head, a sinuous body barbed with protrusions and strange tusks thinned into a long, barbed tail that hung like a piece of dead meat. Wicked talons the length of a man's forearm were curled up against the zoanthrope's torso. Every now and then, they would twitch in palsy.

Alone, this xenos thing was horror enough; but there was more here. Raw-edged wounds filmed with blood that would not clot, seeping from incisions on the alien's spine. Flays of skin peeled back and held in place by heavy iron spikes revealed a swollen bolus of glistening flesh that hung loose towards the floor. Pipes, wet with ichor, penetrated every part of the alien's torso. With each laboured, breathy exhalation the creature made, faint traceries of fine dust were drawn up the tubes, away into sockets on the curved walls.

Rafen dared to take a step closer, and the zoanthrope showed more teeth; but the gesture seemed cursory, and without real intent. Peering at the sac, he saw movement within it, and heard a faint keening. Instantly, the maggot in his chest flexed, making him choke. He saw the same reaction from the others. With disgust, Rafen watched the sac pucker, and from it fell a newborn parasite, shiny with wet mucus.

'They're everywhere,' said Layko, almost gagging on the words. 'Look!' He pointed with his swords. Concentrating on the shadows, Rafen's vision grew definite and he saw what the Crimson Fist meant. What he had first thought might be spoil heaps or piles of shed matter were slowly moving masses of the maggot parasites.

'Little wonder those things Cheyne implanted in us are so agitated,' said Nisos. 'They can sense the closeness of these others.'

Rafen paused, turning back to the wheezing zoanthrope. Closer now, and he could see it was weak and sickly. The flesh of the xenos was pallid, and the surface of its chitin armour was pitted and cracked. A fetid air of necrotic decay shrouded the thing. The alien's head tilted to present him with a jaundiced, milky eye, and he felt a faint wash of telepathic energy move over him. The Blood Angel shuddered, but held fast; the sensation passed as quickly as it had come.

'A creature like this...' began the Tauran. 'It could shatter our minds with a single thought.'

'Perhaps once,' said Vetcha. 'But not now. Bile has made it his slave.'

Rafen nodded. He could see the lines of sutures along the curvature of the zoanthrope's skull, the places where Fabius's chirurgeon had bored into the alien's brain matter and lobotomised it. 'The traitor shows cunning, as ever,' he said. 'Just like this fortress, he has taken what he could find here and perverted it to his own ends.'

'If this zoanthrope is the breed sow for the parasites...' began Nisos. He retched. 'Emperor preserve us! We are tainted by the blood of the alien!'

'Calm yourself,' said Vetcha. 'We'll wail over who is sullied with what when the task at hand is complete.' He turned to Rafen, his blind eye sockets blank and without pity. 'We must kill this thing.'

Rafen nodded. 'Aye. The beast's psychic might is at Bile's command. If he uses it to forge a warp gate, he will be lost to us.'

'But the protection, the pheromones!' snapped Layko, pointing at the tubes. 'I abhor the xenos as much as any Astartes, but if it dies… what then?'

The Blood Angel studied the mechanisms drawing the scent-chemicals from the zoanthrope's gland clusters. 'The veil will fall. Any tyranid predators close by will be drawn to the fortress.'

'So we kill the zoanthrope, and its kindred will come and consume us all!' said the Crimson Fist.

'But if we let it live, Bile will flee.' Rafen shook his head. 'There is no debate to be had here.' He raised the barbed bolter and aimed at the alien creature's head. He tensed, expecting it to lash out, to strike at him in some wild, final effort; instead the zoanthrope folded down its claws and bowed to him, the chains about it slackening.

Nisos hesitated before taking aim with the lasgun. 'Curious. It must know what we are about to do.'

Vetcha nodded. 'It's been a prisoner here longer than any of us. I doubt the arch-traitor's cruelty was any less towards it for its origins.' He coughed and looked away.

'It… wants to die,' said Layko.

'A wish we will grant,' Rafen replied, and fired.

* * *

THE ZOANTHROPE WAS the last of the tyranid master clade still living on Dynikas V. The agonies it had suffered at the hands of the flesh-prey that had tormented it were unbounded; the alien's malleable genetic make-up, the core strength of Hivekind and the key to its victory over the monoforms that infested the galaxy, had been turned against it. The being that had captured it, shackled it, had twisted the zoanthrope with sciences bonded to dark magicks and freakish sorcery. The tyranid became a slave, a breeding machine, little more than a piece of organic hardware meshed into the workings of Fabius Bile's hidden fortress.

If the xenos could have understood the concept, it might have experienced gratitude, or perhaps grasped the incongruity of its fate. But at the end, only one thing mattered; it wanted death, desired it more even than the great unstoppable hunger that lay at the heart of all of its kind.

And in the seconds before its life drained away, even as the bolt shells and laser blasts ripped it open, it gave voice to a final scream of pain that echoed across the planet.

IN THE HALLS of the prison, Brother Ceris cried out and spat blood, flares of bright actinic light flashing about the edges of his psychic hood. He crashed to the stone floor, twitching and coughing, for long seconds caught in the telepathic undertow of the alien's death cry.

THE PSIONIC WAVE of shrieking, boiling pain flashed out across the island in a radial wave, invisible to the

naked eye but blazing sun-bright across the frequen-
cies of the mind. Hundreds of kilometres away,
mind-sensitive psi-slaves aboard the boats patrolling
the Dynikan oceans were killed instantly, and without them the predators in the water began to drift
closer, hunger-lust stimulated by the burst of hate
that the scream kindled in their primitive minds.

At the epicentre of the killing, the psionic shock
touched every single thing that shared a molecule of
tyranid DNA. The clouds of pheromones that had
shrouded the island for so long were suddenly
robbed of any potency, all power bled from them as
the haze of biochemicals quickly discorporated and
congealed, becoming a rain of greasy white ash
falling from the sky.

The wave of rage expanded, like finding like as every
tyranid it touched was abruptly shaken into a ravening,
bloodthirsty frenzy. Creatures that drifted or swam or
flew were immediately aware of something new and
horrible in their midst, as the melange of pheromones
and telepathic blinds concealing Bile's island were
instantly dissipated. For the swarms of the xenos, it was
as if a colossal malignant tumour had manifested itself
without warning in the meat of their body.

All other desires, all other instincts were forgotten.
A towering mad fury reserved for the hatred of
invaders blossomed across the mind of every tyranid
on Dynikas V. They smelled human meat, the spoor
of the unlike, and the drives that ruled their species
took to the fore.

To attack. To kill.

To devour.

* * *

THE ALIEN'S DEATH scream cut into Rafen like a ragged knife, and he threw up his hands to protect his ears. But the sound was no sound – instead it was an *effect*, a field of unseen force rippling about him, through him, into him.

And then came the pain. A fiery churn in his chest that felt like liquid metal pouring down over his flesh, burning him, crisping his skin and bone into blackened gobs of shapeless matter.

The parasite inside him was eating his primary heart; it had to be this. No other agony could be so powerful. The bolter twitching in his cramped grip, he staggered away from the smoking remains of the zoanthrope's body and fell to his knees. Through blurred vision, he could see the others each in the same condition, every man of them clutching at himself in utter agony.

A thin, high-pitched chorus of squealing reached his ears, filling the chamber with every passing second. *The maggots.* All around him, the newborn, unimplanted parasites were lashing at each other and writhing with shock, veins protruding from their glossy flanks, fluids chugging out of their lamprey mouthparts.

The zoanthrope's psychic death throes were killing them; as he watched, struggling to keep himself conscious, the larva-like things burst and shrivelled, vomiting clumps of black cinders into the air. Without the telepathic link to their xenos parent, they were disintegrating as the daemonic elements of their creation were lost back into the warp.

With trembling fingers, Rafen tore open the blood-stained robes across his chest as another sickening roil of repulsion shot through him. He could see the parasite Cheyne had buried beneath his breast, squirming, pressing against the dark clotted matter of scabbed skin where his wound had healed. Then the head of the throbbing, bloody maggot burst from his flesh and hissed at the air, the fronds around its mouth waving. The Blood Angel gagged, but with steely control, he reached up and grabbed the mewling parasite. With a ripping of skin, he tore the thing from him, even as it discorporated into ashen powder.

Rafen spat to clear the taste of acid from his mouth and moved to his comrades. Each of them was stained with the dark powder, their chests bloody and raw.

'We… are free of them…' choked Nisos. 'Free at last!'

The Blood Angel grabbed Vetcha and helped him to his feet, waving a hand in front of his face to disperse the fog of black smoke collecting from the maggot corpses. 'Bile's prison had no need of warders, not while those things were inside us,' said Rafen. 'He will not live to regret his arrogance–'

'Above!' Layko's shout smothered the other man's words.

Overhead, where the ring of gantries circled the circumference of the chamber, a hulking shadow was moving, the glow from an open hatchway silhouetting a figure as tall and as broad as a Space Marine.

'You,' came a voice, as cold as a curse. '*What have you done?*'

* * *

TO THE TYRANIDS' insectile senses, the island seemed to come from nowhere, and the shoal of krakens lurking beneath the ocean surface were suddenly assailed by the vibrations and overspill of prey, so close to them that the proximity was almost maddening.

Their bullet-like bodies exploded out of the shallows, tentacles fanning out in all directions to capture anything that could be consumed and converted into biomass. One dithered over the capsized wreck of the patrol craft, spearing through the boat's internal spaces as it probed for living tissue; others threw themselves on to the hull of the beached *Neimos*, thick ropes of cilia flooding in through open hatches to feast on the morsels of near-human meat cowering within the metal tube. In concert, their coils strangling the steel, they cracked open the submersible, shattering the space-hardened metals and opening it to the saline air.

When they had picked the craft clean, they shifted their mass and altered the configuration of their forms, dragging themselves up the gravel beach and on to dry land, moving with steady purpose towards the gates of the fortress. They could smell the prey, and there was much of it.

In their wake, the waves along the coastline began to froth as countless clades of lictor-sharks, ripper eels and other hungry forms came hunting for the same meat.

'FABIUS BILE!' RAFEN shouted his enemy's name with all his might. 'I name you traitor!' He squeezed the bolter's trigger and sent rounds crashing off the overhead gantry. Nisos joined him, stitching laser fire up in a blazing fan of light.

The Primogenitor snarled as he took a glancing round, and threw himself over the rail ringing the gantry. His skin-coat fluttered open behind him as he fell, and he landed hard and ankle-deep in the mass of a pile of dead maggots.

Rafen was already moving, reloading on the go, putting the support frame and the corpse of the zoan-thrope between him and the traitor. Bile's hand disappeared into the folds of his coat and returned with a wicked-looking weapon.

The Xyclos Needler. Before embarking on the *Tycho's* mission, Rafen had studied all the records he could find of Fabius's methodology and combat prowess; data had been sketchy and often contradictory, but on the matter of the traitor's favoured weapons, there had been a consensus. Bile used a type of archeotech pistol dating back to the Dark Age of Technology, guns whose needle loads could carry a variety of lethal toxins powerful enough to fell even a Space Marine.

The gun chattered and Rafen dodged, feeling the gust of passage as two darts as thick as his finger whispered by his head to bury themselves in the dead tyranid. Beam fire from the Tauran drew the traitor's attention and Rafen broke from cover, looking for an angle of attack. He sensed Layko and Vetcha close by, waiting for their opportunity to strike.

His eyes narrowed; there was no sign of the massive brass-and-steel chirurgeon device Bile often wore upon his back. The machine allegedly supplied the traitor's millennia-old body with warp-tainted chemicals to keep him alive, and on Baal some of Rafen's battle-brothers had learned to their cost that the device had a mind of its own. Still; without it, Bile was denied a key defence, and Rafen would accept every advantage he could get.

'You Astartes fools!' Bile was shouting at the air. 'I wanted to make you part of something great, and now you threaten to destroy everything! Why couldn't you just be good specimens and know your place?'

'We are not yours to toy with, whoreson!' snarled Layko. 'You'll die here in this hell of your creation!'

'Oh, I think not!' came the retort, followed by a hissing storm of needles.

Rafen ducked and sprinted around a stanchion, careful not to lose his footing in the mass of mucal matter and decayed maggot-skin. He fired two rounds and saw Bile take a solid hit in the shoulder that spun him around; but before he could draw a bead a second time, the Crimson Fist was racing from cover, sword blades a web of bright steel. Layko barrelled into Bile with such force that he knocked the Primogenitor off balance and out of Rafen's sight line.

'That idiot whelp!' snarled Vetcha.

Rafen moved, seeking an angle, as Layko connected with Bile, smashing his swords into the traitor with wild, heedless abandon. The expression on the Crimson Fist's face was one of madness. He was lost in the need to strike back at the man who had so tormented him.

Cuts opening across his face and his arms, Bile roared back in anger and grabbed at Layko before the gaunt Astartes could disengage. He dragged the other man off his feet in a burst of speed and strength that Rafen would have thought impossible, and threw him bodily across the chamber. The gesture was not random; Bile tossed Layko straight into Nisos as the Tauran took aim, knocking the other Space Marine down into a wet mass of ashen slurry.

It only took a moment to happen, but it was a moment Rafen employed with the perfect clarity born in hard-fought battle. Fabius recoiled from his attack and found the Blood Angel aiming at his head.

'This ends now, coward,' said Rafen, pulling the trigger.

The sound of the misfire echoed louder than any bullet. With a dull snap, the bolt cartridge mechanism fouled once again, turning the barbed pistol into little more than an ornate club.

A cold smile creased Bile's face as he raised the needler. 'Cheyne never did take very good care of his weapons.'

The traitor's gun chattered; but suddenly the world was turning around Rafen as a lank-haired figure collided with him and threw him to the wet-slick floor. The Blood Angel landed hard, the old Space Wolf's weight upon him. Vetcha gasped and choked, a trio of thick silver spines protruding from his chest.

Furious, Rafen banged the stalled bolter against the deck to free the trapped round and rose up with a roar. Before Bile could react, Rafen pulled the trigger once more and Cheyne's weapon spoke thunder.

The mass-reactive round struck the traitor in the cheek and blasted away a third of his head in a puff of mist. Bile's legs gave way and he dropped into a kneeling position, black blood jetting from his ruptured face.

Ignoring his target, Rafen bent to see to Vetcha. 'Long Fang! You old fool!'

The Space Wolf laughed. 'No way… to speak to your elders, boy…' The poison in the darts was already blackening the veins visible on the surface of the veteran's skin, but still he reached up and pulled open his tunic. There, hidden from sight, was the festering wound from a sword cut. 'Poison was already in me,' he hissed. 'Cheyne… on his bone blade. Better this blind wolf spends his last breath of life well, eh, Blood Angel?'

Rafen gave a grim nod. 'Aye.'

'Tell them on Fenris,' choked the warrior. 'Tell them Nurhünn Vetcha lived to see his enemy die.' The Space Wolf drew in half a breath, and fell silent.

'*Ave Imperator,*' replied Rafen. He stood up, turning towards Bile. Incredibly, the traitor was still alive, his body twitching as jolts of oily fluid spurted from his injuries. The Blood Angel stepped in, touching the barrel of the gun to the ragged wound his first shot had made. He fired again, and this time Bile's skull exploded, flinging his headless carcass to the floor.

Still twitchy with adrenaline, Layko approached the corpse, with Nisos warily training his gun on the remains. 'Is it done?' said the Crimson Fist.

Rafen looked up, towards the circular window in the ceiling. 'Not yet,' he replied.

FOURTEEN

'THERE'S NO WAY OUT!' shouted one of the warriors, falling back towards the main line of the Astartes as las-fire chased him across the sandy ridge. He was a brother of the Salamanders Chapter, and his ebon countenance was set in a scowl.

Tarikus looked up and glanced at Kilan, who gave him a grave nod, confirming the other prisoner's words. The gathering of Space Marines were holding cover in the shadows of the cavern where the enemy had driven them, keeping the modificates out, but only barely. With too few weapons and too many warriors far below optimal fighting strength, they were hard-pressed. The Doom Eagle counted less than ten battle-brothers, and given the choice of them he would have taken only half into war. The death-agony of the parasites had freed the prisoners from the control of the New Men, but the shock had left many of them weakened. Tarikus's hands were still dirty with the blood and ash of the maggot that he had torn from his chest.

'As Vulkan is my witness,' continued the Salamander, 'every splice left in the fortress is marshalling against us!'

'So it's even odds, then,' said Kilan, but his attempt at bravado fell upon stony ground.

'On any other day, I might agree,' nodded Tarikus, 'but we are few, wounded and unfit, and they are many. We can only hold the line.'

Kilan ducked as a laser bolt streaked over his head, slamming into the stone roof. 'Rot their blighted souls!' he snarled. 'We cannot end like this! We are the Emperor's chosen, and for every wound we have taken, all we have lost, we cannot die cowering in the dark!' He fired back, killing a serpent-beast slithering in on its belly. The Raven Guard glared at the Doom Eagle, his eyes aflame. 'The shackles of Bile's prison are broken! If we end here, we will die without honour!'

Tarikus discarded one of the bolters in his hands, the weapon empty, the barrel warped and white-hot with overuse. He loaded his only remaining clip of ammunition into the other gun and whispered words of blessing over it. 'Emperor, I beseech you,' he said quietly, his voice lost in the rumble and screech of the battle, 'deliver us from this.'

'What say you, kinsman?' pressed Kilan. 'Your Chapter welcomes death, does it not? Shall we go out there to find it?' He stabbed a finger at the thronging mass of the enemy crowding the cavern mouth.

'Fate will take us when it is ready,' Tarikus replied.

'Perhaps this is that day—' The Salamander began to speak, only to be cut down by a fusillade of beams spitting from the cluttered entranceway.

Tarikus swore hatred and fired back, killing those who had murdered the battle-brother. He was still cursing them when the pistol breech locked back with a heavy, final snap of metal on metal, the last round expended.

'So be it,' he said. 'Come take me, then, if you dare.' Tarikus listened to the shrieks of laser bolts slashing through the air about him, the bellow and chatter of the modificates, waiting for the sound of the enemy's hooves echoing into the cavern; but instead he caught the unmistakable thunder of massed bolters. Peering out of cover, he saw the modificates being cut to pieces by raging torrents of shellfire and the heavy detonations of krak grenades.

Kilan surged forward, sensing the rout of the enemy as it formed, and Tarikus went with him, charging down towards the cavern mouth.

At the entrance, the smoky light from outside was suddenly blotted out by the shapes of figures in heavy power armour, wreaths of cordite vapour clinging to them like cloaks. Tarikus saw the pointed, feral snout of a Mark VII Aquila-pattern battle helmet, the eye slits glowing red in the gloom. Unbidden, a rare grin burst out across his lips.

'Brothers of the Imperium,' said the figure in black and ruby. 'Stand to.'

'Rafen's comrades, I presume?' said Kilan, laughing.

'The same. We thought you might appreciate some help with this matter.' The Flesh Tearer kicked at a dead minotal and then glanced around at the survivors. 'Is this all that remains?' He removed his helm as he asked the question.

'Aye,' said the Raven Guard. 'A few others with Brother Rafen, but no more.'

'And the arch-traitor?' This question came from a Blood Angel who stood nearby. 'What of Fabius Bile?'

'Unknown,' Kilan admitted.

'I know you.' Tarikus studied the sergeant. '*Noxx*. It's been a while since Merron.'

'Brother Tarikus.' The Flesh Tearer gave him a wary nod. 'It has. Still hold it against me?'

The Doom Eagle shrugged off the question. 'I'll be generous if you tell me you can take us from this place.'

A figure in indigo armour, his head crested with a psionic hood, moved into the cave, turning a penetrating gaze on every one of the freed warriors. 'Our conveyance has been destroyed by the tyranids.' The psyker's hard-edged glare passed over Tarikus and he felt the Blood Angel briefly turning a spotlight on his soul, seeking signs of weakness and taint. 'We need to find another way off this blighted rock.'

'Tyranids...' echoed Kilan. 'The scream we heard...'

'A clarion call,' muttered Tarikus.

'They're coming here,' continued the psyker. '*All* of them.'

'Not the deliverance you were hoping for, I'll warrant,' said Noxx. 'My apologies.'

'On the contrary,' Tarikus replied, thinking again of his prayer. 'We are not dead yet.'

* * *

LAYKO LEVERED THE hatch open and Rafen stalked through, with Nisos behind him. Climbing up to the gantry level where the traitor had entered, the three Astartes had been ill at ease to leave the Space Wolf's body where he had fallen; lacking an incendiary grenade, they could not even grant him a funeral pyre. Rafen took a last look down at the Long Fang as the hatch slammed shut behind him. He resolved to find a way to make sure that every Space Marine who had died unremarked in this place would be honoured in one way or another.

On the far side of the chamber, a heavy airlock was visible, bathed in sickly green light; beyond it had to be the place where Rafen had been interrogated by the renegade. 'We're close to the laboratory level,' he said, noticing the reflexive twitch on Layko's face as he said the words. 'Just beneath it.' His breath made clouds of vapour as he spoke. The near-polar chill of the dimly lit chamber leached the heat from his fingers and through the rags binding his feet.

'What is this place?' said Nisos, squinting. The occulobe implants shared by the Space Marines gave them exemplary night vision, and by degrees the chamber appeared to lighten as their eyes became used to the dark.

There were open-topped tanks crammed into multiple rows, filled with icy cryogenic slush, and overhead dozens of irregular shapes hung from black chains that vanished towards the ceiling. Rafen smelled the faint odour of blood, attenuated by the bite of the cold.

'Dorn's eyes!' cursed Layko. 'This is a meat locker!'

The Crimson Fist was not in error. Each of the objects were corpses – or at least, they were the *parts* of corpses, dangling like cuts of meat in the window of some hive city butchery. Rafen saw gutted modificates of various kinds and things that might have been the raw material for Bile's monstrous New Men. In the tanks too, there were limbs and organs floating in suspension mediums, hearts and lungs connected to electro-stimulators that kept them beating and breathing without bodies.

'Astartes,' said Nisos, in a dead voice. At first, Rafen thought the Tauran was calling them to attract their attention; but he was describing what he saw. Hanging in a line were the legless torsos of figures that could only have been Space Marines, blood still dripping slowly from their opened stomachs into a long fluid gutter below. Visible on the closest of them were the intricate war-tattoos of the Stone Hearts Chapter, each line of text the battle record of the dead man.

Rafen was about to speak, but he glimpsed something that killed his words in his throat. He stepped closer to one of the bubbling tanks.

The air in the chamber was freezing, but what he saw truly made his blood run cold. There, submerged beneath the mantle of slush, Fabius Bile lay naked and dead. His throat was an open, shredded ruin of meat.

'I killed him...' Rafen whispered. 'In the laboratory...'

Layko saw it too. 'How is that possible?' he demanded. 'I saw you blast his head from his neck with my own eyes, and yet there he is... No!' The Fist shook his head wildly. 'This is a trick! Fabius Bile is dead!'

Heavy, sullen laughter echoed across the chamber as a shadowy form detached from the depths of the gloom. 'Am I?' His patchwork fleshcoat rustling as he moved, the traitor moved into the light. With a hissing, chugging whine, the chirurgeon upon his back unfolded its manifold arms. 'You are mistaken.'

No sooner had the renegade spoken, but another, identical voice issued out from the far side of the chamber. Another Fabius, almost identical but for the lack of a chirurgeon-construct, stepped out from behind a towering stanchion. '*Very* mistaken,' said the doppelganger, amused with himself.

Nisos swore under his breath. 'How many of him are there?' he demanded, unsure where to aim his lasgun.

Rafen shook off the shock of what he saw, his hand tightening around the grip of the bolter. It made a horrible kind of sense; the manipulation of genetic material, the creation of replicae and mutant forms of life from nothing, all these things were the meat and drink of the renegade who dared to call himself 'the Primogenitor of Chaos Undivided'. This was a madman who had dared to clone the arch-traitor Horus, who planned to rebuild the gene-code of the God-Emperor of Mankind – by contrast, cutting duplicates of himself, either from raw flesh or by alteration of living beings, would be well within his ability.

'I have killed you twice already,' Rafen spat. 'And if I must, I will cut my way through every single mirror of you until none remain!' He pulled the trigger and fire blazed. His target moved, and the shot thudded into a tank, letting a spurt of supercooled liquids jet into the air. Where the fluid landed, rimes of ice began to form in ragged patches over the walls and the floor.

'You know what must be done!' the first of the duplicates shouted across the chamber to the second. 'I will deal with these animals.'

The other Fabius gave a harsh chuckle and threw himself at the airlock. Nisos fired, but the renegade-double was too quick, slamming the heavy door shut behind him.

Rafen heard a whining grunt of noise, and saw the pistons on the chirurgeon rattle and shift. Oil-filled pods discharged into Bile's spine and he released a hiss of pleasure; then, with jerky, birdlike motions, the brass construct detached from the renegade's back and skittered away on spidery brass legs. It rattled across the metal decking, homing in on the Tauran.

'Come kill me again, if you can, Blood Angel.' Bile goaded him, and with a flourish, the traitor drew a lengthy black rod from a scabbard on his belt, brandishing it like a sword.

The enemy moved, keeping the hanging scraps of corpse-meat between himself and his attackers. Rafen fired on the run, bracketing the traitor with each hit, attempting to drive him, knock him off-balance. The Blood Angel glimpsed the Crimson Fist threading low between the shapes of the fluid tanks and fired again, attempting to draw Bile's attention.

But Layko was too eager, too driven, too wild. The other Astartes burst from cover a moment too soon and struck out with his twinned combat blades, slashing hard and connecting with the traitor's heavy coat. The leathery, tanned hide split and with it Layko carved through armour and into flesh – but the cut was a shallow one.

Smiling, Bile hit back with the rod-weapon and creased Layko's temple with the shimmering tip. The Crimson Fist reacted as if he had been doused in acid, throwing himself aside, his swords forgotten as they clattered to the deck. Every nerve in the Space Marine's body was firing at once, blazing with pain; the smallest caress of Bile's so-called Rod of Torment could magnify the slightest injury into a maelstrom of agony.

Rafen chanced a look towards Nisos, and saw the Tauran engaged in a running battle with the chirurgeon device as it skittered back and forth, snapping at him with barbed injectors and blade-sharp claws. Then Bile was rushing into him, and he dodged with a heartbeat to spare. As the rod cut through the air past his arm, he felt the skin there go tight and stiff with the proximity of the weapon's pain-field.

The Blood Angel fired wildly, shots he knew would not connect, but close enough to keep Bile from grappling him. Following through with a spinning kick, Rafen connected solidly with the traitor's ribcage; but the impact went into a plate of hard armour concealed beneath the flapping coat, doing little more than making his enemy grunt in surprise.

Fabius reacted faster than Rafen expected, and the rod spun around in his enemy's grip like a baton. The tip of the weapon cut an arc downward and this time he was too slow to avoid the hit entirely. The rod connected with his forearm and he bellowed with pain; it was as if his hand had been plunged into a bath of molten metal. Rafen lost the barbed bolter he had taken from Cheyne; in a disconnected way, he vaguely registered it as it tumbled away, falling into an icy slush pool with a splash. The pain resonated through him, robbing his left arm of any function. The limb hung there on the end of his shoulder like a piece of dead meat, numb and useless.

'Come, come!' snarled Bile. 'I want my chance to kill you the same as all the others!'

Others? Again, Rafen found himself wondering how many duplicates of this creature were stalking the stars. Was this the same man he had faced so briefly on Baal?

He tried to work his arm, but nothing came of it. Nisos had his own enemy to fight, Layko was still struggling to regain control of his body; Rafen alone had to make this kill.

Bile held the rod up, slashing it back and forth in the air. 'Ready for another taste?' he asked, circling the Astartes.

A smile as cold as the air in the chamber split the Blood Angel's lips, as he made a daring choice. 'Yes,' he replied, and flung himself at the renegade.

His enemy was taken off-guard, surprised by the frontal attack. Still, the rod slammed straight into Rafen's gut and flooded his body with a torture beyond his experience. He had endured so many different strains of agony, and each had its shade and colour, each a texture unique and equally dire. The power of Bile's weapon was nova-bright and blinding, ripping through him like white fire.

Such a hit would have put him to his knees, had he taken it standing. His headlong rush changed the equation; even as he collapsed, his body wracked with spasms, the force of Rafen's impact against Bile sent the renegade stumbling backward – and there his heavy boots crossed the thick slick of ice across the steel floor. Without traction, Bile's weight turned against him and he fell backward, shouting in fury. Unable to arrest his fall, the traitor crashed through a thin layer of frost atop one of the fluid tanks and plunged into the mix of sub-zero cryogens swirling beneath.

Bile thrashed at the sides of the container, the rod rolling away across the floor, his extremities turning black as frostbite ate into them. The killing cold enveloped him, the freeze marching up his torso as a fungus would spread over the trunk of a tree. Choking, the traitor wrenched himself forward, desperately trying to drag himself out of the tank.

He met the tip of the rod as Rafen, still shaking, blood trickling from his nostrils, ears and eyes, ran it into Bile's chest with all the force he could muster. The renegade's agonised body turned against him and he crashed back into the fluid-filled tank, sinking beneath the surface.

AWARENESS FLED, AND the Blood Angel's mind went dark for long moments. Finally, Rafen felt a hand on his shoulder and blinked back to wakefulness. Ice crystals fell from his face and he looked up from where he had fallen. Layko offered him a hand and he took it. His body ached inside and out, and a fatigue like he had never known lay heavy upon him.

'Lost you for a while, Blood Angel,' said the Crimson Fist. He handed him a lasgun and Rafen's brow furrowed as he registered the weapon.

'Brother Nisos?'

Layko nodded in the direction of the smouldering remains of the chirurgeon; beneath it, eyes wide open and sightless, the Tauran lay dead, pinned to the deck by a dozen of the hellish machine's manipulators. 'He didn't sell his life cheaply.'

'He was an Astartes. We never do.' Rafen began to walk stiffly towards the airlock.

The Crimson Fist gathered up his swords and followed him.

'THIS WAY,' SAID Ceris, pointing into the gloom of the rocky corridor. His voice sounded distant and hollow over the vox link.

Noxx shot him a look. Inside the warren of passageways within the walls of the fortress-prison, every hallway seemed much the same as every other. The crimson flashes from alert strobes impact-bolted to the walls lent everything a hellish, otherworldly air, and the keening sirens sounding down the tunnels were the voices of banshees. Every few feet there were hatchways made of dirty steel, and control lecterns protruding from the walls whose functions he could not determine. They had encountered a few of Bile's New Men here and there, and together they had killed them; but Noxx's skin was crawling with the ominous sense of a threat nearby, and it made him twitchy not to face it head on. 'Rafen is still alive, then?'

The psyker nodded, throwing a glance back at Ajir and Turcio as they flanked the rag-tag group of escapees. 'He is. With the psychic distortion dissipated, I can read him more clearly. He's angry.'

'Aren't we all,' Noxx retorted. 'How far?'

'He's in the tower.'

'And Bile?'

Ceris paused, and Noxx could hear the deep frown in his words. 'Difficult to tell. I sense death, and yet...' He trailed off.

'Sergeant.' Eigen, holding the rearguard, was speaking over the general vox channel. 'Do you hear this?'

Noxx held up his hand and gave the battlesign gesture for 'halt'. Immediately, every Astartes froze in place and fell silent. The Flesh Tearer toggled the gain on his helmet's audial sensors and the noise Eigen had detected became a rushing hiss in his ears. The helm's simple machine-spirit pinpointed the source of the sound within seconds; behind them, closing quickly.

'Like water,' offered Tarikus. 'Could the sea be flooding the lower levels?'

Noxx drew a photon flash grenade and threw it down the corridor, back along the path they had travelled; set to impact-detonate, it immediately blasted a wave of harsh white radiance that illuminated everything as if it were bright daylight.

The floor was a rippling, chittering wave of dark-eyed shapes, serpentine things with massive jawed mouths slithering across the stone towards them. Cracks in the ceiling were allowing streams of them to slip through, more and more of them cascading into the chamber with every passing second.

'Rippers!' shouted Sove, opening fire with his bolter.

'Fall back!' shouted Noxx. 'If we stop to engage them, we'll be engulfed!'

The Astartes obeyed, but one of the prisoners – a young Ultramarine scout – stumbled and fell. The advancing mass rolled over him and began to feed. Noxx fired and moved, the others staying with him.

'We can't outrun these xenos,' shouted Kilan. 'Cover me!' The Raven Guard vaulted to the wall, to one of the control lecterns.

'Do as he says!' Noxx ordered, and the other warriors laid down a fan of fire from bolters and lasguns as the Raven Guard worked. Kilan pulled a set of levers and Noxx saw something move along the walls – metal nozzles at ankle-height, folding out of hidden housings. A familiar smell touched his nostrils through his breath filter: *promethium.*

With a hissing thump of displaced air, the Raven Guard triggered the mechanism and a wall of flame blasted upward, rising to curl along the top of the tunnel. Trapped on the other side, the ripper eels shrilled and died in the hundreds as they were caught by the flames.

Kilan coughed and spat, staggering back to the group. 'Flame jets,' he explained, 'The splices used them to torch the tunnels clean... and to burn the dead.'

'The fire won't last long,' said Tarikus. 'The tanks that feed the nozzles were ruptured in the breakout.'

Ceris pointed again, along a branching corridor. 'This way,' he repeated.

'WHERE IS HE?' said Layko, glaring into the corners of the laboratorium. Rafen stalked forward, the lasgun held out in front of him. It felt small and delicate in his grip in comparison to the bolt weapons he was used to; he had his doubts it would be enough to kill Fabius.

Kill Fabius. The Blood Angel considered the oath he had made, back in the Chapter Master's sanctum, the promise to his battle-brothers and the spirit of his primarch. How many deaths would it take, he wondered? How many good and loyal Space Marines murdered and dissected like animals, how many bullets expended and gallons of blood shed? How much would it take to end this?

'Not here,' Rafen said, finally answering the Crimson Fist's question. Casting his gaze across the chamber he saw a hatchway hanging open, weak yellow light emerging from it in an invitation. 'There.'

'Another horror show?' Layko grimaced.

'A trophy room,' Rafen explained. 'Bile's prizes.' He frowned and gave the Crimson Fist a look. 'I know you want him dead as much as I do, but I ask you to hold your temper, kinsman. We must attack together.'

For a second, Layko's face coloured with annoyance, and he seemed on the verge of decrying the Blood Angel's demands; then his eyes narrowed and he nodded. 'Aye, kinsman. Together.'

'You will not like what you see in here,' Rafen said, making for the open hatch.

Layko followed him in and halted with a jerk on the threshold. Rafen glanced at the other Astartes and saw a series of powerful emotions cross his face – anger, sadness, resignation, horror. The Blood Angel imagined the same expressions had shown on him when Cheyne and the New Men had forced him into this place.

The two of them picked their way through the rows of prize relics, ready for the next attack. Still, Rafen found it hard to keep his focus. At the far end of trophy room, the liquid-filled container holding the stolen progenoids Bile had so brazenly displayed to him glowed, light shimmering through it. He dared not hope that the crystalline vial the traitor had stolen from Baal was still there too – he wanted to abandon all caution and run to it, rescue the sacred blood. It took a strong measure of his self control not to give in; Bile was laying a route for them to follow, that was clear. Somewhere a trap was waiting for them, and any breath could trigger it.

'I do not see him,' Layko whispered, his voice carrying in the quiet. The Crimson Fist moved parallel to the Blood Angel, between racks holding ranks of stolen power armour that stood as mute witnesses to the dishonour of this place. 'He cannot flee.' Layko jerked his head up at the roof. 'This is the upper tier of the tower, and there are no other exit routes.'

Rafen nodded and spoke loudly. 'My kinsman speaks the truth, traitor. You have nowhere to run. Your xenos pet is dead. The warp is closed to you. Your fortress is about to be overrun. If you can still remember what it means to be an Astartes, show yourself. Meet your fate without cowardice.'

He was close to the tank now. A few steps more, just a few steps, and he would be able to reach inside and pluck the vial from the bubbling froth. Rafen's hand clenched and unclenched, and he looked around, trying to see in all directions at once. Almost there.

Layko had halted. 'Blood Angel. Do you see this?' The Crimson Fist bent to examine something. 'This is not Astartes issue. The glyphs on the surface... I have seen them before.' He was studying a canister made of black metal, branded with thick Chaos runes. Through vents in the side of the pod, a stew of emerald mist was visible.

Rafen nodded, his attention on the vial. He was reaching for it. 'Cover me, Layko. I must recover this.'

Both of them heard the creaking. The sound was a familiar one, the sound of ceramite and plasteel turning upon bearings, the working of bunches of artificial myomer muscles beneath the skin of Space Marine power armour.

With sudden, wild fury, one of the dormant suits that lay at rest upon Bile's trophy racks exploded into motion, the fierce red eyes of the helmet flashing into life. A mailed power fist, humming with energy, slammed Layko down and Rafen heard the sharp report of snapping bone. Without a moment's pause, the armoured figure launched itself from the supports and stormed across the metal decking, knocking other cases aside in its headlong rush. Rafen spun away from the fluid-filled tank and brought up the lasgun in his hand.

It was then that he realised the armoured figure before him was clad in the sanguine red of his own Chapter. The wargear was pockmarked by impact hits, battle-scorched and ragged, but it was every inch the holy plate and mail of a Blood Angel. His hesitation froze Rafen's finger on the trigger, his mind racing. 'Brother?' he called.

The harsh laughter echoing from the helmet's vox grille killed that question in a heartbeat. 'Not quite,' said Bile.

Rafen's rage broke its banks at this, an insult piled atop every other offence the renegade had turned against his Chapter. 'You have no right!' he shouted. As Bile crashed towards him, the Blood Angel saw the name of the armour's true owner etched in gold leaf about the chest plate; *Brother Kear*.

'It's a poor fit, I will agree,' Bile retorted, 'but I do not need it for long. I'll shed this paltry skin as I have so many others.' He swung the power fist and Rafen ducked, the impact smashing another display cabinet to splinters.

Through his fury, the Blood Angel registered a moment's sluggishness in Bile's attack, and he understood the reason immediately. Astartes power armour was not simply a layer of clothes a man could choose to don like a robe or a tunic. To correctly mesh the organic machine of an Adeptus Astartes with the perfect function of his wargear took care, time and hallowed ritual; and if a traitor fiend like Bile attempted such a thing... Rafen imagined that even as they fought, the machine-spirit in Kear's armour was working against the renegade, struggling to counter his every input.

His enemy's conceit, his arrogant need for such a grand piece of theatre, could be turned against him. Rafen had an advantage, no matter how slim, and he would use it.

In the next second he was caught by a grazing slap from those heavy, armoured fingers, and he stumbled into a support beam, dazed. Rafen spat thick fluid from his lips and coughed. 'You... cannot despoil and go unpunished. Every crime you commit is added to the tally! Every offence grants you another lifetime in a traitor's hell!'

'Do tell,' Bile said languidly, gathering up a sword from where it had fallen amid the path of his destruction. He examined it, made a swing. 'Will you keep spouting this tired old dogma even as you choke on your own blood?'

'My death will not stop the vengeance of my Chapter!' Rafen shouted back, blasting laser fire at his enemy. 'You cannot escape this time! The xenos will rip you apart or our ships will obliterate you! Death is at your throat, turncoat!'

'Your ships?' Bile laughed, and to hear that hated voice issuing from behind a Blood Angel helm made Rafen's stomach twist in knots. 'How do you think I am going to leave this place?' He came in fast and swung the blade. Rafen instinctively parried with the lasgun and the sword cut it in two, smashing it away in sparking fragments. 'What other reason is there for this loathsome masquerade?' Bile gestured at the armour. 'Look here. I think you know what this is.' His hand pulled a device from the wargear belt, a thick rod etched with runes in gothic script. One end sported a crystal that blinked red-blue in a complex sequence.

It was a summoner, an Imperial teleport transponder. Perhaps it had been taken along with Kear's armour, or perhaps Bile had bartered it from Zellik for some unknown price; it mattered little. The rare archeotech device was encoded with command-level sigils, and correctly manipulated, it could reach through the ether and trigger a ship's teleportarium to automatically lock on to whomever was its bearer.

'You hesitated, didn't you?' said Bile, pushing Rafen back with the point of the sword. 'Your brothers will do the same when I appear among them, up there, on your precious starship. Long enough for me to put that to use.' He nodded towards the canister Layko had discovered. 'Have you ever seen the effects of rot-bane on human flesh, Blood Angel? It is an ugly, sordid death. I have prepared a special variety, just for your kinsmen. One to which, sadly, they will not share my immunity.'

'I will not allow it!' Rafen shouted, turning to attack with his bare hands.

'You have no say in the matter,' Bile replied, and ran the sword into him.

Rafen bellowed and clutched at the blade as it went into his shoulder. The renegade forced him backward until the sword's tip emerged from his back and buried itself in the wall. Bile pinned him there, choking and racked with pain.

'Damn you...' spat the Astartes.

Disregarding Rafen, the traitor punched through the tank of fluids and snatched the vial of sacred vitae, ignoring the precious progenoids as they spilled out on to the floor. Bile continued to ignore him and worked a control lever. A hidden hatch in the ceiling yawned open, and part of the roof descended to form a ramp.

Bile gave Rafen a last look and threw him a mocking salute. 'Remember what I told you before, Astartes. *You have failed*. If you had listened to me, the shame would have been all you lived with. Now, you will be a feast for the tyranids.'

The traitor turned away and climbed the ramp, up towards the cloudy sky and the promise of escape far above.

Rafen's blood-slick hands grasped the razor-sharp blade of the sword and tried without success to drag it back through the wound. He gasped, his breath coming in hard, sharp chugs of air. The abuse his enhanced Astartes physiology had gone through in these last few days was a battle campaign's worth of hurts and injuries, and yet he could not falter, could not rest until his mission was complete. That, or until death itself came to claim him.

And death's touch felt very close at hand for the Blood Angel. Bile had beaten him, time and again, and with each confrontation Rafen felt as if a part of his soul had been chipped away. Defeat was a poison like no other, invidious and corrosive, sapping the morale of good warriors and turning their will to dust. Rafen felt the darkness of it in him at that moment, polluting his resolve.

No. I will not die here. Not like this.

'I will not die...' he whispered, fingers slipping as he tried to dislodge the sword. 'I will not die here...'

'Talk is cheap, Blood Angel,' came a slurred voice. 'Prove it.'

Rafen felt the blade shift and blinked. Layko lurched closer, the right side of his face and torso hanging slack, blood streaming from his nostrils. With his good hand, the Crimson Fist yanked hard on the hilt of the weapon and drew it out, freeing his comrade.

The Blood Angel stifled a cry and staggered forward, barely keeping his balance. 'Layko,' he coughed. 'I saw the hit... Thought you would not rise again.'

'Kantor would disown my name if I let such a love-tap fell me,' managed the other warrior. His words were thick with pain. Rafen saw the misted cast of his right eye; Bile's strike had broken something vital inside the Crimson Fist's skull, and Layko had to know it. He thrust the sword into Rafen's hands. 'Take it. Must finish this. For Nisos. Vetcha. Others.'

The Blood Angel weighed the weapon in his grip. Not since he had been a youth, not since a fateful moment in the shadow of Mount Seraph during the trials of initiation, had he felt so damnably weak. So drained of energy and strength. It would be easy to fall here, he realised. Simple to let his wounds overtake him, sink to the ground and allow fate to choose how he died. It would be fitting for one who had... Who had...

You have failed. The words echoed in his mind, mocking him. If he did no more, then they would be his epitaph.

That would not stand.

'Follow me,' he said, and mounted the ramp towards the roof.

'CLOSE IT!' SHOUTED Turcio, flinging himself across the threshold of the circular airlock. A pack of lictor-shark hybrids swarmed up the tunnel behind him, their dark featureless eyes glittering with hunger. Kayne and Kilan put their shoulders to the cogwheel-shaped hatch and rolled it shut; and as the door was a hand's span from sealing, a scythe of barbed claws rushed through the narrowing gap, whipping back and forth, clawing at the black steel.

Ajir fired off a three-round burst and clipped the talons, giving the others the time to finish the job. The hatch locked home, and immediately the mottled surface began to echo and distend with heavy impacts from the other side.

The assembled Astartes, attackers and escapees, paused to catch their collective breath. The tyranids had overrun the lower levels of the fortress and like a rising flood, they were rapidly claiming every corner of the complex for themselves.

Noxx reloaded his bolter, and without looking up he asked the question that was on all their minds. 'Is this where we will make our last stand?'

Ceris answered, but he seemed distracted. 'The hatch will hold them for the moment.'

'Said that about the fire wall,' Puluo muttered irritably.

'We are inside the inner sanctum of Fabius Bile,' said Tarikus. 'This is his retreat, his laboratory, his house of horrors.'

Gast was moving warily along the metal gangway, peering through armoured viewing slits into chambers that branched off. 'I see cryo-modules. What may be work platforms and operating theatres... Or at least, whatever the archenemy might consider their equivalents.'

'We need to find Rafen and the others,' said Kayne. 'Perhaps together we–'

'Can do what, lad?' Ajir blew out a breath. 'We've exchanged one dead end for another. The tyranids are everywhere, and even if we can last out a siege with them crawling across this blighted place, in a few hours Rafen's standing orders will come into effect. The *Gabriel* and the *Tycho* will blast this place to ashes. Even as we speak, the ships are moving to combat range. Soon they'll engage the gunskulls and the matter will be done, one way or another.'

Kilan pointed at Tarikus. 'I thought his Chapter were the ones who spoke of nothing but death and gloom. My belief in the merry disposition of the Blood Angels is destroyed.'

'Mock if you will, Raven Guard,' Ajir retorted, 'but Sanguinius sires pragmatists.'

Kilan rose to the open challenge in his words. 'Defeatists, more like.'

'You speak of defeat?' Ajir advanced on the other warrior. 'I am not the one who allowed himself to be captured and corralled like a common herd animal–'

'Do not dare to–'

'Be silent, both of you!' snapped Noxx. 'You forget an important fact. You both talk and act as if you have a choice.' He glared around at all the battle-brothers surrounding him. 'Tell me, who here labours under the misapprehension that they will see another dawn? Any of you?' Silence answered him. 'You who escaped this prison, you are free, but you are not. We who came to this world in search of a traitor, are free but we are not. All of us share one goal, in this moment. *Revenge*, and with it the hope we will die well.' Noxx turned his gaze back to Ajir and Kilan. 'If you expect to live, then you are greatly mistaken. There is no way out of here. No egress but to death and the Emperor's Peace.'

FABIUS WALKED TO the lip of the sloped parapet and peered down into the thrashing sea of madness writhing far beneath him. The autosenses of the Blood Angel helmet had proven problematic at first, difficult to put under his control, but at last they were doing as he bid. Bile allowed himself a smile; curious how easy it had come to him, recalling the old mnemonic command-strings to operate the wargear's subsystems. These were skill sets that had lain dormant for ten thousand years, unearthed now and employed as if it were yesterday. The renegade felt a strange sense of disconnection as he tried to frame the events of the deep past in his mind. The memories did not come easily. Irritated, he dismissed his moment of reverie and concentrated on the present.

Far below, all across the central pit of his prison and up around the crater walls, a seething mass of tyranid life was engaged in an orgy of destruction. Whatever was left of his test subjects, his modificates and his New Men, were out there somewhere, if not already torn to shreds by the aliens then within moments of death. Hooting and shrieking and snarling, the xenos were mad with anger; his studies of the tyranid species had shown him that they reacted to an invasion of their territory on an instinctive level with a psychotic degree of violence. Any perturbation in their complex sensoria of pheromones – such as, say, the corruption of their death-scent he had turned to his own ends – drove them to the point of madness. Down there, the myriad variant forms evolved in the Dynikan oceans had come ashore to kill everything they found, and obliterate everything that carried the stink of the non-tyranid.

With the murder of the zoanthrope, the collapse of the aura veil he had laboured so long to construct was the death knell for this secret holdfast. It angered Bile that he was being forced to abandon this place with his work at such a crucial stage. His timetable would be severely disrupted; the project would be set back years, and it would take time to mount a new facility, even using one of the other dozen bases he had concealed about the galactic disc.

But he had long known that the road to conquest was a slow and steady one. Unlike many of the scions of Chaos Undivided, Fabius Bile understood that patience was as much a weapon as brutality and cunning. He understood the need for care and preparation. Why else would he spread his plans so wide? Why else create an army of his own simulacra, each one indoctrinated to believe that *they* were the one and only Primogenitor? For the sake of patience; to ensure that even if a fortress fell, as it had today, no single act of interference from the minions of the Corpse-God could destroy his great strategy.

He would win eventually. It was only a matter of time. Bile glanced down at the summoner where it hung from his belt. The light code had changed; the device was sending to a ship nearby, the pulses growing stronger as the Astartes vessel drew closer. Bile smiled again, and drummed his fingers on the canister of nerve agent maglocked to his thigh plate. He would enjoy the moment when he arrived aboard the Blood Angels ship, the moment when the gas took the crew and turned their lungs to liquid. Any who were lucky enough to survive that would die at his own hands. *Oh yes*, he told himself, *there will be many kills today*.

Then he heard a heavy tread upon the ramp behind him.

RAFEN AND LAYKO emerged on to the battlements atop the tower, and into the dull glow of the daylight threading down from the clouds. The Blood Angel drew a breath and brought up the ornate sword that had been used to cut him so deeply.

'I told you,' Rafen snarled. 'I will not let you escape.'

Bile turned, and his shoulders were quaking beneath the armour as he released a callous, braying laugh. 'By the Eye, you are tenacious little bastards, aren't you? But, it seems, without the intellect to know when they have been beaten.' The traitor gave a mocking bow. 'Come, then. I await your pleasure. If you are so determined to die at my hands, I will gladly accommodate you.'

Layko brandished one of his combat blades; the other would not remain in the nerveless grip of his numbed fingers. The Crimson Fist threw the Blood Angel a look. 'I regret I cannot do as you asked me before, kinsman. I cannot hold my temper any longer.' He saluted him with the short sword.

'Layko, wait–' Rafen's words fell on deaf ears.

The injured warrior broke into a stumbling run that was more a headlong collapse than it was a controlled attack; yet the Crimson Fist was pushed on by a surge of fury that burned through from his heart, a need that drove him like a missile towards his target.

Bellowing the name of his primarch, he connected with Bile's stolen armour and sparks flashed in the air. Layko became a whirlwind of attacks; he spun and sliced, scoring blow after blow across the enemy's torso and chest.

Bile weathered them all, and struck him again with the lightning-sheathed power fist. Layko's body folded like the trick of some conjurer, blood bursting from his mouth and nostrils. His killer followed through, extending the blow to project him up and away, over the edge of the tower. The Crimson Fist spiralled down into the raging mass of the tyranids and vanished.

Rafen rode in on thunder, screaming at the top of his lungs. Layko had to know he was dead, his wounds too great to survive. With his headlong, heedless attack, he had bought the Blood Angel precious seconds to draw in behind and take his assault as close as he dared to the traitor.

The sword sang in his hands, and Rafen slammed the weapon into the points between the joins of battle armour he knew as well as his own. Each cut and thrust he aimed at vital bunches of artificial muscle or feeder conduits from the power pack at the wargear's back. Bile parried with the massive power fist, the blade skipping down the length of the huge gauntlet, tearing gouges in the ceramite, chipping away superheated fragments of plasteel. The Blood Angel ducked beneath the swing of the massive fist, coming as close as he possibly could to the armoured figure, reaching out for him. Ranged against this enemy, for a brief instant he felt tiny, diminished, as if Bile towered over him, as if he were a normal man daring to challenge the death angels of the Emperor.

'Futile,' grunted Fabius, and with a swift grab he curled the fingers of the power fist about the sword and broke it along its length. The shock of the blow threw Rafen backward and he tumbled across the rooftop, landing badly.

Bile laughed again and discarded the pieces of the shattered blade. 'Will you dare to stand up again,

Blood Angel?' he asked. 'Come, I challenge you. Face me once more, if you can!'

Rafen turned over, spitting blood. He could feel the edges of broken ribs grinding against one another inside his chest. The newly-scabbed wound on his breast had split open and he was bleeding there again. When he took in a breath, it felt like stones in his throat.

'Nothing to say?' mocked the traitor. 'No more battle cries or words of power? How sad. I'll be certain to tell your battle-brothers how you died before I choke the life from them…' Bile's hand went to his belt and closed on empty air. 'The summoner…' He stiffened with surprise.

Rafen produced the device from the sleeve of his robe, still gripped in the hand that had snatched it away during his attack. 'Is this what you seek?' With effort, he dragged himself to his feet.

The reply Fabius Bile gave was laced with invective of such venom and potency that Rafen wondered if it might be some sort of daemonic cantrip. 'Give it to me, whelp!' he demanded.

The summoner vibrated in Rafen's hand and emitted a soft chime. He dangled it over the edge of the roof as Bile took a step closer. 'I will drop it.'

'You want me to die with you?' spat the traitor. 'Is that it?'

'No,' he replied. 'I want something else.' Rafen nodded towards a pouch on Bile's belt. 'You know.'

He heard the grin in his enemy's words. 'This, you mean? Your precious relic?' Bile drew the crystal vial from the pouch. 'An exchange, is that it?'

'Aye,' Rafen managed. 'Then you may go and do as you will. Today or tomorrow, you will die. But the blood of Sanguinius is eternal. You cannot possess it!'

The traitor nodded. 'Very well. The vial for the summoner. *Here!*' Without warning, he threw the tube aside.

Rafen bolted forward, the rod device falling from his fingers and forgotten. He went into a dive, arms reaching for the vial as it described an arc through the air. *Emperor, guide me!* The Blood Angel reached out and snatched the crystal tube before it could fall away into the madness below.

Fabius's harsh laughter rose and rose as the traitor stooped to gather up the summoner where it had fallen. 'Pathetic,' he snarled. 'Look at you, giving up your life for a few drops of liquid. It is worth so much to you, isn't it? And yet you do not really understand the potentiality of it.' He walked away. 'Take it! Take it and pray over it for as long as your life lasts, but know that your precious Sanguinius will not save you, nor will your silent, absent Emperor!' Bile glared at him. 'I kept that relic only as a seed for the collection I will rebuild once I leave this place, but in truth it has no value to me. All the data I gleaned from that vitae is in here.' He tapped a finger against the brow of his helmet. 'I have no need of it. It is useless.'

The callous grin on the renegade's face froze as he saw the look on Rafen's face, a look that promised hate and fury. 'You are so very wrong, turncoat,' he replied, drawing himself up. 'Let me show you why.'

Rafen twisted the vial about its length and from the silver detailing about its end emerged a short, thick needle. His eyes never leaving those of his enemy, the Blood Angel stabbed the vial into his chest and injected the contents into his heart.

FIFTEEN

ONCE BEFORE, ON the field of battle at Sabien, when he had joined with the great Mephiston in the final confrontation of the Arkio Insurrection, Rafen had been granted the boon of an exsanguinator. Injectors loaded with the vitae of the high sanguinary priests of the Blood Angels, the fluid within them was a stimulant and strength-giver, said to grant the user a small measure of the power of their angelic primarch. On that day, the exsanguinator gifted to him by the Lord of Death and blessed by Corbulo, the keeper of the Red Grail, had given Rafen the strength to carry that fateful battle to its conclusion. He remembered with perfect clarity the sudden surge of power that had moved through him, the swell of his heart and his will.

He knew now that what he thought to be a moment of communion with his long dead liege lord had only been a pale shadow of the true glory. The contents of the vial, the holy blood from the Red Grail itself, unfiltered and potent, kept alive for millennia by generations of clerics, coursed through his veins. It was gold and it was fire, it was lightning and sun; it was like nothing he had ever experienced before.

Rafen's body was wracked with spasms that went beyond pain. Every muscle went rigid, every nerve sang with the power. His very bones resonated like struck chimes, as the song of his primarch shot into his being. Light crashed about him in waves, bright as a supernova. The gene-matter threaded through his body, induced into him during his rise through the ranks from initiate to battle-brother, was awakened all at once. Every Space Marine carried within them the genetic markers of the primarch that had been their master, bonded to the flesh of the common man they had once been. Every Blood Angel had within them a kernel of Sanguinius's great and majestic power; it lay in the depths of their soul, in the meat of their flesh, there to make them the unmatched warriors of the Emperor's great armies.

And now like called to like. The sacred blood coursing through him merged with Rafen's own, and it echoed to the elements of the primarch's legacy. A unity of power engulfed the Astartes as deep within him, blood mixed with blood as warrior-son and primarch-father were briefly connected across the barriers of life and time.

For one fleeting moment, Rafen knew what it was to be a son of the Emperor; in a storm of sensation and blazing power, he experienced a fraction of that transcendent glory. He went beyond the cage of himself, and into the magnificence that was the bequest of the Great Angel.

He experienced fear; so bright it was, so powerful that he became afraid he would be destroyed by the brilliance of it, like the Terran legend of Icarus voyaging too close to the sun.

Oh fate, what a perfect death that would be. To reach out and touch the face of my primarch.

But even as those words formed in his thoughts, Rafen knew that he could not allow himself to die. Not yet. In the turmoil of the golden, blazing glow, he sensed a truth that was so strong and so clear he could not deny it.

I will not die here. My duty is unfulfilled.

Then he opened his eyes and saw Fabius Bile before him, the traitor cowled in the armour of a good and noble brother, raising his hands to attack.

There was no pain. He felt no wounds, no fatigue. There were no doubts or fears. There was only duty.

'FOR THE EMPEROR and Sanguinius! Death! *Death*!' Rafen attacked his enemy with a speed and a fury that were unmatched. Bile's swing with the crackling power fist seemed clumsy and slow, and it was easy for him to drop beneath it and hammer heavy blows into the renegade's torso.

Time was thick and sluggish, warped through the lens of arrow-sharp senses and bullet-fast reflexes. Rafen felt as if he were speed and power moulded into the shape of a man, unstoppable and untouchable. His bare fists impacted upon the ceramite, each hit coming with all the force he could muster, slamming Bile backward. Cracks in the armour left by previous strikes widened and split, and from within sparks flashed as internal circuitry failed.

Fabius roared with hate and crushed Rafen to him in a lethal embrace, grinding the Blood Angel's head against his stolen armour. Rafen's cheek was opened as it was torn by the sharp corners of the winged sigil across the wargear. The renegade triggered a surge of energy from the power fist and blue lightning crackled through Rafen's flesh, threatening to draw a scream from his lips.

Dizzy with the shock, arms trapped at his sides and his bones cracking with the crushing grasp, the Blood Angel gave a wordless shout and brought down his head upon the brow of the power armour's helmet. He felt the wet snap inside his skull as his nose broke, felt the hot gush of his own spilled blood; but with it came the crunch of shattering armourglass. One of the helm's murder-red visor lenses shattered from the impact and Bile cried out as fragments pierced the soft jelly of his eye. The killing pressure all about him was suddenly gone as the traitor released him, shaking his head vigorously to dislodge the shard of glass.

Rafen coughed up a heavy, dark gob of spittle, teetering. He knew that to hesitate would mean death, and so he attacked while he still could. Riding the power of the blood, he leapt up and grabbed the gorget of Bile's stolen armour with one hand, hauling himself upward, his feet taking purchase upon the legs and abdomen of his enemy.

Clinging to his target, Rafen punched the cracked, damaged facia of the helmet, over and over in rapid succession, blow after blow falling on the same point. Blood streamed from his knuckles and pain rippled along the nerves of his arm, but he went on, beyond reason, beyond endurance, his hand becoming a gory ruin.

He felt the helmet snap and dislodge; driven on, his clawed fingers caught the lip of the helm and tore it free. Beneath, Bile's face glared back at him, white hair now dark with crimson, one eye a torn and ragged pit.

Rafen brought the damaged helmet down like a bludgeon and went on beating the traitor with the cracked orb of ceramite, beating him and beating him with hard mechanical strikes, one after another after another.

Bile toppled and fell to his knees, clutching for the weapons at his waist and finding nothing. He swung at Rafen with the power fist, but the renegade was almost blind now, and could make out only hazy red blurs through his ruined vision.

Rafen staggered backward, dropping the smashed helm. The power of the sacred blood was ebbing from him, streaming out through the hundreds of cuts and contusions scattered across his body. In moments, the strength that had driven him on would be gone, and he would at last succumb. He had only moments left to fulfil the duty.

He had rescued the blood of his primarch and kept it safe. Now he would kill the thief who had dared to steal it.

'No...' gurgled Fabius. 'I am... Unkillable! You cannot... End me!'

Rafen did not answer; instead he bent and gave all his strength to lifting the armoured figure off the blood-slicked roof, hauling him up over his head.

With a last effort, every muscle in his body screaming in distress, Rafen pitched the renegade forward and threw him from the top of the stone tower. He collapsed to the parapet, hanging over the edge as he watched the figure in red drop away, cursing his name as he fell.

The traitor Fabius Bile, sworn enemy of the God-Emperor of Mankind and the Imperium, fell into the ready, hungry claws of the swarming xenos massing far below.

Rafen watched them rise up in a chattering, screeching wave, the black tide of hideous forms ripping his enemy apart.

My duty… is done. Just to form that thought seemed to drain every last iota of his will.

'Not yet,' said a grim voice.

Had he spoken those words aloud? His body was in so much pain, he could barely be certain he was still breathing.

Hands hauled him up from where he had fallen, turned him over. He saw a familiar pale face and dark, dead eyes. 'Noxx.'

'The same. Finished him then, did you?'

He tried to nod.

The Flesh Tearer did it for him. 'At last.'

Other shapes were moving around, casting shadows. He heard Puluo's dour tone. 'Throne of Terra. Is he still alive?'

'He is.' That was Ajir. 'Although there seems to be more of our esteemed sergeant upon the stones than in his veins.'

'The tyranids are inside!' shouted another, unfamiliar voice. 'They're inside the laboratoria!'

Rafen closed his eyes, listening to the reports of bolter fire. Not long now, then. 'Only in death does duty end,' he rasped.

'Not today.' Ceris's words seemed to come from a very great distance. 'Look here. Bile must have lost this in the melee.'

He heard a strange, musical chiming. *The summoner.* The sound brought a smile to his lips.

'Close ranks!' shouted Noxx. 'To me! If you want to live another day, to me!'

Warmth washed over Rafen's flesh, and he let the darkness take him down.

From the window of the chapel, through the panes of stained glass, he watched Dynikas V turning away from him, as if it were afraid to show its face. Nuclear firestorms the size of continents crossed the surface, shock-rings from multiple detonations boring down into the mantle and bedrock of the ocean world. The seas were already boiling into void as the atmosphere dissipated, the orbiting gunskulls consumed by the same fires. Within a day, perhaps less, the fifth planet would be little more than a scorched ember, and everything on it just a memory. The taint of Chaos and of the alien had been scoured clean.

Rafen sighed, wincing slightly at the pain the deep breath caused him. So much had been lost down there. Noxx and Ceris and the others had recovered some small fragments of the trophies Bile had kept in his tower to add to the spoils taken from Zellik's Archeohort – among them the plasma gun that had belonged to the hero Aryon – but so much had been lost. He felt a strong stab of remorse over the destruction of Brother Kear's wargear; he would say a special tribute to the dead man's memory in the Hall of Heroes when the *Tycho* returned to Baal.

There was one loss that he would not mourn, however. The black pall of guilt that had shadowed him since the start of the mission had left him. His duty was done, and his conscience was clear.

Looking away, he bowed and allowed the sanguinary priest to anoint him with the sanctified fluids from the replica of the Red Grail he held in his hands. All of the warriors who had returned alive from Dynikas V had undergone the rituals of cleansing and purgation to undo any lingering mark of the inhuman – but Rafen and those who had been prisoners had more to endure. Each of them had been implanted with one of Bile's demi-daemon/tyranid hybrids, and the priests and chaplains of the Adeptus Astartes needed to be sure that no lingering stigma remained upon their souls. The brothers had already sworn a pact to keep their silence on the full scope of their imprisonment at the hands of the twisted Primogenitor; none of them doubted that the forces of the Imperial Inquisition would look most harshly upon each one of the Space Marines, perhaps even order their summary terminations. But this was not a matter for inquisitors to decide upon. They would be judged when they returned to their Chapters, by the only authority that mattered – their battle-brothers.

At last Rafen stood, accepting a bow from the cleric. He made the sign of the aquila and stepped away, his robes pulled in tight around his body. Crossing the chapel floor, he paused in front of the altar where the statue of Sanguinius rose high towards the arched ceiling. There, a small brazier atop an iron bowl burned brightly, casting firelight upon the wings of the primarch.

He took a step towards it, but halted as he realised another robed figure was approaching. He pulled back his hood. 'Cousin.'

'Cousin,' said Noxx. 'Well met. I come to bid you farewell.' He jerked his chin up at the vast circular window over their heads; beyond it, out in the void the starship *Gabriel* was turning on spears of thruster fire, preparing to depart on a new warp vector. 'The Thunderhawk is ready on the landing deck. My brothers and my passengers await.'

Rafen nodded. The Raven Guard Kilan and some of the other escapees from Bile's prison-fortress were to travel with the Flesh Tearers, to rendezvous with representatives of their own Chapters along the *Gabriel's* course back to Cretacia. Tarikus and the rest were remaining aboard the *Tycho*, and the Blood Angels would do the same for them, quietly guiding them back to their home worlds. Rafen wondered if all of them would be able to recover the lives they had lost to the prison; he had no doubt that many of those captured by Bile's agents had been declared dead. When they returned to their monasteries alive and whole, there would be questions and challenges. For them, their trials had only just begun.

He took Noxx's hand and shook it. 'You have what Lord Seth wanted,' he said. 'In the chronicles of both our Chapters, it shall be written that our enemy was slain by the hands of Blood Angels and Flesh Tearers.'

Noxx's lip curled. 'We both know that isn't so. You killed him, Rafen. The honour is yours.'

'If you wanted it, you could have taken that for yourself. You could have pitched me off that roof, told the survivors yours was the blade to Bile's heart. No one would have known.'

'It crossed my mind,' Noxx said mildly, before nodding towards the statue. 'But *he* would have known. And as hard as it might be to believe, I am not without honour myself.'

'I do not doubt that,' Rafen replied. 'Without you and your warriors… your sacrifices… this mission would have failed. Thank you.'

Noxx released his grip and took on a formal manner. 'The deed is done. This duty is complete. *Ave Imperator.*'

'*Ave Imperator,*' repeated Rafen, as the Flesh Tearer walked away. He stood for a long moment in the glow of the brazier before he realised he was being observed by another. He did not turn to face the figure in the shadows. 'Are you here to try my patience once more, Codicier?'

Ceris stepped into the light. 'No. But I have questions.'

Rafen smiled slightly. 'Of course you do.'

'The sacred blood…' The psyker nodded towards him. 'Your task was to recover it.'

'And I did, in a way. It exists still, in me.'

Ceris frowned. 'I fear Great Corbulo and the other High Sanguinary Priests will not see it that way. There will be consequences.'

'There always are,' Rafen replied. 'I will be called to account when we reach Baal, and I will face it with a clear conscience. I did what was needed. I regret nothing.'

'That much is certain,' nodded Ceris.

'You said you had *questions*,' Rafen continued. 'I would hear them all, kinsman.'

'An uncertainty nags at me and I must give voice to it. You, Brother Rafen, are the only one who will understand why.'

'Go on,' he commanded.

'I fear that Noxx is mistaken, lord. I do not doubt that the man who came to Baal, who robbed our Chapter of that measure of holy vitae, is now dead. I do not doubt that vital essence lives on in you. But I fear the duty is not done. Not to the letter.'

'More riddles,' Rafen said, his mood turning.

Ceris came closer. 'How many times did you kill him, Rafen? The torn throat. The bolter to the head. Drowned in the ice. The feast for the tyranids. How many of them were *him*? All of them? *None of them?*'

Rafen gave the psyker a hard look. 'Do you know the answer?'

Ceris drew back towards the shadows. 'No.'

'Come to me if you do. Otherwise, keep your silence.'

Rafen glanced up at his primarch, at last alone with his thoughts, and bowed low. His bandaged hand reached into his sleeve and returned with a small fold of paper, the creased note he had discovered in the derelict hospital within the tau colony.

Without opening it once again to read the words it bore, he dropped it into the flames and let it burn into dark ashes.

EPILOGUE

ON THE PLAINS of the Crone World, the agony of the modificates was never-ending. It covered the landscape from horizon to horizon, across the fields of the flesh-farms and the cropping houses, though the slaughter tracks and the meat-works. Overhead, the ever-baleful glow of the Eye looked down over everything, and found it good.

The master of this place moved through the rows, sampling the changed and the mutated in the way that a winemaker would wander a vineyard in search of the best grapes for his next harvest. Thus it was, he halted and became irritated beyond all degree to find a perfect circle among his crops, where the flesh of his most recent captures was spoiled.

Some arcane discharge of warped energies had merged the meat of the men and women there into a mess of limbs and faces. It was a ruin, an utter waste of good samples. The master's hand vanished into the depths of his great leathery coat and returned with his rod. He brandished it angrily.

'Show yourself!' he demanded, the great mechanism upon his back reacting to his anger, pumps churning, blades and splines unfolding into the air. 'Give your name to me, creature!'

The flesh-mass quivered, and spoke in a dozen breathy, screaming voices. 'I bring news of value to you, great Primogenitor, first among Chaos Undivided, scion of all–'

He stabbed the meat with the rod and it rippled with exquisite pain. 'Answer me! How dare you break my wards and come here without invitation! I will destroy you!'

'Hear me out,' bubbled the amalgam. 'Know that your grand plan, one of many I do not doubt for so brilliant a mind, your grand plan upon the death world fifth from the Dynikas star has been ended.' The chorus voice simpered.

'Dynikas...' The rod dipped. 'The silence from my proxy...?'

'The servants of the Corpse-God did this, Great Master.' It keened and whistled. 'The Blood Angels.' In saying the name, the morass of flesh vomited with anger.

He laughed coldly. 'Of course. I knew they would come. It was a bold gambit, after all. I should not be surprised they retaliated.' The master glared at the daemon-thing. 'Why do you tell me this? What value does this news have to you?'

'My lord and master only wishes to see you have success in your endeavours,' bubbled the fleshy mess. 'And he wishes to help you overcome this setback.'

'I need no help,' came the angry reply. 'I have many proxies. I will send another. Begin again. No single act of interference can destroy my great strategy.'

'So true. But do not the fires of anger burn in you, great one? Would you not wish to see these Blood Whelps dead?'

He turned away. 'I will kill who I will in my own time. Now be gone.'

'As you wish,' gasped the flesh-form, the magicks holding it together fading, the skin and tissue melting into slurry. 'But remember this offer, Fabius Bile, and know that the Warp Prince Malfallax shares your hate.'

ACKNOWLEDGMENTS

Tips of the helm to BJ and the lads at
GW Bromley, Ben and Phil and the
GW Crawley team, Gareth and the
GW Plymouth crew, along with Peter J.
Evans, Mike Clarke, Peter Clarke and Mark
Lee, with thanks for all the support and
input.

ABOUT THE AUTHOR

James Swallow's stories from the dark
worlds of Warhammer 40,000 include the
Horus Heresy novel *The Flight of the
Eisenstein,* the Blood Angels books *Deus
Encarmine*, *Deus Sanguinius* and *Red Fury*,
the Sisters of Battle novel *Faith & Fire*, as
well as a multiplicity of short fiction.
Among his other works are *Jade Dragon*,
The Butterfly Effect, the *Sundowners* series
of 'steampunk' Westerns and fiction in the
worlds of Star Trek, Doctor Who, Stargate
and 2000AD, as well as a number of
anthologies.

His non-fiction features *Dark Eye: The Films
of David Fincher* and books on scriptwriting
and genre television. Swallow's other
credits include writing for Star Trek
Voyager, scripts for videogames and audio
dramas. He lives in London, and is
currently working on his next book.